Acclaim for Kelly Irvin

"Strangers at first, Maisy Glick and Joshua Lapp find solace in their unhappy circumstances in Kelly Irvin's *Every Good Gift*. Joshua, full of sorrow and doubt. Maisy, full of regret. Together, they forge a path forward in ways that will surprise readers. Irvin's knowledge of the Plain people shines in this endearing tale of love and redemption."

—SUZANNE WOODS FISHER, BESTSELLING
AUTHOR OF *A SEASON ON THE WIND*

"A beautifully crafted story of mistakes, redemption, healing, and grace. Kelly Irvin's *Every Good Gift* will captivate readers and tug on the heart-strings as characters brimming with real human frailty try to work through the consequences of their lives and choices with love and faith."

—KRISTEN MCKANAGH, AUTHOR OF *THE GIFT OF HOPE*

"The second entry in Irvin's Amish Blessings series (after *Love's Dwelling*) delivers an elegant portrait of a young Amish woman caught between two worlds . . . Irvin skillfully conveys Abigail's internal conflict ('How could Abigail put into words the longing that thrummed in her chest? The sense of loss, of missing out, of missing it all,' she reminisces about Amish life). Fans of Amish romance will want to check this out."

—*PUBLISHERS WEEKLY* ON *THE WARMTH OF SUNSHINE*

"Just like the title, *Warmth of Sunshine* is a lovely and cozy story that will keep you reading until the very last page."

—KATHLEEN FULLER, *USA TODAY* BESTSELLING AUTHOR
OF THE MAIL-ORDER AMISH BRIDES SERIES

"This is a sweet story of romance and family that will tug at heartstrings. It is another great story and great characters from Irvin."

—*THE PARKERSBURG NEWS AND SENTINEL* ON *LOVE'S DWELLING*

"*Peace in the Valley* is a beautiful and heart-wrenching exploration of faith, loyalty, and the ties that bind a family and a community together. Kelly Irvin's masterful storytelling pulled me breathlessly into Nora's world, her deep desire to do good, and her struggle to be true to herself and to the man she loves. Full of both sweet and stark details of Amish life, *Peace in the Valley* is realistic and poignant, profound and heartfelt. I highly recommend it!"

—JENNIFER BECKSTRAND, AUTHOR OF *ANDREW*

"With a lovely setting, this is a story of hope in the face of trouble and has an endearing heroine and other relatable characters that readers will empathize with."

—*THE PARKERSBURG NEWS AND SENTINEL* ON *MOUNTAINS OF GRACE*

"Irvin (*Beneath the Summer Sun*) puts a new spin on the age-old problem of bad things happening to good people in this excellent Amish inspirational . . . Fans of both Amish and inspirational Christian fiction will enjoy this heart-pounding tale of the pain of loss and the joys of love."

—*PUBLISHERS WEEKLY* ON *MOUNTAINS OF GRACE*

"Kelly Irvin's *Mountains of Grace* offers a beautiful and emotional journey into the Amish community. Readers will be captivated by a heartwarming tale of forgiveness and finding a renewed faith in God. The story will capture the hearts of those who love the Plain culture and an endearing romance. Once you open this book, you'll be hooked until the last page."

—AMY CLIPSTON, BESTSELLING AUTHOR OF
THE AMISH LEGACY SERIES

"Irvin's fun story is simple (like Mary Katherine, who finds 'every day is a blessing and an adventure') but very satisfying."

—*PUBLISHERS WEEKLY* ON *THROUGH THE AUTUMN AIR*

"This second entry (after *Upon a Spring Breeze*) in Irvin's seasonal series diverges from the typical Amish coming-of-age tale with its focus on more mature protagonists who acutely feel their sense of loss. Fans of the genre seeking a broader variety of stories may find this new offering from [Irvin] more relatable than the usual fare."

—*LIBRARY JOURNAL* ON *BENEATH THE SUMMER SUN*

"A moving and compelling tale about the power of grace and forgiveness that reminds us how we become strongest in our most broken moments."

—*LIBRARY JOURNAL* ON *UPON A SPRING BREEZE*

"Irvin's novel is an engaging story about despair, postnatal depression, God's grace, and second chances."

—*CBA CHRISTIAN MARKET* ON *UPON A SPRING BREEZE*

"Once I started reading *The Bishop's Son*, it was difficult for me to put it down! This story of struggle, faith, and hope will draw you in to the final page . . . I have read countless stories of Amish men or women doubting their faith. I have never read a storyline quite like this one though. It was narrated with such heart. I was fully invested in Jesse's struggle. No doubt, what Jesse felt is often what modern-day Amish men and women must feel when they are at a crossroads in their faith. The story was brilliantly told and the struggle felt very real."

—*DESTINATION AMISH*

"Something new and delightful in the Amish fiction genre, this story is set in the barren, dusty landscape of Bee County, TX . . . Irvin writes with great insight into the range and depth of human emotion. Her characters are believable and well developed, and her storytelling skills are superb. Recommend to readers who are looking for something a little different in Amish fiction."

—*CBA RETAILERS + RESOURCES* ON *THE BEEKEEPER'S SON*

"*The Beekeeper's Son* is so well crafted. Each character is richly layered. I found myself deeply invested in the lives of both the King and Lantz families. I struggled as they struggled, laughed as they laughed—and even cried as they cried . . . This is one of the best novels I have read in the last six months. It's a refreshing read and worth every penny. *The Beekeeper's Son* is a keeper for your bookshelf!"

—DESTINATION AMISH

"*The Beekeeper's Son* is a perfect depiction of how God makes all things beautiful in His way. Rich with vivid descriptions and characters you can immediately relate to, Kelly Irvin's book is a must-read for Amish fans."

—RUTH REID, BESTSELLING AUTHOR OF *A MIRACLE OF HOPE*

"Kelly Irvin writes a moving tale that is sure to delight all fans of Amish fiction. Highly recommended."

—KATHLEEN FULLER, AUTHOR OF THE MAIL-ORDER AMISH BRIDES SERIES, ON *THE BEEKEEPER'S SON*

Every Good Gift

Also by Kelly Irvin

Every Good Gift

AMISH BLESSINGS

KELLY IRVIN

ZONDERVAN

Every Good Gift

Copyright © 2023 by Kelly Irvin

This title is also available as a Zondervan e-book.

Requests for information should be addressed to:

Zondervan, *3900 Sparks Dr. SE, Grand Rapids, Michigan 49546*

Library of Congress Cataloging-in-Publication

Names: Irvin, Kelly, author.
Title: Every good gift / Kelly Irvin.
Description: Grand Rapids, Michigan : Zondervan, [2023] | Series: Amish
blessings novels ; 3 | Summary: "An Amish girl faces an impossible
choice as the consequences from her Rumspringa become all too real"--
Provided by publisher.
Identifiers: LCCN 2022032878 (print) | LCCN 2022032879 (ebook) | ISBN
9780310364559 (paperback) | ISBN 9780310364566 (epub) | ISBN
9780310364573
Subjects: BISAC: FICTION / Christian / Romance / General | GSAFD: Christian
fiction. | LCGFT: Novels.
Classification: LCC PS3609.R82 E94 2023 (print) | LCC PS3609.R82 (ebook)
| DDC 813/.6--dc23/eng/20220721
LC record available at https://lccn.loc.gov/2022032878
LC ebook record available at https://lccn.loc.gov/2022032879

Scripture quotations are taken from The Holy Bible, New International Version®, niv®.
Copyright © 1973, 1978, 1984, 2011 by Biblica, Inc.® Used by permission. All rights
reserved worldwide. www.zondervan.com. The "niv" and "New International Version"
are trademarks registered in the United States Patent and Trademark Office by Biblica,
Inc.® And from the King James Version. Public domain.

Zondervan titles may be purchased in bulk for educational, business, fundraising, or
sales promotional use. For information, please email SpecialMarkets@Zondervan.com.

Printed in the United States of America

23 24 25 26 LSC 10 9 8 7 6 5 4 3 2 1

To Tim, love always.

I praise you because I am fearfully and wonderfully made; your works are wonderful, I know that full well.

Psalm 139:14

And we know that in all things God works for the good of those who love him, who have been called according to his purpose.

Romans 8:28

Glossary of Deutsch*

aamen: amen

aenti: aunt

bewillkumm: welcome

blos: bubbles

bopli, boplin: baby, babies

bruder, brieder: brother, brothers

bu, buwe: boy, boys

daed: father

danki: thank you

Das Loblied: Amish hymn of praise sung at all church services

dawdy haus: attached home for grandparents when they retire

dochder, dechder: daughter, daughters

eck: the corner table where the bride and groom sit at the wedding reception

eldre: parents

Englischer: English or non-Amish

eppies: cookies

faeriwell: good-bye

fehla: sin

fraa: wife

Froh Neiyaahr: Happy New Year

gern gschehme: you're welcome

Glossary

Gmay: church district

groosmammi, groosmammis: grandmother, grandmothers

Gott: God

guder mariye: good morning

gut: good

gut nacht: good night

hallo: hello

hund, hunde: dog, dogs

jah: yes

kaffi: coffee

kind, kinner: child, children

kossin: cousin

maedel, maed: girl, girls

mann: husband

meidung: shunning, excommunication from the Amish
   faith. Shunning is a practice in which church members
   isolate, ignore, or otherwise punish someone for breaking
   community rules.

Mennischt: Mennonite

mudder: mother

narrisch: foolish, silly

nee: no

onkel: uncle

Ordnung: written and unwritten rules in an Amish district

rumspringa: period of "running around" for Amish youth before
   they decide whether they want to be baptized into the Amish
   faith and seek a mate

schtarem: storm

schweschder, schwesdchdre: sister, sisters

seelich gebortsdaag: happy birthday

sei so gut: please (be so kind)

suh: son
wasser: water
weddermann: weatherman
wunderbarr: wonderful

*The German dialect commonly referred to as Pennsylvania Dutch is not a written language and varies depending on the location and origin of the Amish settlement. These spellings are approximations. Most Amish children learn English after they start school. They also learn high German, which is used in their Sunday services.

Featured Families

Jamesport, Missouri

Roy and Peggy Glick

Charlie   Nora   Maisy   Jake   Ian   Martin   Sarah   Shelley   Danny

Chase and Sue Ellen Taylor

Tommy   Hadley   Nathan (Nate)   Kayla

Haven, Kansas

Daryl and Marnie Lapp

Peter   James   Joshua   Hannah   Rachel   Samuel   Michael   Christopher

Amos and Ruth Plank

Bonnie   Nicholas

Isaac and Vicky King

Moses and Alice Coblentz

Kate Maggie Marie Amy Miriam Mark Ephraim Johnny

Bryan (bishop) and Esther Miller

Kylie Seth Richard Julianne

Samuel (deacon) and Anita Zimmerman

Nadine Michael Adam Jana Seth

Delbert (minister) and Loretta Beachy

Emily Carrie Nicholas Chrissie John Robert

Caleb and Millie Mast

Joel Elinor Melissa David Micah Anna

Chapter 1

THE NAUSEA THAT HAD PLAGUED MAISY Glick for three months pummeled her. Her hands went to her still-flat stomach as if she could calm it with a mere touch. She swallowed the bile in the back of her throat.

"Nate, say something. Please."

Nate Taylor was already mentally a hundred miles gone, racing down Missouri's back roads, Jamesport in his rearview mirror. They sat in his pickup, headlights blazing in the darkness, under an enormous bur oak just outside the fence. His lazy grin had disappeared when Maisy said the words "in a family way." His hickory-brown eyes that always warmed her with the slightest glance filled with fear. He didn't meet her gaze.

Instead he got out of the truck and hopped over the barbed-wire fence that separated the dirt road from the meadow where Maisy's neighbors pastured their horses. A quiet place with no ears to overhear. Except the beautiful Morgans that grazed nearby. One raised its head and whinnied.

Nate stopped, but his desire to put space between Maisy and himself had been apparent in his hurried stride through the tall grass and weeds. "I don't know what to say. We were done. I haven't seen you in two months."

1

Say it'll be all right. Say you know what to do.

They'd both known it couldn't last. He was English. She was Plain. He was headed to college in a few weeks. Maisy knew she would never leave her faith—not even for a man who'd stolen her heart in the most unexpected manner.

Nate with his Wrangler jeans and his straw cowboy hat covering his thick tangle of wheat-colored curls. He loved his truck—probably more than he'd ever cared for her. His family went to the Baptist church in Gallatin most Sunday mornings. He called himself a backsliding Baptist when Maisy had asked him if he believed in God.

Maisy slipped through the gate—her days of climbing fences in a dress had passed not so long ago—and followed him. Grasshoppers whizzed past her, their bodies dark against the brilliant headlights. Searching for words adequate to the occasion, she brushed away gnats and mosquitoes with sweaty hands.

Nate still didn't meet her gaze. "This isn't the first time this has happened to a Plain girl."

That didn't make it right. It made it worse. Maisy was stuck. She hadn't been baptized. She wasn't a member of the church so they couldn't officially shun her.

No, but it could be far worse. At least as a member she could do a kneeling confession and be forgiven. If the father had been baptized in the church, they could marry in a quiet wedding and move on. But the *Gmay* held no sway over an unbaptized teenager. Only her family. Her parents. What would they do?

Her father's fierce, stony face loomed in Maisy's mind. If a smart retort to his instruction earned her a whipping as a child, what would the sin of fornication get her? Would he forbid her to speak to her brothers and sisters? Would she be banished from Gmay activities? Church?

Would he send her away?

Forgiveness. Surely he would obey a basic tenet of their faith and forgive her.

Missouri's humid August air pressed on Maisy. Sweat trickled down her temples. If only there were a breeze. "My parents will forgive me. They have to forgive me. What will yours say?"

If he told them. Would he tell them? Would he feel any obligation toward his unborn child?

"What do you think they'd say?" He lifted his hat and ran his fingers through his hair. "Besides, you're the one who called it off."

They'd met at a kegger the previous summer in an English farmer's pasture. Her friend Lana had dragged Maisy to it. She'd turned seventeen earlier in the week. It was a birthday celebration, according to Lana. Nate had strode across the field toward her like a cowboy from one of the western romances she loved to read with a flashlight under the covers after her parents went to bed.

From the first howdy, complete with a bow and a flourish of his black Stetson, Nate had pursued Maisy. He never left her side. He gave her and their friends rides in his pickup—Maisy up front, his high school basketball teammates and the other girls in the bed. He took her to the movies and taught her to bowl. He taught her to line dance to country music.

With each day, with each shared experience, her feelings for him had grown. *Rumspringa* was meant to be a time for finding a spouse. A Plain man. She always knew that, but none of the boys in her district made her feel like Nate did. So full of life.

He'd said he loved her. Even those words couldn't make it right, as much as she told herself they mattered. She'd been deceiving herself. Ignoring the obvious because her heart and her body wanted what they wanted with no thought for the consequences.

"If I hadn't, you would've."

Nate gave her his back. Hands on his hips, he planted his dress-up cowboy boots wide and stared at something Maisy couldn't see. His deep bass voice—the one that sent a pleasant wave of heat through her body every time she heard it—sounded hoarse, unsure. Nate was never unsure.

"The reasons it wouldn't work haven't changed," he said. "I'm only eighteen. I haven't even started college. I'm gonna study agribusiness so I can take over my dad's dairy farm someday. I'm too young to be a daddy. I can't let one mistake derail my whole life."

The breath swooshed from Maisy's lungs. Blood pounded in her ears. Her head floated, disconnected from her body. She was a mistake. Their baby, a mistake. He'd said he loved her when he oh-so-gently laid her down on a plaid fleece blanket in the bed of his truck under a full moon's streaming light and stars so bright they hurt Maisy's eyes.

It was wrong. Terribly wrong. She'd held out for months. A kiss led to a hug to more kissing and more hugging that led them to the cliff's edge. Before she knew it, the cliff crumbled under their feet and they were in a free fall.

She'd promised herself it would never happen again. Then Nate would whisper in her ear how much he loved her, and didn't she love him? She did. She was sure she did. How could something so wonderful be so awful at the same time?

"A baby isn't a mistake. Babies are gifts from God."

Nate paced to the fence and back, his heavy tread leaving a path of smashed weeds bending to his frustration and uncertainty. His dimpled face with its high cheekbones and full lips twisted in sorrow. "I'm sorry. I can't marry you."

He acted as if there were a choice. Maisy certainly didn't have one. "What would you have me do?"

"You think this happened the last time we . . ."

"I think it's at least three months since I, you know . . ." Heat scalded her face. She stepped away from the headlights, mortified, thankful for the darkness. She'd never talked to anyone about such personal things, not even her own mother. "It's likely three months."

Her body had been telling Maisy for a while what she didn't want to believe. She ignored it, sure she was wrong, hoping she was wrong, praying she was wrong. Would she be condemned to hell for praying to God that there be no child growing inside her when the baby was conceived in her sin? God was gracious and merciful. He would forgive Maisy. Her family would be hard-pressed to do it, but they would.

Wouldn't they?

With a groan, Nate climbed back over the fence, then into the truck. No holding her hand, no hug, no expression of awe that they'd made a new life together—however the circumstances. "I guess it's too late."

"Too late for what?"

"Too late, you know, to . . . terminate it."

Horror struck Maisy full force, running into walls and stumbling over its own feet. The man climbing into the pickup truck was a complete stranger. Her decision to break up with him had been the right one. She climbed into the truck and slammed her door.

"I would never do that." Her voice didn't tremble. No tears. "Babies are special gifts from God."

"I get that you feel that way, but it's different for guys like me. You can keep the baby, but you'll be raising it on your own." He twisted the key in the ignition. The truck's engine rumbled to life. "What did you think would happen? I'd marry you and you'd come with me to Columbia? We'd live happily ever after in married student housing?"

She hadn't imagined such a thing. Every road led to a dead end.

They had no options that worked. Her stomach lurched. Vomit rose in her throat. She shoved the door open, hopped from the truck, and fought her way through the tall grass to a spot where she could vomit in private.

After a few minutes, hands grasped her shoulders. They rubbed her back. "I'm sorry, little Amish girl. I'm truly sorry," Nate whispered. An orange-and-black butterfly danced across her periphery until it landed, wings flapping on her sleeve. "You would never be happy away from your mom and dad and the rest of your family. Imagine what it would be like to meet your mom on the street in Jamesport and have her cross to the other side to avoid talking to you. Or leaving Jamesport and never coming back so you don't have to see your brothers and sisters and know you can't ever talk to them."

Nate had grown up around Plain folks. He understood the consequences. At least she should be thankful for that. Leave behind the smell of her mother's peanut-butter-chocolate-chip cookies, the aroma of coffee and bacon early in the morning, the sound of her sisters laughing over the *chug-a-chug-chug* of the wringer washing machine as they did laundry. The women giggling and chatting while they worked on another quilt for the quilt consignment store. The sun shining on Maisy's face while she planted tomatoes, radishes, peas, green beans, cucumbers, and a host of other vegetables in the garden behind the house.

Then there was her father. He followed the *Ordnung* down to the letter. His children never doubted his love, shown in the way he worked hard on a construction crew to feed and clothe them. He wasn't one to crack a joke or offer a hug, but he taught them how to be the Plain people they were born to be.

To tell him how horribly she'd failed seemed unimaginable. He would be so disappointed in her. So ashamed. So angry.

Her father would be even more devastated if she married an English man. Not being baptized in the church led to eternal damnation. Despite the heat, Maisy shivered. "I can't marry you. You can't marry me. So I guess that's that."

They drove back to the intersection with the dirt road that led to her family's farm without talking. Nate didn't even turn on the radio to that twangy country music he loved so much. He stopped the truck and put it in Park. Still he didn't speak.

"This is it, then." Maisy swallowed back sobs. She gritted her teeth. He could simply turn away. She would be left to walk this road alone, the proof of her sin on display for all to see. "Have a good life."

"You too." He bit out the words through stiff lips. "You're a better person than me. Always remember that."

"You'll never wonder if our baby has your eyes? Whether it's a boy or a girl?"

He studied the tops of his hands on the wheel. "I suppose I will, but I'll get over it."

Alone, she started the long trek on the dark dirt road that led to an uncertain future. The hot wind whistled through the sycamore and oak trees that lined the simple thoroughfare. Leaves rustled, keeping her company. A dog howled, a lonesome sound in tune with her heart so heavy she fought to carry it forward.

To be so alone, so bereft, was unbearable.

You're not alone.

The wind whipped the words into a frenzy until they settled in a soft cloak around her shoulders. She raised her face to the moon's light filtered through passing clouds. "It's you and me, *Bopli*, you and me."

Chapter 2

SOMETHING COLD AND WET POKED AT Maisy's fingers. A soft *woof* forced her to open her eyes. Skeeter's tail beat a steady *whap, whap, whap* in the air. His breath stank—as usual. She pulled up the Log Cabin quilt that covered the bed she shared with her sister Sarah until it touched her chin. The light flooding the bedroom window announced that dawn was long gone. The day had begun without her. Another *woof.* "I know, I know. I need to get up."

Woof.

"Give me a minute."

The roly-poly mutt, covered in semiwhite fur that obscured his eyes and usually dripped with slobber around his mouth, sat.

"Gut hund."

Maisy stared at the ceiling. People liked to say everything would seem better in the morning. A good night's sleep could fix what ailed a person. Not so. Nothing had changed overnight. Yesterday's meeting with Nate had left Maisy to forge ahead alone in her dilemma. How to tell Mother and Father? She had to do it soon—before she started to show. But first she had to get up, help make breakfast, and take the buggy to her job cleaning an English family's house.

She threw her legs over the side of the bed and picked up her tattered composition notebook. She kept it within easy reach so she could choose her word of the day to memorize. The list of words she learned in books she'd read was what her mother had called her odd little hobby. Other people collected pretty rocks, thimbles, bird feeders, or coffee mugs. Maisy collected words.

Skeeter spread out on the rag-tie rug at her feet, his head propped on his paws. He knew this would take a while.

Tenacious: tending to keep a firm hold of something; clinging or adhering closely; not readily relinquishing a position, principle, or course of action; determined.

Tenacious. *Ach, Gott. This word?* Maisy had not held closely to her principles, to the Ordnung. She'd relinquished them before she drowned in Nate's gaze, his feel, his everything.

Her family laughed at her propensity—another good word—to use big words. But she liked reading, and reading meant understanding words, small and big. She needed to understand something. Even if it changed nothing.

Woof. This time Skeeter's bark held a worried note. *Woof.*

"I know, I know."

She battled nausea as she dressed and went to help with breakfast. Skeeter followed at her heels like a dog herding sheep. Maybe that was what he was supposed to be doing instead of herding the Glick children. It was hard to say. He'd shown up one day, muddy, flea-infested, and skinny. Mother took one gander at him and sent Maisy to wash him down in the laundry room. That had been that. Now he followed her everywhere.

Her mother, who was bent over the pine table that seated twelve, wiping up food with quick, efficient movements, looked back to see Maisy standing in the kitchen doorway. "I thought maybe you were sick."

"Where is everyone?"

"Breakfast is over. The girls are gathering up the laundry. Jake and Ian went to work. Your *daed* had to pick up a part in town for his boss. Martin is mowing the yard."

"Why didn't you wake me?"

"You seemed like you didn't feel good at supper last night. Then Sarah said you tossed and turned and moaned in your sleep all night. She said it was like sleeping next to a hot baked potato tied to a jumping bean. She begged me not to wake you."

Maisy went to clear the table. Skeeter, satisfied she was where she should be, threw himself onto the faded welcome rug in front of the back door. His favorite spot to monitor *his* children's comings and goings. "What did Daed say?"

"Nothing. He doesn't have a heart of stone."

Humming "I Surrender All," Mother bustled over to the sink with the dirty washcloth. "The boys have such big mouths when it comes to talking in church. I don't understand how they can miss their mouths so often when it comes to food." She dropped cold scrambled eggs and toast crumbs into the sink. "You still look peaked. Maybe you need to go into town to see Doc Nelson. You shouldn't go to work sick."

Mother had a way of running thoughts and words together pell-mell that made it hard to get a word in edgewise. "I'm fine. They're expecting me." Maisy moved to the table and picked up a stack of dirty plates. The mingled smells of maple syrup, fried potatoes, coffee, and eggs gagged her. *"Ach, nee, nee."*

She dumped the plates back on the table, shot from the kitchen, and sprinted to the bathroom. She made it by a whisker. Her belly's sour contents burned her throat. She retched long after it was empty.

"Ach. Nee. *Dochder*, do you have the flu?" Mother touched

Maisy's forehead. "You don't have a fever. How long have you felt bad?"

Her mother's anguished voice, soft and hoarse, surrounded Maisy. She swiveled on the floor so she could draw her knees up and wrapped her arms around them. The loving concern on Mother's face only brought more shame, more regret, more fear. *Tell the truth. Tell it now before it gets worse.* "It's not the flu. I'm not sick. Not that way." She swallowed another wave of nausea. "I'm so sorry, *Mamm*. It's morning sickness."

Mother slipped to the floor onto her knees. She touched Maisy's cheeks with both hands. Her forehead wrinkled. She shook her head. "Nee. It's not possible. You know better. You would never . . . you would never."

"I didn't mean for it to happen."

Her face a deep purplish-red, Mother closed her eyes and bowed her head. "Ach, Dochder, no one in this situation ever does." Tears slipped down her plump cheeks. She didn't seem to notice.

Maisy grabbed a sheet of toilet paper and dabbed at her face. Mother batted her hand away. Her eyes opened. "How long has it been . . . ? How far along are you?"

"I've been feeling poorly for three months and there's been no . . . nothing."

Skeeter whined at the door. "Go away, hund, get." Mother's eyes seemed to devour Maisy as if she could see every inch of her daughter's skin, as if she could imagine the scene of her daughter's downfall. "You're not showing. All the throwing up, I suppose. You never said a word." The disappointment and the shame looming large in her downturned, trembling lips were far harder to bear than anger.

Anger, Maisy could've handled. She deserved anger. She'd brought shame on her entire family. "I thought maybe I was wrong. Maybe it would go away. I prayed I was wrong."

"You prayed to Gott that He'd take away evidence of your *fehla*?" *Mudder* cleared her throat. The disappointment faded into a grim acceptance. "Nee, you must bear the consequences. We all must."

"Just me—"

"The shame is on your daed and me. We failed to teach you. We failed."

"It's my fault."

And Nate's. Mother hadn't even asked who the father was. Because it didn't matter. He wouldn't bear the physical reminder of his sin. He could go about his business each day, the darkness simmering under the surface, hidden.

"*Jah*, but mine also. It never occurred to me that you would do this. No *bu* came calling. I thought you were still searching for your special friend. You said you were going to the singings, but you came home alone."

Parents might give their youngies more free rein during rumspringa, but that didn't mean they weren't paying attention to their comings and goings. And praying they wouldn't stray far from their upbringing.

"Mudder, what's going on?" Sarah rapped on the open bathroom door. Short for a ten-year-old, she hung on the knob with one hand and rested her head against the door. Her blue eyes were bright with curiosity. "The laundry is sorted. I can't reach the soap on the top shelf. Are you crying? Why are you crying?"

Sarah was a mini-mother, with the same blonde curls that refused to be tamed under her prayer covering, the same avid interest in everything and everyone. And the same penchant for talking a person's ear off.

"I'm not crying." Mother sniffed. She used the toilet seat to hoist herself to her feet. "Use the step stool to get the soap. Be careful. I'll be out in a minute."

"Skeeter is whining and crying. What's—?"

"Just never you mind."

"But—"

"Go. Take Skeeter with you."

Sarah went but not without resting her lingering gaze on Maisy.

Maisy put her palms to her cheeks, trying to hide her tears. Not that it really mattered if Sarah found out now. Soon everyone would know. Sarah and Shelly would be painted with the same brush as their older sister. They would bear the brunt of her shame in equal measure.

"I need to leave, Mudder. I need to go away."

"Nee. Your daed and the deacon will want to talk to the bu's parents. He'll need counseling. You both will, before the wedding."

"He's not Plain."

Mother sank back to the floor. "You'll not yoke yourself to an *Englisch* boy."

"He's off to college next week. He wants no part of this."

"That only reflects how poor your judgment and self-control are." Mother spat the words out as if they tasted bitter in her mouth. "You gave yourself to a bu not worthy to be called *mann* or daed. I knew reading those trashy novels would lead to no gut."

"How did you know—?"

"I clean better than you do. I saw them under your bed—behind the suitcase. When you have to hide something, you know it's sinful."

They weren't trashy. They were romantic. Or was that the same thing?

Heavy footsteps sounded in the hall. The *clomp, clomp* of work boots. Mother's pinched face went white. "Your daed."

"*Fraa?* Where are you?"

Maisy scrambled to her feet. Mother did the same. Maisy smoothed her wrinkled apron and set her prayer covering straight.

"I'm here. In the bathroom."

"I forgot the paper with the specs that the boss gave me. What are you two doing in here?" Father filled the doorway. What he lacked in bulk, he made up for in height. "Sarah says Maisy is sick."

"Not sick." Maisy's voice petered out. The words wouldn't come. Her throat closed.

"She's in a family way." Mother thrust the words into the space between them like orphans rejected and thrown out into the world on their own. "She's only just told me."

The concern in Father's face drained away, leaving behind a bleak sickness Maisy had never seen before. His straw hat dropped to the floor. His big hands fisted. "Are you sure?"

"She says jah."

Anger carved deep grooves in his sun-damaged skin. His gaze bounced from Mother to Maisy. "Go to your room, Dochder. Don't speak to your *schwesdchdre* or *brieder*. Don't speak at all."

Mother stepped away from Maisy. The tears and the quiver in her voice had receded. She and Father became as one. Mother clutched her hands together. "The daed is Englisch."

Father seemed to grow taller, his visage more terrible. A muscle twitched in his jaw. "Get out of my sight before I do something far worse."

Maisy edged toward the door. If only she could melt into a puddle that would seep through the pine floorboards and soak into the earth below the house. Mother drew back as if she didn't dare touch Maisy. Father simply stood there, blocking the way.

She sought to squeeze herself between his angular body and the door.

"Roy." Mother touched Father's sleeve. "We have to tell Abel. Word will spread quickly. He'll counsel us."

Mother's plaintive words moved him where Maisy could not. He stepped back.

She slid past him and ran.

His half-muffled sobs chased her down the hallway.

Chapter 3

THE STIFLING AIR IN THE PHONE shack hung heavy on Maisy's shoulders. She shooed away the rooster that had followed her down the dirt road that led from the house to the solar-powered shack. He squawked and strutted away, only to return seconds later. It was too hot to close the door. "Go on, get, get!"

"*Bawk, bawk, bawk.*"

He wasn't any happier than Maisy was. She had to hurry. Mother and Father had left for the bishop's house within minutes of sending her to her room. It wouldn't take them long to sort out the situation with Abel and receive his instructions. The receiver slipped in her sweaty hand. Her own scent wafted in the air. It stank. Hell must be something like it. *Please answer. Please answer. Gott, please let him answer.*

Her half-baked prayers were answered a few seconds later. Nate's hello held a note of trepidation. "Maisy? Why are you calling me?"

Why indeed? He wanted to erase her from his life. He could easily do that. She would never be able to do the same with him. The last thing she wanted in this world was to ask this man for a favor. She had no choice. "I need you to do this one thing for me. I'll never ask you for anything ever again."

"If it's money you need—"

"I need you to take me to Kansas City to the Amtrak station."

Silence on the line sent Maisy's already battered heart smashing against her rib cage. "Today. As soon as possible."

"Why?"

Nate didn't get to ask why. "I don't have much time. My parents are talking to the bishop right now."

"You're running away from home?"

She was sparing her parents months of watching her belly grow and grow until the day when her baby entered this world fatherless. She was sparing her brothers and sisters the bewildering world in which they could have nothing to do with her, not even speak a word to her for months—maybe longer. Sparing them from the furtive, judgmental glances of the entire community. "Could you do this one thing for me?"

"I'm on my way."

"Don't come to the house. Meet me at the intersection."

Where the dirt road on her father's property intersected with the paved one that led to the highway. Where Nate had parked off the road by the gate to wait for her on the nights he picked her up so they could steal away to movies, skating, playing pool, or dancing in St. Joseph—or St. Joe, as Nate called it. "If you see a buggy, turn around."

"I know the routine." He hung up.

Maisy wiped her hands on her apron. Mr. Rooster stuck his head through the door. She stuck out her foot and nudged him back.

"Bawk, bawk."

"Right back at you."

Next up, Mrs. Elliott.

The English woman answered the phone with the same brisk

17

tone she always used. Maisy made quick work of notifying her employer that she would no longer be cleaning her house.

One more call. This one would be simple. An answering machine would pick up. A few seconds later Amos Plank's voice, tinny on the old-fashioned tape recorder, instructed her to leave a message. He might return the call in a day or a week. It depended on how busy he was.

"Ruth, it's Maisy. I'm coming to Haven. I'm taking the train. I'll be there tonight or tomorrow, I hope. I'll find a ride from Hutchinson. If I could stay with you for a bit, I'd be so grateful."

She hung up. It was the best she could do. What if Ruth's husband said her young cousin couldn't stay with them? *Cross that bridge when you get to it.* Grandma Irene's no-nonsense tone delivered that sage piece of advice. She'd been gone for almost two years. Yet her voice still held sway in almost any internal debate that raged inside Maisy.

She settled the receiver back on the phone's base, picked up her oversized, faded canvas bag, and set out for the road. The rooster trotted behind her for a few yards, then changed his mind and headed back.

Danki, Gott, for one small favor.

The hot sun beat down on her head. Sweat trickled between her shoulder blades. Dust bloomed with each step on the dirt road. *Sei so gut, Gott, don't let my eldre come down the road and see me. Sei so gut, let me go without causing them more pain. Sei so gut.*

"Maisy! Maisy! Stop! Where are you going?"

Her head down, Maisy halted in the middle of the road. She didn't turn around. "Go back, Sarah. Go back to the house."

"What's wrong? Why's everyone mad?"

Maisy turned to face her sister. "I'm not mad, but I have to go."

"Go where?" Breathless, the little girl churned toward her,

Skeeter close on her heels. He barked twice as if to repeat her question. Sarah's dress puffed up in the hot wind. Finally she stopped within arm's reach. Her face was covered with sweat. Her skinny chest heaved. "Why did you take your clothes? Where did Mudder and Daed go?"

Skeeter kept coming. Panting, his tongue hanging out, he jumped up and nearly knocked Maisy over. She stumbled back, grabbed on to him, and steadied herself. "Easy, easy, you silly *hund*."

He yipped anxiously.

"I know, I know." She petted and murmured comforting mumbo jumbo. "Settle down. You'll be fine. You'll have Sarah and Shelly and the *buwe*."

"Answer me, *Schweschder*."

"They went to talk to Abel." Sarah would know talking to the bishop meant this was something big, something important. "I did something I shouldn't have done, something bad. So I'm leaving."

"What could be so bad you have to leave?" Sarah's expression grew more bewildered. "Mudder says there's nothing that can't be forgiven. You can come back, right?"

"It'll take some time. Hopefully." Someday. "Mudder will tell you more. Now take Skeeter and go back to the house."

"Where are you going?"

"I'll write you a letter and tell you all about it. Okay?" Maisy drew her sister into her arms for one quick, soggy hug. "Now go."

"You'll be okay?"

"I'll be okay. Go."

"I don't want you to go."

"Sarah. Go make sure Shelly is okay. Hang the clothes on the line. Now."

A fierce frown darkened Sarah's face. She stomped both feet. "That's your job."

"Now it's yours."

Maisy turned her back on her little sister and marched away. Sarah's wails nipped at her heels. Only sheer determination kept her from racing back to comfort her. *Keep going. Keep going. It's for the best. The best for Sarah. The best for Shelly. The best for everyone.*

The wails died away, replaced by an eerie silence. Not even the birds sang. Only the occasional whisper of leaves rustling in a dank breeze that shook the boughs of the sycamore trees offered company.

Good-bye, good-bye, good-bye.

Good-bye to her childhood. Good-bye to her family. Good-bye to the future she'd once thought just around the corner.

By the time Maisy made it to the intersection, Nate's truck idled in the shade of a poplar tree that stretched its branches over the fence toward the road. An almost painful rush of relief flooded Maisy. The passenger door swung open. Nate had reached across the cab and shoved it. She climbed in.

Without a word, he maneuvered the truck back onto the road. They traveled in silence to the highway. The pickup smelled different. It usually made her think of Christmas and pine trees. Now it smelled like sweat and stale beer. She hazarded a quick glance at Nate. His shirt was wrinkled. It was the same one he'd worn the night before. Sweat stains darkened his armpits. His eyes were bloodshot.

He halted at the stop sign and glanced both ways. "So are you gonna talk or what?"

"Talk about what?" Maisy clutched her bag to her chest. Her arms and legs were heavy with fatigue, her eyes gritty with unshed tears and dust. The cool air wafting from the vents dried the sweat on her face. She heaved a breath somewhere between a sob and a sigh. "We said it all last night."

"At least tell me where you're going."

"Why?"

"Because." He beat a rhythm with his thumbs on the wheel. "Because it feels weird to think I won't know where you are. You're carrying around a part of me. I figure I should know where you are."

"I didn't think you cared."

"That's bull and you know it." He ran one hand through his hair. It stood up, tousled like a little boy who'd just gotten out of bed. "I care. A lot. I don't do what we did with just anybody."

"It's hard to tell."

He pulled onto the highway, gunned the motor, and shot past an eighteen-wheeler. "You have a right to be mad at me."

"I'm not mad—"

"Just let me get this out." He wiped at his face with his sleeve and sniffed. "You caught me by surprise. It took me a minute to wrap my head around it."

"So what are you saying?"

"I could tell my parents. We could get married. If that's what you want. I think my mom would be okay with it. She's always after my big brother Tommy to give her grandkids and my sister Amanda too. You could stay with my parents while I finish school. My dad will have a cow, but hey, he's a dairy farmer. What's one more?"

Married to a English man. Living in an English world. Maisy closed her eyes. What would her life be like cut off from her family but living in the same small community? Would she wear pants, drive a car, and go to the Baptist church? She might be able to do the first two, but not the last one. Never the last one. Her plan had always been to join her church. Her rumspringa was a time for finding a man to share her life. Not for finding her faith. That she had.

"I can't. I just can't." She silently ordered her voice to cooperate.

Stop shaking. "It's nice of you to offer, but you don't want to marry me and I can't marry you."

"I figured."

"I'm going to Haven, Kansas. I have a cousin there. She's older, more like an aunt than a cousin, but she was always nice to me. We went to her wedding in Haven. She writes me letters, and she always says at the end that I should come for a visit."

Never dreaming it would be under these circumstances, no doubt.

"Okay. That's good, I guess."

"I'm really tired, Nate."

"Relax. I'll get you to KC, no worries."

Maisy closed her eyes and let the world pass her by. Sleep would be a relief. No need to think, to worry, to wonder about the future. Sweet relief.

"Hey, hey."

Fingers caressed her cheeks. A soft, warm, familiar touch. "Nate . . . Nate?"

Maisy sat up with a start. She opened her eyes.

His handsome face filled with regret, Nate eased away from her. "You were sleeping hard, girl."

"Where are we?"

"The Amtrak station. You slept the whole way."

If only she could sleep away this entire season of her life. Not just eighty minutes. She straightened. Her muscles and bones protested. It had to be how an old woman felt. The view from her window had changed. No more open wheat, alfalfa, and cornfields decorated along the edges with huge, brilliant sunflowers beckoning to the sun. No cattle and horses. Instead, cars, trucks, and taxis clogged the road, moving like snails into the station's vast parking lot.

Nate held up his phone. "I got on the website. The closest you can get to Haven is Hutchinson. There's only one train. It leaves at 10:42 tonight. You'll get there in the middle of the night. I tried Wichita, but it's the same deal. Are you sure you want to do this? What about a Greyhound bus?"

She'd traveled on Amtrak with her family, never a bus. They were already at the train station. Still, the middle of the night? Would she be safe traveling alone? She had the money she'd saved from her cleaning jobs, a tiny nest egg intended for when she married. A sob burbled in her throat. She swallowed it. "How much does it cost?"

His forehead furrowed, Nate did some fancy thumb work on his phone. After a few minutes he shook his head and shrugged. "There's not much difference in the tickets, if you do economy. Like less than sixty bucks. The next bus out of KC to Hutchinson doesn't leave until 8:20 a.m. tomorrow. You'd have to spend the night at the bus station. Or get a hotel room—"

"No, no, I can't do that." A shudder ran through Maisy. She'd heard the horror stories about the big city. And the bus stations. Better to leave tonight and pass the darkness on the train where everyone would be sleeping.

Nate scooched around on the seat so he was facing her. He leaned against his door. "I could stay with you."

"No. You've done enough."

"Too much, I guess."

"No more than I did."

"I can't just drop you off at the curb."

"It costs money to park, doesn't it?"

"I have money." He opened the console divider and pulled out a bulging, white envelope. "Here. It's for you."

He held it out. Maisy didn't move.

"Go on, take it."

"I told you I'm not . . . I'm keeping this baby."

"So you'll need money for stuff, like doctor's appointments, bigger clothes, healthy food and diapers and bottles, baby stuff." He leaned forward and tucked the envelope into her bag. "It's part of the money from the grand champion steer I sold at the county fair this summer."

"That's your college money."

"I've sold a steer or a pig every year since grade school. Plus Mom and Dad will help me. I'll be fine."

It didn't feel right. Or maybe it was. Pride couldn't be allowed to get in the way of what was best for her baby. Not their baby. Her baby. She would have to put him—or her—first from now on.

Maisy sucked in a long breath. She opened her door and took one quick look back at the father of this baby. "Thank you. And thank you for the ride."

"Let me go in with you. I can stay until the train comes."

"You should go home." If she was going to be on her own from here on out, she might as well start now. "I'll be fine."

"You're just a girl. You're hardly even grown up. You'd be a senior in high school if you were—"

"Not Amish? I haven't been baptized yet, but I *am* Amish in every other way. I'm a grown-up." And getting older by the minute. Old enough to make a baby, old enough to take care of him and herself. "Good-bye, Nate."

"Send me a picture."

"We don't take pictures."

Maisy hopped from the truck, hitched her bag's straps up on her shoulder, and set out for her future.

Chapter 4

HUTCHINSON MIGHT BE ONLY A MIDDLING-SIZED town, but that didn't stop it from getting on Joshua Lapp's last nerve. At least he wasn't in his buggy. Doug Haag, the van driver, had whipped through early morning traffic like the veteran driver he was. Joshua's aunt and uncle, with their passel of nine kids, were safely deposited on the train that would take them to Kansas City, where another driver would be waiting to ferry them to their home in La Plata, Missouri.

All that visiting had been exhausting. Time to get back to work, which seemed much less taxing after the weeklong visit. Joshua dodged a man lugging a massive suitcase and helping his wife with her walker. It didn't matter what time of day or night, the train station always teemed with people. People going places. Home was so much better. Quiet, open spaces, bright sunshine, soft winds. A recipe for peace.

He picked up his pace in the long aisle between benches that stretched from one end of the waiting area to the other. Dodged another couple arguing in loud voices, something to do with the cost of sleeper rooms. He plowed forward. His boot hit something in his path. He tripped, stumbled, and righted himself just in time.

A faded canvas bag was the culprit. Unable to hide a scowl, Joshua sought the owner. "You need to move that—"

"I'm so sorry."

The owner of the bag spoke in *Deutsch*. Her voice was low and weary. A Plain woman—a girl really—huddled on a bench. She snatched up her bag and stowed it on the seat next to her. She had dark circles around vivid blue eyes in a pale face. Her apron was wrinkled and her prayer covering askew, revealing more of her honey-blonde hair than she should. Despite being disheveled, she was pretty.

Joshua surveyed the area. No one. No Plain person at her side or nearby. What was she doing alone in the train station at four in the morning? Part of Joshua—the part encased in a stone fortress behind a deep, treacherous, alligator-infested moat—clamored to keep on walking. *Don't get involved.* A tiny sliver of his old self— the best part of him—clamped down on his leg muscles, making it impossible for him to move.

"It's okay." He responded in their native language. "Are *you* okay?"

She rubbed her eyes. "I can't believe I dozed off."

"I haven't seen you around here before." Joshua eyed the empty chairs across the aisle from hers. Should he sit? Would she wonder why a stranger—albeit a Plain one—was bothering her in a train station? His legs made the decision for him. He sat. "Are you waiting for someone or for a train?"

"Maybe you can point me in the right direction." Her voice was so soft and weary Joshua had to strain to hear her words. "I need to hire a driver to get me to Haven, to my cousin's house."

"I'm from Haven. Who might your cousin be?"

"Ruth Plank."

Small world, indeed. Joshua bounced up from the seat. Taking action was easier if a person didn't give it too much thought. "I'll carry your bag for you."

Arms tight around the bag, she shrank back in the chair. "Why would you do that?"

"I work for Amos Plank as a farmhand. I stay at Amos's during the week." Joshua glanced at the enormous clocks on the train station wall above the ticket counter. He introduced himself. "I need to get a move on, or I'll be late to work. My driver's waiting."

The girl stared at him for a long moment. There was something oddly assessing about her expression. As if she was deciding whether to trust him. Most Plain people would find encountering one of their kind out in the world a welcome oasis, a safe touch point. Not this one. "Do you think anyone would object to us traveling together?"

Her meaning took a moment to sink in. "I'll sit up front with Doug, the driver. He'll be our chaperone."

Still clutching the bag close to her body, she stood. "I would be so obliged if you could share your driver with me. I'll pay half his fee."

"No need—"

"I *need* to pay my own way. I don't want to be beholden to anyone."

"It's not a matter of being beholden. My daed paid him in full."

"Then I'll pay your daed."

Her fierce tone and steely glare said the outcome of this dispute had been decided. No need to waste another breath on it. Joshua spun around and headed for the door. He glanced back to make sure she followed. "May I know your name?"

Her pale face suffused red. "Maisy. Maisy Glick."

"Welcome to Kansas, Maisy Glick."

The thirty-minute drive from Hutchinson to Haven passed

mostly in silence. Doug, bless his heart, tried to make conversation with their new passenger, but Maisy seemed engrossed in peering out the window into the darkness as the van sped south along Highway 96. There wasn't much to see even in the daylight. Southeast Kansas was flatter than northwestern Missouri, with few trees, more open fields. If memory served. Joshua hadn't been back to Missouri since his family picked up and moved to Haven from La Plata ten years earlier. His parents went now and then for weddings, family reunions, and funerals. He begged off whenever possible.

"We're passing Yoder." Doug glanced back between the van's headrests in Maisy's general direction. "Blink and you'll miss it."

He hee-hawed with that braying laugh that always made Joshua chuckle—even if he didn't feel like it.

"I've been here before. When Ruth and Amos got married."

Doug's head bobbed in time to the bluesy music barely discernible over the rush of air and the road noise. "Then you and Josh know each other."

"No."

She spoke at the same time as Joshua, but with more force. Why? She didn't know him, but she seemed to hold something against him.

Five years ago. Joshua closed his eyes. She would've been a kid then. He cast about in his memories from that day. He would've been seventeen. His brother Peter, two years older, was married and determined Joshua would find his soul mate among the young girls seated at the table next to the newlyweds' *eck* at the wedding reception.

He'd escaped to the backyard and spent the afternoon cranking the handle on one of the ice-cream makers and spelling his dad at the barbecue pit.

He had no recollection of Maisy's heart-shaped face or searing blue eyes. Why would he remember a kid? She probably played games in the yard or gathered in those thick clusters the way girls that age did, whispering behind their hands, giggling, and day-dreaming about the day it would be their turn to sit at the corner table.

"I have a ham-and-cheese sandwich in my lunch box, a box of raisins, and a Heath bar." Doug took one hand off the wheel to hold up a dented black lunch box. "And a thermos of coffee so strong it'll take the enamel off your teeth. My wife always overpacks. She's sure I'll fall asleep at the wheel or faint from hunger. You'd think I was driving cross-country to Canada. It's not like I couldn't live off the fat of the land, if you know what I mean."

His bray filled the van. His belly, indeed, shook like a bowl full of jelly.

No response for a few seconds. "No, thank you." Maisy's voice sounded choked.

Doug settled the lunch box back on the seat. "It's right here if you change your mind. Just help yourself."

Finally Doug took the last turn and drove up the dirt road that led to Amos's place. Relief blew through Joshua. He could deliver Maisy Glick to her cousin and go back to doing what he knew how to do. He shoved open his door and moved to slide the passenger van's middle door open. "Here we are."

What a silly thing to say.

Her face a peculiar shade of green, Maisy leaned out. A second later she puked all over his dusty work boots.

Chapter 5

MAYBE SHE COULD CLIMB BACK INTO the van. Maybe Doug would drop her at the convenience store they'd passed on the highway. Maybe she could dash past Joshua and keep running until she reached Texas. Better yet, the Gulf of Mexico. Maybe the sky would open up and God would reach down with one mighty hand and carry her away. More like it'd be down, not up.

Maisy hunched over, hands on her knees, unable to raise her head and look at this man who'd shown a stranger an unexpected, likely undeserved, kindness.

"Let me help you into the house." Joshua's voice, soft, almost tender, strummed nerves wound so tight Maisy's fingers and toes hurt. "Ruth will know what to do."

Maisy hadn't come this far by being a coward. "I'm sorry." She tugged loose from his grip. "I'll wash everything."

"Don't worry about it. I'll hose myself down."

His sweetness was almost unbearable. She straightened and staggered past him. Mother never had morning sickness like this that lasted all day. Neither did her sister Nora. Or her sister-in-law, Susie. Or maybe they did and hid it better. Maybe it got better with each baby. Maybe they were stronger.

"Maisy. You made it. Danki, Gott." Ruth shoved through the screen door and bounded down the steps. "I was so worried. To come all this way by yourself."

She threw her arms around Maisy in a tight hug. A badly needed hug, but it almost did Maisy in. *Don't cry. No tears. Not one.*

"Not so far." Her voice was almost unrecognizable, her throat burning with bile, choked with unshed tears. "After Joshua changes I'll wash his clothes."

"Don't you worry none. I'll take care of Joshua."

Ruth's curious gaze skipped to Joshua, who stood as stiff as a fence post, staring at his spattered pant legs and boots. The smell wafting in the air sent Maisy's belly into another spasm. Ruth slid her arm around Maisy. "Go on, Joshua, go change. I'll have breakfast on the table in a few minutes. Amos is waiting."

Joshua nodded. He gave Maisy a long, level look, his dark-blue eyes revealing nothing. "It was nice meeting you."

How could he say that with a straight face?

Ruth's grip tightened around Maisy's waist. "Come on, let's get cleaned up."

With Ruth's help, Maisy made it up the steps to the back porch and into the kitchen. "You need to get breakfast."

"Amos can wait another minute or two. Fact is, he could pour his own cup of *kaffi* if he had a mind to." Ruth's chuckle was blithe, full of airiness. "Your mudder called my mudder, who called me. They figured you were headed this way."

Maisy faltered. "So you know."

"I do, *Kossin*."

"Did she say anything about coming to get me?"

"Nee. Only to let her know when you arrived safely."

Maisy halted in the middle of the kitchen with its sweet smell of fresh cinnamon rolls and coffee. Little Nicholas, his cheeks rosy, brown curls tousled, slept in a playpen in the corner. A calico cat curled up on the open window's sill. A soft morning breeze lifted the forest-green curtains. Ruth's kitchen bloomed with sweet peace. Maisy's presence promised to chase it away. "I'm sorry to bring my troubles to your house."

"We'll figure it out." Ruth had changed in the years since Maisy had seen her. She had merry aster-blue eyes, blonde curls that peeked from her prayer covering, and womanly curves that exuded health and recent childbearing. She bustled to the kitchen counter, where she picked up a package of thick-sliced bacon. "I've always said you could come here any time. I meant it."

"Is Amos amenable to me being here?"

"Amos doesn't say much about anything. He and Joshua are two kernels on a cob." Ruth peeled back pieces of bacon and dropped them into a huge cast-iron skillet. The crackling sound was followed by a scent Maisy once adored. "They both never met a silence they didn't like. I think that's why they get along so well. In fact, I'm amazed at how much he said to you just now."

He'd been quiet on the trip from Hutchinson. Doug had done enough talking for the two of them and then some. Maisy had supposed Joshua couldn't get a word in edgewise. "He said he works for Amos. Is he family?"

"Nee, a hired hand, but he stays here during the week. It's Amos's one concession to the fact that he can't do as much as he did before the accident."

The tractor-trailer driver who had hit Amos's buggy claimed it was all Amos's fault. He pulled out onto the highway in front of him. According to Ruth's letter the previous year, Amos couldn't remember. Such were his injuries. The collision crushed his right leg and left him with a severe concussion. Only sheer stubbornness—Ruth's choice of words—allowed him to walk again.

Now Maisy's presence would add to their difficulties. A wave of fierce regret enveloped Maisy. Her stomach rocked. Her head ached. Her mouth was so dry her tongue stuck to the roof of her mouth. A foul-tasting fur coated her teeth. "Kossin, I think there's something wrong with me."

"Besides being in a family way with the bopli of an Englisch man?" Ruth turned from the stove. Her smile took the sting from her words. "It's normal to feel sickly the first few months. I did both times. Most mudders I know do."

"It's been going on for a couple of months now. Morning, noon, and night." Maisy clutched her bag tighter to her chest. Her heart banged in her chest. "I can't keep food down. I'm losing weight. That can't be gut for this bopli. It's like my body is rebelling. It's sickened by what I've done. Maybe I'm being punished?"

It was a relief to pour out her fears aloud. Ruth had two children. She would know what to do.

Her expression placid, Ruth went to the gas-powered refrigerator and removed a pitcher of water. She poured a tall glass, placed a stack of saltines on a saucer, and carried both back to the table. "That's your guilty conscience talking. I'm no expert, no theologian, but I don't think Gott works that way. That bopli you're carrying is His child. He knows his name. He'll be able to count every hair on his head. You need to focus on getting healthy. That's all Gott wants from you right now. Wash your face and your hands and carry on."

Fresh, hot tears gathered behind Maisy's eyes. She went to the sink and washed them away, along with the grimy aftermath of her travels. "I don't know how I'm going to do this."

"Gott is going to do this. He is mighty." Ruth pointed at the crackers. "And I will help you. Try to eat a few. I'll make you some toast."

"Aren't you afraid others will judge you?" Maisy settled at the table. She nibbled at a cracker. Her throat was too dry to swallow it. Praying it would stay down, she sipped the water. "Will your bishop have something to say about it?"

"You're not a member of this Gmay. You're unbaptized. There's not much they *can* say—not aloud anyway." Ruth dropped the slices of bacon onto a plate and covered it with a paper towel. She cracked a dozen eggs with great efficiency. The smell of frying eggs floated through the air. "You let me worry about that. Every one of us has sinned and fallen short of the glory of Gott. Don't ever forget that."

This was the Ruth who'd passed many long afternoons with Maisy, making fry pies in the fall, embroidering on winter afternoons, and canning peaches and pickles on hot summer afternoons, while imparting tidbits of fledgling teenage wisdom to her younger cousin. "Danki, Ruth. I know you must think I'm a terrible person—"

"I think you're human." Ruth took a stack of plates from the open cabinet and settled them on the counter next to the stove. "I know I am."

"But you never did anything like this."

"I came very close, but Amos is a better person than I am. He never loses sight of right and wrong."

"Who never loses sight of right and wrong?" Amos stood in the doorway. He clasped Bonnie on one hip. She waved and stretched her chubby arms toward her mother. "This little one was calling for you. Didn't you hear her?"

"I didn't." Ruth wiped her hands on her apron and went to take their daughter from Amos. "*Guder mariye*, Bopli. You must be hungry."

"Her daed is." If Amos noticed Maisy sitting at the table, he didn't let on. If Ruth was all curves, light blondness, and blue eyes, Amos was wiriness with almond-brown eyes and dark-brown hair. "I have work to do . . . today . . . this morning."

"Go sit down. It'll be on the table in a jiffy." She took Bonnie from him and brought her to Maisy. "Entertain her for a few minutes."

Maisy took the little girl, still dressed in her nightgown, her tangled blonde curls falling in her sleepy face. All warmth and innocence. And a bundle of wiggles. She was beautiful.

Amos pivoted and limped away.

"Mudder, Mudder." Her dimpled cheeks pink, lips turned down in a pout, Bonnie screeched, "Mudder."

"You're okay. You're fine. Let Mudder finish breakfast." Maisy turned the two-year-old around so she faced Maisy and let her stand on her lap. "You don't know me, but I'm your second cousin Maisy. My family calls me Daisy Maisy because I love flowers so much."

The two-year-old's blue eyes widened. Her fat fingers patted Maisy's face. She giggled. "Daisy Maisy."

"That's me." Maisy gently hugged the little girl to her chest. She inhaled her scent. Had babies always smelled this good? She was old enough to remember the birth and toddler years of Sarah, Shelly, and Danny. Did they smell like milk and sunshine?

Would her own baby smell this good? Maisy's breath caught in her throat. Would it be a boy or a girl? Did it matter? Could she be the kind of mother Ruth was? Her chest ached with uncertainty. She had six months to figure this out. Six months. More than half a year. A long time. Not so long when the mountains yet to be climbed hid the view on the other side—the other world that waited for her there. Her baby would have no father. Every child needed a father. They might not have grandparents either, if Mother and Father chose not to let Maisy back into their lives.

"*Cross that bridge when you come to it.*" Grandma Irene's voice boomed in her head once again. "*Stop getting ahead of yourself.*" "Do you like peanut butter *eppies*? I do."

Bonnie nodded. "Eppies."

"That word she knows. I think she said it before she said Mudder or Daed." Ruth loaded plates with eggs, bacon, fried potatoes, and toast. "Help me carry these out to the other room before the food gets cold. Amos really hates cold eggs."

With Bonnie trailing after her like an undersized shadow, Maisy went to work serving breakfast. Ruth was right. Joshua and Amos had little to nothing to say. They shoveled food into their mouths like starving laborers. Ruth refilled coffee cups when they got low. No one seemed to find the silence awkward. If Amos wanted to know anything about Maisy's situation, he didn't show it. He didn't even ask about the rest of the family. Except for "pass the salt" he didn't address her directly.

Until Bonnie decided to toss a handful of eggs across the table at Joshua, a direct hit on his deeply tanned cheek. From there they dropped into his lap. Another handful followed a second later, this one splattered on his shirt. It left a greasy spot the size of a half-dollar.

"Dochder." Amos's face reddened. The muscle in his jaw twitched. "No more of that."

With a half-stifled snort, Joshua scooped up the eggs and dumped them on his napkin. "I've had worse on my clothes. No harm done."

Was he talking about the contents of Maisy's stomach? Amusement flickered in his face, as if he was reading her mind. "Manure stains and it smells worse."

Maisy breathed.

Bonnie let a piece of bacon fly. This time it landed in Joshua's dark-brown hair. He laughed outright, the sound bright in the somber air. "She's bent on sharing her food, isn't she?"

"Dochder, stop that." Ruth grabbed Bonnie's plate and moved it out of her reach. Despite her attempt at sounding stern, her grin slipped out. "We don't waste food, and we don't throw food."

"Maybe she's trying to tell you she's not hungry." The skin around his blue eyes crinkled with laugh lines, Joshua raised his coffee cup and toasted the little girl. "Or maybe she'd rather have ice cream for breakfast. I know I would. No offense, Ruth, your cooking is mighty gut."

Something about a two-year-old's antics had slain his reticence. For a minute he bordered on downright loquacious. Maisy liked these words. *Loquacious. Slain. Reticence.* She'd found them in her western stories and added them to her notebook of interesting words. Amos, on the other hand, would be laconic. Another good word.

"No offense taken." Ruth grinned. "Myself, I'd like a big piece of pecan pie with whipped cream."

They stared at Maisy expectantly. She groped for the first food to come to mind. "Pizza."

"Cold?"

Of course. Not that Mother ever let them eat it for breakfast. When she had her own home, her own family—if that ever happened now—she would serve it once a month. "Jah. Pepperoni, mushrooms, black olives, bell peppers, onions, extra cheese."

For the first time in months, her stomach didn't rebel at the thought of food.

Ruth and Joshua laughed.

"It's not funny." Amos finally spoke again. Through gritted teeth, his face a grimace, as if he had to chip the words from stone with a chisel. "Throwing food is wasteful. She isn't the day's entertainment. Take her from the table."

Her expression repentant, Ruth did as her husband instructed. Bonnie giggled and blew Joshua kisses. He flashed the toddler a grin. "Bye, Bonnie."

"Bye-bye, Joshua."

"She says your name." Amos's scowl deepened. "She doesn't say daed yet."

Joshua stood. He was a tall man, lean, but thick with muscle. "I'll meet you in the barn. It may rain. I reckon we better get a move on if we're going to cut the silage."

Amos's response was lost in an outraged squeal coming from the kitchen. Nicholas was awake and, from the sounds of his wailing, feeling abandoned. Maisy scooped up her plate and headed for the door. "I'll get him."

Amos's sour expression made his thoughts clear. Maisy's presence had planted a burr under his saddle. The least she could do was make herself useful. But there was something more pointed, something like judgment. "From what I hear, the practice will come in handy."

Maisy slowed. How did she respond to that? She ducked her head and let her gaze bounce to Joshua. His eyebrows lifted, but nothing in his expression suggested he knew what Amos was talking about. His gaze met hers head-on for a fleeting second. Something in his dark-blue eyes caught her by surprise. Sympathy.

It wouldn't last. He would know soon enough. Then he would be sorry he'd shared a ride with her.

"Practice makes perfect, they say." With that ridiculous statement, she fled.

Chapter 6

BLOOD PULSING IN HER EARS, MAISY trudged to the Pack 'n Play in the kitchen. Amos didn't want her here. That she could understand. If he decided she couldn't stay, that was that. Ruth would have to abide by her husband's decision. Maisy couldn't go back home. Where would she go? *Gott, help me.*

What a pitiful, puny little prayer. Was God even listening to her prayers now that she'd committed such an egregious sin?

Egregious: outstandingly bad, shocking. A word from her list. She'd memorized its meaning last week. She concentrated on saying the word in her head, sounding it out. In her haste to pack she'd left her notebook behind. She would have to buy another one. And more books.

Nicholas's wails ratcheted up another notch. "I know, I know, I'm coming." She plucked the baby from his portable bed.

He didn't seem happy to see her. He had his father's round face, long nose, fine dark-brown hair, and almond-brown eyes. Tears flowed down his pudgy cheeks. His arms and legs flailed.

"Goodness, you woke up in a mood, didn't you?" Maisy settled his chunky body against her chest.

The wailing got louder. He arched, his body stiff. His tiny fists punched the air.

"I know, I know, I'm a stranger. I understand." She cooed and murmured sweet nothings the way Mother had done with her brother Danny not so long ago. "Mudder will come for you any minute, I promise."

She carried him into the living room and settled into one of two hickory rocking chairs. "You must be hungry. I can't help you with that. Mudder will be right here, I promise."

An unpleasant odor wafted from the baby. So much for sweet baby smells. "I take it you need a diaper change as well." She stood again. "That I can help you with."

This was what it would be like to care for her own baby. Tears, dirty diapers, middle-of-the-night feedings. To be responsible for a helpless infant who relied completely on his mother. The impending weight of that responsibility settled like a heavy yoke on Maisy's shoulders. Was she up to the task?

"Here I am." Ruth trotted into the room, Bonnie trailing after her. "I had a talk with Bonnie while I changed her dress. She promises not to throw food again—until the next time."

"She promised not to act like a two-year-old?" Maisy couldn't help but giggle at her cousin's matter-of-fact statement. "It *was* wrong to laugh at her throwing food. We don't want her to think it's funny."

Bonnie seemed to know they were talking about her. She giggled, plopped down on the middle of the floor, and burst into a tuneless nonsensical song that might be about cats. Or maybe cookies. It was hard to say.

"Nee, we don't, but neither should we lose our sense of humor. There's plenty of time to instill a sense of decorum and respect in her. I'm not getting much sleep at night thanks to Nicholas, so I'm a little batty. I laugh at the silliest things. I guess it's better than crying."

"I'm on the verge of crying all the time. I've never been a crier. It's annoying."

"It's the hormones. That'll get better too—until after you have the bopli. Then you'll cry at the drop of a dirty diaper all over again."

Not if Maisy could help it. Crying did no good. In fact, it made things worse, what with the headache, the burning eyes, and the pitying looks people were bound to give her.

Nicholas had stopped crying, seemingly soothed by the sound of his mother's voice nearby. Maisy studied his tear-streaked face. He stared back at her, his brown eyes wide and serious. What did it feel like to hold for the first time a baby who'd grown in your body for forty weeks?

The question begged for an answer, but her lips refused to form the words. It was such a personal, private experience. One day she would know. By all rights, sooner than she should. "I'll change Nicholas's diaper. He's one stinky bopli."

"Ach, I'll do it. I need to feed him, anyway. You could start on the dishes, if you feel up to it." Ruth took Nicholas from Maisy with an experienced mother's touch. "I hate scrubbing dried egg yolk off the plates."

"I don't mind washing dishes. It's something I can do without thinking." Maisy followed her into the kitchen, where Ruth tossed a towel on the prep table and laid Nicholas down for the diaper change. A pile of skillets, pans, and dishes were waiting for Maisy to get busy. Being useful was good. It would make her less of a burden. "Whatever you need me to do, just say the word. I'm hoping I can be of help."

"Just having someone around I can talk to is nice." Ruth tossed the dirty diaper into a pail next to the table. "You do stink, Bopli. Worse than a garbage bin."

"I'm so sorry, Kossin. I should've asked first if it was okay for me to come." Maisy plunged her hands into hot, soapy water. She grabbed a skillet and scrubbed with more vigor than necessary. Asking would've given Amos the chance to say no. In her state of panic, she'd chosen to beg forgiveness instead. "If Amos doesn't want me here, I'll go. I'll figure out some other place to be."

"Amos will warm up to the idea. He's a gut mann, a gut daed, and a gut person. It just takes him a while to digest a situation and come to terms with it."

"I don't want to cause a rift between a mann and his fraa."

Ruth laughed. She had a hearty laugh that sounded well used. "Don't worry. It would take more than the likes of you to drive a wedge between Amos and me. We do plenty of tugging back and forth, but eventually we come to a meeting of the minds. He's a fair man. Some find him hard to get to know, but it's just his way. I've sweetened him up a bit. He'll loosen up now and then. Tell a joke. You wait and see."

I won't hold my breath. Maisy didn't give voice to that thought, but Ruth must've seen the incredulity in her face.

Incredulity was another word from Maisy's list. "What about Joshua? Does he live here? Is his family here? I don't remember him from the wedding."

"Joshua is Joshua. Most of the single women in our district watch him from a distance, waiting, hoping he'll ask one of them to take a ride with him, but he never does."

"So he doesn't have a special friend? He must be at least twenty or twenty-one. I wonder why."

Maisy hadn't been able to wait for the day she turned sixteen so she could attend the singings. More importantly she wanted to strike out into the world, try on life in sizes different from her own, and know what it felt like to be someone different from Maisy Glick, Plain girl. Not forever, just for a short while.

Look where that adventure had taken her.

"I don't know and he's not saying. His family moved here about ten years ago, from what I hear at the quilting frolics." Ruth wiped Nicholas's runny nose. He fussed. She pretended to fuss back until he giggled. "I've heard Daryl and Marnie lost a bu before they moved here, but they never talk about it. It's sure not my place to ask. Joshua hasn't been baptized either. There's been talk about that, too, but I have enough on my plate without borrowing from others."

Ruth was wise. How did she get that way so young? Amos's accident, his long recuperation, and the difficulties of running the farm while he was laid up surely had played a part in it. If only her wisdom could be bottled. Maisy would drink a quart of it. No, a gallon.

"Now I've added to your burden."

"Posh. These are sturdy shoulders. You're family, Kossin." Ruth patted Nicholas's diapered bottom, then sat him on the rug next to his sister. He removed his thumb from his mouth and wailed his disapproval. "Hush, Bopli. Play with your schweschder. I'll start the laundry and then I'll feed you. I'm running out of clean diapers. Nicholas is a big pooper, and Bonnie is only potty-trained when she decides she is."

Bonnie perked up at the sound of her name. "Eppies."

"Nee, no eppies."

"Bonnie hungry."

"You should have eaten your breakfast instead of playing catch with it."

Bonnie frowned. "Eppies."

"Nee."

She popped up from the floor and trotted to where Maisy stood. She tugged on Maisy's apron. "Eppies."

Maisy shook her head. Bonnie planted her hands on her tiny

hips and stomped her feet. Ruth laughed. "I guess she thinks you're a softer touch."

"I am, but I wouldn't dare say jah when her mudder says nee."

"Smart woman."

Obviously not. Maisy wouldn't be here now in her cousin's kitchen if she'd been smart. She'd let herself succumb to overpowering sensations that surely meant she was loved. Now she knew better. Lust and love were twins. They were far too easily mistaken, one for the other. "I don't know what I'm going to do."

"I know you don't." Ruth's voice softened. The note of laughter disappeared, replaced with almost unbearable sympathy. "We'll figure it out."

"What did my mudder tell your mudder?"

Ignoring Bonnie, who continued to whine, Ruth leaned against the counter, arms crossed. "That this Englisch man doesn't wish to marry you—a gut thing, everyone agrees. The bishop told them to keep you at home. You're not to go to church or town. Baptism—if you decide you still want to join the church—won't come until after the bopli's birth. They're to forgive, obviously, but it's not an easy thing. You ran away before they could speak to you."

"Did she say if they're coming for me?"

Did Maisy want them to come? Her brain hurt with the effort to imagine what it would be like to go back home now. Nor could it envision what life would be like here for the next six months. Or after that.

"Nee. She didn't say."

"It's better if they don't. It's better if I stay away."

"For you or for them?"

Maisy grabbed another skillet and went to work. The answer to Ruth's question was unclear. Coming here might have been cowardly. At the time, it seemed brave. "I don't know."

Nausea reared its ugly head. She leaned her forearms on the sink and lowered her head.

Ruth rubbed her back. "If you need to lie down for a bit, go."

"I'm fine."

"I figure you haven't seen a doctor yet."

"Nee." She'd been in denial right up until the moment that it simply couldn't be denied. "But there's no doubt."

"You need to get an exam to see if everything is as it should be. My best friend is a midwife. We'll run over to her place this afternoon for a visit. She can help you with the morning sickness."

Better name would be all-day sickness. The thought of talking to a stranger about her situation—and the exam that came with it—was about as appealing as having her arm or leg amputated, but Maisy drew a shaky breath and nodded.

"Gut, it's settled then."

Nothing was settled. Far from it. Maisy went back to scrubbing skillets. At least that was something she knew how to do well.

Chapter 7

NONE OF HIS BUSINESS. JOSHUA STRODE to the flatbed wagon he'd hitched up to the tractor. Really it wasn't. Still, the anguish on Maisy's face when Amos spoke of "practice coming in handy" pestered Joshua.

Ignore it. Check the equipment.

The binder was attached, the gas tank full. His job was to trot along behind it, catching the bound clumps of stalks and throwing them on the flatbed while Amos drove the tractor through the cornfield. From there they'd switch to the corn chopper. A guy needed to keep his mind on his work or find himself getting pulled down the conveyor belt and his legs chopped up in the blades. Good enough reason for a man to mind his own business.

Maisy looked more like a girl than a woman with her bony body and her nose and cheeks dusted with freckles by the sun. Like a lost waif with blue eyes too big for her face and ragged honey-blonde curls that kept escaping from her crooked prayer covering. Why had she traveled alone from Jamesport? Why did that misery peek out from those big eyes? Why did she hurl on his boots?

Maybe she had a bad case of the flu. No, if that were the case, she wouldn't be serving breakfast, sitting at the table, or taking care of the baby. On the other hand, she'd made a single piece of toast last an entire twenty minutes at breakfast, every nibble a study in determined swallowing.

Until Bonnie threw that handful of eggs. Then she'd perked up. Her description of pizza for breakfast had been delivered with genuine gusto.

So who was she? Besides Ruth's cousin. And why did her arrival provoke such distaste in Amos?

Mind your own business.

"She's my fraa's kossin."

Amos rarely offered a comment on the weather, let alone family matters. He was indeed rattled. Joshua climbed onto the flatbed. "So she said."

"Ruth's beholden to you for giving her a ride. I don't know what the girl was thinking—taking a train to Hutchinson with no plan for a driver at this end."

"Worked out, I reckon."

"Gott provided."

Joshua didn't bite. Keeping his thoughts on God's provision to himself was a lesson he learned not long after the fire.

Not long after Jacob died.

As usual his mind shied away from the last two words, as nervous as an unbroken filly wearing a saddle for the first time. Jacob died. Ten years ago last month. "You ready?"

Favoring his right leg, Amos hauled himself onto the tractor. He couldn't hide the grimace of pain that hadn't subsided, even after a year. "Jah. But I need to go see Bryan in a bit."

See the bishop. The puzzle pieces abruptly fell into place. A sharp mental slap on the forehead made Joshua's ears ring. Maisy's situation happened rarely enough that it simply wasn't the first scenario to come to mind. No wonder Amos was rattled. No wonder the woman—definitely a woman—looked so lost. For all intents and purposes, she was—according to her family and her community. "I'll drive the silage to the silo while you do that, then."

"Ruth misses her family."

Amos seemed intent on justifying his decision to allow Maisy to stay in his home. As if Joshua had any business judging him. "My mudder still misses her family in La Plata."

Even after ten years. Not that she said as much, but she'd had that misty look on her face this morning when her family had tromped from the house and loaded up the van for the trip to the train station. Moving to Haven had been his father's idea. He had a brother and a sister with family here. All Mother's kin were in Missouri, but she didn't argue. She was like a pillow that had lost its stuffing in those days.

"I'll tell Bryan you said hey."

Amos's way of saying he knew Bryan was still waiting for Joshua to step up and take the baptism classes. He didn't bother to respond. That wouldn't happen anytime soon. Even the anxious glances from his mother, his father's irritated sighs, the perplexed looks from his brother Peter didn't go unnoticed. Nobody asked Joshua outright, of course. The decision was his and his alone. It wasn't that he didn't believe in God. He did. Whether He was a good God, that was another prickly porcupine of a question.

The morning passed in a blur of engine noise, gas fumes, dust, and sweat that ensured the itchy bits and pieces of stalk stuck to Joshua's wet shirt and neck. His shoulders and arms grew weary. His parched throat ached for a cool drink.

They were only halfway through the rows when Amos halted and turned off the tractor. He wiped at his face with his sleeve. "Time to eat."

Lunch, like breakfast, started out quietly. Bonnie stuffed handfuls of mac and cheese into her mouth, while Nicholas nimbly used his thumb and forefinger to pick up one Cheerio at a time and gum it. The chair Maisy had occupied earlier was empty.

By the time Joshua pulled the last hunk of crisp fried chicken from the bone, sopped up the last of the gravy with a slice of bread, and guided them into his mouth, both little ones were covered with chocolate pudding. To be sure, more was on their clothes and faces than in their mouths—a fact that seemed to leave Ruth unperturbed.

Amos jerked his head toward the empty chair. "Why isn't Maisy helping you?"

"I sent her to rest. She was up all night traveling." Ruth expertly wiped down her son with wide swathes of washcloth. Nicholas's angry squalls suggested he didn't appreciate it. "Plus she was feeling poorly."

"If she's going to stay, she'll need to make herself useful."

"She will." Ruth's acerbic tone matched the sharp look she shot at her husband. "But right now she needs to rest. She has women problems you wouldn't understand."

Amos's face reddened. "No need to be disrespectful of your *mann*."

"It wasn't my intention." She applied the same cleaning technique to Bonnie, who handled it better than her brother. "I just hate to see disrespect toward family members."

Joshua slid back his chair. "I'll just head out to the silo—"

"Nee, have some more cold tea. I have peach pie left over from supper last night." Ruth tugged Nicholas from his high chair and settled him on the floor. "You can't let it go to waste."

Joshua scooted his chair back to the table.

"I'm going to see Bryan." Amos tossed his napkin on the table. "You should go with me, Fraa. Maisy can take care of the *kinner*."

"I had planned to take Maisy to see Kate." Ruth trotted around the table, scooping up their plates, stacking them as she went. "She hasn't seen a midwife yet. She needs to do it right away."

Amos's growl approximated the sound of a bear Joshua had heard once in the mountains when he hunted with friends who'd settled in the far reaches of northwest Montana. Not the least friendly. "And now it becomes your problem."

"She's family."

"I think I'll save the pie for supper." Joshua patted his belly. "I'm full to the brim. Gut fried chicken, Ruth. As gut as my mudder's. Don't tell her I said that. Danki."

This time he scooted his chair out, rose, and beat a quick retreat out the door to the yard. It might be a hot August day outside, but it was far toastier inside the Plank house.

Plain husbands and wives rarely aired their differences in front of others. Usually they saved these discussions for behind closed doors and presented a united front. Especially Amos and Ruth. They never argued—not even playfully. They would regret this discussion.

And it didn't bode well for Maisy if she planned to stay long. It seemed unlikely that her family had kicked her out. Why was she here and not with the father of the baby?

None of your business.

Still he couldn't shake the image of her forlorn, pale face as she sat all alone in the train station. Nobody, no matter her sin, deserved to be that alone in an uncaring world.

None of your business.

Time to work. Work was salve for the soul. That's what his grandpa said.

Amos stomped out the door and down the porch steps. "I'm

taking the old tractor. It'll be faster. I'll be back when I get back. Take the load to the silo."

With pleasure. Joshua stifled a sigh of relief. "Will do."

Ruth had won this skirmish, but the set of Amos's shoulders left no doubt the battle had only just begun.

Chapter 8

"Maisy, wake up! Wake up!"

Maisy forced her eyes open. Where was she? The bedroom wasn't familiar. Her cheeks pink with exertion, Ruth stood over her. Her cousin Ruth. Haven. Amos's house. The baby. It all come flooding back in a sickening wave. Ruth patted Maisy's face a second time. "Your mudder is calling. Joshua walked by the phone shack and heard the phone ringing, so he answered it. Can you go?"

"Jah, jah." Maisy slid from the bed. She stuck her prayer covering on her head and pinned it in place. Hands still on her head, she ran barefooted down the hall and out the front door. "He won't let her hang up, will he?"

"Nee. Your shoes!"

Maisy didn't stop. The hard-packed earth didn't bother her feet. Not when her mother was at the other end of the lane. The phone shack was a twin to the one in her parents' front yard. Squat, small, and sporting a single solar panel on its tin roof.

His expression tentative, Joshua handed over the receiver without a word.

"Danki, danki."

He nodded and slipped away.

Heaving a breath, Maisy sank onto an old caned chair with wobbly legs. "Mudder?"

"Maisy, you made it all right, then." Mudder's voice sounded tinny and broken over the line. "I know it's wrong to worry, but I couldn't help myself."

"It was fine. Nate . . ." She stumbled over his name. She cleared her throat. "The baby's father drove me to Kansas City. He gave me money for the baby."

"Shoo, shoo, you stinkin' vermin!"

Was she referring to Nate as stinking vermin? "Mudder?"

"That rooster thinks he lives here. He won't leave me alone."

"He did the same to me when I used the phone before I left." Maisy laughed—a high, nervous laugh that matched the one her mother uttered from the other side of the world—at least it seemed that far. "He's a pest, isn't he?"

"So is Skeeter. He followed me down here. He thinks you're coming back like always." A *woof* punctuated her words. Mother's sigh filled the line. "How did you get to Haven from Hutchinson?"

Maisy explained.

"Gott provided. He is gut." Some of the angst left Mother's voice. She sounded more like herself. "You shouldn't have left without talking to us first."

"I needed to go. I wanted to spare you and Daed the shame of my presence." Maisy's terrible homesickness couldn't be allowed to matter. "You don't deserve to have me there constantly reminding you of what I've done."

"You're our dochder." Mudder's voice quavered. She paused. Sniffles filled the silence. "I'm being *narrisch*." Another long breath. "You will always be loved. No matter what you've done or do. Don't forget that."

Maisy breathed through the desire to shed her own tears. "That's gut to know."

"Your daed seems harsh and angry, but he's really more disappointed. He didn't want you to go either. No matter what he says."

"It breaks my heart to disappoint him like this." Maisy rubbed her fingers down her throat. It didn't help to assuage the ache. "He's right to be angry. He's tried hard to teach us right from wrong. I'm the only one to blame for this terrible sin."

"Never forget that you sinned, but that bopli is a gift. We would never turn our backs on the bopli either."

"I know," Maisy whispered.

"You could've stayed. The bishop and deacon agreed that you would have to stay away from everyone until the bopli is born. You aren't subject to the *meidung*, but they don't want you to influence the others with your poor choices. You could've stayed in the *dawdy haus* until then. Life would have gone on. We would help you raise your bopli."

"It would be so hard for you and Daed and for the kinner. As it is I can imagine how they felt when you told them why I left."

"Sarah keeps crying. Shelly isn't old enough to understand yet. All she knows is her big sister went away without saying good-bye."

"If everything goes well I can come back after the birth."

"That's what I told them. It's not forever. Just for a season."

"Does Daed know you called?"

"He knows I intended to call. I wouldn't do it without telling him."

Because she was a good wife. She set a good example. Why hadn't Maisy followed it? A few moments of pleasure in exchange for hurting everyone who loved her. "I hope they learn from my mistake."

"It's been my experience that people have to make their own

mistakes." Mother's dry chuckle held little humor. "It's human nature, I suppose."

"I should go. Ruth's taking me to see the midwife who delivered her kinner."

"Tell Ruth your daed and I are thankful for Amos's willingness to allow you to stay with them."

Mother didn't need to know how little Amos seemed to like the idea. "I will. I'll work hard to help Ruth and take care of the kinner. I'll make myself useful."

"Gut."

"I should go."

"I know." More sniffles. "Be gut, Dochder. Write us a letter. Let us know how you're doing."

"I will."

"Faeriwell."

Maisy laid the receiver in its cradle. She covered her face with her hands for a few seconds, then straightened. Mother and Father loved her. Remembering that would help get her through the days ahead. God had blessed her with good parents.

Now she had to be the same for her baby.

Chapter 9

THE STEADY SWAY OF THE BUGGY, its creaky wheels, and the thud of horse's hooves on the hard-packed dirt road lulled Maisy until she could barely keep her eyelids open. Even with the nap she'd taken earlier in the day, she was still bone tired. *Snap out of it.* Sleeping through lunch meant not helping Ruth cook, serve the food, or clean up. Not the impression she wanted to make on Amos. She needed to make herself useful. The last thing Ruth needed was another burden. The thought skittered away. Her eyelids drooped. *Stay awake. Stay awake.*

"Stop fighting it. Take a nap." Ruth swiveled her head to peek at the toddlers inside the boxlike buggy. "Bonnie and Nicholas are."

"I just woke up from a nap. I never nap during the day."

"You spent yesterday traveling on a train and got to Hutchinson in the middle of the night. You're bound to be tired." Ruth patted a canvas bag resting on the seat between them. "I grabbed a package of saltines and a Sprite in case you want them."

Maisy was bound to be tired because of the bopli she was carrying. Ruth didn't have to state the obvious. Maisy pulled the can of pop from the bag and opened it. The lukewarm fizzy drink slaked her parched throat. "Danki."

"No need to thank me. I never had much morning sickness, but when I did it sucked the energy from me. Especially with Nicholas since Bonnie was only eighteen months old. She's always been a handful. A strong-willed child."

No wonder Bonnie tugged at Maisy's heartstrings. "My eldre say I'm strong-willed."

"I made my share of trips to the woodshed."

"I can't imagine spanking Bonnie." Maisy took another sip of pop. Her stomach gurgled. *Nee, sei so gut, not again.* "She's so young. She's still exploring the world. She's still trying to figure out what's allowed and what's not."

Could Maisy still use that excuse? She was eighteen. She knew what was allowed. And what was acceptable behavior. Yet she'd still managed to break the rules. Not just break them, crush them into tiny pieces.

"You do a child no favors by sparing the rod." A pinch of sarcasm dusted Ruth's words. "Or so Amos reminds me at least once a day. I know he's right, but it's a hard lesson."

"My daed didn't spare the rod and I'm still a mess."

"I reckon he's asking himself if he did enough, what he did wrong, what he should've done differently."

Which only made Maisy feel worse. Her father had no blame in this fiasco. "It's my fault. All my fault."

"Yours and the bopli's father."

Only Nate could walk away free and clear in the aftermath. It did no good to dwell on that. Bitterness didn't help. "Where did Amos go?"

"To talk to Bryan, our bishop."

Likely he sought support in sending Maisy home. He didn't

have to have it, but it would help him with Ruth's objections. If asked to leave, Maisy would go. Where, she didn't know.

Back to square one. "Tell me about Kate."

"Kate Coblentz delivered Bonnie, but we were friends long before that. Since I married Amos and moved here. She's a full-time midwife and *aenti* to every bopli she's delivered in this area."

"She doesn't plan to marry?"

"Nee. According to Kate, she loves catching boplin—that's what she calls delivering them—too much to ever give it up."

Not too many Plain women willingly chose the single life, but there were a few. Mostly teachers. "She doesn't want her own?"

"If she feels an emptiness in her life, she never lets it show. She's the happiest, most content woman I've ever met." Smiling as if the thought gave her joy, Ruth raised her face to the sunshine streaming overhead. "She's a gut example for all of us when it comes to making peace with who we are and where we are. She lives with her parents, Moses and Alice Coblentz, and her sister Amy, her husband, and their kids, plus the Coblentz kinner who aren't married and out of the house yet. Their home's bursting at the seams, so I reckon she has little time to be lonesome."

If first impressions could be trusted, Maisy had to agree with her cousin. Twenty minutes later Kate rushed out to the yard to greet them within seconds of their arrival in the Coblentzes' front yard. A flock of small children flowed after her, an enormous, fluffy dog, and a teenage girl with a baby on her hip, like an impromptu parade.

"Hello, hello. It's been forever and a day since you came visiting." Kate trotted toward the buggy with arms wide in a welcoming air hug. She beamed. "Where are those boplin? Let me at them. And who's this with you? *Bewillkumm, bewillkumm.*"

Ruth made the introductions while extracting Bonnie, now

wide awake, from the back seat. Kate took her with a kiss and a hug. "How's my sweet *maedel* doing?"

Bonnie responded by wrapping her arms around Kate's neck and planting a slobbery kiss on the woman's cheek. Despite the din, Nicholas remained sound asleep. Maisy carried him into the house where Kate shooed the other children into the living room with promises of a snack later.

"My schweschder took Mudder and Daed into town for doctor's appointments. Her mann and the buwe are at the cabinet shop." Kate pointed to a long pine table that would seat at least a dozen and a half people. "Have a seat, have a seat, while I pour us some tea. It's hotter than an overused oven this afternoon. You never mentioned you were expecting company, Ruth."

"Truth is, I wasn't." Ruth laid Nicholas in a Pack 'n Play nestled between the table and shelves loaded with foodstuffs, pots, pans, and skillets. "This isn't actually a social visit. Maisy's come to see you."

The pause in pouring the cold tea lasted only a split second. Kate turned and carried two glasses to the table. "Ruth, why don't you take the kinner out on the front porch to eat the watermelon I just sliced. It's cold. It'll hit the spot, and it won't make a mess in the house. Me and Maisy will get to know each other."

Ruth obliged. Maisy's desire to run after her tussled with the knowledge that this was the first of many such moments to come. For the baby's sake. She heaved a breath, determined not to hurl the crackers she'd eaten on the buggy ride.

Kate took a seat on the bench across from Maisy. The hair peeking from her prayer covering was a shiny silver, but the skin on her face was still smooth, making it impossible to guess her age. Her brown eyes were warm behind black-rimmed glasses.

"Do you know how far along you are?"

"I think three months."

"But you haven't seen a doctor or a midwife to confirm you're expecting or if that's right?"

Head down, shoulders hunched, Maisy traced the condensation on her tea glass. She shook her head. "Nee."

"Not a problem. Let's start from the beginning."

Kate left the kitchen and came back with a chunk of paperwork on a clipboard, an oversized backpack, and a plastic cup with a lid. In a soft voice she led Maisy through a series of questions, mostly about her general health and medical history. She took Maisy's temperature and her blood pressure. Both were fine.

"That's a good start."

But only a start. From there it likely would become more uncomfortable. "What I need you to do now is to go into the bathroom and fill this cup for me." Kate pushed it across the table in Maisy's direction. "When you're done I'm going to show you how to use a test strip to measure the level of a certain hormone in your pee. You'll do that each time we visit. You'll also weigh yourself. I'll show you the scale after we get done in the bathroom."

Heat bloomed from Maisy's ears to her toes. Her stomach lurched. She took the cup from Kate. "You do this in your eldre's house?"

"I have for years. I use my bedroom as a sort of office-slash-exam room when need be, but from here on out, I'll come to you."

"How much does this cost?"

"We'll work that out. Let's focus on your bopli right now. I promise I've never turned anyone away ever."

With simple matter-of-fact kindness, Kate walked her through each step, right up to her bedroom-slash-office and the exam Maisy had been dreading most of all. She sat on the very edge of the bed, arms clutched to her chest, and shivered, despite the sweat trickling down her forehead. "Do we really have to do this?"

"We need to know how big that peanut you're carrying is. Women all over the world do this. None has ever died of embarrassment. I promise you."

There was a first time for everything.

Maisy closed her eyes, gritted her teeth, laid back, and stared at the ceiling. She silently repeated the words on her list starting with the a's: *abashed, abdicate, abyss, acrimony* . . . pulling out their definitions and dusting them off, one by one.

"Jah, jah, gut, gut."

Maisy opened her eyes and raised her head so she could see Kate's face. "It's gut?"

"With the information and dates you've given me, the measurements, and what I'm feeling, I'd say you're right on. Twelve weeks. According to my calculations, your due date is sometime in early March. Let's say March first."

Twelve weeks. Only twenty-eight to go. A spring baby.

"Shall we see if we can hear your bopli's heartbeat?"

"We can do that?"

Kate held up a gizmo. "With this portable doppler, we can. At twelve weeks' gestation, we should be able to hear it. Would you like that?"

"Jah. Nee. Jah."

Kate moved the gizmo around on Maisy's stomach. It didn't hurt. It didn't feel like anything at all.

Then it happened. *Whoosh, whoosh, whoosh.* A steady, quick whooshing filled the air. Strong.

A laugh burbled up in Maisy. She came up on her elbows. "It's loud."

"The doppler amplifies it, but your bopli has a strong heartbeat."

"But I can't even tell it's there yet. I can't feel it."

"Nee. Your bopli is about the size of a plum right now. About three inches long. His toenails, fingernails, and bones are forming. He has a fine layer of hair over most of his body."

"You can tell all that from that little gizmo?"

"Nee." This time Kate laughed out loud. "I have a little booklet I'll give you. You can track the development as you go, if you're interested. Not all Plain mudders care to know. First-time mudders sometimes do."

Maisy sank back on the bed. She had a baby the size of a plum inside her. A person could know that but not really know it. A little heartbeat inside her. How would Nate have felt if he heard it? "You haven't asked me about the daed."

Kate held out her hand. "Let's go back to the kitchen and have a glass of tea."

Maisy accepted her help up. Once on her feet, a wave of dizziness swept over her. Nausea rocked her. "I have to . . ."

Once again she raced to the bathroom. Afterward Kate stood outside the bathroom, waiting for her.

"So you're still having morning sickness."

"Morning, noon, and night, for months. That was my first clue . . ."

Kate patted her shoulder and led Maisy into the kitchen, where she instructed Maisy to sit. She prepared a cup of lukewarm tea and set it in front of Maisy. "It's ginger tea. It should help."

Maisy sat across the table and poured out her symptoms. Kate clucked and nodded and took notes on her clipboard. Finally, she laid down her pencil. "Would you be open to seeing a midwife at the birthing center in Yoder?"

"You said you were a midwife."

"I'm a lay midwife. In Kansas, lay midwives don't have to be certified, but we also have certified registered-nurse midwives who are associated with birthing clinics. They have much medical training. And they have associations with nearby hospitals and doctors."

"Just because I throw up a lot, I need all that?"

"Not necessarily. But what you're describing is something with a big fancy name: hyperemesis gravidarum. It can cause you to be dehydrated, like you're not getting enough water. That's bad for you and the bopli. It could get worse if we don't treat it. I'm able to handle what the docs like to call *uneventful births*. Yours might not be."

Knowing a bunch of big words didn't help one iota with this conversation. Her mother delivered all her babies at home with Grandma Irene and Grandma Liza's help. They'd had eighteen babies between the two of them and delivered a few others. No one thought too much of it. "My *groosmammis* delivered all my brieder and schwesdchdre. They weren't midwives. They didn't have that gizmo or strips or scales."

"That's true. Lots of Plain women decide to do it that way. I'm somewhere in between, I reckon. I figure if we have ways to make sure boplin are healthy and mudders are healthy, a little extra help don't hurt. In your case, we need to make sure you drink lots of water. You might need some medicine. The ladies at the birthing center could help with that."

"Can't you just tell them about me and see what they say?"

"They'll want to do some lab work and take a peek at you." Kate slid her hand across the table and patted Maisy's hand. "I know it's a lot for a youngie like you to take in. But the birthing center is run by a *Mennischt*. She's a nurse and certified midwife. The Plain folks got together with the Mennischt folks and had a frolic to build the center. It's meant for women like you. Lots of Englisch women go there too. They take all kinds."

"Can I think about it?"

"Of course. Talk to Ruth. She's been there."

"I thought you delivered Nicholas and Bonnie."

"Bonnie came along with no problems. Ruth had some problems when she was carrying Nicholas. The only reason I delivered him was because he came too fast for us to get her to the clinic. That bu was in an all-fire hurry to see the world."

Kate went to the counter and cut a slice of homemade bread. She toasted it on the stove, all the while talking. "In the meantime I'll give you a pamphlet that has some suggestions that should help. Like no greasy, spicy, and fatty foods. Hard to do, I know, the way we Plain folks like to eat. Eat small meals several times a day instead of three big ones. Try bananas, rice, applesauce, and foods that have ginger in them."

The opposite in every way to what Maisy was used to eating. And what about all the time spent around food cooking it? Some things couldn't be helped. "Like gingerbread or gingerbread cookies?"

Chortling all the way, Kate traipsed to the table with a saucer that contained the dry toast and a lollipop. "I like the way you think. Eat this toast if you can, wash it down with the tea. Then suck on the ginger pop. If it helps, I'll give you some more to take home."

So much information, so much to learn. Her notebook sure would come in handy.

"Don't worry. It's all in the pamphlet. The important thing is to drink a lot of fluids. Water, ginger ale, 7-Up, Sprite—whatever whets your whistle. Six to eight cups a day—but no caffeine."

Whoa, Nelly. Back up the buggy. "No kaffi?"

"Unless it's decaf. Even then it's better to avoid it."

The one thing that had helped Maisy stay awake after sleepless nights these last few months. "What would be the point of that?"

"I'm right there with you, my friend. Kaffi is acidic, and the caffeine dehydrates you more. You'll feel better without it."

That didn't seem likely. "Ach. Okay."

"There's one more thing. I'm hoping these suggestions help, but if you still end up on the bathroom floor, be sure to brush your teeth afterward. All that stomach acid is hard on them too."

Such a fine conversation for a sunny afternoon. The tea and toast did help, though. That and the fact she'd survived her first appointment with the midwife. Giving up coffee would be worth it if it meant not going to the birthing clinic in town. Kate, a Plain woman, a friend of Ruth's, she was enough. No exams by any other strangers.

Maisy's stomach settled. All was good.

"So I need a little bit of information about the bopli's father."

The stomach gurgle returned with a vengeance. Maisy breathed, in and out, in and out. Fingers tight around her mug, she recited the basic facts. "What else do you need to know?"

"That'll do. He's not in the picture. If we need to know more of his medical history down the road for any reason, you know where to find him. That's gut."

If Kate had any thoughts about Maisy's lack of judgment or her moral deficits, they didn't show on her face. Maisy choked down another bite of toast and sipped her tea. When she was sure she could speak without her voice quivering, she formed the question. "Why would you need his medical history?"

"It's not for sure, but sometimes babies inherit genetic conditions or diseases from their parents—either parent. It's just gut to know where to find him."

This having a baby seemed more complicated than Maisy remembered. "Ruth says you called delivery catching the baby."

"Jah. All I do is catch that little whippersnapper. You do all the work. Women have been having babies since the beginning of time. Your body knows what to do. Especially if you eat gut and take care of yourself from now until then. I stay out of the way, unless I'm needed. Mostly I'm not."

Maisy tugged her bag from its spot on the chair next to her. She pulled out the envelope Nate had given her and held it out. "You still haven't said how much your help will cost."

Kate didn't reach for the envelope. "Save that money in case you need it for the clinic."

"But I can't let you do this—"

"I get to decide when and where I get paid. That's one of the things I love about my job." She waved away the envelope and Maisy's objections. "Just mind your manners and stick that back in your bag for when you really need it."

People could be so nice. So nice it was almost unbearable. A person who'd done what Maisy had done didn't deserve nice. Tears clogged her throat. She gulped down the rest of her tea and reached for the ginger pop.

"How's it going in here?" Ruth poked her head in the doorway. "The kinner polished off every bite of watermelon and decided to wash off in the horse tank. You can imagine how that went."

"Come in, come in." Kate stacked up her paperwork and slipped it into a folder. "We're just nattering on. Who fell in and who needs dry clothes?"

"They're all sopping wet." Ruth held Nicholas on one hip and tugged Bonnie, who had a dirty face and watermelon juice down the front of her dress, toward the sink. "They decided to drip dry in the sun, so they're all lying in the grass trying to outdo each other finding animals in the clouds."

"Ah, kinner do live the life, don't they?" Kate chuckled, a sound like the tinkling of wind chimes in a hearty breeze. "They're so eager to grow up. If they only knew."

If they only knew. Growing up had been fun when Maisy had been running around. Now it was a thicket full of prickly thorns.

Ruth finished cleaning up her two little ones. Neither appreciated her effort. "Are you ready to go home, Maisy?"

Home. The single syllable pressed on Maisy in a way that none of her big, highfalutin words could help. Not home. A haven.

Haven: a place of safety or refuge; an inlet providing shelter for ships or boats; a harbor or small port.

For now.

Chapter 10

No one talked much at the supper table. Mindful of Kate's advice, Maisy put a roll, a banana, and applesauce on her plate. Her belly accepted most of it without complaint. What she didn't eat she shared with Bonnie and Nicholas. Amos's eyebrows got a workout, but he said nothing when she passed the platter of roast beef and the fried potatoes without helping herself to them. Ruth said little. Joshua said nothing. Finally it was time to clear the table. Maisy stood and reached for the bowl of potatoes.

"Wait, Maisy. Before you clear the table, we need to talk." Amos pushed his plate away and leaned back. "Joshua, do you mind?"

"I've got some harnesses to repair." He shoved back his chair and stood. "*Gut nacht.*"

Maisy's stomach clenched. *Here we go. Did she need to pack her bags? Where would she go? How far would Nate's bundle of cash take her?*

"Gut nacht." She slipped back into her chair.

Ruth put both children on the floor and gave them each their own stack of wooden blocks. Nicholas rolled over on his tummy and smacked one across the floor. Bonnie giggled and ran over it with a metal tractor. This activity might give the adults five minutes of uninterrupted conversation.

"I spoke with our bishop this afternoon."

"Ruth said you planned to do that." Maisy bunched up her apron between her clenched hands. "I understand why you needed to do that."

"Bryan is a kind man, a gut man." Ruth moved to sit next to her husband. A united front. As it should be. "He is learned as well. His time as bishop has given him experience in how to deal with issues that come up in a way we hope is pleasing to Gott."

Now she was an issue that "came up." Maisy forced herself to nod. She'd created a problem for her sweet cousin and her husband. Whatever came next she'd brought upon herself. "That's gut. I'm glad to hear it."

"Our deacon and minister also sat in on our meeting."

Amos was having trouble getting to the point. Or Maisy's nerves were shredded. She took a sip of now-lukewarm water. Sweat beaded on her forehead. A feverish warmth settled on her face. "Gut."

Ruth leaned forward and stretched her hands across the table as if to touch Maisy. The remaining space was only a few inches, but it seemed insurmountable, a vast divide filled with a raging river of self-recrimination, fiery brimstone, and the disappointment of everyone Maisy cared about. "It's going to be all right, Kossin. We love you. We will love your bopli. Remember that."

The iron grip on Maisy's throat tightened. Unable to speak, she nodded.

"Bryan and the other elders agreed. You will not attend church with us. There's no harm in your staying here, however. The kinner are too young to understand why you're here. They'll not be affected by your decisions."

"You're not to talk with the district's youngies about why you're here." Ruth's gaze was downcast. She didn't like where this was going. "'So as not to tarnish them' is the way he phrased it."

"Understood." As if she would go around spouting the joys of premarital relations and how she'd come to be in this predicament. "I wouldn't."

"I know, but Bryan wanted it stated so there would be no misunderstanding."

"He also suggested you get a job in town." Amos's voice turned gruff. His ears were bright red. "At an Englisch business."

Parade around town for all to see. The English wouldn't think twice about a single pregnant woman working. Whether they would hire a Plain woman with no experience remained to be seen. Maisy knew how to cook, clean house, take care of children, sew, and can. Did these skills translate into a paying job? She could clean English houses again—if she stopped throwing up.

"Why get a job?" she asked.

"Because you'll need funds to cover your medical expenses, even if Kate delivers your bopli." Ruth withdrew her hands and stuck them in her lap. "We don't have the money ourselves." Suddenly a strange mixture of regret and delight fought on her pretty face. "And we might be needing it ourselves not so long after you deliver."

Another baby so soon. A blessing to be sure, but Ruth would have her hands full with two toddlers underfoot. The ping of a wooden block hitting the rung on a chair followed by delighted giggles underscored that truth. Bonnie toddled over to Ruth's chair and held up her arms. Ruth tugged her into her lap.

"Pat-a-cake, pat-a-cake."

Ruth obliged, but her gaze returned to Maisy. It was full of loving regret.

Down the road, Maisy could help. Working elsewhere would also minimize her contact with the Haven Plain community. "That's *wunderbarr*. I understand. I have some . . . funds to start. I'll see what I can find. Maybe there are English families who need a babysitter or their houses cleaned."

"It's possible." Amos took a long drink of his tea. He wiped his mouth with a wilted napkin. "No one is passing judgment on you. Your fehla is forgiven. The elders want to minimize the effects it might have on others in the community."

"I do understand." Maisy straightened in her chair. "I'll do my best to find a job quickly."

"You haven't been feeling well. It's understandable if you need a little time . . . to adjust." Ruth sideswiped Amos with a pleading glance. His nod was so slight a person could've missed it. Ruth's gaze traveled to her other little one. Maisy's followed. Nicholas chewed on the corner of one slobber-drenched block. He lifted it over his head and cooed. "The sooner the better, though."

"Understood."

Amos stood. He went to the rack by the door and picked up his hat. This family meeting was over. "I have chores to finish. I reckon so do you."

Maisy waited until he slapped the hat on his head and disappeared out the door to move. She concentrated on clearing the table instead of waiting for her cousin to say something. Ruth settled Bonnie on her hip, scooped up Nicholas, block and all, and headed for the kitchen.

Maisy followed with a stack of dirty dishes.

The only sounds for a while were the babbling of babies and the clatter of dishes in the sink. Ruth deposited her toddlers on the floor, this time with an array of stuffed animals that included a cow, a horse, a cat, and a dog.

"Moo-moo-moo." Bonnie chortled. "Meow, meow. Neee— neigh, bark, bark."

Ruth sighed. "She calls the animals by the sound they make instead of their names."

"It's a start."

"She doesn't even say Bonnie yet. She calls herself bopli."

"She's only two."

"I hope you know—"

"I do know." Maisy turned, wet, sudsy hands and all, to receive Ruth's hug. "I'm so sorry I brought this on you. I'm so happy for your gut news."

"Gott is gut." Tears slid down Ruth's cheeks. "I'm happy, but also overwhelmed. So soon. I love my boplin, but I'm still getting up at night with Nicholas. Both are still in diapers. Bonnie is teething so she wakes up at night—when Nicholas is sleeping."

Maisy hugged her harder. What else could she do? Plain women put up a brave front. They loved their children. They wanted many. But that didn't mean they shouldn't be able to vent now and then. That's all Ruth was doing.

"Sit down. I'll take care of the dishes."

"Nee. I'll help."

"Sit."

Ruth sat.

Maisy slid a serving dish into the dish tub and applied elbow grease. "Are you having morning sickness yet?"

"Jah. But only in the morning. Danki, Gott."

"I'll share my ginger tea and lollipops."

"Much appreciated." Ruth's rueful tone reflected Maisy's own love-hate relationship with all things ginger. "Frying eggs first thing in the morning has not been fun."

"Or smelly sausage."

"And not being able to drink kaffi when a boost of caffeine would be so nice."

They both sighed. Then laughed.

"I'll help with everything." Maisy added the last plate to the drying rack. She grabbed a ginger lollipop and took it to her cousin. "Dessert is served."

Sighing again, Ruth accepted her offering. "Danki. Where's yours?"

"I'm saving it for later."

Maisy finished the dishes and helped Ruth get the children ready for bed. She read stories to Bonnie until the little girl nodded off. A peek into Ruth's bedroom revealed Nicholas asleep in his crib and Ruth curled up, still dressed, asleep on the bed.

"Sweet dreams," she whispered.

Quiet descended. It seemed loud in its own right after the children's noisy play. Maisy wiped down the cabinets one more time, grabbed her lollipop, and headed out the front door. Amos sat at his desk in the living room, scrutinizing a stack of papers. Maisy slipped past without a word. She, too, could be laconic.

Rolling her eyes at her own thoughts, she ambled down the steps and wandered through the yard. The sun hovered on the horizon, still deciding whether to make its nightly descent into darkness. A soft breeze lifted the leaves in the sycamore trees that lined the gravel road to the corral and barn. A harbinger of fall just around the corner. *Harbinger: a person or thing that announces the approach of another.*

She stuck the lollipop in her mouth and raised both arms over her head in a lovely stretch. The tight muscles in her back, shoulders, and neck eased. A movement caught the corner of her vision. Joshua stood at the corral fence, one boot propped on the lowest railing. Two of Amos's horses—beautiful tawny brown Morgans—enjoyed each other's company in its confines.

Maisy dropped her arms. She spun around.

"Out for a walk?"

Too late. She turned back toward him. "Just a stretch."

"Long day."

"The longest."

He went back to staring at the horses.

Something about the slump of his shoulders kept Maisy from retreating. She slipped closer. One of the horses dipped his head in her direction and whinnied as if to say hello. If she loved dogs and cats first, horses were a close third. Maisy learned to ride not long after learning to walk. "Friends of yours?"

"Jah." He straightened and stuck his arm across the railing. His hand opened, revealing several slices of apple. One of the horses immediately ambled over to the railing. "Hey, Pete. Care for a nibble?"

The horse took his time. He nibbled slowly, politely.

"If Ruth notices her stash of apples is shrinking, you can tell her I'm the thief." Joshua's tone was unrepentant. "Pete, this is Maisy. Maisy, meet Pete."

Maisy smoothed Pete's forelock. "Pleased to meet you, Pete." She chuckled. "You don't talk to people, but you talk to horses?"

"They're nicer."

"It's okay, I guess, as long as they don't talk back."

"Of course they talk back. Not in Deutsch, but they talk." Pete had finished off the snack. He snorted, tossed his head, and trotted away. "They are gut friends. The best."

"They have personalities, don't they?"

"They do. They're faithful, intelligent, and hard workers. They'll work themselves into the ground for the right owner."

His tone was light, but his gaze was filled with a strange melancholy. Maisy leaned against the railing a ways down from him.

Not getting in his space. "What were you thinking about when I so rudely interrupted you?"

"Nothing really." He wiped his hands on already dirty pants. "Daydreaming, I reckon."

"A penny for your thoughts."

"Big spender."

"I'm saving for . . . the future."

"My *bruder* and me used to talk about how we would train horses for a living when we grew up." The timbre of his voice deepened. He shifted and lowered his head. It made it harder to see his expression. "We'd have our own farm for breeding them too."

"What happened?"

"I grew up. He didn't."

"I'm so sorry."

"It was a long time ago."

The unrestrained longing in his deep voice said not so long ago. "You could still do it."

He shook his head. "You're so young."

"Not so young. Not anymore."

The emotion in Joshua's face shut down, like a barn door closing in a gust of wind. He pushed away from the fence. "Gut nacht."

"Gut nacht."

She'd reminded him of her sin and he'd drawn away. Just as he should. So why did it hurt so much? He was a stranger.

A stranger caught in a similar tempest of emotions. Sadness. Regret. Should-haves. What-ifs.

Chapter 11

THE SINGER DREW OUT THE FIRST few syllables of "Das Loblied" with great feeling in long, low notes. Joshua halted in the hallway that led from the Planks' upstairs bedrooms to the staircase. Plain folks sang "The Praise Song" in every church service on every Sunday in every district throughout the country, maybe throughout the world. A person didn't expect to hear it sung at home on a Sunday morning. Leastways not when he was alone—or so he thought.

Joshua followed the sound to the other side of the second floor. It grew louder and more spirited. "Das Loblied" likely had never been sung quite like this before. The bedroom door stood open. He peeked in. Maisy Glick had her back to the doorway. She pulled up the quilt and smoothed it. Then she plumped the pillows and laid them side by side on the double bed. She stepped back and surveyed the results, all the while singing at the top of her lungs.

Her presence this past week had been a welcome addition to the Plank household—at least to Joshua's way of thinking. She bantered with the children at the supper table, getting them to eat when Ruth couldn't. She didn't say much, but when she did it was something good. Sometimes her voice mingled with her cousin's in song in the kitchen while they cooked and cleaned. Their laughter offset Amos's dark moodiness.

Such a voice. Joshua leaned against the doorframe. His sister Rachel would be about the same age as Maisy and just as able in the singing department. No one ever said as much. A person didn't sing "Das Loblied" for an audience or to show off a talent. For God and God alone.

Maisy turned. She shrieked, backed up, and landed on her behind on the bed.

"Sorry!" Joshua straightened and held up both hands, palms up. "I didn't mean to scare you."

"What are you doing here?"

"I stay here. I thought you knew that."

Maisy put one hand to her chest as if to capture her heart before it leaped to freedom. "Ruth said you were here only during the week."

"I was off last week because of family visiting so I decided to stay over and make up for lost time." She didn't need to know the whys and wherefores. "I thought I was here alone."

"So did I." Maisy popped up and edged away from the bed. Her pale face reddened. "I should get downstairs. I told Ruth I would clean up the kitchen. She was running late, what with getting the kinner ready to go."

The question of why neither she nor Joshua had gone to the service hung in the air. He saw no reason to answer it. Nor did she seem interested in sharing her story. He could guess. Joshua spun around and headed for the stairs. Her footsteps said she followed.

His plan to grab a cup of coffee and enjoy the rare moment of aloneness while the Planks were at church disappeared into the great outdoors.

"Have you eaten?"

At the sound of Maisy's soft voice, Joshua stopped in the middle of the kitchen. She followed so closely she nearly butted into him. He swerved toward the stove and the coffeepot. "Nee. Kaffi is all I need."

"I could make you breakfast."

"Nee." He grabbed a mug, poured the coffee, and headed for the back door. "Not necessary."

"I understand."

Joshua turned and paused, his free hand on the doorknob. "Understand what?"

"You're not wanting to be here with the likes of me."

"What do you mean, the likes of you?"

She sped to the stove, slapped a teakettle onto the burner, and turned up the flame.

What now? He'd shamed her without even trying. This had nothing to do with her condition. A single man and a single woman, unrelated, shouldn't be alone in the house. His father's voice rang in his ears. "I thought I'd drink my kaffi on the front porch before it gets too hot out."

Without waiting for a response, he went outside and settled into a canvas camping chair. That had been a stupid thing to say. The last day of August in Kansas would be nothing but hot, beginning to end. Hot, humid, still air. As long as he didn't move, he wouldn't sweat. Until that first sip of hot coffee. His little sister once asked him why folks drank coffee when it was so hot. It made a person sweat. Which cooled his body.

His teacher would've called that science. He called it common sense.

The screen door creaked. Maisy stuck her head out. Like a crab checking for predators. Joshua took a sip of his coffee. "Come on out. It's a free country."

"I don't want to bother you none."

"No bother."

Hardly any at all.

Instead of taking the battered lawn chair next to Joshua, she scooted over to the steps and took a seat. Her mug held a tea bag. Her head raised to the morning sun, she dipped the bag up and down.

He sought a topic of conversation. None came to mind. That was nothing new for him.

Maisy left off messing with the tea bag and took a quick sip. A calico cat trotted across the yard, paused, one paw in the air, meowed, then proceeded to climb the steps and sprawl on the porch next to Maisy. With a soft chuckle, she stroked its thick fur. "You must be even hotter than we are, kitty cat."

Cats didn't make Joshua chuckle. They made him sneeze. He leaned back in his chair and contemplated his companions. If Maisy stopped petting, the cat would meow and nudge her hand until she started again. The cat had her under its thumb or paw, as it were. "I think you made a friend."

"Funny how some cats are standoffish and others want to be your best friend right off the bat." The cat rolled over onto her back. Maisy obliged by rubbing her belly. More pleased meows. "Like people, I reckon."

Joshua didn't need friends. Regardless of Maisy's intent, the remark stung. He concentrated on the coffee. It could've used some doctoring. Served him right. He ran out of the kitchen without the usual tablespoon of sugar and dollop of milk.

"Do you have a name?" Maisy tugged the cat into her lap. "Hmm, let's see, you're orange, and black, and white all over. Calico isn't very original. What does Ruth call you?"

"Mostly she calls her Kitty."

"Not very original either."

"I reckon Ruth doesn't have time to worry herself over a stray cat."

Maisy's hands stilled. "Not when she's got a stray girl who invited herself to the house with no warning, you mean. If I could go somewhere else and save her the bother, I would, just so you know."

This was why he didn't make conversation. Sinkholes and quicksand lurked everywhere. "I'm just saying since Amos's accident she's taken on a lot more of the outside work. Besides the produce stand and the jams and jellies for the gift shop in town and the quilts for the furniture store."

Maisy's gaze bounced his direction and back out to the yard. "I reckon I'm still figuring out what to expect from people."

"Don't assume the worst, for starters."

"Sometimes I can't help it." Her nose wrinkled as if in concentration, as she smoothed the cat's fur. "So far most folks haven't given me a reason to do otherwise."

"I reckon you expected that."

What Joshua hadn't expected was to sit on Amos's front porch and make stilted conversation with a half woman, half girl who'd shown up all of a sudden, looking like she needed a friend or someone to talk to. That someone couldn't be him. She had Ruth, didn't she?

"Can I ask you a question?"

Joshua studied a swollen bite on the back of his thumb. Mosquito or chigger? It itched like crazy. He hazarded a sideswipe glance at her. She'd gone back to spoiling the cat. "If you really need to, I suppose you can."

"Are you baptized?"

"Nee."

"Why didn't you go to church?"

"That's two questions."

"Ruth was right."

"About what?"

"About you. She said you never met a silence you didn't like." Maisy picked up her tea. She set it down without drinking. "Have you always been like that?"

"Not always." Joshua couldn't contain a sigh. This conversation had tuckered him out, and the day wasn't even half over. "People jaw at each other too much. They use way too many words, to my way of thinking."

"I like words. I make lists of them. I study them and memorize their meanings."

"Why?"

"Why not? It's gut to be able to use words to make yourself understood." She kissed the cat's nose. It snuggled closer. "I figure the more words you know, the more you can tell people what you mean and understand what they're trying to tell you."

"I know words in three languages, and I still don't understand half of what people are talking about."

"Maybe you just don't know the right words."

"Could be."

The cat stopped meowing. The only sounds were her purr and the chirp of the blue jays scolding each other in the sycamore tree across the way. Occasionally a bee made itself known with its incessant buzzing. A dragonfly zipped through the air and landed on Ruth's pink rosebush that hugged the porch railing.

A sweet silence a man could enjoy.

"I miss my family. I miss them so much even my teeth hurt with it." Maisy whispered the words as if sharing a terrible secret no one but Joshua could know. "I even miss my dog."

She was determined to confide in him. She couldn't know that confiding in Joshua was like telling her life story to a tree stump. He was no good at this. He slid down in the canvas chair and hunched his shoulders in order to better bear the weight of her sorrow. "What's your dog's name?"

It was the best he could do.

Maisy cocked her head in his direction. She smiled. Everything about her changed in that split second. The wretched girl drowning in her own guilt disappeared, replaced by a pretty woman with blue eyes and sunshine on her lips.

"Skeeter. He's dumb as a doorknob, but he's brave and fierce—when he's chasing a squirrel. He makes a gut pillow. Boplin love him. He loves them."

More words than Joshua had ever heard spoken about a dog. She felt about dogs the way he felt about horses. Skeeter sounded like a better friend than most people. Animals often were. "Huh. Skeeter."

"Jah."

"I reckon I see why you miss him."

"I better get in there and finish cleaning the kitchen." She kissed the cat's nose again. "I dub thee Sunny because you have a sunny disposition."

The cat yawned widely, revealing a wicked set of incisors and a skinny pink tongue.

"We moved to Haven when I was twelve." Dangerous territory, but something about her lament over a dog had touched him. Whether he liked it or not. And he didn't. "I still miss my friends. But I see them once in a while when they come up for a visit."

"And you made new ones."

He shrugged.

Maisy seemed to ponder his revelation like a puzzle missing some pieces. The silence stretched, this time more companionable.

"Kate says my bopli is the size of a plum." She didn't whisper this time. Her tone was curiously flat. "I'll never eat a plum again. I would feel like a cannibal."

Even more dangerous territory. They were better off talking about dogs. Why tell him this? Why not Ruth? Plain people liked to pretend babies appeared from one day to the next, fully formed, squalling and pooping. Even the women who carried them, tucked neatly away for safekeeping until the right time, didn't talk about them.

"She gave me a pamphlet. It has a chart. At thirty-five weeks the bopli is the size of a honeydew melon." Her expression morose, Maisy plucked cat hair from her apron and deposited it with a flick of her fingers in the sun-fried, brown grass that framed the steps. "At forty weeks, we're talking a pumpkin or a watermelon. Why did it have to be fruit?"

Only one response came to mind. "Ouch."

"Jah." She rose and moved toward the door. The cat stretched and followed. "I'd better go clean the kitchen. What big plans do you have for today?"

"I'll sit here and think about how pumpkin used to be my favorite pie." He offered a smile in hopes she would understand it was his poor attempt at a joke. "After a while I'll mosey down to the creek and go fishing. Maybe we'll have catfish for supper."

A pained look passed over her face. Her hand went to her mouth. She jerked open the screen door and disappeared inside. The door slammed behind her.

See, that was why it was better for him to keep his mouth shut.

Chapter 12

THE DAYS SETTLED INTO A SEESAW of ups when the nausea faded and downs when it hit like a flu epidemic. The household was a truce held together by twine and determination. Maisy was determined to make herself useful until she could find a job—which remained elusive. Ruth was determined to take care of Maisy. Maisy took care of Ruth, who had her own share of morning sickness—thankfully confined to the mornings. Amos appeared determined to ignore Maisy's presence as much as possible.

She changed diapers, gave baths, read stories, and sang songs. She helped with laundry, cooking, cleaning, and canning. She worked in the produce stand at the end of the dirt road, selling corn on the cob, zucchini, radishes, tomatoes, green peppers, eggplant, and watermelons. She worked with Ruth in the kitchen, dripping with sweat, making jams and jellies from strawberries, peaches, apples, and pears, to sell in the gift shop in town. At least one day a week, she went into town in search of work. No one was hiring a Plain woman with no retail experience. That's what they called it. Working in stores. Yoder and Haven were small. The pool of jobs in non-Plain stores even smaller.

Hard work kept fearful thoughts and loneliness at bay—except for the wee hours, when she stared at the darkness and longed for Skeeter's stinky doggie breath on her cheek and Sarah's early morning giggles.

Maisy missed her father's voice when he told stories to the kids by the fireplace on cold winter nights. She missed her mother's off-pitch humming as she cooked and cleaned.

She missed her friends. She didn't miss cleaning Mrs. Elliott's toilets. She didn't miss Nate either. But then he was her constant companion. He was there in the nausea, the fatigue, and the vomiting. Which she did everywhere. In the backyard while hanging laundry on the line. In the weeds behind the produce stand. In the kitchen sink after washing dishes. She kept plastic bags next to her bed, along with a glass of water and a sleeve of saltines. She gave up her beloved coffee and drank ginger tea instead. All that did was give her a headache.

Even if she found a job, how would she manage to work with a body openly rebelling against the child it was supposed to nourish?

None of Kate's suggestions for taming the nausea helped.

At the four-month mark, a rain-cooled September morning, Kate appeared at the screen door that led into the kitchen. "Hello, hello. I come bearing gifts."

Maisy pushed the door open and held it for her. Kate bustled in and kept going toward the table with a foil-covered plate in her hands. Maisy followed. "If it's food, I'm afraid I won't be able to eat it."

She'd just vomited her breakfast into the trash can.

"It's gingerbread. It's warm, fresh out of the oven."

"I'll try."

Kate turned and gave Maisy a thorough once-over. She frowned. "Where's Ruth?"

"She's in the garden picking tomatoes. She wants to have a canning frolic tomorrow. The kinner are with her."

"Go brush your teeth and grab your bag. I'll run out and tell her I'll visit with her when we get back. She'll understand. She's been through this before. You haven't."

"Where are we going?"

"To the birthing clinic in Yoder."

"But—"

"No buts. You've lost weight. You have dark circles around your eyes. I suspect you're dehydrated." Hands on her wide hips, Kate tut-tutted. "Why didn't you ask Ruth to call me? I would've come sooner."

"I did everything you told me to do." Mostly. "It just didn't help. I can't let it get in the way of helping around here. Plus I'm supposed to be getting a job. The bishop wants me to work and pay for my medical bills myself."

Kate snorted. "I reckon Bryan has never had morning sickness. If men had to birth babies, they'd be a whole lot more understanding."

The mental picture of Amos with a watermelon-sized belly, wearing a maternity-sized dress made Maisy smile—for the first time in days. "So what now?"

"Now we're going to see Miss Betsy at the clinic."

Her no-nonsense tone gave Maisy no room to argue. Besides, she didn't have the strength.

An hour later they pulled Kate's buggy into the clinic. The stout, one-story building with a brick facade had a warm, welcoming feel. Bright purple, red, and yellow flowers paraded alongside the sidewalk. Another buggy and horse occupied one of the buggy-designated parking spots.

The ever-present knot of nausea lodged in the pit of Maisy's stomach. She breathed through her nose, in and out. In and out. Another swig from the water bottle Kate handed her didn't help. The thought of a saltine only caused the knot to expand. She couldn't do this. She couldn't walk into a clinic and talk to a stranger about this baby growing inside her body.

"I don't want to do this."

"I know you don't." Kate patted her hand. "Betsy is nice. You'll like her. So is Leeann, the other midwife. And the nurses. They only want to help. They're women. They understand. Ask Ruth. She knows."

"I can't do this."

"Jah, you can."

"I don't mean this." Maisy waved at the building. She pointed at her belly. "I mean this."

The words came out despite her best effort to restrain them. She hadn't even expressed this horrible misgiving to Ruth. Plain women had babies. It was what they did. What was wrong with her?

"You're having a rough time now, but when you hold your bopli in your arms, you'll feel differently."

How would her bopli feel when he grew older and realized his mother wasn't married, or that his father was English and could never be a part of his life? Would he feel like an outcast? Would he hold the circumstances of his birth against her?

"Do you think I'm being punished?"

"Do I think Gott punishes women who have boplin outside the confines of holy matrimony?" Kate hopped from the buggy. She tied the reins to the railing. "I'm just a woman. My itty-bitty brain doesn't know much about matters of theology, but I do know about boplin. Every bopli is a gift. Gott wouldn't punish a bopli for your sin—not to my way of thinking. But who am I to try to fathom what Gott thinks or does?"

She strode around the buggy and held out her hand to help Maisy down. "Regardless, you have a responsibility to take care of this bopli. Starting with gut prenatal care. That's what they will give you here."

Maisy stuck the water bottle into her bag. With a sigh, she took Kate's hand and descended. Together they walked into the center. A bell tinkled when they opened the door. It looked like a doctor's office except for the framed photos of cute babies and Scripture wall hangings. Almost immediately a woman dressed in green medical scrubs swooped down on them. "Hi, Kate, it's so good to see you. Who's this?"

Kate introduced Hope, one of the center's registered nurses. She handed her a manila envelope. "This is Maisy Glick and this is a copy of my report from her first exam. She's expecting and she's having severe nausea. She'd like to get checked out."

She would not. Maisy shook her head and opened her mouth.

"Why don't we sit down in the kitchen and you can tell me all about it?" Hope spoke before Maisy could. "Betsy and Leeann are catching a baby right now. Betsy's been up all night with this one, and Leeann will do the postpartum."

Hope's eyes were tired and surrounded by dark circles. The midwives weren't the only ones who'd been up all night. She grabbed a clipboard from the front counter and led the way down a short hall to the kitchen. White, lacy curtains adorned windows that allowed the sun to flood the room. A huge Boston fern took up one corner, a sofa another wall, and more green plants dotted the room. It smelled like vanilla cake. Maisy inhaled the scent. Her shoulders relaxed a tad.

Just as Maisy sat at the round table covered with a tablecloth that matched the filmy curtains, a loud squall split the air. Hope grinned. The weariness in her face disappeared. "It sounds like the baby has decided to join us after all. That makes three in the last twenty-four hours. It's a baby boom for Haven."

Another RN trotted into the room. "It's a girl." She and Hope exchanged an exuberant high five. "They already have two boys so they're thrilled. I hope I didn't burn the cake. I almost forgot it."

A nurse was baking a cake in the middle of delivering a baby?

"They make a birthday cake for every baby born here." Kate sniffed the air like a retriever. "Don't you love the aroma of cake baking? The parents light the candle and sing 'Happy Birthday' before they go home."

"They go home today?"

"In a few hours." Hope settled at the table across from Maisy and Kate. She shuffled through the paperwork on the clipboard, kept some of it, and pushed the rest toward Maisy. "Here's some forms for you to fill out after we talk."

Her questions mirrored the ones Kate had asked Maisy the first time they spoke. When they arrived at the reason for today's visit, Hope's forehead wrinkled. She nodded and took notes. "There's a good chance you're dehydrated. If you are, so is your baby." She tapped her pen on the table. "I'll ask Betsy to come talk to you. She should be done by now. Leeann will take care of mom and baby from here."

"But Betsy's tired. She's been up all night." Maisy would be happy to skip the exam that would be sure to follow. "She should sleep. I can come back another day."

"Nee, you cannot." Kate shot her a severe frown. "Try to think about this from the perspective of what's best for your bopli."

"That's good advice." Hope jumped up from her chair. She hustled to the refrigerator and returned with a large bottle of water. "Sip on this while I talk to Betsy. And fill out the paperwork. I'll be back in a jiffy."

"No rush. I'm not having my baby here, just so you know."

Hope paused in the doorway, then trotted back to the table. "Don't worry. This is all about what you want. Having babies is a natural part of life. It's not a sickness or a medical condition. We understand that." She patted Maisy's shoulder. "But you might need some help along the way since your body is being such a stinker about the pregnancy."

She was off before Maisy could respond.

"See, I told you they're super nice." With a self-satisfied grin, Kate clasped her hands together on the table. "You should see the birthing rooms. They're set up like regular bedrooms. Each one has its own bathroom with a tub that has jets so you can sit in the water and let it massage your back."

"Why would you want to do that?"

"It eases the pain."

Maybe Maisy deserved to feel every stab of pain.

After a few minutes, a woman in a pale-pink and yellow flowered dress strode into the kitchen. She wore a large white handkerchief over her steel-gray hair and wire-rimmed glasses that magnified her blue eyes. She was as tall and thin as Kate was short and round. She wiped her hands on a towel as she walked. The two women exchanged hugs, and Kate made the introductions.

"Maisy, we need to do some blood work this morning." Betsy jumped into the conversation as if she'd been there since the beginning. "It's likely we'll need to get you started on an IV after that. Just until we can get you rehydrated."

From there it went downhill. The same routine with weighing and peeing on a stick—only this time Maisy did it all herself. The blood draw didn't hurt much. And then the exam. Kate cheerfully pointed out that the exams would become routine as the months rolled by.

That remained to be seen.

Maisy's blood pressure was too high and the baby's heartbeat too fast.

"Being dehydrated will do that."

Before she knew it, Maisy was tucked into a double bed covered with a flowered quilt in the "Pink Room," an IV needle strapped to her arm and the water bottle on the end table next to her. Betsy explained everything as she went. Fluids and antinausea medications were the order of the day.

"I should be at home helping Ruth get lunch ready." Maisy squirmed. The IV tape pulled at the skin on her arm. It hurt. "I was supposed to work in the produce stand this afternoon."

"Ruth got on fine before you came to stay with her." Kate glanced up from the *Mothering* magazine she was reading. She had the nearby recliner tilted so she could lean back, her sneaker-clad feet up. "She'll manage without you for one day."

"They haven't said how much this will cost."

"They offer payment plans for folks who don't have insurance."

Which would be all their Plain moms. The difference being that the community helped its members with their medical costs whenever possible. At least Maisy had the money Nate had given her. "I won't be coming back after today."

"That's up to you. I can take care of you if we can get your nausea under control *and* if that takes care of your high blood pressure."

Hope popped into the room now and then to check the baby's heartbeat and Maisy's blood pressure. Both started to right themselves quickly. Hope also brought in a snack of peanut-butter toast and then a pamphlet with all the tips for dealing with nausea. And a paper bearing the names of two supplements Betsy wanted her to take. "Betsy can write prescriptions for these, but the over-the-counter vitamins are less expensive if you don't have insurance. B6 and B1."

"We'll stop by the store before we head back to Amos's." Kate intercepted the note and tucked it into her bag. "Your face is already starting to have more color."

Her words disappeared into the quiet hum of the central air-conditioning. Maisy's bones melted into the cocoon of cool sheets. The soft pillow smelled like clothes that had been hung on an outdoor clothesline. Her eyelids refused to stay open.

"Maisy. Maisy, honey, time to wake up."

Maisy started and forced her eyes open. Smiling, Kate loomed over her. Maisy sat up. Where were they? The birthing center. She had slept. Hard and long. She rubbed her eyes. For the first time in weeks they didn't burn. "I can't believe I slept."

"You needed it."

Maisy threw off the sheets. A small bandage covered the spot where the IV needle had been. "You should've woken me. I need to get back to the house."

Then it struck her. For the first time in months, no nausea. She sank back on the bed. "I feel . . . better." She laughed. "Much better."

"Wunderbarr." Kate helped Maisy stand. "It won't last forever, but it will give you time to get some protein in your body and start to build up your strength again."

At the front desk, a different woman shuffled charts with a phone tucked between her chin and her shoulder. "Yes, yes. That's fine. Come on in. Betsy went home to get some sleep, but Leeann is here. We've got you covered."

She hung up the phone. Her gaze bounced from Kate to Maisy. "I'm Candy, the administrative assistant. You must be Maisy Glick. Betsy wants to see you again in one week."

No, no. "That's okay. I'm fine now."

Kate's hand squeezed Maisy's. "You lost five pounds in the last month. You can't keep doing that. It's not gut for your bopli. Or for you. Let them help me take care of you."

The sound of sobbing caught Maisy before she could reply. A Plain man plodded through the lobby with his arm around a tearful woman. Her wrinkled prayer covering was askew over pale-blonde hair that had come loose from its bun. His face lined with pain, the man rubbed the woman's back.

"Let's go home, Fraa. You'll feel better there."

"I'm fine." The woman wiped her face with a sodden handkerchief. "I'll be fine."

Her words strangled on a sob. The sound reverberated from Maisy's fingers to her toes. It made her bones ache. Such heartache. A person couldn't let it pass by without acknowledging it.

"I'm so sorry," she whispered even though she had no idea what had happened to the couple. "So sorry."

"Gott's will be done." The man's eyes reddened. His voice broke. "He can use all things for our gut."

Both true according to Scripture, but that didn't make some trials easier to bear.

Kate stepped into their path. She held open her arms. The woman, who was much taller, bent down and walked into them. They huddled in a hug in the middle of the waiting room. "I'm so sorry, Vicky. It must be heartbreaking."

"I know there's a reason for all this, but I can't for the life of me imagine what it is." Vicky pulled away from Kate. She swiped at her face. Kate handed her a fresh tissue from the box on the counter. "In four years no bopli. Then the adoption fell through. How could she change her mind like that at the very last moment after all those months of saying yes? Now yes is no. And now I thought . . ." Her voice dropped to a whisper. "I thought I was expecting, but I'm not. Wishful thinking. Betsy says it was probably stress."

"Gott's timing is His timing." Vicky's husband studied his boots. His Adam's apple bobbed. "We aren't to question it."

"Gott has a plan for us." Kate shook her head. She had tears in her eyes. "Sometimes it's hard for us to wait for it to unfold."

"I've tried so hard to be patient." Vicky hiccupped a sob. "If we're not meant to have our own kinner, so be it. Gott's will be done. But I thought surely we'd be allowed to care for a bopli whose mudder cannot. What would be wrong with that?"

"Nothing, nothing at all," Kate soothed. "As Isaac says, Gott's will and Gott's timing."

"Let's get you home." Isaac's arm encircled Vicky's waist again. "Tomorrow's another day."

Then they were out the door and gone.

Candy's happy-go-lucky grin had disappeared. "I've been praying for them like crazy. I've got calluses on my knees."

Kate grabbed a fresh tissue for herself. "It's the most important thing we can all do. For some of us, it's the only thing."

"I'm sorry I got distracted." Candy tapped on the monthly calendar that lay on the desk in front of her "So come see us at ten o'clock next Tuesday, Miss Maisy?"

"Okay." Maybe.

"I see that you don't have insurance. That's fine. We'll set up a payment plan." Candy laid yet another stack of papers in front of Maisy. "This is what you owe for today. Just fill out the form and put on there how much you want to pay and how often. We've had folks pay weekly, monthly, lump sum, and bigger installments, depending on their resources and whether they plan to deliver with us."

The amount owed was mind-boggling. For one day. What would a delivery cost?

Her answer was on the next page. She couldn't contain her gasp.

"Don't worry, really. However long you need to make payments is fine. There's no pressure tactics or anything like that."

Nate's money would be a down payment at best if she had to deliver at the clinic. She would not let that happen. She counted out enough cash to pay for today's services. The stack of bills shrank.

Back in the buggy she tucked the bag close and closed her eyes for a few seconds. Bryan and Amos were right. She needed to get a job. The Gmay couldn't be expected to pay her bills. It was tantamount to approving of her actions—even if they dutifully forgave her.

"Try not to worry about the money."

So Kate was also a mind reader.

"I know it's wrong to worry, but I have to pay for these vitamins and get material so I can sew bigger dresses. I can't deliver at the clinic."

"You still have six months to go before this bopli comes along." Kate shook the reins and clucked her tongue. Her horse neighed and took off. "Let's not borrow trouble."

"What kind of trouble do Vicky and Isaac have, if I may ask?"

"Everyone in the district knows so there's no reason I can't share their troubles with you." Kate guided the buggy onto Red Rock Road. "Vicky had a miscarriage in the first year after they married. She's never been in a family way since."

"Do the doctors know why?"

"That's between them and the doctors." Kate pulled into the grocery store parking lot and guided her horse into a parking spot set aside for buggies. "They decided to try adoption. The agency connected them with a young Englisch girl who wanted to give up her bopli. Last month they went to Hutchinson to fetch the bopli, a little bu, at the hospital. Only the mudder changed her mind after his birth."

"That's why they're so brokenhearted?"

"They spent a lot of time with the mudder. Vicky made clothes and crib quilts. Isaac built a cradle with his own hands. They made all the plans any parents who are about to have a bopli would make. They had all those dreams. Now they have nowhere to put them. They're gut people. They gave the cradle to the mudder and the bopli things to one of Vicky's friends who's due this month."

Almost all Plain women wanted babies—lots of them. Few were like Kate, happy to be single and engrossed in a job like midwifery or being a teacher. Maisy had wanted as many as God would give her—until this happened. Now it seemed unlikely God would find her deserving of her dream. "No wonder she's so distraught. Both of them."

"Our bishop has met with them several times. He's trying to help them through this painful season. We all are. But it's as if they had a baby who died. It's that kind of grief. It takes time to overcome it."

No wonder Vicky's dress hung on her. No wonder Isaac's shoulders were hunched.

Kate climbed down from the buggy. "We better get a move on. Ruth will start to worry."

Maisy didn't move. Her heart thrummed with Vicky and Isaac's hurt. It made no sense. Life didn't make sense. She rubbed the spot under her breastbone where her heart lay. In the heady rush of freedom granted to her by her rumspringa, she'd made all the wrong choices. Done all the wrong things. Now she bore the burden of responsibility for her actions. She carried a baby inside her, now the size of an apple or an avocado, according to her pamphlet. He—or she—would double in size in the next few weeks. His legs were growing, his heart pumping, his hair starting to grow, finger-nails and toenails too. He would become more and more a baby.

While Isaac and Vicky had none.

"Are you coming?" Her expression quizzical, Kate stared at Maisy from the sidewalk. "Are you feeling bad again?"

"Not the way you mean. It's so unfair. I'm eighteen, not mar-ried, with no prospects, and I'm expecting. Vicky wants so badly to have a bopli, and she can't. It's sad."

"Whoever said life was fair? Scripture says we will have trouble in this world, but to take heart. Jesus has overcome the world."

Did that Scripture give Vicky and Isaac comfort? Did they wonder how God could use this season of pain, loss, and sadness for their good?

Two steps in their shoes and anyone in her right mind would wonder.

Chapter 13

MAISY DIDN'T NEED ANOTHER VISIT TO the clinic. Really, she didn't. She tossed back her vitamins and gulped a big swig of 7UP. She tried on her best air of well-being coupled with contentment. The sun shone through the open windows. A warm September breeze floated through Ruth's kitchen. Sunny stretched out on one of the windowsills, sleeping. The kitchen smelled of coffee, sausage, fried eggs, and hashbrowns, none of which bothered her stomach this morning. Progress, indeed.

Kate didn't appear convinced. She sashayed through the kitchen to the rack next to the back door where she selected a canvas bag—Maisy's bag. "Let's go. It's been a week. Your appointment's at ten o'clock. We don't want to be late."

"I feel better. I'm getting ready to make pies to sell at the produce stand. Ruth needs help with the laundry. We're canning tomatoes this afternoon."

"We need to see how much better." Kate held out the bag. "We'll only be gone a couple of hours."

Maisy planted her feet and stuck her hands on her hips. "I haven't thrown up once today."

"It's only nine o'clock. What about yesterday?"

Maisy took the bag. "Okay. Twice."

Her expression triumphant, Kate went to the arched doorway that led to the laundry room. "Ruth, do you need anything from town?" She lifted her voice to be heard over the *chug-a-chug-chug* of the wringer washing machine. "We're headed out."

Ruth came to the door with Nicholas on one hip. Bonnie clutched a doll in one arm and toddled after her. She immediately trotted over to Kate for a hug. "Katie, Katie, Katie."

"You have my name down, don't you, little one?" Kate picked her up and planted a kiss on her cheek. "Are you helping your mudder do laundry?"

"More like she's trying to climb in and take a bath. She loves to play in the water." Ruth's pink face shone with perspiration. Her hands were wet and soapy. "We need more pectin for making the peach and plum jelly if you get a chance. A twenty-pound bag of sugar, too, if you don't mind. I'll pay you when you come back."

"Absolutely." Kate pulled a list from her purse and added the requests. "How are you feeling?"

"Better." Ruth already had that glow expecting moms often had. Envy tried to slip in the side door, but Maisy kicked it out. Ruth had her hands full. She didn't need to feel crummy too. "I weighed this morning. I already gained two pounds. At this rate I'll be huge."

"You gained thirty-five pounds with both your boplin." Kate shook her head. "Nothing wrong with that as long as your blood pressure cooperates. I'll check it when we get back."

"Tell Betsy and Leeann I said hi." Ruth shifted Nicholas to her other hip. The little boy's eyelids drooped. Nap time would make chores easier. "Tell them no offense, but I'm hoping not to see them anytime soon."

That would be a blessing. Maisy had to fight off envy again.

It kept trying to whisper in her ear *No fair, no fair.* This was all her fault—hers and Nate's. Ruth and Amos had done everything according to the rules. "We better get going. The sooner we go, the sooner I'm back here making pies."

"While you're at the grocery store picking up the pectin, you should apply for the cashier job that's open."

The first wave of nausea of the day rolled through Maisy. She'd applied for a maid job at a bed-and-breakfast and for a receptionist job at a fencing company, both in Haven. So far neither had left a message for her to come in for an interview. The receptionist job didn't surprise her. She had no experience answering a phone. But the B and B was another story. She knew how to clean, make beds, and cook breakfast. "How did you know they have an opening?"

"Word gets around. My friend Diana told me about it at church."

Another reason to get moving and get it over with. It seemed unlikely the owners would hire a woman with no experience running a cash register. How did a person get experience if no one would hire her? At least it would be an opportunity to buy a new composition notebook. Maybe they would have paperbacks for sale there. She'd been itching to start a new list of words, but she'd had no time to go to the Haven library for books. Westerns were okay as long as they weren't romances. Maybe a good mystery.

Reading books would give her something else to think about. An escape.

An hour later Maisy fought nausea while Betsy thanked Kate for the bag of chocolate-chip-walnut cookies she'd brought for the whole staff.

"Your color is better." Betsy set the cookies on the counter and led Maisy down the hallway. "Get your weight and take care of the strip. I'll meet you in the exam room."

She'd gained eight ounces. "It's only been a week."

Maisy settled into a chair in the exam room.

Her iPad in hand, Betsy took a seat on a stool. She wheeled closer. "It's certainly better than losing weight." Her smile lit up her face. Fine wrinkles decorated her eyes and mouth, like accessories. "Your blood pressure is better too. Maybe you're not quite as nervous today."

Maybe. Maisy rose. "So I can go home and Kate can take care of me?"

"How do you feel?"

"Better."

"I don't mean physically. When you were here last week, you seemed almost distraught."

She sat back down. "I don't like being so . . . exposed."

"Some of our other Plain ladies feel the same way. You're not alone. It'll get easier, I promise."

Maisy's situation was different. Completely different.

"You can talk to me, Maisy. I've delivered many babies for single moms. You'll get no judgment from me. I'm here to listen and help so this delivery is as natural and wonderful as possible."

A darkness threatened the corners of Maisy's mind. Her throat tightened. Her heartbeat quaked in her ears. Wonderful? And then what? "I don't think I can do it."

"Many first-time moms feel that way. Your body knows what to do."

"I'm not talking about the delivery."

Compassion filled Betsy's face unadorned by makeup. Completely natural. In some ways the Mennonites weren't so different from Amish folks. But then Betsy had a degree in nursing. She'd spent years as a missionary and midwife in El Salvador. She drove a car to the clinic and used a computer. "You have the ability to take care of yourself and a baby, even more than English girls your age, because of all the vocational training you get in your community. I imagine you have several younger brothers and sisters you've taken care of since they were babies. The experience serves as on-the-job training for when you have your own."

All true. Maisy drew a long breath and let it out. The quaking didn't ease. Pounding in her ears like beating drums made it hard to hear. "That's also how I know I'm not ready. I know what's involved. Also the fact that I got involved with an English man tells me I'm not making wise, grown-up decisions."

"The fact that you recognize that tells me you've learned a lot from what you've been through."

"I have. I don't think I'm ready to be a parent yet. I'm not mature enough." Maisy sought words that could express the depth of her misgivings and found none. The sound of Vicky's sobs filled her ears. Could she not take a bad situation and turn it into something good—for her baby and for the Kings? "I've been thinking of another possibility. What about adoption?"

Betsy cocked her head. Eyes squinted, forehead wrinkled, she nodded slowly. "That's another option, but it's a difficult one. Giving up your baby is a hard road, one that requires a steadfast willingness to endure the pain of that separation."

"But it's also a chance to give a woman who's desperate to be a mother that gift, isn't it?" Maisy smoothed her wrinkled dress over her belly. Sometimes at night when she relaxed in bed, a strange, small flutter would surprise her. Not a kick, not yet, but a little wave to say, "Hey, I'm here." It would be hard, very hard. "I'm just thinking about it right now. This baby's father isn't Plain. If I decided to give him up, I would want the couple to be Plain."

"Of course. We have Plain couples who are struggling with infertility just like Englisch couples."

Maisy knew of one such couple. What would Ruth and Amos say about such a decision? Her own parents? The Gmay? Her stomach clenched. "I better . . ."

She jumped up from her chair and ran to the bathroom.

A knock on the door several minutes later forced Maisy to pull herself up off the cool tile floor. "I'm fine. Really, I'm fine."

"May I open the door?"

"Yes."

Betsy opened it a sliver, peered at Maisy, then opened it wide. She held out a new toothbrush and a travel-sized tube of toothpaste. "Get washed up and I'll get you a ginger ale, if you like."

"Thank you."

When Maisy returned to the exam room, Kate had joined Betsy, who held out the glass of ginger ale. "There's a saucer of crackers on the desk." She patted Maisy's back. "No decision has to be made today or tomorrow, for that matter. Ultimately it's your decision. Give yourself time to think about it and pray about it."

"Okay." Maisy forced the two syllables through dry, cracked lips. She cleared her throat. "But the sooner I make a decision, the sooner I can learn to live with it. And the sooner the couple can have some relief from their heartache."

"Are you thinking of someone specifically?"

"Vicky and Isaac."

"Ah. You saw them here."

"They were so lost and sad."

"They are." Betsy guided Maisy to the exam table. "Let's check on the baby's heartbeat."

After a sip of ginger ale, Maisy hauled herself onto the table and lay back. If only she could curl up in a ball and stay there until this baby made an appearance.

"It's really important that you make sure this is what you want to do before there's any discussion with Vicky and Isaac. They've been through so much. We don't want to be responsible for more pain."

"Me neither," Maisy whispered. "Me neither."

The *whoosh-whoosh* of the baby's heartbeat filled the small room. Maisy closed her eyes. The baby was the size of an avocado. He would fit in the palm of her hand. Babies were sweet and squishy and smelly. They needed more than dry diapers, milk, and clean clothes. They needed a father and a mother who would keep them safe, teach them about God, and guide them to adulthood.

Maisy could barely keep herself on the straight and narrow.

"The heartbeat sounds good. Strong and steady." Betsy laid the doppler aside. She held out her hand to help Maisy up. "I'd like to schedule an appointment in one month. Kate will check your weight and blood pressure every week in the meantime. Any problems and we'll get you right in. That will also give you time to think about the other thing as well."

Maisy thanked her again, made a payment at the front desk, and followed Kate out to the buggy.

"Did I understand that you're considering adoption?" Kate insisted on giving Maisy a hand up, even though she didn't really need it. "That's a big decision with lifelong repercussions."

The happy-go-lucky Kate had disappeared. Maisy drank the ginger ale Betsy had sent with her. Her stomach didn't care much for it. "Do you think it's wrong of me to consider it?"

"Nee. I think it's brave." Kate held the reins, but she didn't give her horse the signal to move. "People will talk. It's human nature, no matter how much we try to change it. You must do what is best for your bopli, not what others think is best."

"Would it be selfish of me to give my bopli to someone else to raise?" Maisy dug her fingernails into her palms. She concentrated on the pain to keep from crying. "Would I be taking the easy way out?"

"Ach, maedel. There's nothing easy about handing over a bopli you made and grew in your own body to another person." Scowling, Kate pushed her glasses up her nose. She tut-tutted. "That's how I know you're not ready for this. Think hard on it. Pray. Then decide."

"I will." Maisy's head throbbed. Her back hurt. Her heart hurt. Now that she'd opened the door to the possibility of giving the baby up, she couldn't close it. She rubbed her belly. *What do you think, Bopli? Would you be better in the arms of another woman?*

The truth hurt worse than any pain she'd ever experienced.

"I don't think you're up to applying for jobs today." Kate clucked and snapped the reins. "I'll run into the store and get the application. Amos will have to be happy with that."

"Bless you." Maisy dug through her bag for her billfold. "Would you mind getting me a composition notebook?"

"No problem whatsoever."

Kate didn't ask any questions and returned in less than ten minutes. For a woman who loved to chat with everyone who came within twenty feet, that was a lightning-fast trip. She handed a bag to Maisy before settling a big bag of sugar on the floor behind the buggy's seat. Maisy dug through the bag. Pectin, a notebook, and a Janette Oke novel.

"How did you know?"

Kate held out Maisy's change. "I saw a book on the dresser the other day. I hope you haven't read that one."

"I haven't." Maisy smoothed her hand over the cover. A romance, of course. She was only eighteen. She couldn't swear off romance. But now she knew the stories were just that—stories. "Did you forget the application?"

"Nee. They'd already filled the position. The new cashier starts tomorrow."

Maisy leaned back on the buggy's bench. To her chagrin relief flooded her. The thought of making conversation with customers was scary. She'd only been in the grocery store a few times. She didn't know which aisle had the cereal or which one had the canned vegetables.

"You'll get the hang of this."

She hadn't so far. "I know."

"Just know you can always count on me and Betsy and Leeann. And Ruth. You can always count on her."

Until Amos laid down the law. "I don't want to create discord in her home."

Any more than she already had.

"Give Amos time. He'll come around. He's a gut man who's hurting. Don't forget that. And remember. You'll catch more flies with honey than vinegar."

Maisy raised her face to the sun. She closed her eyes. Who wanted flies, anyway? What she wanted was peace.

"Amos wants peace too."

"Stop doing that!" Maisy sat bolt upright. "It's scary."

"What?"

"Reading my mind."

Kate laughed. "Rest. I'll get you home."

What a nice thought. Rest. Home.

Not her home, but the next best thing. For now.

Chapter 14

A BABY FACTORY. THAT'S WHAT THE Plank farm seemed to be these days. Joshua smiled to himself. The women acted like it was a big secret. But even a bachelor like himself—one with five younger brothers and sisters plus cousins, nieces, and nephews—recognized the symptoms. Both women gave up coffee and sipped ginger tea. They both sucked on lollipops like grade school kids. Their faces were green around the gills while serving fried eggs, bacon, and sausage for breakfast. Once Joshua suggested pancakes might be a nice change of pace, knowing his sister-in-law served mountains of pancakes and waffles last year before his first niece came along, but Amos deep-sixed that idea. A man needed protein to farm.

After another long day bringing in the last load of hay for the year, Joshua was in no mood to argue. He stalked into the house to wash his hands and face before supper. All the windows were open to let in a breeze. The summer heat had faded into fall breezes—especially in the evenings. Soon the harvest season would be over. It would be time for Joshua to switch to his other job—working for Caleb Mast at the furniture store.

Joshua splashed water on his face again. If only he could wash away the feeling that time was getting away from him. Caleb was a good furniture maker. He taught well. But he had his own sons to work with him. Everything was slightly off-center. A man Joshua's age should be married and starting a family of his own, not living at home and eating supper with his parents—nice at it was. He should be plying a trade of his choosing, not one he fell into when nothing else materialized.

Wide-open spaces. Horses. Working outdoors. The dream that died with Jacob—that Joshua allowed to die. What would Jacob say about that if he were here?

You're not here. That's the whole point.

Joshua dried his hands, refolded the towel, and laid it over the rack. This wasn't a new or unexpected dilemma. So why did he avoid thinking about it? Dealing with customers was uncomfortable, but he did it because it was a job—like working for Amos was a job. Hard work kept his mind occupied.

Still pondering the future, he trudged to the table. Maisy looked up from setting down a platter piled with corn on the cob. She smiled. She did that more now. Her sickness must be abating. "Just in time. I hope you like tater-tot casserole."

"I do."

"Gut."

Amos strode into the kitchen and headed for the sink. Maisy's smile disappeared. She hustled to the counter where Ruth dumped pickled beets from a Ball jar into a serving dish. "Shall I take the casserole to the table?" Maisy grabbed two pot holders in preparation for the task. "The men are chomping at the bit to eat."

"Surely. Danki. Whoops!" Ruth hopped back from the counter. Purple juice splattered her apron and hands. "Ach. I splashed the beets."

"That'll stain. I can presoak it tonight. We'll wash it tomorrow."

"Gut to see you're making yourself useful, Maisy." Amos's voice held a note of approval. "I saw a help-wanted sign in the window at the hardware store today. Did you go into town this afternoon to apply for jobs?"

"Nee, I didn't." Maisy set the casserole on the table. "Bonnie had tummy troubles all day. I stayed here to take care of her while Ruth sewed. Both boplin are growing so fast. Plus Ruth needs bigger—"

"I know what Ruth and the kinner need." With a grunt, Amos plopped into his chair at the head of the table. "I also know what we talked about almost six weeks ago."

"I can't imagine the owner hiring a woman to work in his hardware store." Maisy picked up the water pitcher and trotted around the table filling glasses. She reached past Joshua. She smelled like diaper rash ointment and gingerbread. "I don't know anything about nuts and bolts, hammers, farm implements, or stains, or sandpaper."

"Joshua could help. He could walk you through the store. He could show you what's what before you apply." Ruth buckled Nicholas into his high chair. "He's an expert."

True, but the expectation that Maisy could get a job at a hardware store with no prior experience seemed far-fetched. Plus it meant spending time alone with Maisy and making conversation with her. By this time of day Joshua was out of words. "It seems unlikely that Harvey would hire someone with no experience."

"Maisy's been around construction workers her whole life." Ruth's tone was airy. Optimism bloomed wherever the woman went. "She'll pick it up quickly. Harvey's a friend of yours. Your recommendation would go a long way."

"I couldn't put Joshua out." Maisy's cheeks had turned as red as the fresh, sliced tomatoes on the plate next to the corn on the cob. "He has more important things to do than teach me about tools."

"Maybe he should speak for himself." Ruth swiveled in her chair to glare at Joshua. "Would you be willing to help out Maisy, knowing her situation?"

Amos and Maisy joined her in staring at him.

When she put it that way—which was her intention—Ruth knew there was no way Joshua could say no. "I reckon I could start with a run-through of the tools in your barn, Amos. After that we'll make a trip into town."

"You better do it tomorrow." Ruth grabbed a napkin and wiped up Bonnie's spilled milk without missing a beat. "Someone else might apply. Harvey's surely in a hurry to fill the position, now that his son has gone off to college in Manhattan. The hardware store is always busy, and he likes his long lunch hour so he can take a nap after he eats his salami-and-Swiss cheese-on-rye-bread sandwich and barbecue chips."

Apparently everyone knew about Harvey's love of salami and Swiss cheese. "If Amos doesn't object, we'll do that."

"Amos, you don't object, do you?" Ruth cast her encouraging gaze widely to include her husband. "After all, you're the one pushing for Maisy to get a job. Her bills will start to add up at the birthing clinic pretty quickly."

Why didn't she simply have the baby at Amos's house? Nope, better not to dig into those details. Joshua kept his mouth shut.

"I reckon that's fine." Amos tugged at his beard, his expression thoughtful. "It's worth a try. You might as well start after supper. After the kitchen is clean."

Joshua took a bite of his tater-tot casserole. It wasn't as tasty as it had been a few minutes earlier. Bonnie's merry tune involving an itsy-bitsy spider and Nicholas's gibberish were the only sounds besides forks clinking on plates for the rest of the meal. Maisy finished first. She rose and picked up a plate that still held food.

"You're wasting food." Amos pointed his fork at her. "Don't put it on your plate if you don't intend to eat it."

The flush on her face deepened. She nodded but said nothing.

"Why don't you bring out the brownies left over from yesterday?" Ruth's tone was soft, the voice of a long-suffering mediator. "Amos needs some sweetening."

Joshua kept his amusement to himself. Ruth did know how to say what she had to say without actually saying it. "The food was gut." He pushed back the bench and stood. "I'll meet you in the barn, Maisy, when you're finished in the kitchen."

Again, a simple nod. The few pounds she gained in recent weeks filled out her face, taking away the gaunt look of a sickly person. Her cheeks were plump, her blue eyes bright, and her skin clear. She was a pretty woman.

Forget it. Just forget it.

He whirled from the table, stomped through the living room, and out the front door. How could he be having these thoughts about a woman expecting another man's baby?

Half an hour later, that pretty woman slipped into the barn, her steps slow, hesitant. The calico cat trailed after her. He wound himself around her feet. She picked him up and settled him in the crook of her arm. "I'm sorry I kept you waiting. I didn't think it would take so long to clean the kitchen."

She was always apologizing. She shouldn't do that, especially when it was because she'd been working hard to clean the kitchen. Joshua cocked his head toward the tools Amos had hung on the far wall with shelves underneath for others. "We can start here."

"We don't have to do this right now if you're busy or tired." She stroked Sunny. His purr revving like an engine, the cat meowed his pleasure. "You've had a long day."

"So have you." Joshua moved to the shelves that contained the bulk of Amos's tools. "The sooner we get started, the sooner we'll be done."

"I'm sorry you got stuck in the middle of this." Maisy didn't move. "I know you don't want to be here doing this with me."

"I don't mind."

"Jah, you do."

Joshua forced a smile. "Not for the reasons you think."

She couldn't know how hard it was for him to carry on a conversation, how little desire he had to talk to anyone.

Joshua picked up a piece of sandpaper from a row he'd arranged on the counter above the shelves. "Do you know what grit is?"

Maisy deposited Sunny on a hay bale and trudged over to the shelves. "You mean dirt?"

A woman would think of that. She mopped a lot of floors. "The roughness of sandpaper is graded in a measure called grit. The lower the grit the more abrasive it is. Customers will come in and ask for coarse, medium, fine, and super-fine sandpaper. The grade corresponds to how big the grit is."

Joshua handed her the sandpaper. She ran her fingers over it. "Why is that important?"

"Because the customer wants to use the right grade for his project. The coarse-grit paper gets the material off faster, but it leaves scratches. You follow up with a fine sandpaper for a smooth finish. Using the wrong grade could mess up a piece of furniture."

Maisy walked along the shelves, touching hammers, saws, buckets of nails, a gas-powered drill, screwdrivers, wrenches, and a variety of implements she likely would be hard-pressed to name. "It's too much to learn by tomorrow."

"Then we best get started."

"You obviously know everything there is to know about tools. Ruth says you are about done working for Amos until next spring. How come you don't apply for this job?"

"I already have a winter job. I work for Caleb Mast at the furniture store until Christmas. He's teaching me to build furniture."

"Instead of training horses."

"Instead of training horses." He shouldn't have told her about Jacob. "Harvey Lipton is a nice man. A fair man."

"And I have to work for someone Englisch."

"Amos might have mentioned that." His boss hadn't actually told Joshua. Amos had been talking to his brother about Maisy's unwanted presence in his home when Joshua walked in on the conversation over coffee one day last week. Far be it for him to criticize Bryan, but Plain businesses had many English customers. English businesses had both. What point was made by limiting Maisy's options? "You'll have to wait on both kinds of customers at the hardware store."

"But mostly men." She shook her head. She probably didn't even realize she was doing it. "Many Englisch men."

Which was how she'd gotten into trouble in the first place.

Likely it was a moot point, anyway. Harvey would have to be feverish to be foolish enough to hire her.

Maisy stopped in front of the saws hanging from the wall. "Why does Amos need so many saws?"

This was a topic Joshua could wrap his head around. "It depends on what he wants to cut. When Amos bought this property, it was a fixer-upper. He did a lot of the work himself." He pointed to a hacksaw. "He had to move and repair some of the plumbing so he needed a hacksaw. It cuts through pipes, both plastic and metal. Trees needed to be trimmed. He used a crosscut saw and a bow saw for that. He has two gas-powered saws—the jigsaw and the chainsaw—for bigger projects. The smaller saws were for his woodworking projects. He made several pieces of the furniture you've been using in the house."

The saws hadn't been used in a long time. The lingering effects of Amos's injuries kept him from doing many of the jobs he'd previously relished. That fact likely accounted for his prickly attitude and brusque way of talking. His brother helped when he could. The rest of his family lived in Jamesport, as did Ruth's. If Amos ever thought about moving back to Missouri, he never mentioned it.

"I feel for him." Maisy took a hammer from its hook. She hefted it up and down a few times. Her gaze swept across the tools, some covered with a fine coat of dust. A spider wove an intricate web between the gas-powered drill and the rip-cut saw. "He's young to have such limitations placed on him. It must be so frustrating. He wants to be a good daed, mann, and provider. It must hurt his heart to know he caused the accident that resulted in his injuries—if the tractor-trailer driver is to be believed."

"Either way it was an accident and forgiveness is the only recourse." Joshua studied the array of screwdrivers to keep from staring at her delicate features. As hard as Amos was on her, Maisy still saw through to his pain and suffering. She had a sweet soul.

He picked up the biggest screwdriver and held it out to her. "Do you know the difference between a Phillips-head screwdriver and a regular screwdriver?"

"Nee." Frowning she came a few steps closer and accepted his offering. "It never came up when I was learning how to cut the flour and shortening for a tender piecrust or to add yeast to warm water so the bread dough would rise."

Surprised, Joshua laughed. A sense of humor would go a long

way in Maisy's situation. He picked up the Phillips and held it up. "I suppose you could use the Phillips-head to crimp the piecrust edges."

Maisy grinned. "Or to poke the holes in the top."

"I'm glad to see you two getting on so well." Amos's tone held surprise and a sliver of concern. Joshua turned. His boss stood in the barn doorway, a dark shadow silhouetted by the setting sun behind him. "I hope it hasn't gotten in the way of learning what you need to know to apply for the job tomorrow, Maisy."

"We're making progress." Joshua forced himself to stand still. He wasn't too close to Maisy. They were only talking about screwdrivers. He had no reason to feel caught in the act. Caught in the act of what? "We've covered saws, screwdrivers, and sandpaper."

"You've barely scratched the surface, in other words."

"There's no way I can learn everything I need to know by tomorrow." Maisy laid the screwdriver down. She crossed her arms as if hugging herself. "Just about any other applicant will know more than I do."

"Don't take that attitude with you to the store." Amos stepped into the barn. His horses nickered and neighed as if greeting their owner. He held up a handful of carrots. "I'm coming, I'm coming. Bonnie got into the tube of diaper rash cream. She got it all over herself and Nicholas before Ruth noticed. I guess someone left it within the maedel's reach. She wants your help bathing them, Maisy."

She nodded at Joshua. "Danki for tonight. I'll be ready to go to town tomorrow after breakfast—or whenever is best for you."

She gave wide berth to Amos as she left the barn. Sunny unfurled, stretched, and followed her out. Amos said nothing. Joshua began returning tools to their rightful spots.

"A strange pairing, indeed."

Joshua's body stiffened. He swiveled. "Pardon me?"

"She's an outcast because of her fehla. You keep putting off a decision regarding baptism. You don't go to church. It's a match not made in heaven."

Anger gathered steam. Joshua bit his lip and gritted his teeth. This man was his boss, but they'd also formed something akin to friendship over the past year. "There's no pairing. You asked me to help Maisy learn about tools. That's what I was doing. She's trying hard to please *you*."

Amos's face reddened. "And I'm trying to do right by my fraa's cousin while following Bryan's rules."

"You're caught in the middle." And now so was Joshua.

"I am."

"I was only trying to help."

"Understood." His tone grudging, Amos moved so he could lean against a stall. "I don't say it much, but I appreciate you taking the job working for me. I know you do it to help me out, not because it's the kind of work you want. Helping with Maisy is way beyond that."

A vast number of words bordering on an expression of feelings welled up. "No worries. I like working with my hands. Outside."

"Gut. Gut nacht."

Joshua stalked from the barn. Had he been entirely truthful with Amos? All this time Joshua had worked to keep his distance from people. He couldn't remember the last time he went to a singing or a Gmay picnic. He liked not having to make empty conversation. How had Maisy gotten under his skin? Their conversation on the porch ran on repeat in his head. She missed her family. She missed her dog. She made friends with a cat. She was an adult by Plain standards, but she'd made a terrible mistake that had sent her life in an entirely new and scary direction. She questioned God's presence in all this turmoil.

They were more alike than different—except for the cat. That wasn't a bad thing. No matter what people thought.

Chapter 15

Harvey Lipton's skeptical expression told the story. Maisy plucked a sales flyer from the hardware store's glass countertop. The sale featured paint, stains, wallpaper, brushes, and other supplies needed for renovating a room. Also footstools, ladders, and riding mowers. Joshua's running commentary on the quick tour of the store after the previous night's equally brief tutorial bounced around in her head. The difference between varnish and stain. Indoor and outdoor paints. LED lightbulbs. Critter traps. Hoses. Hammers, saws, axes, socket sets, rakes, pruning shears, lawn and garden insecticides and herbicides. Work boots. And a huge display of flashy red Radio Flyer wagons, tricycles, and bicycles, alongside a display of dark-green John Deere toy tractors.

Toys in a hardware store. Who knew? Maisy sorted through her childhood memories. Not one time had she entered a hardware store with her father. Her parents drew the lines clearly. Girls with Mother to the grocery store, bakery, sewing-goods store, thrift shop, and so on. Boys with Father to the hardware store and the farm and feed-supply store.

Did they think children didn't have enough room in their brains for both?

Harvey had a right to be doubtful. He pushed the application across the glass counter toward Joshua. "You're the one applying, no?"

"No, she is." Joshua waved his hand toward Maisy. "Meet Maisy Glick. She's Ruth Plank's cousin. She moved here from Jamesport."

The loose skin on Harvey's sun-damaged forehead crinkled. He scratched his oversized nose, took off his black glasses, held them up to the light streaming from the windows, then returned them. "It's nice to meet you."

"Likewise." Maisy's throat was so dry, the word came out like a croak. Heat curled itself around her neck and cheeks. She took the application from Joshua. "Can I fill this out now and return it right away?"

His expression said *don't bother*, but he nodded. "Let me ask you this, what's a miter saw?"

A million images collided in midair. Maisy concentrated. A miter saw. She seized a definition from the dozens Joshua had drilled into her on the drive. "It's a saw that lets you make cuts at different angles. It has a blade mounted on a swing arm that pivots left or right. You use it to make cuts for crown molding, doorframes, window casings, and such."

Memorizing word definitions had trained her mind to hold information. She sounded like she knew what she was talking about. Joshua winked at her. She stifled the urge to laugh. "I saw it on aisle four."

"That's right." Harvey ran his hand over thinning gray hair that didn't quite cover a sun-reddened bald spot. "What about caulk? Where do you find it?"

"Over by the paint, paintbrushes, and such."

"Hey, Harvey." A man in white painter's pants splattered with half-a-dozen colors of paint leaned on the counter next to Joshua. "I need some clear epoxy. Where're you hiding it?"

"It's on aisle five with the stains and varnishes." Maisy was on a roll. "Is there anything else I can help you with?"

"That'll do, little lady." The man ambled away with a wave at Harvey.

"What do you think, Harvey?" Joshua tapped the application. "How about giving her a trial run? Go have your lunch and your nap. Let Maisy take over for an hour—or two. I'll teach her to use the cash register."

"It doesn't really count if you're here coaching her." Harvey tugged at his ragged salt-and-pepper goatee. "I wager you've been hanging out in hardware stores since you were knee-high to your daddy's britches."

"I promise not to cheat. My job is to teach her to run the cash register. Everything else is on her. If she can't handle it, she'll come get you."

"I sure am hungry." He stared wistfully toward the back of the store. "Janie packed me my favorite lunch."

"And that salami-and-Swiss-on-rye sandwich is calling your name."

"Sure as shootin'." He sighed. "I'll be right back there behind door number one if you need me."

"Enjoy."

Maisy waited until Harvey trekked from sight to beam at Joshua. "I can't believe you did that."

He shrugged. "I've known Harvey for a while, that's all."

The painter was back with his can of epoxy, paint stirrers, a roller brush, a dozen rolls of blue tape, and liners for paint pans.

Joshua held open the swinging gate so Maisy could go behind the counter. He followed. It turned out not to be that hard. The scanner did all the work. As long as she pushed the right buttons, could find the UPC to scan, and didn't miss any of the merchandise, she was fine. She'd made change often at the produce stand where she didn't have a cash register to calculate the correct amount.

The store had its version of a lunchtime rush—workers who stopped in while on their break. Joshua claimed it was a perfect time for her to "show her stuff" for Harvey. It also meant she didn't have time to worry or think about how she felt. The time passed quickly.

At two o'clock Harvey reappeared. He rubbed his eyes and yawned. "All is well?"

"You'd be proud." Joshua held out the store's receipts for a dozen sales. "Once I showed her how to work the scanner, she was good to go."

Harvey pushed his glasses up his nose and perused the receipts. "Not a bad haul. But I need to see it for myself."

"So you want some more free help." Joshua flashed Harvey a grin, so there'd be no doubt he was joking. He had a nice smile. It transformed his face. Maisy dropped her gaze to the counter.

Joshua helped himself to a peppermint in a jar next to the register. "I'll come back at five to pick you up, Maisy, if that's okay with Harvey."

His expression still doubtful, Harvey nodded. Joshua headed for the door. Just like that, they'd decided her future. Men did that. Maisy gritted her teeth and summoned a suitably grateful expression for Mr. Lipton. "I'll be right back."

She followed Joshua to the door. "What will you do for the next three hours?"

"Talk with Caleb across the street."

"I'm sorry to take up so much of your time—"

"Stop apologizing. It's a bad habit." Joshua pulled open the door. "I'll be back in three hours."

The time passed quickly. Harvey took a seat on a stool behind the counter and gave Maisy directions. Sweep the floor. Straighten the shelves on aisle one. Restock the batteries. Wipe down the glass countertops. He waited until almost five to let her ring up a few customers, which she managed to do without a hitch. By that time Maisy's shoulders, back, and feet hurt from standing. She sneezed half a dozen times from the dust. Her throat was parched.

"So what do you think?" Harvey reached under the counter and brought out a jar of assorted jelly beans. "Help yourself."

Maisy scooped up a handful. The first one was butterscotch. "I guess the question is, what do you think?"

"Pleasantly surprised, I'd say."

Her shoulders relaxed. The ache in her feet subsided. "Really?"

"You seem surprised."

"I don't have a lot of experience."

"That's obvious. Joshua wanted me to give you a try before you filled out the application. That's a dead giveaway. But you've never been in jail for anything, right?"

"Never."

"You've never stolen from an employer?"

"Of course not."

He picked out a green jelly bean and tossed it in the trash. "I don't like the sour-apple ones."

Neither did Maisy. Her next one was watermelon, then cinnamon. Her sweet tooth wanted to burst into song.

"There are some things that by law I can't ask you." He wiggled on the stool. It teetered. Maisy edged toward it in case she needed to catch him. "But some things are obvious, if you know what I mean."

She did know. *Here it came.*

"You Amish folks don't wear rings."

"No we don't."

"But wives don't usually work outside the home."

"No they don't."

"You think you'll stick around after, say, February or March?"

"I honestly don't know. The truth is, I'm single. I'm taking this one day at a time, figuring it out as I go."

"So Joshua's not . . ."

"No, no, no. No, he's not." For the first time all day, nausea reared its gut-spilling head. "My kossin Ruth Plank asked him to give me a ride into town."

Really it was Amos and it was more than a ride. He'd asked Joshua to do the impossible.

"I like hiring Amish folks. They work hard, they're honest, they show up on time, and they're clean." Harvey smoothed his thinning gray hair. It didn't help. The hair tended to fall more to the right side than the left. "On the other hand, they don't have a lot of experience with some of the newfangled electric tools we get in every day."

"We're quick learners." Maisy cast about for other good qualities. "We don't mind getting our hands or our clothes dirty."

"Finish filling out the application. I need all your particulars." Still looking mystified, Harvey pulled a folder from under the counter and opened it. "Here's a time card. Fill it out with today's hours. You'll make eleven dollars an hour. Thirty hours a week. I can't offer you benefits like paid leave, but if you need time off for doctor's appointments, you've got it."

She had a job. A real job. In a store. Maybe Amos would unbend enough to carry on a conversation with her. It wouldn't be so great for Ruth. Maisy had tried to be helpful by cooking, cleaning, and taking care of the children. Amos didn't seem to think that was important. What was important was doing what the bishop had instructed.

"Thank you, Mr. Lipton."

"Just Harvey."

The bell over the door dinged. Joshua held the door open for a red-faced English woman dressed in overalls and a tube top, then came in behind her. The woman rushed toward the counter. "I couldn't remember what time you closed, Harvey." She put her hand to her chest and panted for a few seconds. "I need four bags of cement mix. We started pouring the concrete for the addition and we ran out. I must've miscalculated."

"Aisle eight." Maisy grabbed a shopping cart from the row lined up near the register. "I'll help you."

"No you won't." Joshua put a hand on the cart. "Those bags weigh ninety-four pounds apiece. You shouldn't be lifting those in your . . ."

His face turned tomato red. Maisy shook her head. *Don't. Don't draw attention to the bopli.*

"I think I just discovered a drawback to hiring you." Harvey pushed through the swinging gate. "A little pregnant girl can't lift heavy stuff, and we have tons of heavy materials."

Was he going to take the job back? Maisy pushed Joshua's hand away. He should've kept his observation to himself. "No worries, I can help. I have a stout back. I've lifted heavier."

Plain women expecting babies worked in the fields, they planted gardens, they mowed the yard with push mowers—they did whatever needed to be done. No need to coddle them. No need to coddle her.

"I'm capable of lifting my own bags." The woman flexed her bare biceps. She did have some impressive muscles. She grinned at Maisy. "Men. They insist on seeing us as the weaker sex."

Maisy scowled at Joshua. She turned her back on both men and followed the woman to aisle eight where together they lifted the bags into the cart. Harvey and Joshua apparently couldn't help themselves. They peeked around the endcap of stepladders and aluminum buckets as if they thought the women couldn't see them.

Flashing them her best smile, Maisy pushed the shopping cart with all 376 pounds of cement mix toward the front. Her shoulders ached. Sweat dampened her dress and hair. She stopped under the ceiling fan that cooled the area behind the register. "Let me get you rung up."

"Thanks for your help." The woman dug a wad of bills from the front pocket of her overalls and laid them on the counter. "My husband had a conniption fit when he realized we were short. He wants to finish tonight because there's a chance of rain tomorrow." She rolled her eyes and shook her head. Her purple-and-red curls bounced. "Of course it was all my fault we ran out. Women always take the blame and do the dirty work."

In that respect the lives of Plain women and English women didn't sound all that different. Maisy took her money, made change, and handed it over with her receipt. "Good luck with your addition."

"Thanks. Good luck with the baby."

A total stranger had wished her luck. That was more than most of the people who knew and loved her had done. This job might work out. That little flutter below her belly was a reminder that she had no choice. This had to work out.

"Time to go." Joshua tossed the words over his shoulder as he strode toward the door. "By the time we get out to Amos's, supper will be on the table."

No congratulations for getting the job. Fine. Maisy removed the red HARVEY'S HARDWARE apron, stowed it on the rack near the storeroom door, and said good-bye to Harvey.

"Be here tomorrow at nine o'clock. Don't be late. I'll open and close." Harvey tapped his index finger on the counter as if to punctuate his instructions. "I want you here for the middle shift. You'll be off at three thirty. Thirty minutes for lunch. I recommend you bring something. It takes too long and costs too much to eat in the restaurants around here."

Three thirty would get her home in time to help Ruth with supper and clean up afterward. Would Amos loan her a horse and buggy? He could always use a tractor if he needed to come into town. A luxury they didn't have in Jamesport. "Thank you for the job. You won't regret it."

"It's obvious you have gumption, missy. I just hope you stick around. You better not make me regret it."

Maisy had no intention of doing that. She had enough regrets of her own.

Chapter 16

JOSHUA DROPPED MAISY OFF AND WENT home. To his father's home. Helping Maisy get a job felt good. Too good, maybe. She didn't belong in a hardware store. She stood out like a Plain girl in a rock 'n' roll band. But she was so happy about it. She kept thanking him for helping her. By the time they were halfway to the farm, she'd dozed off. She gradually listed to one side until her head leaned against his shoulder. Of course she apologized for it as her face turned scarlet. She jumped from the buggy and practically ran into the house.

Truth be told, Joshua hadn't minded. He should've moved her away, but he didn't want to wake her. She was exhausted and she needed even a few minutes of relief before doing the chores that surely awaited her in Amos's house.

Joshua shouldn't be entertaining thoughts about how nice it was to have Maisy's soft cheek leaning against his shoulder while she slept. How sweet she looked with her mouth half-open and her long eyelashes resting against her white skin.

Stop it. Stop it right now.

Joshua hopped from his buggy and unhitched his bay Standardbred. Job—so named for his patience—tossed his regal head in appreciation. His black tail swished. He neighed. Joshua patted his muzzle and smoothed his forelock. "I know. I'm glad to be home too."

"Glad to hear it." His dad popped up from inside one of the stalls. "It's gut to know my *suh* likes to come home."

"I didn't see you there."

"I figured as much." Pitchfork in hand, Dad pushed through the stall gate. He was a tall man, fit, without an ounce of fat on him. Daryl Lapp's only concession to his age of forty-six was a new pair of wire-rimmed glasses. "You aren't much for sharing your thoughts with two-legged animals. How long are you here?"

"I thought I'd stay for a while."

"Your mudder will be happy to see you."

And Dad wasn't? Joshua's presence only reminded his father that his son still hadn't chosen to be baptized. Nor did he attend church. That meant a cloud of uncertainty and tension followed Joshua into the Lapp house.

Not that Dad would say any of that. Joining the Amish faith had to be Joshua's choice.

Joshua led Job into the nearest empty stall and grabbed a brush. "Did you get supper at Amos's?"

"Nee. I wasn't hungry."

"Your mudder made that taco casserole you like for supper. She'll be itching to warm it up for you." Dad hung the pitchfork on the wall and headed for the door. "It'll make her day."

Joshua lengthened his strokes over Job's withers. "That's his way of saying that despite everything, he's glad to see me too."

Job nickered. Joshua chuckled. "You're right. The apple doesn't fall far from the tree."

Joshua took his time. He finished grooming the horse, enjoying the companionable silence. He fed him, visited with the two

Standardbreds and the four Percherons in the other stalls, and finally headed for the house.

Sure enough the spicy aroma of onion, garlic, cumin, and jalapeños hung in the air like a welcome committee. Joshua went to the sink and washed his hands. By the time he picked up the towel, his mother bustled into the room. "You're here, you're here."

"I am."

She hugged him. Joshua let her. Marnie Lapp was a hugger in a community where folks tended to be more reserved. She was the only one in his family who did it. He would never deny her that pleasure. "That casserole smells so gut. I hope you had a lot left over."

"Ach. You know your little brothers. They eat like they have hollow legs. But I made two because everyone says it's even better left over."

She ducked past him and opened the oven door. The aroma deepened and enveloped Joshua. The concoction of corn tortillas, layered with Monterey Jack cheese, spicy crumbled hamburger, salsa, and sour cream with golden-brown cheddar cheese melted on top was perfect.

"Did you know I was coming home today?"

"Ruth talked to Alice, who mentioned it to Hannah, who told me you were done at Amos's until the spring." A welcoming grin splitting her deeply tanned face, Mom set the casserole dish on a trivet and snagged a spatula from the dishes drying on the counter next to it. "Sit, sit. I want to hear all about your day. Hannah's friend Carrie Beachy said she saw you in town today with Ruth's kossin. What's her name . . . ? Maisy. She said you were in Harvey's with her, of all places. How did that happen?"

The Haven-Yoder grapevine never ceased to amaze. Joshua settled onto a bench at the black walnut table long enough to seat twelve. "It's a long story."

"I have all evening. The boys went night fishing. Hannah and Rachel are hatching some plans for seeing their beaus that they think we don't know about. Your daed will be asleep in his chair in another half hour. You have me all to yourself."

She set a plate filled to the edges with casserole, black beans, and a pile of tortilla chips in front of him, followed by a tall glass of water and a bowl of salsa that added the enticing smell of cilantro and lime to the mix. "Go on, you can eat and talk at the same time."

Between bites too good to hurry, Joshua told his mother the whole story. She sat transfixed, not saying a word, until he finished. "Knock me over with a feather. No wonder Ruth and Amos have said little about her."

"Not wanting to spread gossip, I reckon." Joshua emphasized the word *gossip*. His mother would get his drift. What he shared with her would not be repeated. "Maisy made a mistake. We all do. I won't throw the first stone."

"Me neither." Mom helped herself to a tortilla chip and dipped it in the salsa. "I'm glad you were able to help her out. Harvey has a heart so big it's a wonder it didn't burst when he offered her the job. He'll end up doing twice the work while trying to teach her what she needs to know."

"I don't know. She's a quick learner and a hard worker."

Mom snatched another tortilla chip, but this time she paused with it in midair. Her sharp blue eyes lit up in concert with a cheeky grin that shaved years from her age. "You sound . . . smitten."

"What? Nee, I don't. I'm not." Joshua concentrated on dipping his own chip. He was not smitten. No way. He'd never been smitten in his life. Finding Maisy at the train station had somehow made him responsible for her—in his head. "Just helping her out."

"If you hadn't rescued her at the train station someone else would've. Poor thing." Mom leaned back and adjusted her wilted prayer covering over dark-brown hair only just beginning to include silver strands. "However, I can see why you'd get attached. After all, she barfed on your shoes."

Her kind attitude toward Maisy warmed Joshua. And her chuckle. She could be counted on to see the humor in every situation. "I'm not attached."

"How does that saying go? 'Methinks he doth protest too much.'"

Only his mom could quote from an author none of them had ever read. "You can thinketh whatever you liketh, but I just did Amos a favor. He's my boss. It'll keep Bryan and the elders out of his hair."

"When did you start caring about making the elders happy?" Dad stood in the doorway. He had *The Budget* newspaper in one hand and an empty glass in the other. "The last time I checked they were making noise about you not coming to church. That doesn't seem to bother you." He came the rest of the way into the kitchen and set the glass on the counter. "Do we still have lemonade?"

Mom shot from her chair to the refrigerator before Joshua could open his mouth to answer his father's first question. She beamed at Dad as she poured without spilling a drop. "Have a seat, Daryl. Joshua has been filling me in on the goings-on at Amos's house."

"You know what Scripture says about gossip." Despite his comment, Dad sat across from Joshua. Mom added another bowl of chips to the assortment on the table. Dad studied the chips, selected one, and laid it on the napkin she'd provided for that purpose. "You haven't answered my question, Joshua."

"I can't come to church."

"Can't or won't?"

Joshua pushed his plate away. He'd eaten too much. What he

needed now was his bed—not a discussion with Dad. "I still haven't made my decision about baptism."

"Are you thinking of not joining the faith?" The fear on Mom's face etched lines where her smile had been earlier. "I know we're not supposed to say anything, but how can we not? You're our suh. We don't want to lose you—"

This conversation had gone south far too quickly. Joshua couldn't lie to her or his dad. "I can't. It would be wrong."

They knew why, even if they didn't want to admit it. They didn't want to talk about it. They never had.

How could God allow a boy, only twelve years old, to burn to death in a house fire because he was determined to save his dog and her puppies? What kind of God couldn't be bothered to save Jacob but made sure a momma dog named Buttercup and six puppies escaped before he went to find them?

Their mom was the kind of woman who had allowed Buttercup to have her litter in the sewing room upstairs—mostly because she'd done so without asking. Jacob had loved Buttercup. He loved those puppies. So did Joshua, but he had been busy helping the men haul buckets of water, trying to keep the fire from spreading. He never even noticed Jacob was gone. Until it was too late.

The stench of burning wood and rubber filled his nostrils. Joshua squeezed his eyelids shut, trying to block out the images. The moment he realized Jacob was nowhere to be found. The ugly, sinking feeling in his gut. The impossible struggle to break free from his father's muscled arms. He had to go in. He had to find his brother. His twin. His mirror image born two minutes before Joshua. Always the daredevil who jumped into the pond from the highest tree branch, who climbed higher, ran faster, and never blinked.

He was okay. He had nine lives.

But no.

Backlit by flames that towered toward the sky, the volunteer firefighter carried out Jacob's limp body. His head lulled back. His clothes were burned, the rubber on his sneakers melted. His face was covered with red, angry blisters.

Dad ripped him from the firefighter's arms. He was sure he could be revived. He carried Jacob to the ambulance. The paramedics tried everything. Finally, they stopped.

Dad demanded they keep trying. They said he died of smoke inhalation before the fire got to him—as if that made it okay.

Mom fell to her knees in the mud. She raised her fists to the heavens, as if beating on God's door. Her anguished screams still reverberated in Joshua's nightmares ten years later. Dad sank to the ground and took her in his arms. They huddled there, their tears mingled. Peter consoled Hannah and the little ones.

Joshua did nothing. Said nothing. His body refused to move. No tears fell. The pain pinned him to a wall he couldn't see. Every breath should've been his last one. The desire to walk into the flames, to be consumed by them, was so palpable he tried to run toward it. Nothing worked. Nothing moved.

Move. No. Not until Jacob does. He'll open his eyes. He'll get up. He'll say he's fine.

Only he didn't.

Then his brother Peter turned. His face wet with tears, he stumbled toward Joshua. Joshua didn't want to be comforted. He didn't want someone to say it would be all right. That God knew the number of days Jacob would live on this earth. His death was part of God's plan. Joshua pushed Peter and his trite words away with both hands.

How? *How?* The silently screamed question beat against his brain. His head might explode. He ran into the dark night. He ran until his side hurt and his bare feet bled. He stayed away until Dad found him, forced him into the buggy, and took him to his uncle Samuel's house.

Joshua's sisters found Buttercup and her babies in the barn after the sun broke over the horizon, casting its light on the smoldering pile of debris that was all that remained of their two-story, four-bedroom, wood-frame house that had held all their earthly belongings. Buttercup had led her puppies to safety—probably before Jacob tried to find them.

All the Lapp family had left were the clothes on their backs and the contents of the barn. Dad still had a way to support his family. Buggies, horses, farm equipment. A silver lining, according to the bishop.

None of that mattered. A precious life had been lost and could never be restored.

Mom blamed herself for not keeping track of her boy. How could she not have known he went back in after Dad forbade it? Jacob wasn't the kind of kid who disobeyed his father. Joshua was. He should've noticed. Jacob was his identical twin. Their teachers had trouble telling them apart. Even Grandma and Grandpa were hard-pressed sometimes.

They did everything together.

He should've felt it in his own lungs when Jacob struggled to breathe. Joshua should have felt the terrible pain when flames licked his brother's skin. His heart should've stopped when Jacob's ceased to beat.

Instead he was still here and still wondering why.

"Not going to church doesn't make it any easier to make a decision about baptism." Dad would avoid the searingly painful bonfire in the middle of the room. "Bryan has offered to counsel you. All you have to do is show up at his house. He wants to help."

"It's been ten years." Mom was braver than Dad. That wasn't surprising somehow. Women had to bear the brunt of childbirth. Having a child she'd borne from her own body die must've been like losing a limb. "It's long past time to let go of your anger and your pain."

"Have you let go?" Joshua wasn't playing fair. He had no right to plumb her pain. She'd carried it so well for so long. "Have you forgotten?"

Without a word, Dad rose. He stomped out the back door.

"He can't even talk about it. He wants to pretend it never happened. That Jacob never existed."

"That's not true." Mom's cheeks turned scarlet as if she'd been slapped by his words. "Don't take your anger out on him. He still has nightmares. He left because he doesn't want you to see how the memories torture him."

"Why can't he say that? I have nightmares too. Why can't he offer—"

"Words of comfort? He has no more words than you do. You two are cut from the same cloth. That's why you butt heads." She rose and took Joshua's plate. "Don't ever question his feelings. They're as real as yours are. He blames himself."

So they all blamed themselves. Jacob's legacy. His foolish—yet understandable—decision to run into a burning house left all of them with pieces of their hearts and souls missing, burned away, unable to grow back.

Mom removed the rest of the dishes and wiped down the table. "We don't want to lose you too. Talk to Bryan. If you can't do it for yourself, do it for your daed. At least try, for our sakes. You have to join the faith for your sake, I know that, but you can talk to Bryan because I asked you to."

Joshua stared at her. He had her blue eyes and dark-brown hair, but he had Dad's height and lean build. She claimed he had Dad's personality. If only he could be more like her.

"Bryan will say Gott's will be done. He'll say we have to be obedient and accept Gott's plan for us. I already know all that."

"If you're such a know-it-all, you should know we aren't smart enough to understand Gott's plan. We won't get our questions answered until we enter heaven—Gott willing."

It was the most she'd ever said about Jacob or that night. Jacob was only twelve, but he was old enough to understand the risk. He loved animals that much. If only he'd loved his family more. He would've thought twice and he'd still be here, tussling with Joshua for the last cookie, catching the biggest fish, and teasing Hannah about her freckles.

"I'll think about it."

"Don't think too long." Mom touched his cheek with her warm, callused hand. "Life will pass you by."

Maybe it already had.

Chapter 17

THE CHILDISH HANDWRITING ON THE ENVELOPE offered the first clue. The letter postmarked Jamesport, Missouri, had been lying on the dresser in Maisy's bedroom when she returned from her trip to the hardware store. She lifted it to her nose. It smelled like the post office and crayons. A letter from Sarah. Just holding it sent homesickness racing through Maisy. She settled on the foot of the bed and tore it open. Sarah had used a red crayon to write the letter in simple block letters. Her handwriting had improved since the previous year. Her teacher would be proud.

Dear Schweschder,

Mudder says you're staying at Kossin Ruth's for at least six months. That's a long time. I don't understand why you had to leave home. Your friends miss you. Mudder and Daed miss you. I miss you. Shelly misses you. Even the boys miss you. Skeeter whines because you're not here. I wish you were here to read to us before we go to bed. Mudder is doing it, but she doesn't do the voices like you do.

Mudder says I will understand better when I'm older. I get so annoyed when people say I need to be older to know stuff.

137

Don't you? You're having a bopli. You're not married. That's bad. But you're still my schweschder. I would like to have a niece to rock and play with. A nephew, too, but not as much.

I have to go now. Nora is teaching me to make bread. I like kneading it. Nora says it works out all your mad feelings when you punch it down. She's right. I think Daed needs to punch down some dough too.

Write me a letter, sei so gut. We miss you.

Love,
Sarah

Sarah and Maisy were cut from the same cloth. Maisy understood rules, but she also had her own opinions about many things. Being opiniated made life harder for Plain women, unless like Ruth, they learned to tamp their thoughts down, be diplomatic, and let the men in their lives think that good ideas came from their own selves. An art form all its own. Some might call it devious, but it wasn't. If a man did it he was smart, a good businessman, a good leader, a good provider. That was true in the English world too.

Maisy touched the red crayon strokes. She held the letter to her chest and closed her eyes. Sarah was only ten years old. She still had much to learn. What Maisy had done was a sin. The Gmay couldn't ignore her actions. Her family and community would forgive her, but she would also be an example to girls and boys about the consequences of such a sin. Forgive but not forget, or the lesson would be lost.

How did a person tell a naive childlike Sarah this hard truth? A return letter would require a finesse Maisy lacked. She went to the kitchen where she found Ruth making a pitcher of lemonade.

"It's so hot. Are you hot?" Her cheeks pink, damp strands of loose hair plastered to her forehead, Ruth waved her fingers like a fan in front of her face. "I feel like running down to the pond and jumping in."

"*Wasser, wasser!*" Bonnie must agree. She wanted water—or something to drink. The little girl called all liquids water. "*Wasser.*"

"Patience, maedel."

Neither of the Plank women sounded as if they had much patience left.

"It's September. The days are getting shorter and the nights are already starting to cool off. Hang in there." Maisy held up Sarah's letter. "Can I borrow some of your stationery? I want to write a letter to Sarah."

"Sure. It's in a basket with my pen pal letter stuff on Amos's desk."

Maisy made a quick trip to the living room and returned to the kitchen with a pen, a few sheets of paper, and a matching envelope. Ruth favored flowers on her stationery, including sunflowers, one of Maisy's favorites. "I need your help."

"I'll do my best." Ruth handed a sippy cup to Bonnie, who plopped down on her diapered behind and took the cup in both hands. Blessed silence. "Did Sarah have any news of your family?"

"Nee, she spent the whole letter lamenting about how much I'm missed." *Lament: to feel or express sorrow or regret. To mourn for or over.* Such a good word for Maisy's feelings as well. She lamented the error of her ways. She mourned the loss of her life in Jamesport, the loss of time with her family. The loss of their respect and trust. How could she explain all that to a ten-year-old? "I need to make her understand why what I did was so wrong that I shouldn't be around her and Shelly and the boys for a while. If I had been baptized I'd be in the meidung now. She couldn't talk to me or even see me."

"A hard lesson for such a small girl."

"She has a mind of her own. She reminds me of me." Maisy settled at the kitchen table. She stared at the blank piece of paper. "Which worries me. It's hard to be obedient, to bend to the will of Gott, to be humble, when you think the rules don't apply to you."

"Is that what happened to you?" Ruth set a glass of lemonade on a napkin in front of Maisy. She took her own glass and sat across from her. "I never thought of you like that. You always seemed so happy. When you came for our wedding, you were like a sweet, pretty butterfly, flitting from one fun thing to the next."

"I didn't count the cost of my actions. I wanted to try out the world. I told myself that's what rumspringa was for. To try anything and everything to see if it fit me better than the life I'd grown up in." Maisy held the cold glass against her cheek. The coolness did nothing to assuage the heat of her embarrassment at her own hubris. *Hubris: excessive pride or self-confidence; arrogance.*

"Even so, I always intended to join the church. I'm Plain through and through. I just haven't done it well. And now my little schweschder is suffering for it."

Ruth opened her mouth. An outraged cry from the Pack 'n Play by the door to the laundry room made her wince. "Hold that thought." She fetched Nicholas and brought him to the table. "He isn't happy that I'm weaning him to a bottle. Where was I? Oh, so you still intend to join the church once the bopli is born?"

"I do. If I'm allowed."

"You can't expect a little girl to understand the whys and wherefores of this situation, I reckon." Ruth's nose wrinkled. She lifted Nicholas from her lap and sniffed. "You stink, little bu. No wonder you're so cranky. You need a diaper change."

She stood and hoisted the boy to her hip. "Tell Sarah you love her and you miss her. You'll be home before she knows it, and in the meantime, she should be extra nice to your mudder and daed.

They're suffering with you. They don't stop loving you because you mess up. They love you more because you are their dochder, and they hate seeing you in this predicament—even if it's one of your own making. Don't tell her she'll understand when she's older. That's so annoying when you're a *kind*."

"Your perspective on things always helps." Maisy managed a smile. "I hope Sarah grows up to be like you. Smart, knowing what to say and how to say it. I never learned to do that. I just blurted out stuff. It gets me in trouble."

"I hope Sarah grows up to be like her big schweschder." Ruth swooped down and planted a kiss on Maisy's prayer covering. She was right. Nicholas stank. "Brave. Honest. Loyal. Willing to admit her mistakes and try to make them right. Keep an eye on Bonnie while I change Nicholas?"

"I will. And danki for being such a good kossin."

Ruth curtsied and grinned. "At your service."

She left Maisy to figure out what to say to her little sister.

Dear Sarah,

I miss you too. All of you. Even the buwe. (That's a joke.) I know it's hard for you to understand why I'm in Haven, but believe Mudder and Daed when they say it is the right thing for me to do. Remember it was my idea. If you listen really hard to the messages on Sunday (which I know you do), you know how Plain maed and buwe, whether grown up or not, are supposed to act. It's all about the rules Gott made for how He wants us to behave. I behaved badly. I'm very sorry about it, but sorry doesn't make it right. I have to live with my mistake. I'm so sorry because it means you and Shelly and the whole family have to live with it too. I'm learning a hard lesson. I wish you could learn from my lesson, but wiser people tell me we mostly learn from our own mistakes.

I will see you again so don't fret. I will read you stories again. We both have to be patient. I reckon that's part of the lesson too.

Give Mudder and Daed extra hugs for me. This is hard for them too.

Give Skeeter hugs for me too. Take care of him for me. You could even tell the buwe I miss them if you want to. They won't admit to missing me, but that's okay.

Write to me again, but tell me news. I miss not knowing what's going on. How is school? Are Daed and Mudder taking produce to the auctions on Thursday? Are you seeing any purple martins passing through on their way to South America? Did you have a birthday celebration for Danny last week?

I'm glad to know you would welcome a niece or nephew. I will need my family's help to raise a bopli without a daed. That's one of the many reasons what I did was wrong. My bopli won't have a daed who loves him and provides for him. Think about that when you are wondering why what I've done is so frowned upon.

Hugs and kisses.

Maisy

Maisy reread her words. For ten years, since birth, Sarah had attended church, first in Mother's arms, then in Maisy's lap, and now seated next to Mudder, tending to the littler ones. She'd heard all the same messages as Maisy. She knew God's laws. She knew the rules Plain folks were expected to follow.

Would Sarah do better than Maisy? Maybe Sarah couldn't learn from Maisy's situation, but Scripture said God could use all circumstances for His children's good. *If something good could come of this situation, let me be an example, Gott. Let me handle it with more grace, with more love, with what's best for my bopli.*

A squawk forced Maisy to open her eyes. Bonnie slung her sippy cup into Maisy's lap. The toddler attempted to climb up her skirt. "Wasser, wasser."

Maisy hoisted Bonnie into her lap. The little girl wrapped her arms around Maisy's neck. "Maye!"

"Maisy."

"Love Maye."

"I love you, too, sweet maedel." Maisy returned the hug. "Stay little for as long as you can. Stay sweet and innocent. You're blessed to have Ruth for a mudder. She'll teach you all you need to know about life."

If only Maisy could be as good a mother.

Chapter 18

Amos didn't mind loaning Maisy a horse and buggy for transportation. After all, she had a job. Even though that left Ruth without a buggy. Maisy contemplated this dilemma as she pulled into the buggy-only parking space in front of the hardware store the next day. Ruth said she didn't mind. She also said she could drive the tractor if she needed to go someplace while Maisy was at work. The Haven Gmay's use of tractors was mystifying. The Jamesport Ordnung didn't allow it. Most Gmays didn't. If Maisy drove a tractor, would she be in trouble if she decided to join the Jamesport church?

She hadn't been baptized. At the moment she could carry a cell phone and not be banned. Not that she would. What if she decided to be baptized in a Haven district? Leaving this sticky wicket behind in the buggy, Maisy hustled into the store. She'd left with more time than necessary. A new employee shouldn't be late on her first day.

"Good. You're here." Harvey trotted from behind the counter. He wasn't wearing his hardware-store apron. "My wife wants me to go with her to a last-minute doctor's appointment. You're still wet behind the ears and I hate to do it, but do you think you can handle the store for an hour or two while I hold her hand?"

"Of course. Anything to help." Dealing with customers by herself on her first full day on the job? Maisy plastered an encouraging expression on her face and ignored the familiar heave-ho in her stomach. *Be good, Bopli. We need this job.* "Is there anything you want me to work on between customers?"

Harvey handed her a list. "Now that you mention it. Sweep and mop the floors. Straighten the shelves. Break down the empty boxes and stack them in the storeroom. Just go down the list. It'll be the same every day."

Sweeping and mopping—that she knew how to do. Maybe there wouldn't be too many customers on a Tuesday morning.

That proved to be wishful thinking. Within ten minutes of Harvey's departure, the doorbell dinged and didn't stop dinging for the next two hours. Which gas grill was a better deal? Could the customer return a kerosene lamp that didn't suit after all? Another needed two pounds of nails, three grades of sandpaper, and two kinds of varnish. Two customers needed keys made. They would have to come back. Harvey hadn't taught Maisy how to make keys. They weren't happy.

Using the credit card machine proved to be the biggest challenge, though. It was touchy. Maisy didn't know anything about internet and Wi-Fi connections. A man dressed in painters' pants and shirt wanted to buy four gallons of white exterior latex paint. He tapped his paint-stained fingers on the counter for five minutes while she tried to get his charges approved.

"You must be doing it wrong." He planted both meaty hands on the counter and hoisted himself up and over to peer at the machine. His belly hung over his belt and rested on the glass. Amazingly, it didn't crack. "It can't be rejected. I have lots of credit available."

Sweat trickled from Maisy's temples, tickling her cheeks. The ceiling fan didn't help. She gritted her teeth and inserted the card again. No go. "I'm sorry, sir. Your card's been declined."

"Where's Harvey? I want to talk to Harvey."

"He had a family matter he had to take care of." Maisy moved the paint to one side. "I could hold this for you while you go get cash or a checkbook."

"You must be new around here." With a scowl, the man puffed up his chest and moved the paint front and center again. "Harvey knows me. He'd let me take it on credit."

"Come on, Bill, you're holding up the line." The lady behind him had a cart filled with bags of peat moss, mulch, and winter fertilizer. "Give us a break."

"Keep your pants on, Cheryl." Bill swiveled long enough to shoot the other customer a frown. "I need this paint now if I'm gonna finish the Wileys' house today."

"I can't let you leave with merchandise you haven't paid for." That seemed like common sense. Harvey hadn't mentioned letting certain folks run a tab. He didn't seem like the kind of businessman who would do such a risky thing. "Harvey should be back any minute, if you want to step aside and let this lady pay."

"I was in line first."

"What's going on here?" Joshua's familiar voice cut through the waiting customers' grumbling. Smiling, he strode up to the counter and waved at Maisy. "I have experience with credit card machines. Maybe I can help."

"That would be wunderbarr." Maisy spoke in their native language. She shouldn't, but she didn't want these folks to know how intimidating the situation really was. "I don't know what I'm doing wrong."

"Probably nothing. If it's declined, it's declined." Joshua slipped behind the counter. He examined the card, inserted it, and pushed all the necessary buttons. The result was exactly the same.

He turned to the customer. "Let's call the company. They'll tell us why it's being declined."

"Naw. You know what, just give me my card back." Bill snatched it from Joshua's hand. "Harvey don't want my business, I'll go down the road to the store in Hutchinson."

"Whatever you think's best." Joshua's mild tone didn't waver. "You'll put a lot of miles on your truck, though, driving to Hutchinson for something you can get right here."

"We'll see." Bill brushed past the lady, still muttering to himself. "We'll see."

"Don't worry, honey, we're not all like Mr. Jerk." With a smirk, the lady held up a billfold. "I have cash and I'm ready to pay whenever you're ready."

Thankful for an understanding customer, Maisy rang her up. Joshua helped the woman cart the bags out to her car. He was back a few minutes later. "How does the saying go? All's well that ends well?"

"Something like that. Danki for the help. What are you doing here?" The question sounded like Maisy was accusing him of something. "I mean, why did you have to come to town again so soon?"

"I'm doing inventory for Caleb. We're figuring out what pieces of furniture we still need for the Christmas season." Joshua glanced at the oversized clock on the back wall. "I thought I'd see how you're doing on your first day."

"It's been busy. I didn't expect to be on my own, but Harvey had to go with his wife to the doctor."

"That may happen a lot. She has cancer."

"Ach. He didn't say."

"Harvey says she's doing okay, hanging in there."

Maisy grabbed a bottle of glass cleaner and squirted the counter. Bill had left his greasy fingerprints all over it. She concentrated on wiping it down. Joshua's presence was a mixed blessing. His store of knowledge would be a great help. On the other hand, she should be able to do this job without him. She shouldn't get in the habit of depending on him—or any man. "You don't have to hang around. I'll be okay."

"I know you will."

Maisy studied Joshua's face for signs of sarcasm. His blue eyes were full of kindness and something else—more unexpected. Want. He wanted something from her.

This was not good. What could a man like Joshua possibly want from her?

Maisy tossed the paper towel and stowed the glass cleaner on the shelf. "I need to break down some boxes. I've been too busy to do it. Harvey will wonder what I've been doing."

"He knows how busy it gets."

"He said he'd be gone an hour. It's been almost two."

"Doctors' offices are like that. They're called waiting rooms for a reason."

Maisy had little experience with doctors. She'd been a healthy child. "I hope his wife is all right."

"Me too."

Silence descended.

Joshua shifted on his feet. He glanced at the clock again. "I should go. Caleb's sons are bringing in a load of furniture. They'll need help unloading."

"How many sons does he have?"

"Two who are helping out. They build furniture at the shop on his property."

"I just wondered because it's a blessing that he needs your help too. It's nice that Gott's plan—"

"I know what you mean. Gott's plan and Gott's will and all that." This time undisguised sarcasm ran through his words and matched the curl of his lips. "I appreciate the sentiment."

He didn't believe in Gott? Shock and understanding sparred while Maisy sought the right response. Only a hurting person would be so cynical. His brother didn't grow up. Where was God's plan in that? "I'm sorry you're hurting."

The sarcasm fell away, leaving behind something that could only be uncertainty. Joshua ducked his head. "You're a kind person."

She'd thought the same of him. "My mudder says Gott takes care of us even when we don't believe He will."

"Now's not the time for such a weighty discussion." He held open the gate for her. "Go break down your boxes."

"So we'll be working across the street from each other?" She almost said it would be nice.

Joshua's ears turned red. He ducked his head again. "I reckon. I better go."

He practically ran out the door.

Maisy put her hands to her warm cheeks. She hadn't meant anything by the observation. It would be nice to have her only friend in Haven across the street. He was a friend, wasn't he? The question became whether having Joshua nearby was a gift from God or a temptation from Satan.

Maisy threw her hands in the air. "Gott?"

Before God could answer—if He actually deigned to answer such a lowly sinner full of uncertainty like Maisy—the bell dinged. Maybe Harvey had returned. Maisy whirled. Nope. Isaac King entered and grabbed the closest shopping cart.

What would Isaac say if he knew Maisy was thinking of giving her baby to Vicky and him? What did she really know about him? Right now his hair was ragged under his sweat-stained straw hat. His eyes were red. He was a farmer, a hard worker, and a good husband. Which meant he could provide for her baby. But would he be a good father?

How could she know? Isaac stood on the store's welcome mat, studying her as if searching for some sort of sign. More like a simple hello.

"Hi there, welcome to Harvey's Hardware." Ignoring the tempest welling up in her, Maisy concentrated on infusing her greeting with warmth, the way she'd heard Harvey do. "Is there anything I can help you with?"

If Isaac remembered her from the birthing clinic, it didn't show on his face. He shook his head and headed down the first aisle. Squelching the desire to follow him, Maisy turned to a display of toy tractors that had entertained a customer's two sons while she bought out the garden aisle earlier in the morning. They needed straightening. She couldn't talk to Isaac about her dilemma—not until she was sure of her plan. So no thinking about it while he was within earshot.

Her thoughts turned to Joshua. No. That wasn't good either. She'd embarrassed him. She'd read too much of her own loneliness into his expression. Now he might not come back to visit her.

The thought caused a painful hitch in her heart's rhythm.

"*Nee, nee. None of that, maedel.*" Grandma Irene's voice boomed in her ears. "*Behave yourself. Remember what liking a bu got you.*"

So true. Still a small voice whispered something entirely different. Joshua was no boy. He was Plain. He was solid. He wasn't ashamed to be seen in public with her. He didn't seem bothered by her current situation.

On the other hand, he wasn't baptized. He didn't go to church.

He'd as much as admitted he struggled with his faith. If he never found it, having feelings for him would only end in heartache.

Who said anything about having feelings for him? She'd had enough heartache to last a lifetime already. From the looks of Joshua, so had he.

The conversation whirled around in her head until it made her dizzy.

"Excuse me, I'm ready to check out."

Startled, Maisy dropped the tractor she'd been dusting. Isaac picked it up for her. The small, green toys were perfect replicas of the real thing. Her brothers would love them. They loved all things farming. She held out her hand.

Isaac didn't seem to notice. He cradled the tractor in both hands. His thumb traced the words *John Deere*. His shoulders hunched. He shook his head. He probably didn't realize he was doing it. His lips trembled. He pressed them together.

"Isaac, are you all right?"

His head jerked up. "Jah, I'm fine." He thrust the toy at her. "It's sturdy. I don't think you hurt it."

"Gut." Maisy sought words that might offer him comfort. She had none. She couldn't begin to imagine his pain. Trite phrases like God's will, God's plan, God can make good from all things teetered on her lips and burst like bubbles. "Could I get you a bottle of water?"

He shook his head again. His gaze seemed to focus on Maisy for the first time. "You know my name? I've met you before, haven't I?"

For a second the urge to deny it threatened to overwhelm her. Why add to his pain or the awkwardness of this situation? "I was with Kate at the birthing clinic a while back when you were there with your fraa."

His blue eyes filled with pain. His gaze swept toward her belly and then fell to the floor. He nodded. "On second thought, I'll take the bottle of water, if you don't mind."

Maisy rushed to the cooler Harvey kept by the door to his office. She carried the icy-cold bottle to Isaac, who'd taken a seat on a lawn chair in the summer barbecue display. "I'm so sorry. I didn't mean to intrude on your grief."

Isaac removed his hat and laid it on his knees. His flaxen-colored hair was wet with sweat and plastered to his head. "This is the first time I've gone anywhere in a while. Bryan says we need to get out, go about our business, and it'll get easier with time."

How could Bryan possibly know that? Maisy had never met the bishop. She shouldn't pass judgment. "How is your fraa doing?"

"She's canning today with her mudder and schwesdchdre. Keeping busy is the only thing that helps."

Keeping busy to stave off dark thoughts. Maisy had experience with that too. "If there's anything I can do to help, please let me know."

His forehead crinkled. "I'm sorry. I don't remember seeing you around before that day at the clinic. Are you new to Haven?"

The tipping point. Their conversation would be over. "I'm Maisy Glick, Ruth Plank's kossin."

Understanding didn't flash across his face. No sudden stiffening. Isaac sipped his water and nodded. "Welcome to Haven."

"Danki."

Isaac and Vicky had been so caught up in their own lives they hadn't heard the gossip or engaged in the conversations after church. Maisy was just Ruth Plank's cousin. He would find out one day, and that would be the end of any conversations with her. Unless she decided to give up her baby. Then they would be linked together forever. Even if Isaac and Vicky decided to never tell their child who his biological mother was. All the possibilities rushed at Maisy, taking her breath away.

Work, just work. "Why don't I ring up your items while you finish your water? Vicky will be wondering what's keeping you."

"When did you start working here?"

"Today."

"I'll be sure to tell Harvey he chose well."

"Danki again."

He looked as if he wanted to ask another question, but he didn't. Instead he held out the toy tractor. "Add this to my purchase, sei so gut."

The ache where Maisy's heart should be thrummed so hard her hand went to her chest. Isaac hadn't given up hope. He couldn't, not and keep on living, keep on getting up each morning, putting one foot in front of the other, day after day. He was that kind of man. A good man who would make a good father. "I'd be happy to do that."

How she managed to say those words without a quiver involved a small miracle and supernatural, ironclad control. Maisy took the tractor to the counter, where she wrapped it in butcher paper and added it to the bags of insect repellent, birdseed, vegetable and flower seeds, and a new rake. The Kings were seeking a way forward to a season of planting and renewal. First they had to get through a long, dark winter. Their journey felt familiar.

How was it possible that Maisy had this baby growing inside her when the Kings wanted one so desperately? *Gott?*

Isaac came to the counter as she finished ringing up his purchases. He set the empty bottle on the counter. "Be sure to add the water to my bill."

"It's on the house." She tossed it in the recycle bin. "It's what Harvey likes to call complimentary for customers who buy something."

"That's nice of Harvey."

Isaac carefully counted out his payment in cash. With equal care he placed his bags in the cart. He moved as if each task required his complete concentration. As if he'd never done these things before and had to think about how to do them now. Maisy gripped the counter with both hands. They wanted to brush his away so she could do this work for him. He wouldn't appreciate her interference. No man would.

Finally he finished and rewarded her with a nod. His effort to smile tore at her heart. "It was nice to meet you. I expect we'll see you at church one day."

Maisy scraped up her own semblance of a smile. If he knew, he'd never speak to her again. He would see the horrible unfairness she represented. It would break his heart all over again. "Maybe, one day."

Confusion flitted across his face, but a second later it was gone. He took his receipt and left her to ponder how life could be so hard.

The ding of the door faded away. She took a deep breath and let it out. She'd survived. A sudden dull ache caught her by surprise. She sucked in air. Something didn't feel right. She rubbed her belly with one hand. The ache intensified.

She needed to go to the bathroom, but she couldn't leave the counter unattended. She breathed in and out, in and out. If only Ruth were here. Or Kate. Or her mother. *Mudder, I miss you.*

The minutes ticked by slower than catsup from a bottle. Maisy leaned her forearms on the counter, head down. *Breathe. Breathe.* The door dinged. *Please, Gott, not a customer.*

"I'm sorry I took so long." Harvey trotted on spindly legs too skinny for his round body through the gate. "I hope everything went well."

"I need to run to the back."

"Of course you do. I should've told you. If you're here by your-self and nature calls, lock the door, put up the sign that says CLOSED until whatever time, and fix the clock."

Maisy was already moving toward the back. Five minutes later she rushed from the bathroom. "I have to go to the birthing clinic. I know my shift's not over but—"

Harvey must've seen something in Maisy's face. "Go, go."

Maisy flew out the door and hurled herself into the buggy. This baby she hadn't wanted, who turned her life upside down and inside out, was trying to come out.

Sei so gut, Gott, sei so gut, don't let that happen.

Chapter 19

The drive seemed to take forever. Amos's horse had a mind of his own. Maisy's arms ached. Her head hurt. *Sei so gut, Gott, sei so gut.*

She slipped from the buggy and shot into the center. Candy sat at the front desk. "I need help. I need help."

Candy popped up. "Betsy, Betsy!"

Then Betsy was there, holding Maisy's hand, rubbing her back, leading her to the exam room. "Deep breaths, in and out, one, two, three, four, in, one, two, three, four, out."

She helped Maisy onto the exam table and patted her leg. "Just take a breath and tell me what's going on."

"There's blood." Maisy whispered the words. Saying them out loud would make it real. "I'm spotting."

"Okay. Okay. Just relax and I'll examine you."

Maisy leaned back. She clasped her hands together and closed her eyes. When had something she didn't want become so important? Betsy did the exam. Her touch was gentle, like a feather.

"Let's listen to the heartbeat."

Sei so gut, Gott, sei so gut.

There it was. *Woosh, woosh, woosh.* Strong, steady.

"Hear that? The baby's fine." Betsy squeezed Maisy's hand. Her grip was firm and reassuring. "Just to be sure everything is good, I'm going to do an ultrasound."

"Whatever you need to do. This baby needs to stay in there."

"Agreed. We want him to be fully baked before he pops out."

"I'm working at the hardware store now. I lifted a bunch of heavy bags yesterday." She'd been so determined to prove to Harvey that she could do the job as well as any man. She'd put the job ahead of this baby. "Joshua and Harvey didn't want me to do it, but I was showing off. It was stupid. Did I cause this to happen?"

"You're a strong, healthy woman. Women in Third World countries work in the fields right up until the day their babies are born. Lifting bags isn't going to cause a miscarriage in a healthy woman. Especially after the first trimester."

"Unless you're like Vicky King."

Betsy cocked her head and nodded. "Some women have a much harder time, yes."

She rolled a machine closer, then settled onto a stool on wheels. She squeezed warm jelly on Maisy's stomach, then began to push a wand around. "The heart appears to be good, everything looks good, right on track for the baby's developmental stage."

How could she tell? A black-and-white blob floated on the screen. "Are you sure?"

"There's the baby's head." She pointed. "See that line there, that's its spine. Arms, legs."

"If you say so."

Betsy chuckled. "Do you want to know the baby's sex?"

"You can tell that?"

"I can."

"No. No, it's not right to know these things before a baby is born. It should come as a surprise."

"Lots of parents feel that way—especially Amish couples. But a lot of English couples want to know so they can decorate the nursery and buy clothes. Gender-reveal parties are really big these days." Betsy wiped away the jelly and pulled down Maisy's dress. "Let me give you a hand up."

Maisy sat up. "So the baby's okay?"

"Yes. Everything's good. Now that you've calmed down a little, I'll take your blood pressure and do some blood work. I'd also like you to give me a urine sample. Just routine tests to make sure everything is good."

Whatever it took. That moment in the bathroom had been just a tiny peek into what it must've been like for Vicky to lose her first baby. When the adoption fell through, she had to experience the loss in another way but still every bit as painful.

Maisy moved quickly through the steps Betsy had outlined. The midwife's thoroughness was reassuring in its own right.

After drawing the blood, Betsy slid the vials into a plastic bag with writing on the outside. She sealed it and laid it aside. "Okay. We're done for now. Go home. Rest. Put your feet up. If the spotting doesn't stop or gets heavier, come back right away and I'll refer you to an obstetrician. Otherwise I want to see you in one week."

Plain women didn't put their feet up. And they rarely went to obstetricians.

Her expression must've revealed her uncertainty. Betsy leaned forward, hands on her knees. "It's okay, Maisy. You did the right thing coming here. If there's a problem I'll go with you to the obstetrician or we can ask Kate to go with you. How does that sound?"

Betsy and Kate were on the same wavelength. They read minds. "It sounds good."

Maisy hauled herself up from the lab chair. Legs like soggy

noodles, she staggered. Betsy grabbed her arm. "Maybe you should sit down for a few minutes before you go." She guided Maisy toward the kitchen. "I'll pour you a glass of orange juice."

The clock over the refrigerator read three o'clock. Still time to get home and help Ruth with supper. Maisy sank into a chair and gathered up her courage. "I was going to come see you anyway before this happened."

Betsy pulled a bottle of orange juice from the fridge. "I'm glad you feel comfortable doing that. What did you want to talk about?"

Here we go, Gott. "Isaac King came into the hardware store this afternoon."

"It's good that he's getting out of the house. I hope Vicky is able to do the same."

"He's still very sad."

"That's not surprising." Betsy poured the juice and brought it to Maisy. "There's no time line for dealing with grief and disappointment heaped upon grief and disappointment. They've had more than their fair share."

Maisy traced the fine lines on the lacy tablecloth. She forced herself to meet the midwife's gaze. "Seeing him . . . it only reinforced my thoughts about giving my baby to Vicky and him. I know they would be good parents. They're ready. I'm not. I want what's best for this baby. That would be a couple like them."

"It's good that you're giving it careful consideration." Betsy took a seat across from Maisy. She clasped her hands together, fingers entwined. "The decision to give up a baby is terribly difficult. Some mothers regret it later—when it's too late. Some change their minds at the last minute. Some are tortured by their guilt over it. I wouldn't wish that on my worst enemy. But there's another side to this story.

"There's the joy and the satisfaction of knowing you've done the right thing for your baby. You've given him or her to parents who will love and cherish him. There's the joy of knowing you've given two people the most precious gift anyone can give them. You've given them the chance to be parents—an opportunity they might not have had otherwise."

The sword cut deep on both sides of the argument. Keep the baby, hear his first words, watch his first steps, teach him to love God, and be there to watch him grow up. On the other hand, Maisy's baby wouldn't have a father. Yes, he would be loved by her family. They would never hold her failings over him. But his life would be different than the other children's. The shadow of her sin and failure would follow him everywhere.

Or she could give a couple like Isaac and Vicky the chance to be parents. Her baby could grow up with both a father and a mother. He could be surrounded by love, never knowing how his real mother had failed him. Isaac and Vicky wanted children so badly. Maisy wanted them, too, but when the time was right. She could have more babies one day when she'd met and married the right man. Isaac and Vicky couldn't.

"What are you thinking?" Betsy touched Maisy's hand. "If you have questions, please ask me. Anything."

"I can't imagine seeing my baby with them and knowing that he thinks Vicky's his mother."

"If you make this decision, Vicky *will* be his mother. Whether you'll be able to cope with being close by will be something you'll have to figure out." Betsy hesitated. Her blue eyes were dark and serious. "You would have to be able to let go of this baby. To know he's where he's supposed to be. To know he's in a good place. And you would have to be able to go on with your life."

Maisy gulped down the orange juice, trying to swallow a hard knot in her throat. What would her family think? The bishop? Did Nate have a say in this? Surely not. She cleared her throat. "I really need to think more about this."

"Pray about it." Smiling, Betsy relaxed back in her chair. "First things first. Pray. I'll pray for you as well."

Good advice.

"If I decide to do this, how will it work? How is it done?"

"Since there's no adoption agency involved, the Kings would have to get a lawyer to draw up a contract for everyone to sign to make it legal. You can have as much or as little contact with the Kings as you want before the baby comes. When he arrives—whether that's at the Planks or here—the Kings would be there to take him home. Your part would be done."

What would she do then? Where would she go? Could she simply go on with her life back in Jamesport? Could she stay in Haven a few miles down the road from the child she gave away? The questions pelted Maisy like rocks flung in anger. "It's a lot to think about."

"Yes, it is."

"You won't say anything to anyone about this—especially not the Kings?"

"Absolutely not. You can count on that." Betsy walked Maisy out to the lobby. "Anything you say to me here is confidential. If you have any more questions or you just want to vent, come see me."

"You kept saying he and him. Is that what you saw on the ultrasound? A boy?"

"No, no, don't draw any conclusions." Grinning, Betsy shook her head and put both hands up, palms out. "It's just easier to say *he* than *he or she* every time. I wouldn't let the cat out of the bag that easily. My lips are sealed."

It didn't matter. Not to Maisy. Certainly not to the Kings. "Thank you."

"It's my pleasure to help any way I can." She held open the door. "I'll be praying for you."

Maisy needed all the prayers she could get.

Chapter 20

THE STEADY PATTER OF RAIN AGAINST the store windows kept Joshua company as he pushed a dust mop around the furniture on display in the store. Rain meant fewer customers at Mast's Furniture and Antique Store, but the peaceful sound was a sign autumn had arrived with cooler weather and much needed moisture for the plants and animals in farming country. October was quickly slipping toward November and winter. Gone were long days in the broiling sun working side by side with Amos in the fields. Instead Joshua dealt with English tourists who wanted to negotiate down prices for beautiful handmade quilts that had taken months of painstaking needlework to complete. They wanted deals on handcrafted curio cabinets and bed sets. Or they wanted to take selfies with Joshua. They wanted to grill him on being Amish or have him speak in Pennsylvania Dutch so they could record it and play it back for their friends.

That was where Joshua drew the line. He was polite. He did his best to be a good employee, but he didn't feel obligated to be chatty. As if he could. For that he called Caleb, the store owner, out from his office at the back of the store. Let him be the Yoder goodwill ambassador. Humming, Joshua stowed the mop and picked up a dustrag. The bell over the front door jangled. He dropped the rag and strode to the front.

Bryan stood on the rug, closing his dripping umbrella. Raindrops splattered his black jacket and straw hat. His glasses steamed over from the humidity. For a split second Joshua considered whirling around and hiking to the back of the store. Let Caleb deal with him.

Only Bryan hadn't come to the store to buy furniture or quilts. He was a saddlemaker by trade so he didn't have pieces on consignment here either. Smiling, he took off his glasses and wiped the lenses on his shirt. "Just the man I came to see."

"When did you start wearing glasses?"

As if that was an important piece of information. Anything to put off the coming discussion.

"Last week. When I couldn't see the street signs anymore, it was time." Bryan perched the wire-rimmed specs on his nose. "I thought you might be due for a lunch break about now. I have a hankering for a bacon cheeseburger and onion rings at Bull's Eye Grill."

"It's only eleven o'clock." A weak response. Everyone knew it was best to get to the Bull's Eye early before the lunch-hour rush filled the small restaurant to capacity. "I'm out here by myself while Caleb takes care of paperwork in his office."

"I reckon Caleb intends for you to take lunch."

"He knows I bring my lunch. It's too expensive to eat in a restaurant every day."

"This lunch is on me." Bryan leaned his umbrella against the wall. He took off his hat and shook it. Raindrops scattered on the rug. "I'll browse while you ask Caleb."

Bryan knew no one in his right mind would turn down a free meal at the Bull's Eye. Nor could Joshua say no when it was the bishop asking. Not really asking. Telling.

Joshua trudged back to Caleb's office. His boss was perfectly happy to give Joshua a long lunch hour when he heard it was the bishop calling. Bryan wasn't Caleb's bishop, but he understood how these things worked. "Enjoy your lunch," he called out as Joshua opened the door and let Bryan go first.

"Very funny," Joshua muttered.

"What?" Bryan lifted his umbrella to cover them both. "Did you say something?"

"Nothing. I was just commenting on how the rain has cooled the air. It feels gut."

"Indeed. Fall is my favorite season."

They left Bryan's buggy parked in the lot next to the furniture store and walked in the rain, which had turned into a drizzle, to the Bull's Eye. Bryan seemed focused on avoiding puddles and the splashing of cars as they drove by so conversation was minimal. Even at this early hour most of the tables at the red barn-style restaurant were taken. The volume of chatter nearly raised the roof. The aroma of burgers on the grill, fried chicken, and grilled onions mingled in a mouthwatering scent. At least it would've been mouthwatering if Joshua's stomach didn't rock with every step closer to this conversation.

Bryan pointed to a table for two by the kitchen door. "That will work."

Despite the crowd, a waiter descended on them not one minute later with ice water and menus. Bryan reeled off his order and handed the menu back to him. "What's your poison?"

A knot in the pit of Joshua's stomach didn't bode well for enjoying a meal with Bryan sitting across from him. Joshua swallowed hard and ordered his usual—a mushroom Swiss cheeseburger with sweet potato fries. Maybe a root beer would settle his stomach.

"There's no reason to be so mortified." Bryan slurped his water.

He leaned back in his chair and sighed. "People didn't used to look so alarmed when they saw me coming."

"You've been bishop for three years now. You must be used to it."

"I have no more qualifications to be bishop than you do."

"But Gott chose you through the lot."

"So you do believe." Bryan's dark-brown eyes lit up. "Or are you just parroting what you've been taught?"

"Is that what you want to talk about?"

"Among other things. Your daed and I had a conversation after church yesterday." Bryan's gaze shifted over Joshua's shoulder. He waved and hollered a greeting. People liked Bryan. "That's the thing about eating here. We'll know everyone."

"We don't have to do this now."

"We're both busy people. I figure a man has to eat, so this is as gut a time as any. Your daed's concerned. He's between a rock and a hard place. He feels like he can't say anything. Yet as a daed he can't help his feelings. I'm the bishop. I have more leeway."

Here it came. Joshua lined up the catsup bottle, salt and pepper shakers, toothpicks, and sugar dispenser in a buttress against the coming attack. "Leeway for what?"

"To talk about three things." Bryan held up one stubby finger. "First, the time you've been spending with Maisy Glick and why." Another finger went up. "Second, the fact that you still haven't been baptized, and third, you don't come to church."

"So I've had an extended rumspringa." Better to talk religion than about his ambivalent feelings regarding Maisy. They were his feelings, and Bryan wasn't entitled to know about them. Besides, Joshua couldn't explain them to himself. How could he explain them to another man—especially the bishop? "I haven't broken any rules. I don't drive a car or date Englisch girls or carry a cell phone. I don't go to movies or drink alcohol—"

"Stop right there. I'm fully aware you obey the Ordnung like a faithful Plain man. No one can fault you for that. What I don't understand is why you don't take the next step and commit yourself to the faith. You aren't Plain until you do. If you wanted to pursue a life outside the faith, you would've by now."

An astute observation, but Bryan had no right to demand that Joshua unpack his wounds and share them like show-and-tell. "No one is to take the vow of baptism until he is sure of his faith."

"What questions do you still have?"

Joshua paused while the waiter placed his pop on the table, along with an iced tea for Bryan. When he walked away, Joshua tore the paper from his straw, dunked it in the root beer, and sipped.

"You're stalling."

"I am." Joshua set his soda on a cardboard coaster. "Do you know why we moved to Haven?"

"I do."

"Then you know what my questions are."

"It's been ten years."

"People keep saying that like there's a time limit for grief."

"Do you trust that Gott knows what He's doing?"

"If He does, He has a cruel streak."

"The fundamental pillars of our faith are obedience and humility." Bryan's tone didn't change. "Do you think you're smarter than Gott, that you know more than He does? That you can thumb your nose at Him and go about your life without Him because you're miffed at the way your life is going?"

"Nee—"

"It sure seems that way. Who are you to question Gott's plan? Who are you, Joshua Lapp?"

He was a twelve-year-old boy standing in front of a blazing inferno started by lightning, by an act of nature, watching it consume the only home he'd ever known, watching it devour the life of his twin brother without mercy, without grace, without thought for the consequences. "A man with questions."

"I don't think so. I think you're stuck. Stuck in a time warp. You're still twelve, and you're still mad. You're mad at Gott." His brown eyes full of empathy, Bryan spoke softly as if afraid of scaring off that little boy. "I think it's time for you to grow up."

The words stung. The ache in Joshua's throat made it impossible to respond. It throbbed in concert with his aching heart. He rubbed the heel of his hand across his chest.

The waiter showed up with their food. Maybe God was watching over him, after all. Bryan said nothing while the waiter distributed their food, asked if they needed anything else, and trotted away.

He bowed his head. Joshua did the same. *Gott, please get me through this meal. Don't let me crack. Sei so gut.* No matter what happened, he still had conversations with God, most of them surly and morose on his part.

"Amen." Bryan unrolled his silverware and spread his napkin on his lap. "Let's let that topic lie while we eat. It's far too heavy. I, for one, would like to enjoy this greasy pile of goodness. I can feel my arteries hardening as we speak."

Grateful, Joshua nodded. His hamburger tasted like cardboard. Only a mound of catsup made it possible to swallow several sweet potato fries washed down with pop.

Bryan wiped his greasy lips with his napkin. Crumbs dotted his dark-brown beard. He didn't seem to notice. Or care. "It's been brought to my attention that you've been seen with Maisy Glick."

The gossipmongers struck again. Joshua laid down his hamburger. "Since I'm not a member of the Gmay, I didn't think there was a prohibition. She's alone here except for the Planks and her midwife."

"There's not. This is more of an offering of advice to proceed with caution." Bryan's piercing gaze no doubt saw too much. Or saw what he wanted to see. "You seem to suggest you can be her friend. You're a man. She's a woman, a woman who's put herself in a precarious position with a fehla that will follow her throughout her life."

"She's made a mistake. She's paying for it. She only has to ask to be forgiven and she will be. At least that's the way it's supposed to be."

"Agreed." Bryan dunked an oversized onion ring in catsup. He rolled his eyes in feigned ecstasy as he bit into it, chewed, and swallowed. "Is it your intention to save her from herself, then?"

"Nee. There are no intentions." None that he could explain. Joshua threw his napkin over his uneaten food. "I brought her to Amos's from the train station. Somehow I feel responsible for her."

"She's responsible for herself. If she needs help, she has family."

"They seem more inclined to judge than to help."

"They're protecting their kinner from being infected by Maisy's fehla."

"I thought boplin were never mistakes."

"*They* aren't. The adults make the mistakes. That doesn't mean we get to ignore Gott's Word regarding the rightful order of things when it comes to love and marriage."

Joshua snatched his napkin from his plate and refolded it. He didn't disagree. What did Bryan want from him? "What would you have me do?"

"I can only advise you, one man to another. Be careful with your heart. Be careful with hers, which is surely bruised and hurting as well. Think carefully of the consequences."

"No one said anything about love."

"Maybe not yet, but maybe a longing for more. Your face gives you away."

His mother had said something similar. They were wrong. They had to be. "Amos asked me to train her so she could get a job at the hardware store. I did that. There's no more to it than that."

Sure, he stopped by the store regularly now. They sat at the picnic table in the back, ate their sack lunches, and compared notes on the crazy antics of their customers. Like friends would.

A Plain man and a Plain woman couldn't be friends.

"Gut to know." Bryan mopped up a puddle of catsup with his last onion ring. He'd demolished his burger. "I sure could use a hot fudge sundae to top off a good meal." He patted his small paunch. "But I better not. My eyes are always bigger than my stomach."

Danki Gott for small favors.

"What can I do to help you with your questions?"

"Let me find my own way."

"We've done that."

"Pray."

"We continue to do that." Bryan counted out several bills and laid them next to the ticket. "Come to see me with your questions instead of brooding. Talk with me man to man. Take the baptism classes with Samuel. Face your anger instead of wallowing in it."

Easy for Bryan to say. *Walk a mile in my shoes. I'm not wallowing, Gott. Am I?* "There's more to it than just the baptism."

"I know."

He probably did. Joshua took a last swallow of soda. He breathed. "I can't think about having a family until I have a better handle on my livelihood."

"The district appreciates the work you do for Amos. We know it comes at a cost to you."

"It's also not a job that will sustain a family. Nor is the job at the furniture store a few months out of the year." Joshua unwrapped one of the peppermints that had come with the bill and popped it in his mouth. Maybe it would calm his stomach. "Caleb has sons who work for him. I suspect he hired me because he has a good heart and wanted to help me in a way similar to how I help Amos. To get unstuck I need to pursue a vocation that will support my family."

Bryan shook a toothpick from the jar on the table and applied it to his teeth. After a few seconds, he nodded. "What did you have in mind?"

"Making saddles and leather goods puts you in contact with many folks who own horses." Joshua studied the bishop's face. Understanding and concern mingled in his eyes. "Jacob and I wanted to train horses when we grew up." His voice cracked on the last two words. He took a long breath and let it out. "I still do."

"Good to know." A grin stretched across Bryan's face. "I know just the person. John Shirak. He has a horse farm over in the East District. I'll put in a gut word for you and see if he has a need for a hired hand eager to learn the trade. This is a step in the right direction."

A baby step. "I'd appreciate that."

Bryan stood. "You better get back. Caleb will have my hide if I keep his employee away for too long."

Not likely.

Together they walked back to the store. The sun tried to break through dark, heavy clouds. The cool air had turned warm and humid. "Danki for the meal." Joshua had one hand on the door. As anxious as he'd been to avoid this conversation, he now saw it for what it was. A flicker of light in the darkness. "I appreciate that you made a trip into town to talk to me."

"*Gern gschehme.* You didn't eat much of it. You wish I hadn't stopped by, I know." Bryan took the toothpick from his mouth and grinned. "You think I'm a nosy busybody, but I'm not. It's not just my job as bishop to care. It's my job as a fellow brother in Christ, a member of the body of Christ."

"I know that and I appreciate it." Joshua's body felt strangely buoyant. "Faeriwell."

He slipped inside before Bryan could respond. After he closed the door, he glanced out to make sure Bryan had walked away. Maisy sat on a bench outside the hardware store. She'd probably wondered why he hadn't come by at lunch. Not anymore. Bryan probably saw her too.

In fact Bryan didn't head toward the parking lot and his buggy. Instead he waited for a car to pass and then headed across the street toward the hardware store. Straight for Maisy.

And there wasn't a thing Joshua could do about it.

Chapter 21

DON'T GET TOO COMFORTABLE. DON'T RELY *on a man.* The voice in Maisy's ear kept telling her that, but she had never been good at taking advice. Obviously. When Joshua didn't show up for lunch, the odd wrenching feeling in the vicinity of her heart was unwanted, unneeded, and unwarranted. She hadn't chosen to eat lunch on the bench outside the store instead of in the break room because she might see him. It was cooler outside now that it had rained. That was all. The breeze smelled of rain and earth. It blew away the aches and pains of a morning on her feet.

Seeing Joshua walk up to the store with another Plain man answered the question of why he'd stood her up. Not that they had a firm commitment—like a date—for lunch. Just a habit, really.

Maisy studied her peanut butter and honey sandwich, concentrating on how good it tasted. It didn't cause her nausea to flare up or its friend heartburn.

She would give the extra brownie she'd slipped into her lunch bag to Harvey. He had a worse sweet tooth than she did. A sip of cold water helped clear the stupid lump in her throat. She'd been far too weepy lately. Kate said that wasn't uncommon. It was the hormones. Maisy could cross bananas off the list of fruits she would no longer eat. At twenty weeks the baby was now the size of a banana.

"You must be Maisy Glick."

Maisy jumped. She'd been so deep in thought she hadn't noticed Joshua's visitor crossing the street toward her. She laid her sandwich on her napkin and raised her hand to her forehead so she could see him in the early afternoon sun that finally decided to make an appearance. "I am."

"I'm Bryan Miller, the bishop for Amos and Ruth's Gmay." He settled onto the bench next to her. "I saw you sitting here, and it occurred to me that I should make your acquaintance."

"Have I done something wrong?"

"Nee. Not that I know of." He set his umbrella against the wall and leaned back against the bench as if he planned to stay awhile. "You tell me."

"Nee, I don't think so. I'm working at an Englisch-owned store. The rest of the time I'm at home helping Ruth with her kinner."

"Amos mentioned that."

Amos had talked to Bryan about her again. Why? It didn't matter. She stayed out of his way as much as possible. Bonnie and Nicholas loved playing with her. Ruth appreciated her help. "Would you like a brownie? I have an extra one to share."

"I don't mind if I do." Bryan accepted her offering. "A sweet hits the spot after a big lunch. Too bad you don't have an extra one for Joshua. He didn't eat much of his lunch. He seemed to be down in the dumps."

Maisy took a big bite of her sandwich and chewed vigorously. She had nothing to say about Joshua, his lunch, or his dumps. Not to his would-be bishop.

"Have you thought about returning to Jamesport?"

Maisy's stomach clenched. She stuck the rest of her sandwich in its plastic bag. A long swallow of water didn't help. "Nee." The single syllable came out in a whisper. "I can't."

"Your eldre would be happy to see you. I know if you were my dochder, I would be."

He wasn't old enough to be her eldre. He seemed even younger with brownie crumbs in his beard and frosting on his upper lip. However, being a bishop aged a man on the inside. "I made a choice to come here to spare them the pain of watching . . ." Her throat closed. She heaved a breath. "Are you saying I must go?"

"Nee. I can't do that. I'm only offering a suggestion. You would have gut family support there. Your Gmay elders know you and can counsel you."

"Everyone there knows me. That's the problem. Here I can help Ruth. I'm useful. And I have a gut job."

"Ruth has Amos's family to help her. Jamesport is bigger than Haven and Yoder combined. It has much more for tourists to see and do. You could easily find a job there."

He'd given her situation much thought. It might be a suggestion, but it sounded more like a command. Maisy couldn't go. Not when she had a plan for her baby that would ensure he had a good life with two parents who loved him. Should she tell Bryan? No, her family should know first. And then Isaac and Vicky. "I have other reasons for staying."

"Like Joshua."

"Nee. Nee, I didn't say that."

"Then what might they be?"

"It's not something I can tell . . . you. Not yet."

Eventually everyone would know. Then they would judge her for different reasons. No one could know what walking in her shoes was like. They had no right to judge her. Human nature, that's what Grandma Irene would call it.

"Ah. Forgive me for prying." Bryan said the words with such sweet humility. It made him likable even when a person didn't want to like him. "Just know that Joshua has his own row to hoe. You wouldn't want to make it harder."

No, she wouldn't. A cold, hard wind blew through her, filled with disappointment. She'd known better than to let Joshua in. It was wrong. Unlike Nate, Joshua was Plain. All the more reason to keep her distance so he could find a woman who hadn't given herself away with no regard for the consequences. "I understand."

Her voice didn't shake. *Danki, Gott.*

"Gut. I better get moving. I have a saddle to finish. Danki for the brownie. It was tasty."

"Gern gschehme." Maisy held out a napkin. "You have frosting on your upper lip."

"Danki for telling me. My fraa says I'm an oversized kind. At least I eat like one. I tell her I'm saving it for later."

"I'll think about what you said."

Bryan doffed his hat. "I'm hearing that a lot today."

Maisy gathered up her lunch bag and dumped the detritus—her word for the day—into the trash can a few feet from the store's doors. She stretched, rubbed her belly, and squared her shoulders. She would get through this. On her own. Without dragging anyone else in to her wretched quagmire—another good word.

Only three more hours. Then she would go home. Funny how after a few months she'd started calling Amos's house home. She would talk to Ruth. Together they could talk to Kate.

And then Betsy, who could smooth the way with the Kings.

The baby moved inside her. A faint flutter. Hand on the door handle, Maisy closed her eyes. She strained to feel more, to know more. Was she doing the right thing? Once she gave the baby to the

Kings, she would go back to Jamesport—not back to her old life, but maybe she would be allowed to forge a new one.

"Are you okay?"

Startled once again, she opened her eyes. Her hand dropped. She turned. "Joshua, what are you doing here?"

"I saw you talking to Bryan." His face somber, he paused a few feet from Maisy, one foot on the sidewalk, one on the street, as if poised for flight. "Was he giving you a hard time?"

Maisy pushed the door open so an elderly man wearing a bright-yellow rain slicker could get in. She moved closer to Joshua. "We ate brownies."

"The man must have a hollow leg."

"And a sweet tooth."

"So you didn't talk about anything important?"

Just everything important to her in this agonizing, limbo-like season. Maisy told him about Bryan's "suggestion" that she return to Jamesport.

"He also suggested I shouldn't drag you into my problems because it will make it harder for you to find your way to baptism."

"Bryan has never walked in your shoes." Joshua's face darkened. "Like he's never walked in mine."

"He took you to lunch so he could make 'suggestions' about joining the church?" The urge to smooth the hurt from his face assailed Maisy. She clasped her hands behind her back. "He thinks you should get over whatever is holding you back and get on with life?"

"Jah. I appreciate his concern, but he has no idea what it's like to be in my situation or yours. What you decide to do about the bopli and about your life has to come from your heart. Gott's will be done, not Bryan's."

"Maybe he's right."

"Nee." Joshua flung that one syllable at her with a ferocity that startled Maisy. His Adam's apple bobbed. "Don't leave. Sei so gut."

"Why? Why would you want me to stay?"

"Just don't go. See this through." Joshua backed away. "I told Caleb I would only be gone a few minutes. I better go."

He whirled away and strode across the street.

The most words he'd every strung back to back in her presence. It was also the first time he'd ever referred directly to the baby. Maisy curled her fingers around the awning column and held on tight. Why did he want her to stay? Why did she desperately want to stay?

See what through?

Chapter 22

WASHING DISHES AFTER LUNCH WOULD SERVE as a good time for conversation. Maisy could scour a skillet and not have to make eye contact with Ruth. She had Sundays and Mondays off from the hardware store, which was good. She could help with laundry on Monday. She waited until Amos went out to mend a hole in a pasture fence and her cousin put a sleepy Nicholas down for a nap in the playpen near the prep table. Wearing most of her mashed potatoes and gravy on her dress, Bonnie sat on the floor, playing with wooden cows and horses her father had carved for her. Ruth set a stack of dirty plates on the counter. Maisy slipped them into the hot, soapy water. No more postponing it. "Can I ask you something?"

"Anything." Ruth picked up a washrag and knelt next to Bonnie to wipe her daughter's face. "I reckon you already know about the birds and the bees."

She chuckled, which made Bonnie giggle. Ruth had a gift for finding humor in the most difficult situations. Amos and Bryan wouldn't think it was funny. Of course it wasn't, but life would be an awful hard journey without the ability to laugh at one's self.

Her hands still sudsy, Maisy turned around and leaned against the counter. On second thought, seeing Ruth's reaction would be important. No point in pussyfooting around. "What would you think if I decided to give my bopli to Isaac and Vicky King?"

"Give away your bopli?" Ruth stumbled back on her behind. Bonnie crowed and clapped her hands. Little ones were easily entertained. Ruth sat up and crossed her legs. "You mean let them adopt him?"

"Jah."

Ruth pulled Bonnie into her lap and wrapped her arms around the toddler. "I can't imagine giving up our boplin to anyone."

"Your situation is different from mine." Maisy grabbed the stack of plates and slid them into the tub to soak. "I did things in my rumspringa I should never have done. I showed my immaturity in everything I did. I'm kidding myself if I think I suddenly grew up because now I'm having a bopli. He deserves parents who are mature enough to be parents."

"I can understand that, I reckon. Though Plain women your age have boplin regularly."

"They get married first. They don't give themselves away to an Englisch man." Harsh words, but ones that had to be said and faced before Maisy could grow up. "I'm thinking about giving this bopli to Vicky and Isaac. They're ready. More than ready."

"But to give up your bopli. Wouldn't it break your heart?" Ruth kissed Bonnie's forehead. The little girl tried to crawl away from her lap. Ruth didn't let go. "I feel for Vicky. I really do. I pray for a bopli for them if it's Gott's will."

"Gott's will might be a different path to parenthood for them."

Bonnie squawked. Ruth set her free. The little girl toddled over to Maisy and held her arms up. Maisy sighed. She was such a cute baby. A tiny replica of Ruth with her blonde curls and blue eyes. "Come on up, sweetie."

Maisy pulled her up onto her hip. She pumped a puddle of dish soap onto her fingers and ran them under the water. Bubbles floated over Bonnie's head. Laughing, she tried to catch them with both hands. *"Blos, blos."*

"Jah, die blos."

Maisy captured one on her fingertip and deposited it on Bonnie's nose. The toddler's mouth opened wide. She tried to grasp it, but it popped. "Blos, blos."

"All gone." Maisy touched her nose. "Blos all gone."

Bonnie snuggled against Maisy's chest. "More, more."

"I think you're tired, Bopli."

"You're gut with boplin." Ruth dragged herself up from the floor. Her belly had become more prominent too. Her cheeks had turned pudgy. Three babies back-to-back did that to a woman, but she wore it well. "I understand why you might think it would be best for you to give yours up, but you're the mudder. You'll be gut at it. Don't let anyone shame you into thinking otherwise."

"It's not a matter of shame. It's a matter of truth. Plus I want this bopli to have a daed."

"You're assuming you won't marry. You will. I just know you will."

"Who will want to marry a woman who committed the sin of fornication with an Englisch man?" The words sounded so ugly spoken aloud. "What man will want to marry a woman who already has a bopli who came from that sin?"

"A gut man who knows he isn't perfect." Ruth took Bonnie from Maisy. The little girl laid her head on her mother's shoulder. Her eyelids drooped. "We've all sinned and fallen short. That's what Scripture says."

"So why do I feel like I'm the only one in the world who has messed up? Why do I feel like some people are staring at me like I'm such a poor excuse for a human being?"

"Because everyone likes to feel as if they're superior, like their sin is less than yours. Bryan says all sins are equal in Gott's eyes." Ruth rocked Bonnie as she talked. The little girl's eyes closed. "And she's out. I'll put her down for her nap. Whatever you decide I'll support you. If you keep the bopli, you can stay here and we'll raise our kinner together."

"I don't think Amos would like that."

"Amos isn't as hard-hearted as you think. He'll warm up." Ruth planted a soft kiss on Bonnie's cheek. "I know it's hard for you to understand, but Amos's entire view of himself changed after that truck hit his buggy. He struggles to feel like the man he was before, when his leg was strong and whole. He doesn't want to have to rely on others for help. He has pain all the time and doesn't sleep well. He needs to walk a mile in your shoes, but it might help if you did the same for him. He wants to feel in control of something—anything."

"I do understand." Maisy dunked the washrag in the soapy water and wrung it out. "Joshua told me a little about that when we talked about all the tools in the barn."

"Gut. As for your bopli and the adoption, will you talk to Kate to see what she thinks?"

"She is so full of wisdom and grace." Maisy pushed the washrag across the counter, contemplating. Kate had never been married, never had a baby. She couldn't truly know what it felt like. Yet her opinion mattered, somehow. "Having her thoughts can't hurt. After I finish here, I'll go see her."

"Whatever you decide, I'll be here for you."

"Danki." If it weren't for the sleeping toddler in Ruth's arms, Maisy would've hugged Ruth. "It's nice to know I can count on someone."

"I'm pretty sure there's someone else you can count on." Ruth paused in the kitchen doorway. "Just give it time."

The mischievous twinkle in her eyes said Ruth wasn't talking about Amos. "What have you heard?"

"Just a whisper here, a whisper there."

"Gossip is a sin."

"Just keep an open mind."

Joshua was a kind, stalwart—her word of the day—man, but she'd made an error in judgment before. She couldn't afford to do it ever again. Plus, Joshua had his own problems that needed sorting out. Not the least of which was his inability to commit to his faith.

"Maybe you can help him with that." Grandma Irene's voice surfaced again. Not a whisper. More like a shout. How could a sinful, shamed woman like Maisy help a reluctant believer like Joshua?

The question plagued Maisy as she finished the dishes and headed to the barn to hitch up the buggy. The afternoon sky was such a brilliant blue it hurt to look at it. A few wispy clouds floated on a breeze that sang autumn's praises. The horse, a beautiful bay, tossed his head and whinnied at her approach. "So you're eager for some exercise. That's gut." She crooned to him as she led him from the stall. "I could use some fresh air myself."

"Where are you going?"

Maisy turned to find Amos coming through the barn door, carrying a post digger under one arm. Pain etched lines around his mouth and eyes. Sweat soaked his faded blue shirt. She stifled the urge to offer to help him carry the digger. "To see Kate. And possibly to the birthing clinic."

Maybe Kate would go with her.

"Are you feeling poorly?" He leaned the digger against the workbench in the corner. Panting slightly, he picked up a bandana and wiped down his face and neck. "I can drive you to Kate's or to the clinic, either one."

"Nee, no need." Maisy ran her hands down the horse's gorgeous, long neck. "I just want to talk to them about something."

"Are you thinking you'll deliver at the clinic?"

The first ever question he'd asked about her plans for her baby. More of that thawing. "I hope not. I'd rather be here with Kate to help." Maisy drew a long breath. "I'm thinking about giving my bopli to Isaac and Vicky King."

Amos stopped moving. His forehead wrinkled. His face darkened. "You've spoken to your eldre about this?"

"Nee." *Because it's my decision, not theirs.* Maisy swallowed back words that would sound prideful and angry. "I'm trying to do what's best for the bopli."

"And easier for you?"

Spoken like a man who would never have to know how it felt to make such a hard decision. "Nothing is easy about this."

The ire in his face dissolved, replaced with an embarrassed flush. "I suppose not." He grabbed his toolbox. "Would you like Ruth to go with you? The boplin are napping. I could keep an eye on them."

A lovely, kind offer. There was the man Ruth married. A nice human being lurked behind the crusty exterior. "Danki. She knows about it. We've talked. I can do this part on my own."

"Be careful on the highway. Some of those farmers' teenagers in their monster diesel trucks don't know when to slow down."

"I will. Oh, and what is this horse's name?"

"Violet." Amos chuckled. "Don't ask me why. Ruth chose it."

Maisy waited until Amos left the barn to slump against Violet's warm body. "Will wonders never cease, Violet?"

Violet neighed.

"No kidding."

Chapter 23

FINDING KATE PUTTERING IN HER FAMILY's flower garden came as no surprise to Maisy. The woman blossomed wherever she stood. Mums, asters, and daisies, among Maisy's favorite fall flowers, lifted their colorful faces to the early afternoon sun. Purples, blues, pinks, oranges, and reds bloomed bright and cheerful. The sight of them slowed the thoughts racing through Maisy's mind like a spooked herd of horses.

Kate straightened, stuck her gloved hands on her lower back, and stretched. Her smile bloomed, a flower all its own. "Hi there, my friend. I wasn't expecting to see you today." She sauntered down the row between the dahlias and the cosmos. "It's my therapy day."

"Therapy?"

"Jah, weeding, planting, and plotting gives me time to work out problems." Kate stopped and touched the perfect purple petals of a luscious aster. "The sweet aromas of the flowers mingled with the smell of dirt reminds me Gott is sovereign and the Creator of all that is beautiful in the world."

Everyone needed that reminder now and then. Maisy closed her eyes and inhaled her favorite scents. The tension eased in her shoulders. Her back ceased to ache. She stretched and opened her eyes. "I see what you mean."

"I'm so glad you came." Kate had a way of making a person feel so welcome, so loved. It was a gift. "Do you want to help me plant some bulbs while we talk?"

"I'd love to."

"Feel free to take your shoes off."

Maisy glanced down. Kate's bare toes wiggled in the loose dirt beneath her feet. How nice. "I believe I will."

She sat on the ground to remove her shoes and socks while Kate arranged plastic containers filled with three kinds of bulbs along a row where she'd already troweled the earth several inches deep. The containers were marked with labels that read TULIPS, DAFFODILS, and HYACINTHS. What a feast for the eyes these flowers would be in the spring. "I really love flowers."

"Me too." Grinning, Kate waved her trowel in the general direction of the mums and daisies. "I try to plant so we have flowers blooming each season to greet our visitors. The flowers from these bulbs will pop up in the spring. They'll be so welcome after a long, cold winter. I favor perennials. They're less work, but some annuals are too gorgeous to ignore. Besides, gardening isn't work for me; it's food for my soul."

A perfect way to sum up how Maisy felt about flowers. "My mom calls me Daisy Maisy because I love flowers so much."

Kate dropped the first tulip bulb in a hole about six inches deep. "I love that. Daisy Maisy." She handed the container to Maisy. "You drop them in, and I'll cover them up. So tell me, Daisy Maisy, what do you want to talk about?"

Talking about babies in the middle of a garden where life bloomed seemed the most natural thing in the world. "I would like Isaac and Vicky to adopt my bopli."

Kate dropped her trowel. Her gloves softened the thud as she clapped. "You sweet *maedel*. What a beautiful idea." She threw her hands in the air. "Gott is faithful. He has a plan for you and for Vicky and Isaac."

Such enthusiasm. It left little room for Maisy's doubts and worries. "You think this is Gott's plan?"

"I think Gott uses what we give Him." Kate scooped up a mound of earth and let it crumble between her fingers. "We only have to stand back and watch the Master at work."

"It's not an easy decision for me."

"It shouldn't be. This is your *bopli* we're talking about." Kate raised her face to the sun and smiled. She was the smiley-est person in all of Haven, maybe in all of Kansas. "In all things He works for our gut, but that doesn't mean we don't have to use our noggins to do what is right and gut."

"This feels like it's right and gut."

"That's a start."

Maisy worked in silence for a few minutes, dropping the bulbs six inches apart. At the end of the row she straightened. Humming tunelessly Kate worked her way down the row, covering the bulbs. At the end she surveyed their work. "We'll plant the hyacinths next and then the daffodils. After that we'll need to water, fertilize, and cover with mulch."

"You said it was a start." Maisy picked up the container filled with hyacinths bulbs. "I'm not sure what's next."

Kate's expression turned somber. She cocked her head and sighed. "I know you know this, but it's so important that you be certain before you breathe a word of this to Vicky and Isaac. They're fragile souls right now. Have you given adequate thought to what it will be like to hand over your newborn *bopli* to another woman? To what that will feel like? Are you sure you can go through with it?"

"It's hard for me to imagine." If ever there was a time for absolute truth, it was now. Maisy turned to the next row. She dropped a hyacinth bulb into the trench. Planting new life, knowing the fruit—or in this case the flower—of their labor would not be seen until spring. Patience, food, water, light, all the ingredients were needed to grow a beautiful, healthy plant.

"I used to wonder how women could give their boplin up for adoption. It seemed unfathomable. It seemed wrong. It seemed like something an Englisch woman was more likely to do than a Plain woman. Which is judgmental in itself, I know."

Kate crouched next to the bulbs and covered them. "It's gut that you're examining your feelings so carefully." She stood and removed her gloves. "I think we need to pay a visit to some friends of mine."

"What friends?"

Maisy followed Kate into the grass, where the other woman plopped down and brushed dirt from her feet. She reached for her shoes. "Friends who have some experience with what we're talking about." She pointed at Maisy's shoes. "Better put them on."

"What about the bulbs?"

"I'll finish when I get back. This is an urgent matter. The sooner you have all the information you need to make a decision, the better for you and for Isaac and Vicky." She studied her shoes for a second. "And especially for the bopli."

They decided Maisy should follow Kate in her own buggy so she wouldn't have to come back to Kate's to get it afterward. Forty-five minutes later they pulled into Freeman Bontrager's farm. Kate's short explanation of the trip had simply been that Freeman and Lorene adopted an English girl's baby at birth. They never told the girl she was adopted. Then Abigail Bontrager's birth mother showed up one day and wanted to be a part of her daughter's life.

How that played out, Kate said, would best be explained by the Bontragers.

Maisy's situation was different. Everyone involved was Plain—well, not everyone. Nate was English, but he wasn't part of the equation. Should Isaac and Vicky tell the baby he was adopted? Did Maisy want the baby to know? Would he grow up feeling sad or rejected because his birth mother chose to give him to a couple? How would he feel about a birth father who never claimed his right to fatherhood? So many questions, so few answers. Maybe Kate was right. Maybe Abigail Bontrager, who was now Abigail Kurtz, could give her some insight in to the pros and cons of her situation.

Her stomach churning, head pounding, Maisy slipped from her buggy and followed Kate up the steps to the Bontragers' front door. A second later a young woman not much older than Maisy opened the door. She, too, was expecting—only much more so. "Hi, Kate, what a nice surprise." Her curious gaze bounced to Maisy. "And you brought a visitor. Wunderbarr. It so happens that Mudder just pulled a pan of pumpkin bars from the oven. Come in, come in."

Kate made the introductions as they followed her inside. Despite her girth, Abigail Kurtz moved with enviable grace. She was a pretty woman with strawberry-blonde hair peeking out from her prayer covering and deep-blue eyes. Kate grilled her on her health, who was delivering her baby, and all the womanly things associated with childbirth.

Abigail seemed to take it in stride. She said another local midwife would do the honors here at the Bontrager house so her mother could help as well. "It's a super-busy time for Owen with the sunflower harvest, so he wanted to make sure I'm not alone when the bopli decides to make an appearance."

She was so blessed to have a husband who cared so deeply and a mother eager to help. Maisy swam through a treacherous wave of envy that threatened to drown her. She, too, had family and friends who would help her—she was blessed even in these trying circumstances. She needed to remember that.

In the kitchen they made the acquaintance of Lorene Bontrager. She and her daughter could be twins, making it hard to believe Abigail was adopted. She bustled to the table with a platter of the pumpkin bars. The aroma of cinnamon and nutmeg calmed Maisy's nerves and made her mouth water.

"It's so gut to see you, Kate." Lorene's gaze rested on Abigail. Something about her expression suggested she knew exactly who Maisy was. "You're Ruth Plank's kossin from Jamesport?"

"Jah." Maisy stifled the urge to wiggle in her chair. "I've been staying with her for a few months now."

Despite her troubled expression, Lorene said nothing more as she handed out napkins and offered the bars. Maisy took one. Maybe she could simply eat bars and let Kate do the talking.

Abigail poured glasses of cold tea and brought them to the table. "So what brings you out this afternoon?"

"We're hoping you'll be willing to share your hard-earned wisdom with us." Kate nodded encouragingly at Maisy. "Maisy is considering asking another Plain couple here in Haven to adopt her bopli."

Understanding flashed in Abigail's face. She sank into the chair across from Maisy. Her hands rested on the table's top, fingers splayed. She sat very still. "That's a big decision."

"It is." Maisy willed her voice to remain steady. "Kate has told me a little about your experience—both of you. I'm trying to imagine what it'll mean for my bopli to grow up adopted. How he'll feel when he finds out. Should the couple tell him when he's little or wait? What if he decides he wants to know me? I know every situation is different—"

"Not so different." Lorene slid into a chair next to Kate. The lines around her mouth and eyes deepened. She squeezed her daughter's hand and let go. "Abigail's biological mudder was unmarried like you. She was also very young. Her parents didn't want her to marry the bu. They were the ones who pushed for the adoption. Stephanie didn't want to do it, but they didn't give her a choice. Stephanie knew me and Freeman. She came to us. She asked us to adopt her bopli."

Maisy grasped the cold glass for a few seconds. Then she put her hands to her hot cheeks. To have her situation compared to the English woman's in such a matter-of-fact tone was like ripping the scab off a partially healed wound. "The daed of my bopli is Englisch. We agreed we couldn't marry because of this. I won't leave my faith."

"You're still unbaptized, though." Lorene's lips thinned. Her frown deepened. "Because of that you aren't shunned, but our bishop did say for us to avoid contact with you."

"True, but Bryan would also want what's best for this bopli." Kate jumped in. "He's aware of the couple's predicament. This would be a great blessing for them. Surely you would want Maisy to benefit from your experience as she figures out what to do."

If Lorene took Kate's words as castigation, it didn't show on her face. She plucked at the pumpkin bar on her napkin, her expression pensive. "When all this happened, my mann and I were concerned we might not have our own bopli. When Abigail's birth mother approached us, we prayed and we talked to our bishop. Freeman and I agreed it was the right thing to do for us and for the bopli. Within a year our dochder Jane was born, but that didn't change a thing. We loved our first bopli, our Abigail, from the minute she was born. We never thought of her as our adopted dochder. She was simply our firstborn."

"If anything can be learned from hindsight, I would say it has to do with not telling me I was adopted." Abigail slid an arm around her mother and gave her a quick, one-armed hug. "I know it's easy to criticize in hindsight. I was so hurt and angry and confused when my biological mother showed up here out of the blue. To find out at twenty I was adopted and my biological parents were Englisch was a blow I almost didn't recover from."

"We would do it differently if we had it to do again." Tears wet Lorene's eyes. She sniffed and wiped her nose with her napkin. That it was still a delicate subject after all this time reflected how painful a period it had been. "But we can't. It will be different for you, I reckon, with Plain parents taking the bopli."

"They aren't able to have their own. At least they haven't yet. They almost adopted a bopli and the birth mudder backed out. It broke their hearts. That's why I need to make sure this is the right thing for me to do."

"Ach. You're talking about Vicky and Isaac. Vicky's mudder is a gut friend of mine." Lorene sat up straight. The anguish melted away, replaced with enthusiasm. "Indeed it would be a gift, a blessing, for them to adopt a Plain bopli. Not dealing with an Englisch mudder should make it easier."

If Maisy could be sure she could go through with it. "Are you okay now with being adopted, Abigail?"

Her expression distant and intent, Abigail brushed crumbs from the table. "I am. Lorene and Freeman are my eldre. They raised me. They loved me. They disciplined me. They never let me want for anything. They taught me to be true to Gott and the Ordnung. I've been blessed with a gut life. I visited my biological family and I realized I'm Plain through and through. It's not a bloodline. It's a way of life.

"That doesn't mean I regret getting to know my biological

family. I'm related to them, too, but in a different way. Knowing them has given me another perspective on life. It's another part of who I am. Knowing their family tree and history gives richness to my life."

"Well said, my dear." Kate clapped softly. "You have gained wisdom from your experiences."

Vicky and Isaac would give Maisy's baby that same loving, caring upbringing. There was no doubt about that. They could give him so much more than Maisy could. It was for the best. So why did the pain of that realization threaten to bring Maisy to her knees? "I hope I can be as brave and as wise."

"Don't measure yourself by another person's yardstick." Lorene's features had relaxed. She spoke with a gentleness that brought a lump to Maisy's throat. "If I learned anything through this experience, it's that speaking openly about it is so important. Talk to Vicky and Isaac about the future and whether you want to be involved in your bopli's life after the adoption. Don't base that on your feelings and your wants. Think of the bopli first. What's best for him."

"Gut advice. Danki." Maisy managed to whisper her response without a quiver in her voice.

Why was she so emotional? Because the response to what was best for her baby stared her in the face. The baby would be better off with Vicky and Isaac. He would have a good life with two loving parents. She wasn't ready to be a mother. Her baby deserved parents who were.

Her decision was made for her.

Chapter 24

ONCE BETSY WAS CONVINCED MAISY WOULD remain steadfast in her decision to give her baby up for adoption, she agreed to broach the subject with Vicky and Isaac—alone. She told Maisy to go home and wait. And wait. And wait. After what they'd been through, they might not be ready to consider trying to adopt again. Days passed. Maisy stayed busy at work and at home. Every time the bell dinged at the hardware store, she jumped and turned. No Betsy. Until finally, three days later, it was indeed the midwife standing on the welcome mat.

Maisy's heartbeat blew through a stop sign and galloped for the highway. "Well?"

Betsy waved her hand toward the door. "Ask Harvey if you can have a few hours off."

As usual Harvey was amenable. Twenty minutes later Betsy and Maisy pulled into a neat wooden A-frame house a few miles from Amos and Ruth's place. Mums and marigolds added yellow, orange, and reds to the flower boxes that lined the front porch. Everything was neat and clean. Betsy put the car in Park and removed the key. "Are you okay? You're awfully quiet."

"They didn't seem concerned about my . . . character?"

"They have no concerns about your character. Isaac has other concerns, but Vicky thinks you can convince him that you're serious about the adoption. That you won't do to them what the previous mudder did."

Maisy's stomach clenched. Even now nausea reared its ugly head at least once a day. She put her hand to her mouth. "I might need . . ."

She hopped from the car and made it to the wind-tousled weeds that lined the dirt road before she vomited.

Betsy rubbed her back. When it was all over, she held out a package of spearmint gum. "Don't say I never gave you anything."

Maisy managed a nod. "I won't."

By that time Vicky had come out to the front porch. Betsy propelled Maisy forward. "It'll be fine."

Easy for her to say. Vicky looked much better than she had the last time Maisy saw her. Still too thin, but the dark circles around her eyes and the puffiness of her face had receded. She waved at Betsy and smiled. "Thanks for coming." Curiosity in her pale-blue eyes, she turned to Maisy. "Bewillkumm."

"Danki."

Betsy made the introductions. They followed Vicky into the house, where everything was as neat as the yard. She offered them lemonade and a seat at the big kitchen table. "I'll ring the dinner bell."

She stepped out on the back porch. A bell sounded. A few seconds later she scooted back to the table. "That will confuse him. I usually only ring it when it's time to eat."

Sure enough Isaac ambled up to the house a few minutes later. "It's awfully early for lunch . . ." He stopped wiping his boots on the rug. His gaze first landed on Betsy, then on Maisy. "You're here."

"I asked Betsy to bring Maisy out so we can talk some more." Vicky went to her husband's side. She put one hand on his arm. "I know you think it's too soon, Mann, but at least hear her out. Sei so gut. For me."

Vicky's soft, sweet tone loosened the knotty nerves that made Maisy's neck and shoulders hurt. She breathed easier. The nausea subsided. So did Isaac's frown. He followed his wife to the table and sat by her side. "Go ahead. Speak your piece."

Maisy cleared her throat. She licked her chapped lips. "Betsy says you're worried that I'll change my mind. I don't blame you, considering what you've been through. But I want you to know, I've made up my mind. I want you and Vicky to have this bopli."

"Why?"

Her mouth went dry. She gulped down lemonade. "I'm not ready. I know I should be. I'm eighteen. I'm considered an adult, but I haven't even been baptized. I can't help thinking I wouldn't have . . . done what I did, if I was fully formed as an adult and as a Plain believer. I can't be a gut mudder if I'm still capable of doing what I did."

"I've known one or two other maed who've been in your situation." Sadness softened Vicky's face. Her voice quivered. "It's so hard for me to understand. We want a bopli so badly, and there you are . . . with one conceived under the wrong circumstances."

Tears slid down her face. Pain drew deep lines on Isaac's sun-beaten face. He slid his big hand over Vicky's small one. She hid her face in his shoulder. Isaac hugged her close, but his gaze never left Maisy's face. His fierce concentration burned through her thoughts and fears and concerns. He needed to know if she meant it.

She picked up her glass and drank the rest of her lemonade. No amount of lemonade or tea or water could wash away the agonizing pain that came with letting go of something so precious. Now that the words had been said, they couldn't be unsaid. To take them back would do terrible harm to Vicky and Isaac.

"It's a generous offer, one that I know costs you greatly to make." Isaac's hoarse voice trembled. "You know we've been down this road before. You can see what it's done to us."

Unable to speak for fear her voice would break, Maisy nodded.

"It nearly killed my fraa the first time. I won't put her through it again."

"Isaac." Vicky raised her head. "This is different."

Her words were a whisper so faint Maisy had to strain to hear her.

"How is it different?"

Vicky swiveled so Maisy could see her tearstained face. "She's Plain."

That word represented so much. The differences between the English and Plain world were likely incomprehensible to the average outsider. In today's world an English girl might not face any repercussions. She might or might not marry the baby's father. Some folks thought nothing of a single mom. The girl who changed her mind would have support for that decision. Her life would go on. Maisy would always be the woman who sinned and bore a child out of wedlock. English teenagers likely had never heard that phrase.

"You still have time to make a decision," Betsy said gently. "Vicky just wanted you to meet Maisy so you can get a sense of who she is. She's halfway to her due date. Take as much time as you need. Talk about it. Pray about it. Talk to your bishop, if that helps. Right, Maisy?"

"Right." She tried to smile but couldn't quite manage it. "I know it's a huge decision. It is for me too."

"How do we *know* you won't change your mind?" Isaac's expression turned stony. "You say this is what you want now, but when the time comes and you hold that bopli in your arms, you won't be able to do it. We've seen it before. I can't. I won't do it again."

"Isaac."

"Nee." He untangled himself from Vicky's arms and stood. "I have to get back to work. Betsy, you probably have patients waiting for you at the clinic. It was nice to meet you again, Maisy."

Shoulders stiff, he stalked through the back door.

Vicky laid her head on the table and sobbed. Betsy scooted around the table to comfort her. "Give him time, Vicky. He'll come around."

She raised her head. Her eyes were bright red, her nose running. "I don't blame him for feeling like he does. I'm scared too." Her gaze flew to Maisy. "Please don't offer your bopli to another couple. Give me time to talk to him."

It wasn't like that. Maisy had no intention of approaching an adoption agency. Her bopli needed a Plain mother and father. "I would never do that. I promise."

Vicky's body shuddered. She wiped at her face with the back of her sleeve. "It's an incredibly kind thing you're offering to do. Danki."

"Gern gschehme."

"You can call me at the clinic or come by anytime." Betsy hugged Vicky. "You know where to find Maisy if you want to talk to her."

Vicky rose and came to Maisy. She held out her arms. Maisy's heart shattered in a dozen pieces. The tears threatened to spill out. She accepted the hug. The other woman smelled of clothes dried by the sun, vanilla, and heartache. "I'll pray for Gott's will in this," she whispered. "I'll pray He softens Isaac's heart."

"Danki. I'll pray Gott eases your pain," Vicky whispered back. "I can't imagine how much this will hurt you."

They huddled together for a few more seconds. Finally Vicky broke away. She grabbed a napkin from the table and wiped her face. "Come back soon. I'll make doughnuts. Do you like home-made doughnuts?"

"I love them." Maisy led the way out of the house. At the front porch steps, she turned and waved. "Talk to you soon."

The soon-to-be mother of her unborn child waved back. "I'll be in touch. I promise."

They'd both made promises. But what happened next rested on the shoulders of a man. Strange how so often that seemed to be the case.

Chapter 25

THE MORNING DRAGGED. CUSTOMERS HAD BEEN few and far behind this fine autumn day. Joshua straightened the display of homemade pot holders and place mats. Some people got spring fever. He had fall fever. The wind had shifted to the north overnight. The leaves were changing colors. The weather in Kansas in late October sparkled. He'd worn a light jacket when he left the house. People should be outdoors in this kind of weather. Not stuck inside dusting and mopping and entertaining tourists who wanted to know all about the "Amish way of life" while they tried to decide if they really wanted to spend that much money on a quilt.

"You sure have been antsy this morning." Caleb stood behind the counter putting the finishing touches on a clearance-sale flyer. "Is there some place you'd rather be?"

Riding a horse, fishing, hunting, harvesting alfalfa, shucking corn, digging fence-post holes—anywhere but here. Fortunately those words didn't escape from Joshua's mouth. Not that his boss and owner of the furniture store wouldn't understand. Joshua wasn't a kid waiting for the school bell to ring.

"It's the weather. It feels like we should be outside."

Joshua couldn't blame it solely on the weather. He had Fridays and Sundays off. Maisy was off on Sundays and Mondays. Now she hadn't shown up for her shift today until almost lunchtime. He hadn't talked to her in four days. Somehow he'd started to look forward to their lunches. This scary thought disturbed his sleep at night. Everything about her situation demanded he keep his distance. Including his bishop. Something in Joshua's character was either lacking or more inclined toward grace and mercy than others in the Gmay. Only God could decide which it was.

"I wish we could be, too, but playing hooky won't feed my family." Caleb flashed a good-natured grin. "Are you sure it's just the weather?"

"What makes you say that?"

"You keep glancing out the window. Like you're waiting for something to happen." He dropped a black marker on the counter, hitched up his pants, and grinned. "Or you're waiting for someone to show up."

"Nee. Nothing. No one." Joshua purposely turned his back on the front of the store. He rearranged the carved wooden toys on the shelves next to the counter. Kids loved the horses, cows, dogs, and cats. Having children one day would be a gift. A sudden wave of yearning caught him by surprise. Somehow his heart had arrived at this place before his head. "You're dreaming."

"You forget I have youngies of my own." Caleb held up the flyer, cocked his head to one side, frowned, then laid it back on the counter. "I recognize the lovelorn look when I see it."

Joshua didn't plan to have this conversation with anyone, let alone his boss. On the other hand, if the stories were true, Caleb had some experience with painful relationships destined to break a heart. Not that Joshua had any intention of bringing up what had to be hurtful memories.

"I'm not so old that I don't remember what it's like to court." Caleb seemed determined to bring it up himself.

"I'm not courting."

"Of course not."

His forehead furrowed, Caleb studied his handiwork, but it was obvious his mind was elsewhere. "You know Mason Keim is my suh."

"Jah."

"He was brought up English, but he returned to his Plain roots and married Cassie Weaver after his mudder died."

Mason and Cassie were members of Joshua's Gmay. They were good folks. When Georgia Keim's six children, ages four to twenty-two, showed up with a social worker at Job Keim's house, word had spread to the far corners of Haven. Caleb had courted Mason's mother, Georgia Keim, before meeting the woman he eventually married, according to some folks. Georgia realized she was expecting his child and left Haven. She never came back. By the time Mason came into Caleb's life, his father was married and had six children with his wife.

Caleb knew something of what Maisy was going through. Only from the man's perspective. "I've heard that."

"People like to talk."

"They do."

Caleb picked up his coffee mug and took a sip. He sighed. "People are fallible. All people."

"True."

"People like to think they're better than those whose mistakes are on display for all to see."

Where was Caleb going with this? "Also true."

"If I've learned anything from my mistakes, it's that nothing is more important after living a godly life than making a life and a family with the right woman."

"That can be a hard lesson to learn."

"It can be." Caleb studied his coffee as if he'd find relief from those hard lessons there. "The other thing that is true is that Mason didn't have a daed in his life to model faith for him. His mudder didn't do it either. Yet he still ended up here, still embraced his legacy of Plain faith. I didn't do that. Georgia didn't do it. Job and Dinah didn't do that. Gott did."

Caleb had a point. A good one. "Understood."

"Do you? He can do that for you. You can't do it on your own. No one can do it for you. You have to give up the idea that you're in control."

Caleb was right, but it was so easy to say and so hard to do. It was prideful for Joshua to think he could control any part of his life. "Jah. Working on it."

Smiling, Caleb lifted his mug toward the front door. "In the meantime don't let your friend down. Don't let yourself down. Go see how she is."

Joshua eyed his jacket on the coatrack. "You haven't had your lunch."

"You should go first. Take your time. It's been slow this week, and I don't think it's going to get any busier."

Joshua sped to the break room, grabbed his lunch box, snatched his jacket, and forced himself to adopt a more dignified pace through the store. Once outside, he sucked in the crisp fall air and tried for a leisurely saunter across the street.

The hardware store had more customers than the furniture store, but Harvey's clientele was mostly local. Harvey waved from behind the counter and went back to ringing up a customer in an

HVAC repair uniform. Maisy stood in the paint aisle poring over paint chips with an English woman Joshua didn't recognize. Maisy looked up just as he rounded the corner. A smile transformed her face. "Hey, Joshua."

Her cheeks had filled out. The extra weight agreed with her. The sickly cast to her skin had disappeared. She was still indisposed regularly, but she didn't jump up and run for the nearest trash can quite as often as she had once done. She was prettier than ever. Joshua waved and pointed toward the picnic table in the back. She nodded.

A few minutes later she plopped down across from him. "Harvey says he has watermelon in the ice chest if we want some."

"He's a gut man."

"A man after my own heart. Too bad he's taken." She laughed. A sweet sound. She'd changed so much since that day in the van when she'd barfed on his boots. That she could laugh about such things was a testament to her resilience. "I'm blessed to work here. I would never have imagined myself doing this in a million years."

Joshua unwrapped his ham and Swiss cheese on sourdough bread. His mother's liberal use of spicy mustard made his day—as she knew it would. "I'm glad it's worked out for you. Life does take some crazy, unexpected turns."

Maisy's face filled with a somber uncertainty. She laid her peanut butter-and-honey sandwich on its plastic bag. "I've actually been thinking about that."

"I hope it didn't hurt." A little joke in hopes of making her relax. It didn't work. "Just kidding."

Her gaze dropped to the bag of barbecue potato chips she'd laid next to her sandwich. She opened it and dumped out the chips next to the sandwich. "Can I tell you something?"

"Sure. What are friends for?"

Many in the community would debate whether Plain men and women could be friends, but what else could they call this thing between a wayward unbaptized man and a woman living with her sin on display for all to see?

"It might make you uncomfortable."

"I can take it."

"I've asked Isaac and Vicky King to adopt my bopli. That's where I was this morning. Betsy, the midwife from the clinic, took me to talk to them."

The simple statement, delivered in a soft, almost beseeching tone, knocked Joshua back a country mile. Something in her words and her face wanted his opinion or his blessing or simply his support. He concentrated on chewing longer than necessary, then took a swig of his grape pop.

"That was the last thing I expected you to say."

Her anxious expression begged for his approval. Why did she care what he thought? This was her decision and hers alone. The right words dangled in front of him like a thick rope. He could use them as lifesavers or to hang himself. "That's a hard decision."

"Very hard." Her voice quivered. She broke a chip into pieces with her fingernail. "Isaac's afraid to trust that I'll go through with it. He keeps saying no. He doesn't want to put Vicky through it again. She's trying to convince him I can."

"Do you think you can?"

"I would never have offered if I didn't." Her eyes bright with unshed tears, she gulped down water. "It's best for the bopli. And they want boplin so badly. They've been through so much. Maybe this is Gott's plan. I want to believe it *is* Gott's plan."

God's plan. How could Joshua tell her he'd lost faith in that concept a long time ago? Had God planned for her to give herself to the wrong man at the wrong time so she could be the answer

205

to a childless couple's prayers? What lesson was she learning from this trial? How was her character being honed? And what about Joshua's? Did he have a role to play in her redemption? He gritted his teeth. *Answer me that, Gott, sei so gut.*

"You're so quiet." Her voice dropped to a whisper. "Don't make me sorry I told you, sei so gut."

She'd confided in him the way no other person ever had—man or woman. Taking a long breath, he pushed away his sandwich and stared her in the eye. "You know I had a brother who died?"

"You told me."

"He was my twin. He was twelve." Haltingly, Joshua told the story in as few words as possible. Maisy's eyes mourned with him. Her hand crept toward his. Despite the agonizing pain in the vicinity of his heart, Joshua forced himself to keep going. "When I was old enough to decide for myself, I stopped going to church. I kept asking how Gott could let a bu die because he ran into a burning house to save a hund and her puppies. Especially knowing the hund had saved them and herself."

"It's a hard question." Her fingers were warm and comforting over his. Touch. Touch had been missing from his life for so long. She started to withdraw her hand. He grasped it. He needed it. Not just anyone's touch. Hers. Maisy's. Her expression startled and she stared up at him. Alarm bloomed there. Like a bird caught in a net. "I can't."

Joshua let go and sat back. A shiver shook him. A want he'd never known before or maybe hadn't acknowledged took hold and wouldn't let go. With all his problems, he had no right to insert himself in her life with all its problems. The only way for him to have a glimmer of a chance with Maisy would be for him to face his past head-on. As soon as possible. "I know. I'm sorry. I didn't mean to make you uncomfortable."

"I made a terrible mistake." Maisy stuck her hands in her lap far from Joshua's reach. "I have to be very careful not to make it again."

"Understood. You won't."

She shook her head. "How do you know that? I was weak. I exercised terrible judgment. I did something because it felt gut with no thought for the consequences. Bryan was right. You shouldn't even be close to me."

"I'm not a fair-weather friend."

A faint smile crept across her face. "Aren't we quite the pair of outcasts?"

"Who better to help each other find our ways?"

"Bryan doesn't agree." A sadness, so profound it made Joshua's bones ache, enveloped Maisy's features. She hunched her shoulders. "He's right. You should stay far away from me. You should go to singings, attend baptism classes to shore up your faith, and move on to the life Gott intends you to have."

"Bryan and I have talked. I don't agree with him. I reckon he's had his trials, but they weren't mine or yours. Don't let his words stand in the way of something gut."

"This isn't gut. I know you think it is, but it's not." Maisy grabbed her sandwich and stuck it in her lunch box. She gathered up the rest of her lunch. "Associating with me only makes it harder for you to become the Plain man you should be."

"Don't back away, sei so gut." The urge to slide his arm around her and smooth away her pain hit Joshua like a surge of flood-waters. It would be the last thing she wanted. He gripped the table's edge with both hands. "I'm the one with the problem, not you. Bryan says I'm stuck. I'm still that little bu who wants to save his bruder."

"Does he have a prescription for getting unstuck?"

"It sounded like the one you just gave me."

"Then you should do it."

"And you do the same. After this bopli is born, you'll take your baptism classes, join the faith, and move on to the life Gott intended you to have."

Maisy straightened. She picked up her lunch box, then set it down again. "Does that life include keeping my bopli or trying to live without him?"

"That is between you and Gott." Joshua scrambled to line up his thoughts. They wanted to focus on her smooth, soft skin, her blue eyes, even the curves of motherhood that sat on her so well. "You should do what you think is right. To give this gift to Isaac and Vicky is brave."

"I don't feel brave. I feel sad. I'm happy for my bopli, though. He'll have eldre who are prepared to be his mudder and daed. Every bopli should have that."

No one could argue with that. Although some would try. It seemed to be human nature to criticize others as a way to feel good about themselves. "When will you talk to Isaac and Vicky again?"

"That's up to Isaac. In the meantime Vicky and I made plans to go to garage sales in Hutchinson on my day off. Ruth and Kate are coming."

"A girls' day."

"Jah." A smidgen of joy crept back into her face. She brushed crumbs from the table with her napkin and dropped it in her lunch box. "Kate's sister is going to watch Bonnie and Nicholas. It'll be fun."

"I hope you have fun."

Her gaze bounced over his shoulder. "I have fun eating lunch with you."

"Me too. With you, I mean."

"Gut."

"Gut."

"I better get back. Caleb will wonder what happened to me."
Joshua slipped his half-eaten lunch back into the lunch box. "Same
time, same place tomorrow?"

"Same time, same place."

Joshua almost said, "It's a date," but he didn't. It might scare
Maisy away. That was the last thing he wanted to do.

Chapter 26

"THE ANSWER IS JAH."

Maisy's legs teetered. A sudden maelstrom—her word for the day—of relief, fear, anxiety, strange delight, and happiness for Vicky and Isaac buffeted her at Isaac's words delivered with a bright grin. Light-headed, Maisy put her hand on the porch railing.

Kate's arm came around her. "Are you all right?"

"I'm gut. I'm gut." Maisy swallowed tears. "I'm so glad."

This was supposed to be a get-to-know-me outing. A fun day for the women. Instead Isaac and Vicky had been sitting on their front porch swing, waiting for Maisy, Kate, and Ruth to arrive in the van they'd hired for garage sale day. Vicky had stood and waved for them to get out.

As soon as Maisy traipsed up the steps, Isaac had delivered the verdict. And the baby kicked. Not just a flutter, but a kick. "Oh, my goodness."

"What is it? Is it the bopli?" Vicky sprang from the bench, slipped past Ruth, and reached for Maisy. "Is he all right?"

"He's fine, but I think he agrees with your decision." Taking a deep breath, Maisy rubbed her belly. *One step at a time, one day at a time.* They would get through this. "Danki for doing this."

"Nee, danki to you." Isaac stood as well. His fingers tightened around his suspenders. "It's not an easy decision for you or for us. I called Betsy at the clinic this morning. She's helping with the lawyer and all the paperwork."

"Gut. Gut." What else could she say? Isaac and Vicky would be part of her life for the next four months. Then she would fade away, leaving them to raise this baby growing in her womb. Would they tell him he was adopted? That was none of her business. "We'd better go. You know how picked over everything gets at these garage sales."

Isaac nodded. "Have fun. Don't spend too much money."

Vicky shot him a brilliant smile. She was a different woman. She glowed. The misery, disappointment, and grief were barely discernible next to the hope that shone in her face.

Gott, sei so gut, don't let her be disappointed again. Give me the strength to do this.

They piled into the van and took off for Hutchinson. Kate had a *Hutchinson News* folded to the classified-ad page. She'd circled and highlighted a half dozen garage or yard sales, which she had shared with their driver, Doreen Schmidt. Doreen loved a good garage sale as much as the next gal. She'd used her GPS to map out the most efficient route to hit all the sales and still be back in time to fix Amos's and Isaac's suppers. Doreen said her husband could grill his own steak.

"I'm hoping to find some decent bedding." Ruth leaned back in the seat and fanned herself. She claimed to be hot all the time despite the brisk fall weather. "I have all of Nicholas's and Bonnie's clothes so it doesn't matter if this bopli is a bu or a maedel. But the sheets for our bed are so threadbare you can see through them."

"I'm hoping to find a deal on canning jars." Kate ran her finger down the row of garage-sale ads. "This one says they have board

Kelly Irvin

games, kids' baseball equipment, and gardening tools. I'm always searching for things for my nieces' and nephews' birthdays and Christmas presents."

"We gave away most of the baby things we'd gathered for . . ." Vicky's gaze swiveled to the countryside whizzing by. "Anyway, we don't have anything. We're starting from scratch."

"It'll be fun to find some bargain baby things." Ruth waved a section of the newspaper in the air like a flag. "I love picking them out for someone else."

"Two of the sales list baby stuff." Kate passed the classified to Vicky. "Usually you can get it super cheap."

"What about you?" Vicky turned to Maisy. "What are you shopping for?"

Maisy wiggled in her seat. What could she say? She didn't need to buy baby things. They wouldn't have clothes suitable for a Plain woman. She didn't need household goods. She didn't have her own household. That didn't leave much. "I'm just along for the ride." She managed to sound cheerful. "I like to watch other people spend their money."

All three women laughed. They giggled and talked and teased each other all the way to Hutchinson while Maisy struggled to stay awake. Something about the hum of car motors, the cool AC air, and the motion made her sleepy. It could also be how little she'd slept the night before, wondering if she was making the right decision and whether the Kings would accept her offer.

"Are we keeping you awake with our boring chatter?" Kate nudged Maisy with an elbow. "Are you feeling all right?"

Her expression alarmed, Vicky sat up straight. "Jah, are you feeling all right?"

"I'm fine. Just sleepy."

"I can fall asleep at the drop of a hat." Ruth leaned back and

212

rested both hands on her belly. "Of course the kinner are my alarm clocks. I don't have to worry about oversleeping."

"I can't wait to have a bopli to wake me up during the night." Vicky ducked her head. "I know I'll regret saying that, but no amount of lost sleep will be equal to the joy of having my own bopli."

Maisy's fingers itched for her notebook. She was keeping a list of all the reasons giving the bopli to the Kings was a good idea. Recording Vicky's statements would allow her to read them later on if she started to have misgivings.

"We should be coming up on the first sale in the next block," Doreen called out. "I hope we can get a parking space close by."

Cars were parked end to end in front of the house where the owners had spread their treasures across the driveway and front yard. Customers crowded tables covered with large-sized women's clothes, old mismatched dishes, puzzles with pieces missing, and dog-eared paperbacks mostly of the science fiction variety. The big draws were furniture and electronics. The women hopped back in the van and moved on.

But the next one was, as Doreen put it, the mother lode. English women bought such a wealth of baby things, far more than a Plain mother needed. Vicky bought a wooden high chair, a diaper pail, crib sheets, baby blankets, a battery-operated baby monitor, some board books, and a huge bag of cloth diapers. The owner, a chubby woman with a sleeping redheaded baby in a sling across her chest, explained she'd tried cloth diapers, but they'd been too much trouble so she switched to disposable. "No fuss, no muss."

Nodding in agreement, Ruth slung the bag of diapers over her shoulder. "When it comes to dirty diapers, it doesn't matter whether they're disposable or cloth. There's always a mess."

"True. Speaking of which." The lady held her nose. "Pee-yew. For a little squirt she sure does make a big stink. I'll be right back."

At the next sale Kate scored the canning jars she needed, baseball mitts, balls, bats, and a Monopoly game that had never been opened. "I love a bargain." She lugged the box of canning jars to the van while the owner brought up the rear with the sports equipment. "The kinner will be so excited."

After one more sale they made a pit stop at a McDonald's for Quarter Pounders with cheese, fries, and milkshakes. By that time Maisy's feet, back, and head hurt. The chocolate milkshake hit the spot, though.

"You're sure quiet." Kate dunked a fry in a big puddle of catsup. "What are you thinking about?"

"Nothing in particular. I'm having fun watching you all spend money." She sipped the milkshake and savored the cold chocolate goodness. No need to spoil their fun. Or let on that this was harder than she'd expected. Watching from the sidelines was bittersweet, and they were just starting down this road. "I haven't seen anything I can't do without, that's all."

"Could you be thinking about a certain fellow who's spending a lot of time at the hardware store these days?" Ruth shot her a sly look. "I hear he has a sudden need for tons of sandpaper."

"I don't know what you're talking about." Heat toasted Maisy's cheeks. "I have lots of customers in need of sandpaper." She chomped on her burger and occupied herself chewing.

The other women laughed. "Come on, Maisy. Is something going on we should know about?" Kate grinned and snatched one of Ruth's onion rings. "I don't have any romance in my life, so I love hearing about everyone else's."

"Gossiping about them, you mean." Ruth stole one of Kate's fries and dipped it in mustard. She insisted her baby preferred mustard to catsup these days. "And there are at least two older bachelors I know of who would love to add a little romance to your life, Kate."

Kate huffed. "I'm perfectly happy as my old spinster self."

"You might be happier as a married self. You never know." Vicky picked up her grilled chicken sandwich, then laid it back down. "I thought I would be a schoolteacher forever. I loved teaching. Then Isaac came along, and I knew being his fraa was everything I ever wanted."

The ache in Maisy's chest ballooned. Vicky had her cross to bear concerning children, but she traveled that road with a man who loved her. She wasn't alone. That kind of love was a precious thing. Maisy took a long draw on her milkshake to wash away the taste of sadness tinged with envy.

"Joshua is a kind man." Ruth held out a strawberry and crème pie. "Split this with me. My eyes are bigger than my stomach."

"Jah, he is." Maisy took Ruth's offering, slid the pie from its sleeve, and broke it in half.

Baby was getting his share of sweets today. That moment at the hardware store picnic table was never far from her mind. It had been a mistake to touch Joshua. A mistake to get close to him. Not just for her, but for him too. The bishop had spoken. Joshua needed to reclaim his faith and live his life. Her need for his friendship couldn't get in its way. In a moment of selfish weakness, she'd allowed a small piece of her heart to show itself to him. He would only end up disappointed.

"He's smart, he's a hard worker, and he's a gut listener. He also doesn't pass judgment."

"It sounds like you've given his gut qualities some thought." Kate's sly grin brought out dimples that made her round face all the more appealing. "Is the feeling mutual?"

"Once he makes up his mind to be baptized, he'll be a gut catch for one of the maedel in the Gmay."

Maisy concentrated on the sweet, creamy pie filling, a pale

imitation of the taste of homemade cakes and pies for birthdays, celebrations, and happy memories of her childhood. No store-bought fast-food pie could compare.

Don't think about Joshua. Don't think about him. The last time she'd let her feelings get away from her, she ended up in a family way.

Joshua was Plain, but he didn't go to church. He was mad at God. Having feelings for such a man would only cause her more pain. He seemed to want to spend time with her despite her failings. He shouldn't. He needed to get unstuck and find a woman worthy of his love and companionship. What Plain man would want a woman who gave herself to an English man and then bore his baby?

"You made one mistake, Maisy." Her tone fierce, Kate leaned closer. She tapped on Maisy's hand. "Don't think you're forever stained by it. Gott's plan for you is still unfolding. You don't know what He has in store for you. A mann, boplin, a family, or a calling like mine, you just don't know. Don't close any doors."

"What she said." Ruth slid her arm around Maisy. "Our little raisin-sized brains can't begin to understand His plan. We only have to know there is one and be obedient in embracing whatever comes."

Easy for her to say.

Maisy shut the door on the naysayer who had taken up residence in one corner of that raisin-sized brain. She swallowed fears, self-doubts, and ugly recriminations. "I hope you're right," she whispered.

"You should talk to Bryan." Her cheeks wet with tears, Vicky plucked a napkin from the table, wiped her face, and blew her nose. She sighed. "It was hard for me to go with Isaac to talk to a man about our . . . dilemma, but I felt better after I did. He says he's just a man like any other, but there's a reason Gott chose him in the lot."

"Bryan has made it clear he thinks I should go back to Jamesport." Maisy pushed the pie back into its sleeve. "He doesn't want me around to taint others with my sin. That includes Joshua. Joshua already has enough doubts and issues with the church."

"Gott knows now what you plan to do, how you plan to help us." Vicky wadded up the napkin and tossed it in the bag. "Give Bryan another chance. I think you'll find his view has changed. He is in favor of you staying—"

"Until the bopli is born. I'm sure he'll still advise me to avoid Joshua."

"One thing at a time." Kate stood. She gathered up their trash onto one tray. "Bryan's heart may soften when he sees the gut you are doing for Joshua as well as for Vicky and Isaac."

"The gut?"

"Don't you see it?"

"See what?"

Kate took a last sip of her Mountain Dew through a straw, making a terrible slurping sound. Her hand went to her mouth to cover a ladylike burp. "He's got a lilt in his step he didn't have before. He smiles more often. He's not so broody."

"I've seen it too," Ruth added. "He's almost, not quite, but almost borderline talkative when he comes around to see if Amos needs help with anything. He's taken to spending a lot of time playing with Bonnie and Nicholas. He's gut with kinner."

Maisy couldn't be responsible for Joshua's newfound happiness. He would only be hurt in the end. So would she. "And after he's baptized he'll seek out a woman to be his fraa, they'll marry, and make a family. All I want for Joshua is whatever happiness Gott has planned for him."

"Gott has plans for you too." Ruth and Kate spoke in unison, laughed, and fist-bumped like teenagers. "Count on it."

Maisy helped Kate take their trash to the trash can. They were back on the road a few minutes later. Now all of them had the after-lunch sleepiness. "Wake me up when we get there." Ruth settled back and closed her eyes. "I need toothpicks to prop up my eyelids."

Two more sales netted a set of silverware for Vicky's sister who was getting married in two weeks and a complete dish set for Kate's cousin, who was doing the same next month. Still nothing for Maisy.

Until the last sale on the itinerary. The afternoon sun radiated heat. The breeze had died down. Sweaty and thirsty, Maisy considered staying in the van with Doreen, who'd declared her shopping done after she'd snagged a hardly used electric coffeepot, four like-new blouses in her size, and a set of six cut-crystal wineglasses she said would be perfect for that empty spot in her curio cabinet. Not that she drank wine. It gave her a headache. She simply liked the way the glasses sparkled in the sun.

"Come on, you can do one more." Ruth tugged at Maisy's arm. "Don't be a party pooper."

The books were front and center in two long rows on the first table situated on the driveway. "Oh, how perfect." Kate elbowed Maisy. "Just your cup of tea."

Indeed they were. Two long rows of paperback romances neatly arranged with spines up. Maisy ran her finger over the authors' names. Kim Vogel Sawyer, Denise Hunter, Rachel Hauck, Janette Oke, and more. All romances. All sweet. She didn't recognize the titles so they weren't ones she'd already read. She'd had nothing to read for more than a month now. The sweet release of a good story—whether a western, a mail-order bride, or a contemporary tussle over a cupcake shop—called her name. The sign read 25 CENTS OR 5 FOR $1. The price was right too.

"We'll take the whole lot." Kate waved a five-dollar bill at the owner, a gray-haired, portly lady decked out in a matching purple sweatshirt and sweatpants. Even her sneakers and her scrunchie were purple. "Do you have any more books beside these?"

"That's it, my complete library." The woman jerked her thumb toward the house. "I had to get rid of them so I could make room for more. I'm a romance junkie."

Like Maisy. "Nee, don't buy them for me." She pulled on Kate's sleeve like a toddler. "I told myself I wouldn't read any more romances. They're so unrealistic. They just get you into trouble."

"You can't blame romances for your current situation." Kate stacked the books in a box provided by the romance-reading Englisher. "These are just for fun, and you know the difference between real life and fiction."

She was right. Kate usually was. "Then let me pay for them."

"Consider them an early birthday present."

"My birthday isn't until March."

"A very early present."

"Danki."

A person didn't get far arguing with Kate. Maisy carried the box to the van and returned to find a like-new pair of black sneakers in her size for only two dollars. A foray into the garage where more tables had been set up revealed several pristine composition books and half-a-dozen packs of unopened, sharpened pencils. "I retired from teaching school last spring," the lady in purple explained. "I'll give you the whole kit and caboodle for five bucks."

Another bargain. That was the beauty of garage sales. Maisy hugged the writing supplies to her chest. Something about making lists helped her get through each day. What would Bryan have to say about that?

Ruth bought two bed sets for ten dollars each and they were officially done.

"It's a gut thing that was the last sale. I've had it." Ruth plopped onto the van seat and wiggled out of her sneakers. "I think my feet are swollen to twice their normal size."

"So are mine and I'm not even expecting." Kate dug cold bottled waters from her ice chest and handed them out. "We need to stay hydrated. That will keep our skin young and dewy."

Ruth burst out laughing. Maisy joined in. "Have you been reading those Englisch magazines again?"

Kate grinned and leaned her head against the headrest. "Maybe. Drink your water."

So they did. "I feel more dewy already." Vicky joined Ruth in removing her shoes. "I'm sorry if my feet stink. They're sweaty."

"You're among friends," Ruth murmured. Her head lolled to one side. "So tired . . ."

The ride home was much quieter than the ride to Hutchinson. Maisy leaned her head against the window and watched the countryside whizz by. The air wafting from the vents smelled of pine. It mixed with the car scent of vinyl and whatever cleaner Doreen used to scrub the upholstery. A nap would be nice, but sleep didn't come. Maisy had friends in Haven. They accepted her despite the error of her ways. In fact they embraced her. If she went back to Jamesport, would she still have friends there? She'd written to a couple of them. So far no response. The girls who'd been her classmates in school would soon join the faith and get married. They'd wonder what happened to her baby. She'd have to explain. They'd give her that perplexed look that even Ruth had given her. How could she?

Maisy opened her eyes. She peeked at Vicky. Her head nodded forward. Occasionally, she jerked and raised it. But seconds later she flopped forward again. Poor thing. She was tired. How tired would she be once she had a baby? Maisy's baby.

Maisy turned back to the window. If she felt this empty now, how would she feel when the day came and she no longer carried her bopli in her womb?

Gott, help me to surrender all. Thy will be done.

So much more needed to be said, but that short prayer was the best she could do. She snuck a notebook from the plastic bag the lady in purple had kindly supplied. A recap of the day's events would pass the time until they were home. To Amos's house. It would be best to stop thinking of it as home.

Twenty minutes later they rolled into Haven. Doreen dropped off Kate first, then Vicky, who thanked all of them for a wonderful time. "Danki for including me. It's been a long time since I laughed so much."

"We'll talk soon." Maisy waved at Isaac, who stood on the porch waiting for his wife. "My next day off is Sunday. Maybe we can get together in the afternoon."

"Wunderbarr." Vicky waved at them until the van turned off their dirt road and headed for Amos and Ruth's house.

A quick five minutes later, Doreen whipped the van on to the gravel road that took them right up to the Plank house. Someone had parked an oversized fire-engine-red diesel pickup truck at an angle next to the long row of yellow and pink rosebushes in front of the porch.

"We're here." Maisy patted Ruth's knee. "You have company."

Her cousin jerked upright. Her eyes opened. She rubbed them and yawned so widely her jaw popped. "Company? I hope we have enough leftover meatloaf to feed whoever it is."

"We can do meatloaf sandwiches. It'll go further."

They gathered up their purchases, thanked Doreen, who'd been paid up-front, and headed into the house. It was strangely quiet. The children weren't in the living room. Amos sat in one of the recliners. A tall, thin lady dressed in a black western-style shirt with pearl snaps, Wrangler jeans, and black cowboy boots sat on the couch across from him. Turquoise-and-silver earrings dangled from her ears. Turquoise rings decorated several fingers.

They both rose when Maisy and Ruth approached. Maisy adjusted the box of books. They were heavy. The woman seemed vaguely familiar with her dark-brown eyes and curly wheat-colored hair. Then her full lips turned up in a smile that brought out her dimples. Nate's dimples.

Maisy dropped the box.

"You must be Maisy." The woman trotted across the room. She knelt and began picking up books. "I'm Sue Ellen Taylor, Nate's mother. I came to see about my grandchild."

Chapter 27

"*MY GRANDCHILD.*"

The clock on the fireplace mantel *ticked, ticked, ticked* so loud in the silence that followed Mrs. Taylor's announcement. Thoughts ran pell-mell through Maisy's befuddled brain. Nate's mother wanted to talk about her grandchild. Sue Ellen Taylor had driven from Jamesport, Missouri, to Haven, Kansas, to talk to Maisy about *her* grandchild.

"Come to the kitchen, Ruth. Lottie has the kinner upstairs playing." Amos strode toward the hallway that led to the kitchen. "Let's give Maisy and her visitor some privacy to talk."

No, please don't. Please don't.

"I could fix some coffee or some iced tea for you." Ruth edged toward the hallway. "You've come a long way. I have apple pie made fresh yesterday."

"You're so sweet, but I'm fine." Mrs. Taylor dropped a Denise Hunter book into the box. "I'm watching my carbs and my curves."

Ruth telegraphed Maisy a hang-in-there look and followed her husband from sight, leaving Maisy all alone with Nate's mother. He'd told her about the baby. Did that mean he'd decided to push being a part of his baby's life? He was English. A relationship between them would never work. They'd agreed on that. If Mrs. Taylor was here, where was Nate? Maisy glanced around. "Is Nate here? Did he come with you?"

"No." Mrs. Taylor didn't meet Maisy's gaze, but her cheeks turned pink. The chunks of turquoise in her necklace clinked when she moved. She smelled like flowers. "He's at school. He doesn't know I'm here."

If it wasn't his idea, then whose? What exactly did Mrs. Taylor want? Did she have rights in this situation? What would she think of Maisy's decision to give the baby up for adoption? Blood rushing in her ears, Maisy sank to her knees and stacked books in the box. "It's okay. You don't have to help me."

"You shouldn't be carrying a heavy box in your condition." Mrs. Taylor pushed Maisy's hands away. A faintly condescending expression descended on her carefully made-up face. "Romance novels. I would think you'd had enough romance for two or three girls."

"It's just something I do to pass the time." Heat scorched Maisy's cheeks. She picked up the last of the books and slid the box toward the corner. "It's good for my vocabulary."

Maisy moved to the rocking chair farthest from the couch. Instead of going back to her old seat, Mrs. Taylor chose the glider rocker only a few feet from the rocking chair. She clasped her hands in her lap. "Nate didn't tell me about your situation until recently. He came home unexpectedly on a Friday night. He seemed way too tuckered out. I thought it was because of all the studying and burning the candle at both ends the way college students do."

"But it wasn't?" Hearing about Nate's college life wasn't at the top of Maisy's list. "Is he sick?"

"He said he was having trouble sleeping." Mrs. Taylor twisted a ring sporting a diamond the size of Maisy's big toe around her ring finger. "He sat in my kitchen that Friday night and poured his heart out to me while his dad was at a poker game. He told me he feels guilty about letting you come to Kansas by yourself—"

"Mrs. Taylor—"

"Sue Ellen."

"Sue Ellen, he doesn't have anything to feel guilty about. We agreed that me being Amish was an obstacle that couldn't be overcome. I plan to be baptized after the baby is born. I'm not leaving my faith. I've realized I need it more than ever."

It was true. The bigger the baby grew inside her, the clearer it became. Only God was big enough to carry Maisy through this. He showed mercy and grace even when a person didn't deserve it.

"I understand it's totally unacceptable for an Amish woman such as yourself to have a baby out of wedlock. That used to be a moral certainty embraced by everyone. Not so much in this day and age." Sue Ellen fluffed her curls and brushed back bangs that belonged on a much younger woman. "Now women frequently have babies and raise them on their own as a matter of choice."

"Not in my community."

"I understand. Which is why I have a proposition for you." She smoothed her shirt collar, first one side, then the other. "Give the baby to me and my husband to raise until Nate finishes college. In four years he'll come back to Jamesport. He can be a part of his baby's life, and you won't have to worry anymore about trying to raise a baby in a culture that sees what you've done as a terrible sin."

The *tick-tick-tick* of the clock resounded in Maisy's ears. Sunny wound her lanky body around Maisy's legs. She picked her up. Sunny settled in her lap and purred. Laughter floated down the hallway from the kitchen. Fussing—likely Nicholas—wandered down the stairs. The baby in her womb now belonged to Isaac and Vicky. The image of Vicky's glowing face in the van earlier in the day shone in Maisy's mind. She would be a good mother. The baby would have a Plain mother and father.

"We thought you would be thrilled with our offer, truly." Frowning, Sue Ellen leaned forward. "My husband and I thought this would be a perfect solution to your problem. And Nate would be able to focus on his education, knowing his baby is with grandparents who love him—do you know the baby's gender yet?"

Not trusting her voice, Maisy shook her head.

"We can find out later. We'll have a big gender-reveal party. Those are so much fun." Sue Ellen clapped as if the fun had already begun. "You have nothing to worry about. You can stay with us until you have the baby. Then you can go home to your family. Problem solved."

"I'm sorry, Mrs. Taylor—"

"Sue Ellen."

"Sue Ellen. I can't do that." Maisy chewed on her lower lip. How could she put this so Nate's mother understood without being offended? So she understood how important it was. "I want my baby to be raised Plain."

Sue Ellen's forehead wrinkled. She cocked her head to one side. "That's a funny way of putting it. You mean you plan to raise my grandchild in the Amish church?"

"I won't be raising my baby." Maisy's heart slammed against her rib cage like it wanted out. Out of this situation. There was no way out. "I've decided to let an Amish couple here in Haven adopt my baby. They can't have babies of their own—"

"You mean yours and Nate's baby." Sue Ellen's scowl raked Maisy from head to toe. "You plan to give Nate's baby away to strangers?"

"They're not strangers to me."

"How long have you known them?"

"A few weeks, but—"

"You dated my son for at least six months. You know him well enough to have his child. Does this couple have the means to support and care for my grandchild like we do? My husband is a successful dairy farmer. I design western wear clothes and jewelry quite successfully."

"It's not about money."

"It's about religion." Sue Ellen shook her head so hard her earrings jangled. "We're members in good standing at our church. We believe in the same God you do. We believe Jesus Christ died on the cross so we can have eternal life. What more do you want?"

Confusion twisted Maisy's tongue. If only she'd taken those baptism classes. She couldn't debate theology with this woman. Or with anyone. The Plain faith was a way of life. Her baby wouldn't grow up to wear jeans, dance, play music, go to movies, drive cars, watch TV, and attend college. If it was a girl, she wouldn't wear the jewelry or clothes designed by her grandmother. Either way, her baby's life would be a simple one filled with faith, family, and community.

"I've made a commitment to this couple. They're desperate for a baby. They've already had one birth mother change her mind. It nearly broke them." Maisy poured heart and soul into the words. Sue Ellen had to understand. She had to agree. "You've already had your children. You've raised them. Your children will have other grandbabies for you to spoil. You don't need mine."

"He's not yours alone. He's also Nate's."

"Nate agreed to let go."

"He didn't sign anything, did he?"

"No."

"Do you have a signed contract with these people?"

"Not yet, but—"

"Good." Sue Ellen grabbed her purse and stood. "I'll discuss this with my son. I'm sure when he knows about your intentions, he'll want to step forward and claim his parental rights."

What rights would they be? He'd agreed they could never marry and be a family. Would he change his mind now that his mother was involved? "Nate agreed our relationship could never work. We can't marry."

"Heavens no. I told him I totally agreed with his decision not to marry you. You're from two different worlds." Sue Ellen tucked the fringed leather purse's strap over her shoulder. Her long fingernails were painted a pale pink. "I plan to consult a lawyer about his rights as the biological father. I'm sure he's willing to take a paternity test. If you don't want the baby, he does."

"It's not that I don't want the baby." The world spun topsy-turvy, making Maisy's stomach lurch every time it rolled downhill and tumbled sideways, back and forth. She put her hand to her mouth. The taste of fries, hamburger, and chocolate milkshake gagged her. She swallowed and let her hand drop. "A baby needs a father and a mother who are married. Who plan to stay together no matter what trials life brings them."

Don't vomit. Don't vomit.

"Isaac and Vicky will love and care for this baby like he's their own because he will be their own. Nate's just starting out in life. He'll get married and have children when he's ready. That time isn't now."

Sue Ellen's finely plucked eyebrows rose. "We'll just see about that, won't we."

Chapter 28

LAWYERS COST MONEY. PLAIN FOLKS DON'T get involved in lawsuits and court cases. Sue Ellen Taylor wanted to take her grandchild. Maisy's baby would grow up in an English world. Isaac's and Vicky's hearts would be broken all over again. They trusted Maisy. They were counting on her.

The thoughts chased one another around Maisy's brain at neck-breaking speed until her head threatened to explode. She'd spent most of the night reliving the conversation with Sue Ellen and reframing all her responses into an argument that would convince Sue Ellen not to interfere.

Maisy had failed again. She'd failed her baby. She deposited a large box of work gloves on the floor next to the shelves in the hardware store's tool aisle. She paused. What next? Her brain couldn't hold simple tasks and the amusement park ride of her thoughts in the same small space.

"Unpack the gloves. Hang them up," she whispered. "Be good at something."

"Are you talking to yourself?" Harvey pushed a wheelbarrow filled with a new style of flashlight he planned to feature in an endcap display. "Don't worry about it—unless you start answering yourself."

"Just muttering to myself, but no, I'm not answering myself. Not yet anyway." Maisy maneuvered the box's flaps so they would stay open. As Harvey's employee, the least she could do was pay attention to her work. "I was going to put these gloves on the aisle with the tools since they're to be used with construction work. Or do you want all the gloves in one place, like with the gardening gloves?"

"According to the work they're used for." Harvey set down the wheelbarrow. He straightened the boxes Maisy had planted on the shelf. "You seem distracted this morning. Is everything all right? Are you feeling okay?"

"Yes. No. Not really." She couldn't tell this older English man her problems. This was a hardware store, not a counselor's office. He was her boss, not her mother. "Business has been slow this morning."

"It'll pick up when the rain stops."

The skies had opened in a cloudburst of rain so heavy it filled the roads as Maisy drove into town earlier in the day. The downpour suited her mood. A blustery north wind blew it into the buggy. She'd arrived cold, wet, and shivering.

Harvey had supplied towels, a warm jacket, and a hot cup of cocoa. Then he'd driven her buggy around to the back of the store so Amos's horse would have shelter under the awning next to the loading dock. "People don't like to get wet, but I reckon you can relate to that."

She could.

The bell over the door dinged. A customer, finally. Maisy wiped her dusty hands on her red hardware store apron and trotted to the front of the store. Betsy stood on the welcome rug with an oversized man in a too-tight blue suit and a skinny checked tie. Both closed umbrellas and wiped their feet on the welcome rug.

"Betsy, what are you doing here?" Maisy cast a glance backward.

Harvey had rolled the wheelbarrow to a spot by an endcap where he could see the newcomers. "I'm working."

"I got your message. I was delivering a baby at the time and another after that or I would've come sooner. Candy said you sounded distraught. And I know you wouldn't have used the phone unless it was something really important." She cocked her head toward the man standing next to her. "This is Charles Simmons. He's an attorney who handles family court matters, including adoptions and paternity suits."

The lawyer doffed his blue fedora, revealing a smooth, bald head. "Please to meet you, Miss Glick. Betsy has told me quite a bit about your situation, but I need you to tell me your story directly and fill in some of the holes."

"There's been a misunderstanding, Mr. Simmons." Maisy gripped her hands together. How could Betsy have done this without asking her first? This was embarrassing. "I can't afford a lawyer. Besides I'm working. I can't just drop everything to talk to you."

"What's going on here?" Harvey materialized next to Maisy. The man could employ stealth when he wanted to. "Hey, Charlie. I heard the word *lawyer* and I wondered if it was a shyster like you."

"Maisy needs to talk to a lawyer about a matter involving her baby." Betsy spoke up before Maisy could. "It's urgent, Harvey. Do you mind giving her a few moments to talk to Charlie? You know him from church, don't you?"

"I do. I knew something was up." Harvey shook his finger at Maisy. "Take your break early, Maisy. Talk to Charlie. Use my office."

"There's no point in it." Maisy kept her feet firmly planted on the hardwood floor. "I can't afford a lawyer."

"Let's just consider this an initial consult, free of charge."

Mr. Simmons rubbed his hands together. He picked up a leather briefcase from the rug. "It's cold out there. Is that coffee I smell? Let's have some coffee, talk, and then we'll work from there."

It was no use. They were determined to overrule her. The nest egg Nate had given her was dwindling fast with the clinic payments. Her checks from the hardware store helped, but lawyers cost a lot. Maisy didn't know much about the law, but that she knew. She marched behind the counter, poured Mr. Simmons his coffee, and ushered her two visitors behind the counter.

Harvey's office was the picture of Harvey. At least a dozen fishing trophies lined one shelf along with a multitude of fishing photos. Mr. Simmons laid his briefcase on top of a pile of invoices and folders. He settled into the chair behind the desk like he owned the place. Maisy perched on the edge of a straight-back chair, leaving the more comfortable padded chair for Betsy.

"I don't know what Betsy told you, but Plain folks don't have much to do with lawyers and court."

"I do understand that. I practice in Hutchinson, but I've had some dealings with Amish folks. Adoption comes up more often than a person would think."

"I wanted Isaac and Vicky King to adopt my baby, but then the baby's grandmother showed up—I guess Betsy told you about that. Can you work with Isaac and Vicky to find them another baby?"

"If I have to do that, I will." Mr. Simmons opened his briefcase and produced a stack of papers. "But first I want to see if there's a way I can help you. This is about you and your wishes for your baby to be raised by an Amish couple. Why don't you run through the details for me to make sure I have all the facts?"

Maisy glanced at Betsy. Telling this English stranger the private details of her life was even more painful than telling Betsy.

It seemed as if she'd repeated it to the whole world in the last two months.

"You can trust him. There's nothing you can tell him that he hasn't heard before." Betsy flashed an encouraging look at Maisy. "You're not the only woman to go through something like this. He's not going to pass judgment. He just wants to help."

Maisy started at the beginning. Mr. Simmons leaned back in his chair, steepled his fingers, and occasionally nodded. He didn't write anything down.

"So that's where we are now." She heaved a long breath and stared at her hands. Her knuckles were white. She unclasped them. "Now I don't know what to do."

"Maisy—may I call you Maisy?"

She nodded.

"I can help you. We'll work out a payment plan."

"I'm already making payments to the clinic."

"I use a sliding scale, depending on how much a client can pay. You'd be surprised at how reasonable I am."

"So what would you do for me?"

He slid a pamphlet across the desk. "This is a brochure that explains how unmarried fathers in Kansas establish paternity. It's important for you to understand that if you and Nate aren't married at the time of the baby's birth, Nate is not the baby's legal father. He doesn't have any rights. He would have to establish paternity."

"He's not in Kansas."

"I understand that. How long have you resided in Kansas?"

"Two and a half months."

"And you plan to remain here until the baby is born?"

"Yes, if Mrs. Taylor doesn't force me to move in with her in Jamesport."

"She can't force you to do anything. She has no legal standing in this matter." Mr. Simmons tsked. "Don't let her bamboozle you. The only people with skin in the game are you and Nate Taylor. You'll be a resident of Kansas and so will your baby. Nate will have to establish paternity here."

"How does he do that?"

"He can request genetic testing immediately after the baby is born. If you decline, he can file for court-ordered testing. You go to a lab and they swab your cheek and the baby's cheek. The Kansas Department of Children and Families offers this as a free service."

"There are some positive reasons for having Nate establish paternity," Betsy said.

Mr. Simmons nodded. "For him, yes. It would give him a say in the adoption."

Nate was the baby's father. Maybe he should have a say, but to stand in the way of a Plain couple adopting the baby seemed wrong. Or maybe Maisy could only see it through the lens of her upbringing. "Why else would it be positive?"

"Having access to his medical history, for one. I mentioned that to you before." Betsy leaned forward, hands on her knees. "It also gives your baby a relationship with his biological father in the future. If you choose an open adoption, he could know how the baby is doing and where he is as he grows. Get pictures of him. Letters from the adoptive parents. Or if you decide to keep the baby, he can provide financial support for the baby."

Isaac and Vicky wouldn't be sending Nate photos of their baby. "I can see how the child would want to know who his biological parents are, but later when he's old enough to understand."

"By law in Kansas you have to wait twelve hours after the baby is born before you can sign the consent-to-adopt form. That gives you time to be sure this is what you want." Mr. Simmons pushed a sheaf of papers toward Maisy. "The adopting couple can still be at the birth. You can make plans with them for all the details like car seats and a going-home outfit and who holds the baby first, but you can't actually consent immediately."

"That's not enough time for Nate to get the paternity test done, is it?"

"He could go to court and ask for an injunction to halt the adoption until his paternity is established."

"This is so complicated." A fierce pain stabbed Maisy between the eyes. She rubbed the spot as if she could rub away her problems. Her stomach returned to its old ways, lurching until bile burned the back of her throat. "I don't want my baby to be born into a fight between her biological parents. The Gmay here won't like it. My parents back home won't like it."

What strange phrases. *Biological parents. Birth mother. Adoptive parents. Legal father. I'm sorry, Gott, this is all my fault. If I had been stronger none of this would've ever happened. Sei so gut forgive me.*

The pain in her head eased.

"From a legal perspective there's nothing we can do right now, not until Nate makes the first move. My suggestion is you talk to Nate directly. Cut his mother out of the equation. It sounds to me like he was sure he didn't want to be a part of the baby's life until his mother got involved." Mr. Simmons picked up his cell phone and touched the screen. "Sorry, just checking the time. I have to get back to Hutchinson for a custody hearing. Read through this paperwork so you have some understanding of how this works."

"I have to tell Vicky and Isaac."

"Not yet." Mr. Simmons and Betsy spoke in emphatic unison. "Not yet."

"It's wrong to keep it from them. The longer they think the baby is theirs, the more they'll imagine their life with this baby. They're making plans. They're buying baby things. The sooner they know, the sooner they can come to terms with the change in plans."

"Talk to Nate first."

Maisy closed her eyes. She opened them. Her baby deserved to have two parents. He had to be raised in a Plain community. It was up to her to convince Nate of that. No one else could. "I have his cell phone number. I'll call him tonight."

Her baby depended on her. So did Vicky and Isaac.

Chapter 29

PRIDE LEFT A BITTER TASTE IN Joshua's mouth. Job tossed his head and whinnied.

"Hush your mouth." Joshua hopped from the buggy and tied the reins to Bryan's hitching post. The Standardbred stomped his feet. He wasn't living up to his name on this cool, wet autumn evening. "You're such a complainer. This may be a short conversation."

The front windows in the bishop's house were bright with the gleam of kerosene lamps' light in the gathering dusk. Supper would be over. No point in procrastinating. It was time to set aside his pride and ask for help. So why did his legs move slower than a schoolboy's on the first day of class?

Because he'd been avoiding this discussion for years. He would gladly keep on avoiding it if it weren't for a woman named Maisy Glick. She'd gotten under his skin. He didn't like it, but he couldn't shake her. When he'd gone over to the store earlier in the day to have lunch, she'd been closeted in Harvey's office. According to Harvey, who was itching to tell someone, she was talking to a law-yer and one of the midwives from the birthing clinic.

"It looked real serious," Harvey had said. "Maisy was wound

so tight I thought she might spontaneously combust right there in front of me."

So no lunch. Which was probably for the best. Despite her mixed messages the last time they had lunch, Maisy's petrified face had told the real story. She was scared spitless of doing the wrong thing. And he was the wrong thing. Not just because he was a man, but because he was a Plain man who was spiritually alienated and hanging on to his alienation with all his strength.

Go on. Get it over with. He gritted his teeth and raised his hand to knock.

The door flew open. Bryan peered out. "I was beginning to wonder if you were still there. I thought maybe you chickened out and went home."

"If you knew I was out here, why didn't you open the door earlier?"

"I figured I'd give you time to mull it over." Bryan opened the door wider. "Come on in and take a load off."

Inside, Bryan's house was set up like most every other house in the district. Hardwood floors, a few simple pieces of furniture. Kerosene pole lamps. A desk in the corner for paying bills. Green curtains on the windows. Esther sat on the couch with knitting needles in hand. She said hello, and then took her knitting somewhere else.

"So what can I do for you?" Bryan plopped down in an overstuffed chair next to an empty fireplace. "You either have an important issue to discuss, or you have a serious case of indigestion."

Joshua took a seat in a glider rocker. The sausage-and-rice casserole he'd eaten for supper sat like a boulder in his gut, but it wasn't his mother's fault. Nor was it the reason for his expression. "I wondered if you had a chance to ask John Shirak about horse training."

"Actually I did. He doesn't have a need at the moment, but he expects to in the spring." Bryan cocked his head to one side, then the other. He grimaced. "I told him about your interest. He said to come around and see him sooner rather than later."

"Gut. Gut."

"Working toward the vocation you desire is a start, but I hope that's not the only reason you're here."

Joshua shifted in his seat. He stopped just short of wiggling like a little boy. "I need to figure some things out."

"Gut." Smiling like an expectant father, Bryan rubbed his hands together. "Gut. Wanting to talk is a gut start."

"Don't expect miracles."

"Why? Gott is in the miracle business."

"Not so I've noticed."

It only took a second for the frown to overtake Bryan's face. "Tread carefully."

Off to a bad start. "We talked about why my family moved to Haven."

"We did." Bryan leaned back and crossed his arms. He had the remnants of supper on his shirt—most likely gravy—and bread crumbs in his beard. "You know how I feel about that."

"I do." Bryan hadn't been there. Joshua had. Losing a brother to a fire couldn't simply be buried under a mountain of better memories. "I want to move on."

"What's changed?"

"What's changed?" Joshua tugged at his shirt's collar. It suddenly felt too tight. "What do you mean?"

"Joshua."

Joshua's leg bounced. He stilled it. "I don't want to be a bachelor with no family, living with my parents forever. I want to get on with my life."

"Why?"

"Because it's what we're expected to do. Get married. Have kinner."

"That's not why you're doing it now. If it was you'd have done it a long time ago."

"I can't have the life I want unless I'm baptized."

"True. But you can't choose baptism because of a woman." Bryan cocked his head, then shook it. "Especially a woman who hasn't been baptized herself."

The crux of the matter. "She will be. After the bopli is born."

"Isaac and Vicky have consulted with me about their plan. After the bopli is born, I'll instruct Maisy to go home to Jamesport. She belongs with her family."

Not here, stirring up trouble. "Why is it so wrong for me to have . . . an interest in her?"

"She's off to a poor start. She needs to make amends at home and then be baptized there." Bryan's tone sharpened. "There are young women here in your Gmay who would make gut fraas. Why seek out someone who isn't in a position to reciprocate?"

"What if she did?"

"She knows better."

Maybe she did. Maisy was trying so hard to keep her distance. Not because she didn't like him. Joshua was sure of that. As sure as a man with so little experience with women could be. She didn't trust herself. She feared being hurt. If Joshua couldn't resolve his own problems, he would never be the man she could trust with her love and her life.

"How do I do it?"

"Get unstuck?"

"Jah."

"Let's start with you telling me why you're so angry with Gott."

Joshua's heart sped up just as it always did when the memories threatened to destroy his defenses. The intense heat threatened to blister his cheeks' tender skin. The stench of burned wood and rubber filled his nose. The cracking of flames, the crash of walls tumbling down, the shouts of the firefighters, the intense spray of water from the hoses—a cacophony of noise filled his ears.

He ducked his head and cleared his throat.

"Go on, Joshua, you can tell me."

Joshua raised his head and stared at Bryan. Anger leaped higher than the flames that consumed every stick of furniture, every stitch of clothing, every memento that reminded them of relatives who'd passed away. All gone. None of that meant anything next to the specter of Jacob snared by the smoke and the flames. Did he have time to be afraid? Did he writhe in agony as the flames consumed him? Did he cry out for Joshua or Dad or for God?

"I keep thinking of Meshach, Shadrach, and Abednego when Nebuchadnezzar had them thrown into the fire. They didn't burn up. Gott was in the fire with them." Joshua wrangled his voice into submission. A grown man did not cry. A grown Plain man accepted events as Gott's will. Why couldn't he? "Where was He when Jacob died?"

"It's prideful to expect to know and understand Gott's plan for us." Bryan spoke softly. "I suspect you've heard all the usual answers about honing of character. Gott doesn't cause tragedy to befall us in this broken world full of sin. He does promise to walk through it with us. Jacob's days were numbered in the Book of Life. It's not for us to know why."

"I can't feel Him." Joshua studied his fisted hands. He forced himself to meet Bryan's gaze. "He's supposed to be the light. Everything is dark."

"I've never been through what you went through, so I won't

claim to know how you feel." Bryan tugged at his shaggy beard. The bread crumbs fell in his lap. He shook his head. "Have you ever talked to your daed about this? Your mudder?"

"A little. I've tried. Mudder barely spoke for months after it happened. After the funeral Daed stopped talking about Jacob." Mourning doves cooing had been the only sound as the pallbearers lowered the unstained wooden casket Dad made into the black hole. Mom sagged against Dad. His arms held her up. Neither shed tears. The smell of wet earth was overpowering.

"A few weeks later they sat us down and told us they'd decided to sell the farm to an English family that wanted to build a new house on the land. They'd decided to move us to Haven for a fresh start. Daed's kossins were here. It was like Jacob never existed."

"They may not talk about it, but they still mourn your bruder. They're older and wiser than you are, my friend. They know they must go on with their lives. For the sake of their other kinner and for each other. They know Jacob would've wanted that. Jacob wouldn't want you to miss out on life because you're back there at that fire."

"My birthday is next week."

His expression earnest, Bryan leaned forward, elbows on his knees, hands clasped. "And every birthday is another one you can't share with Jacob."

"Mudder insists on baking my favorite carrot cake with cream cheese frosting."

"What was Jacob's favorite?"

"German chocolate."

"Maybe this year you can ask her to make Jacob's instead."

Maybe. Would she get it? Would she understand?

Joshua closed his eyes and lowered his head into his hands. *The smell of chocolate cake wafted on an autumn breeze. Grinning like a silly monkey, Jacob elbowed Joshua. A pile of presents stacked on the table accounted for his grin. "I bet there's a new mitt in there. What do you think?"*

"I think you hinted around enough that even the bopli knows you want one."

"If you get a bat and some balls, we're all set."

Joshua liked basketball better, and he really wanted a fishing pole and lures, but he didn't mind if Jacob was better at getting what he wanted. Either way was good. Chocolate cake was good, second best to carrot cake but still tasty.

Dad had made vanilla ice cream, cranking the machine by hand until it was cold and creamy. Mom bought all the toppings for sundaes. A double birthday warranted double desserts, she said. She said that every year.

Sure enough there was a bat, balls, and a mitt. But also a new fishing pole and lures for Joshua. Somehow Mom knew. She knew everything.

Except for one big detail. That would be the last birthday they celebrated with Jacob at the table, stirring his ice cream until it was soupy and slurping it up, all the while grinning like a silly monkey.

Bryan's living room was quiet, peaceful. His kids had gone to bed. He probably longed for bed himself.

Footsteps sounded. Bryan's hand touched Joshua's shoulder. "Go home. You're tired. You need to sleep. On your birthday celebrate the time you had with your bruder, not the time you wanted to have. Be thankful for twelve years of shared birthdays."

Joshua didn't trust himself to speak. He simply nodded.

Bryan's compassion shone like a star on a dark night. A light. "I'll pray for Gott's will to be done for Maisy. And for you. If those two paths are to come together and stay together, Gott will make it known."

His throat so tight with tears he couldn't breathe, Joshua stood and moved to the door.

"You took a step in the right direction tonight." Bryan opened the door and moved onto the porch ahead of Joshua. "Small steps forward will get you where you need to go. Take heart. It won't always be dark."

"How do you know?"

"Because Scripture says so. Jesus is light in the darkness. You have to open your eyes to see the light."

Joshua plodded down the steps and into the dark night. He looked back. Bryan had extinguished all but one lamp. Its light shone brightly in one last window.

Chapter 30

Maisy shivered. A cool evening breeze didn't account for the chill that ran through her. The phone shack door was closed. No one needed to hear this conversation. Almost three months had passed since she last saw Nate. Yet it seemed like a hundred years ago. Her life had changed so much. His likely had as well. He studied at a university now. She worked in a hardware store. They'd had so little in common before. Now they had even less. Despite the chill, she wiped dampness from her temples with her apron. She'd lost her supper in the weeds before entering the shack, so that was done. Now came the hard part.

She unfolded the piece of paper she'd kept tucked in her bag since the first time Nate approached her in that farmer's pasture. He'd insisted she take it even though she didn't have a phone. He'd drawn a smiley face wearing a cowboy hat next to his name under the number. *Gott, sei so gut, let him answer.* The number rang and rang, one, two, three, four.

"Hello."

Danki, Gott. "Nate, it's Maisy."

"Are you all right?" Suddenly he sounded more alert. "Is the baby all right?"

He cared. Somehow it made this call harder. "The baby's fine. That's why I'm calling. Did you know your mother came to see me?"

"What?"

"She came to see me yesterday. She wants me to give the baby to her so she can raise him until you graduate from college."

"Seriously?" Nate huffed. He said some words he shouldn't say in a voice loud enough to make Maisy hold the phone away from her ear. "I knew I shouldn't have told her."

"Why did you? After all this time."

His breathing sounded quick, angry. "Because I kept dreaming about the baby. It was so weird. So real. Like I had a car seat in my truck and this baby was crying because she was hungry. She had blonde hair and blue eyes like you. I couldn't see any of me in her. I needed to tell somebody. It's not like I can tell my buddies here, 'Hey, man, I got a girl pregnant. She's having my baby.'"

He dreamed about the baby. But not about Maisy. "Is it because you want to be in the baby's life? Be his father?"

"I don't know. I can't interpret dreams. I want to be a dad someday. I want kids. But not now. I mean, I don't have to decide now, do I?"

Maisy's heart jerked in a fierce *rat-a-tat-tat*. Light-headed, she gripped the receiver in her sweaty hand. "I've decided to let an Amish couple here in Haven adopt the baby."

No response. Maisy waited. The silence stretched. "Nate?"

"Yeah. I'm just thinking."

"What are you thinking?"

"About strangers raising my baby."

"They're not strangers to me. Unless you claim paternity, you're not legally the baby's father."

"You talked to a lawyer about this?"

Now he sounded mad. She was making it worse. "Only after

your mother came to see me. She said she would get a lawyer and help you establish paternity so you could keep the adoption from going through. She wants me to live with your family until the baby's born and then leave him there with her."

"Wow. She's a piece of work."

On that they could agree. "So you didn't know anything about this?"

"No. You and me agreed to part ways. You're Amish. I'm not." He groaned. "My mother's always been a busybody, but this takes the cake. I'm a freshman in college. I'm taking English 101 and algebra and basic courses like that. I'm going to football games and drinking beer on the weekend. The last thing I'm thinking about is being a daddy."

At least consciously. "This Amish couple desperately wants a baby. They've lost two and an adoption fell through when the birth mother changed her mind. I've already talked to them. It would be horribly mean to back out now and put them through that again."

More silence. Maisy drew circles with the toe of her sneaker in the shack's dirt floor. Nate hadn't changed his mind about the baby. That was good. Now all he had to do was tell his mother that. Everything would be fine. "Are you still thinking?"

"Yeah, I'm thinking." Noisy laughter filled the line. A man's voice shouted something about a party. Someone else said dough-nuts and beer. "Everybody just shut up!"

"Nate?"

"Sorry. My roommate and his jock friends just wandered into the room." A noise like a door banging hurt Maisy's ear. Nate's breathing deepened. "Okay. I'm in the closet."

"What are you thinking about?"

"I'll go home this weekend and talk to my mom."

"You'll tell her you want the adoption to go through?"

"I didn't say that. When do you sign the adoption papers?"

"I can't sign the consent form until twelve hours after the baby is born."

"Then I still have time."

"Time for what? You said you aren't ready to be a father."

"I'm not, but this is messing with my head." Nate's voice went hoarse. "Sometimes I feel like I'm losing my mind. Don't you ever feel that way, Daisy Maisy?"

Daisy Maisy, prettiest girl in Daviess County. I do love you, Daisy Maisy.

Maisy closed her eyes. Nate's face shining against the dark night sky like another moon accosted her. They did have something in common. Those moments when they connected like she'd never connected with another human being. Would she ever again?

"Yes, I do. Especially now when I'm trying to do the right thing. I have to do what's best for the baby. It's not about me. It's not about you. It's about the baby."

"In my dream she was the spitting image of you."

"Whether it's a girl or a boy, the baby deserves parents who are ready to be parents. That's not you or me. Think about that, Nate, please. Remember that when you talk to your mother."

"I will." He cleared his throat. "Call me Sunday night."

More sleepless nights and restless days lay ahead. "Okay."

"I have to go. I have a biology test to study for."

A biology test. Was he learning about genes and DNA and how the color of a baby's eyes was determined? Such things were a mystery to Maisy. What did it matter how a baby came to have blue eyes? It only mattered that he saw clearly with those eyes.

Would Nate learn that science didn't determine the true parents of a child? Love did.

Chapter 31

THE SECOND WEEKEND IN NOVEMBER DAWNED a cool forty degrees with clear skies and a brisk north wind. Maisy needed a winter coat. The one Ruth loaned her didn't quite cover her belly. She added a black scarf Ruth had knitted and tucked it in front of the coat to make up for it. The cold air nipped at her nose and cheeks as she pulled into the slot next to the hardware store's loading dock. Cold weather made her miss coffee all the more. Not just for the taste either. Obsessing over what Nate would decide kept her from sleeping at night. It was only Saturday. She still had to get through another night and day before she could call him.

Her brain in a fog, she hopped from the buggy and trotted inside. At least she pretended to trot. It was more like a waddle. The scale tattled on her. Despite the bouts of nausea, she'd gained seventeen pounds. Not bad, according to Kate, who said the baby was now the size of a full ear of corn, weighed a little more than a pound, and was somewhere between eight and eleven inches long, crown to rump. At least Maisy had until next summer to regain her taste for corn on the cob.

Inside, Harvey presented her with a cup of hot cocoa. How the man knew when she'd walk in the door remained a mystery. "How are you today?"

"My sciatica is acting up." He rubbed one hip as he hobbled to the counter. "I always know when the wind shifts to the north."

"Anything special I should work on today?"

"We got another shipment of fireplace logs, fire starters, and lighters." Harvey wrapped his knobby fingers around a coffee mug with the words THE BOSS on it. "You can restock the endcap display to start with."

Maisy hung her coat and scarf on the rack. "Will do. On my lunch hour I need to run over to the thrift store to see if I can find a bigger coat."

"I don't think there will be any running involved." Harvey chuckled at his own joke. "But that's fine. No lunch with your buddy then?"

"My buddy?" Maisy pointed to the boxes stacked next to an order of mops, brooms, and dust mops. "Can you help me move those? You're talking about aisle six's endcap, right?"

Harvey straightened and set down his coffee mug. "Yep, and sure thing. You can pretend all you want and change the subject, but you know who I'm talking about."

She had been avoiding Joshua since Sue Ellen's visit and the conversation with Nate. Why? Because she was carrying the baby of another man? Because Nate might come tromping back into her life right behind his mother? Joshua's life was complicated enough without her mess. "I'm sure Joshua's busy too."

"Today's his birthday. It'd be a shame to thumb your nose at him on his special day."

"I'm not thumbing my nose at anyone." Maisy dragged one of the boxes toward aisle six. Maybe Harvey would get the hint. "How do you know it's Joshua's birthday?"

Because he knew everything. He was a busybody like Sue Ellen. Only in a good way.

"His little sister was in here yesterday. She and her brother went together and bought him a new hunting knife."

"I'll sure he'll appreciate that."

His birthday. Also his twin brother's birthday. How hard it must have been for his parents to strike a balance between celebrating one son's birthday, while mourning the death of the other. After ten years, surely they'd learned to walk that fine line. Had Joshua?

Harvey picked up the box with ease. Maisy followed him to the endcap. He used a box cutter to open it. Without pausing, he began handing her artificial fire logs. She never understood why folks used them instead of real wood. She stacked as quickly as he handed them to her. Maybe he was right. She would go to the thrift store at lunch, pick up cupcakes from the bakery, and then swing by Mast's Furniture Store to present them to him.

How old was he now? At least twenty-three. Old compared to her. The unspoken pressure to be baptized and marry would only increase. Mulling over his problems kept her mind off her own. The time passed quickly. At noon Harvey let her go with the promise that she'd bring him back a jelly roll from the bakery. She didn't ask how he knew she'd be stopping at the bakery. Wild guess, no doubt.

The thrift store was doing a brisk business in coats, scarfs, stocking caps, mittens, wool socks, and winter boots. Eager to make a selection and get back to the store so Harvey could enjoy his lunch, Maisy zeroed in on the women's coats. A Plain woman stood in the middle of the aisle holding up a dark-blue sweater to see if it fit her companion, an older woman using a cane to steady herself.

Maisy tried to squeeze by.

The older woman saw her first. Her eyebrows arched. She nodded. Maisy cast her gaze at the floor. Mennonites ran the store, but these were Plain women. She wasn't to engage with them.

"You're Ruth Plank's kossin, aren't you?" The younger woman spoke despite the older woman's frown of disapproval. "You two could be sisters."

Maisy nodded and kept moving.

"You're not to talk to her." The woman with the cane scolded her companion. "She carries her fehla everywhere she goes."

"*Mammi*, she's not from our district." The woman spoke lightly. "It's not like it's catching."

The women's voices followed Maisy as she searched the rack of coats two sizes bigger than she would normally wear. They didn't seem to make any attempt to talk quietly. In fact the older woman's voice grew louder and more insistent.

"She should be at home with her family, not adding to Amos and Ruth's burden. Poor Ruth's in a family way, taking care of two kinner, and Amos with his bum leg. Now this maedel."

"Mammi! Scripture says we're not to judge."

"Nor are we to mingle. Let's get this sweater and go."

Finally they moved away. Bile burned Maisy's throat. She swallowed hard. Did all the local Plain folks feel this way? Was she a burden? She helped in every way she could. Sewing, cooking, cleaning, bathing the babies. Taking care of them so Ruth could rest when she felt poorly. Was it enough?

Maisy tugged a black wool coat from its hanger. She tried it on quickly. Shame made her fingers thick. She fumbled with the buttons. It would have to do. Her pleasure at doing a bit of shopping had disappeared under an avalanche of uncertainty. A thick woolen scarf and mittens completed her purchases. She rushed from the store wearing the new-to-her coat.

A Plain family from Amos and Ruth's district owned the bakery across the street. Instead Maisy trudged back to the hardware store and her buggy. They had cupcakes at the grocery store owned by an English family. Fifteen minutes later she had half a dozen cupcakes in assorted flavors and a jelly doughnut for Harvey. Her stomach rebelled at the thought of eating either one. For herself she bought a ginger ale.

Outside the furniture store, she took a breath and fixed her face in what she hoped was the perfect happy-birthday expression. It was Joshua's birthday. He didn't need to hear about her troubles.

Joshua wasn't at the counter. Caleb was. The owner looked up from a catalog. He immediately straightened and closed it. "Maisy, right? I've seen you coming and going at Harvey's store. Joshua's always in a hurry to have lunch with you."

Should she be talking to Caleb? Only long enough to ask for Joshua. "Is he here?"

"He went across the street to Harvey's, searching for you." Caleb's face lit up. He looked like a kid contemplating a holiday from school even though he had to be around the same age as Maisy's father. "It's his birthday, you know. He's been very quiet—more than usual—lately. I reckon you can cheer him up."

"I don't know about that." Maisy did an about-face and headed for the door. "But I'll try."

"If anyone can, you can," Caleb called after her. "Tell him not to rush back. We haven't had one customer in the last two hours."

"I'll tell him."

Maisy picked up her pace. She waited impatiently for a car to pass, then traipsed across the street just as Joshua pushed through the hardware store door.

"There you are." His smile seemed half-hearted. "Harvey said you were running errands, but I thought you were still avoiding me."

"I'm not avoiding you." *Not much.* Maisy shifted the grocery bag from one hand to the other. *"Seelich gebortsdaag."*

His smile died altogether, replaced with a somber stare. "How did you know it's my birthday?"

"Harvey told me. I brought you something." Maisy gestured toward the bench on the sidewalk in front of the store. "Can we sit? Caleb said to tell you not to rush back. He hasn't had a single customer."

"Sure."

He planted himself on the end of the bench, leaving Maisy plenty of room to carve out space between them. Plain people from the Gmay driving by would probably object to them sitting together in public, but neither of them were members. What could they do to them? Talk behind their backs?

Maisy shut the door on the thoughts that milled around in her head. Letting the women's spiteful conversation at the thrift shop bother her gave them too much power over her. She opened up her grocery bag and took out the six-pack of cupcakes. "I didn't know what flavor you like so I got one of each. There's chocolate, vanilla, strawberry, spice cake, cherry, and pumpkin."

This time Joshua's smile was real. "That's a lot of cupcakes. Are you going to help me eat them?"

"Or we can give one to Harvey and one to Caleb."

"I don't know. You did say they were my cupcakes." He perused the box. The frostings matched the cupcakes in flavor. Each one had sprinkles in different flavors. "Now all we need is ice cream."

"It's a little chilly to sit outside and eat ice cream."

"True. I like carrot cake so the spice cake is probably the closest." He took Maisy's offering and licked off some frosting. "Aren't you going to sing happy birthday?"

"You don't want me to sing. I can't carry a tune in a bucket."

He laughed. "You didn't do so bad with 'Das Loblied,' as I recall."

That Sunday morning at Ruth's house seemed a hundred years ago. "How're you doing?"

His gaze swung in her direction. "Birthdays are hard." He did her the favor of not pretending he didn't know what she meant. "But this year it's a little easier."

Maisy took a small bite of the chocolate cupcake. Her taste buds crooned happy notes. "I'm glad. I can't begin to imagine how you and your family find a place beyond your sadness where you can celebrate. I'm glad the passage of time makes it easier."

"It's not just the passage of time."

Something in his tone made Maisy study his face. Sadness still resided there, but something else did as well. Hope. A sudden wariness caused a hitch in her breathing. "What is it then?"

"It's you."

"Joshua."

He polished off the cupcake in three bites. Frosting decorated his upper lip. "I know you're afraid, but I'm not an English teenager with only one thing on his mind. I'm a man who's been through some things and not handled them the way a Plain man should. I'm ready to start fixing myself, but I'm not perfect. I don't expect you to be."

"Joshua, sei so gut—"

"Let me finish. I talked to Bryan about you. He's praying for Gott's will. He wonders why you and not one of the maed in the Gmay." Joshua selected the cherry cupcake, but he didn't take a bite. "I don't know. I feel something for you that I've never felt for anyone."

"I can't. I can't think about such things in the middle of carrying a bopli I'm giving away because I committed a fehla that I can't ignore. I'll always be that woman who carried an Englisch man's bopli."

"Nee. You won't. You'll be forgiven. You will live the life Gott has planned for you."

"You sound so sure."

"I am. I've never been surer of anything in my life."

"I don't understand how you can even look at me with that spark in your eyes." Maisy set the box between them. No amount of sugar could sweeten her words. "Don't you see what I've done every time you gaze at me?"

"I see a woman who's repentant, who's asked Gott for forgiveness, and who'll go and sin no more. You'll do what's best for the bopli because that's who you are."

A herd of emotions ran willy-nilly through Maisy, a stampede so wild she couldn't sort them out—grief, joy, guilt, fear, anticipation, uncertainty, a sort of fear-joy that snatched her breath away and made her breastbone ache. "I don't know what to say."

"Say you feel something for me."

Cars drove past. A truck honked. An elderly couple went into the hardware store without glancing their way. Joshua represented everything she'd ever wanted. A husband. A family. A Plain life as it was supposed to be. But how could he look at her, her belly swollen with another man's baby, and think of her with anything more than disgust or pity?

"This isn't the time or place for this."

"Then at least tell me this, will there come a time and a place when we can have this conversation?"

The anguish for all her indiscretion had cost her tumbled down on Maisy. She staggered to her feet under its weight. This hadn't gone as planned. Cupcakes. Simply cupcakes. She slipped past him without answering. She should do the right thing and say no, but the single syllable word refused to be said. Her feelings for Joshua couldn't be allowed to stand in the way of doing the right thing.

"Maisy?"

At the door, she stopped and forced herself to turn back. "I don't know, but I hope so. I really do. Seelich gebortsdaag, Joshua."

Chapter 32

THE HOUSE SMELLED LIKE BIRTHDAY. JOSHUA followed his nose into the kitchen. The sweet yet spicy scent of carrot cake conspired to keep him from burying his feelings after his conversation with Maisy. *Stupid. Stupid. Stupid.* He'd jumped the gun. Now she really would avoid him. His stomach clenched. Maisy had gone to the trouble to buy cupcakes for his birthday. Why hadn't he simply accepted her sweet gesture and enjoyed the moment?

Because he was self-centered and acting like a lovelorn teenager. The feelings were so new to him he didn't know what to do with them. Maisy was in no position to think about courting another man. He hadn't even asked her how she was doing. She was sad and worn out and he'd made it worse.

Stupid, stupid, stupid.

"Goodness. What happened to you?" Joshua's mother stood at the kitchen table frosting a cake. She waved the plastic spatula at him. "You have a face full of thunderclouds."

"I'm just smacking myself around for doing something stupid today." He snatched a glob of frosting from the bowl with one finger. "That's gut stuff."

Smiling, Mother swatted playfully at Joshua's hand. "I hope

your fingers are clean, Suh. Wait until I finish and you can lick the spoon. A person can't go wrong with butter, cream cheese, vanilla, milk, and powdered sugar. So, does this stupid thing you did involve a woman?"

His mother always said she had eyes in the back of her head. "What makes you ask that?"

"My friend Lottie drove down Switzer Street today and saw you sitting outside the hardware store with a Plain woman who's not from our district. You know Lottie. She taxis every family in Haven. She didn't recognize your friend."

Lottie was a busybody English woman who hired out as a driver after she retired from teaching school. Joshua's mom had taken a liking to her, and now they visited over iced tea and pie in the summer and hot tea and muffins in the winter. "So she had to drive out here lickety-split to tell you about it?"

"Nee. She was coming out anyway to bring me a pumpkin. She bought several at a church pumpkin patch and wanted to share."

And gossip.

"So, who was she?"

Joshua stopped to peruse gifts wrapped in plain brown paper stacked on the kitchen table. It was a nice haul—one of the perks of having so many brothers and sisters. How much could he tell his mother? He went to the sink and washed his hands. He grabbed a towel and turned to lean against the counter.

"You're stalling."

Might as well dip his toe in the water. Maybe she would have some advice. Mother had an opinion on everything. "Maisy."

"So this stupid thing you did involved Maisy?"

"Yes, it did."

A hint of worry crept into her expression. "Have you talked to Bryan about her?"

259

"Jah."

Her eyebrows popped up. "Gut. I reckon it's a complicated situation. Her not being a member of this district and not being baptized. He's told us not to socialize with her."

Since Joshua didn't belong to the Gmay, that prohibition didn't apply to him. The grapevine was nothing if not efficient in Haven. "She plans to be baptized after the bopli is born."

"The poor girl has enough problems to work through without adding a man who isn't baptized to her burden." Mom used her sleeve to push back a lock of silver and brown hair that had escaped her prayer covering. "She chose poorly once. I can't imagine she wants to do it again."

"She doesn't."

"So she's learning from her mistakes."

Maisy saw him as another mistake, another burden, a man who could break her heart all over again. Changing that might be impossible. "I'm not a mistake."

"Nee, you're a man with a soft heart and a hard head."

She didn't want to talk about courting. She wanted to talk about his faith—or lack thereof. The topic of Maisy was closed for now. Instead the real topic of the day still had to be broached. Joshua folded the towel and laid it next to the cake. His mother opened the oven door. The aroma of garlic, oregano, tomato sauce, and sausage filled the air. Lasagna. Another one of his favorites. His stomach rumbled. Lunch had consisted of two cupcakes. "That smells gut."

"I'm glad you think so. I made two. Your *onkel* and aenti and kossins are coming for supper." She closed the oven door. "Another fifteen minutes are so. What's really on your mind?"

"I talked to Bryan about something else."

Mother took a pile of leaf lettuce from a strainer in the sink and began tearing the leaves into bite sizes and tossing them in a bowl. "What was that?"

"I'm considering the possibility of hiring on as an apprentice at John Shirak's horse farm in the spring. I think it's time for me to seek the vocation I've always wanted."

Her hands stopped moving. She ducked her head. After a few seconds she went back to tearing the lettuce, but with more vehemence. "The vocation you and Jacob always wanted."

"Jah. It's always been too painful to contemplate, but I realize now Jacob would've wanted me to go after our dream—not throw it away."

"So you talked to Bryan about Jacob?"

"Jah."

"Did it help?"

"Some. But Bryan wasn't there. He doesn't know. Not like you and Daed." After so long it was strange to talk so much about Jacob. "You and Daed never talk about him. Daed leaves the room if I bring him up. Peter and the others don't talk about him either."

"There's nothing to say."

"It's like you want to pretend you never had another suh."

"That's not true. And it's hurtful that you would say such a thing." She dropped the lettuce and turned to face him. "I think about Jacob every day. And then I remind myself he lived the exact number of days written in Gott's Book of Life. Gott knew how long he would live and how he would die. I don't know why Jacob died that day, but Gott does. I trust and I obey. To do otherwise is sinful and arrogant."

The certainty in her tone left no room for argument. She clung to her faith, which was exactly what she was supposed to do. That a twelve-year-old boy had trouble doing the same shouldn't have surprised her or his father.

The pressure of his father's hand on his shoulder as they had watched the casket being lowered into the ground returned as if his father stood in the kitchen now. His hand was heavy. His fingers tightened until it hurt. Unspoken words, unspoken strength, unspoken comfort. His father had no words for what he felt. That didn't mean he didn't mourn or question or rail at God.

"I'm sorry."

His mother turned back to the counter. She picked up a paring knife and a tomato. "Don't be sorry. I'm the one who's sorry. You were a little boy. He was your twin. I was selfish. I thought only of my own pain." Her voice quivered. "I was your mudder, but I didn't know how to help you. I couldn't even help myself."

And every time he walked into the room, she saw Jacob again. Missed him again. Castigated herself again.

Her shoulders slumped. She stared at the tomato in her hand as if she had no idea what to do with it.

Joshua's mind said a million words of comfort. His mouth didn't open. His arms wanted to give her a hug. His legs wouldn't move. Every beat of his heart hurt until it seemed better that it should simply stop.

He cleared his throat. "It's okay. You suffered from a mudder's grief."

A grief so deep they'd moved to another state to try to outrun it. Instead the grief followed and compounded itself. They had no photos of Jacob, no mementos of his life. Instead they were reminded daily by Joshua's presence of how tall Jacob would've grown, how broad his shoulders would've become, the deepening of his voice, the first whiskers on his chin. They saw his mirror image sitting at the supper table every night.

That thought propelled Joshua forward. He took the tomato and the knife from his mother's hands. He set them aside. "I'm sorry for your loss."

She looked up at him, her blue eyes wet with tears. "I'm sorry I couldn't make it better for you. I expected a young bu to figure it out all on his own. You must've felt so alone."

"It's okay."

"Nee, but maybe it will be a little better tomorrow, a little more the next day, until one day when we'll wake up and think only of the baseball game where Jacob hit a home run every time he batted or the time he stole an apple pie from the windowsill and ate the whole thing before I found him or the time he was five and took the buggy for a drive while we were eating lunch after church."

"Or when he put a bean in his nose and you had to take him to the doctor to get it out. And the time he put a bowl on his head and cut his own hair so he could look more like Daed."

Mom hugged Joshua, a hug so quick he almost missed it. "Happy birthday."

"Danki."

"Joshua, Joshua!" Samuel and Michael, inseparable as brothers so close in age tended to be, shot into the room, talking over each other the way they always did. Samuel, older by a year, took the lead. "Daed said you were home. Seelich gebortsdaag!"

"Danki."

"You can't guess what we got you." Not to be outdone, Michael climbed on a chair and stood for more height. "You'll really like it. Mudder helped."

"Don't tell. It's a surprise." Samuel rocked the chair. Michael hopped off and shoved his brother. The two were joined at the hip and they never stopped bickering. But let someone say something about one of them, the other was his biggest defender. "Guess, Joshua, guess!"

All the sadness in Mother's face disappeared in a split second. She pointed the paring knife at Joshua. "Take your brieder in the living room while I finish supper. Rachel and Hannah will be home from work soon. Peter and his fraa will be here any minute with their boplin." The remnants of their earlier conversation settled into the lines around her mouth and eyes. "Let the party begin."

A person didn't know how many birthday parties he would get or who would be around for the next one. A morbid thought, true. But people who'd suffered a loss understood this and knew that each moment had to be plumbed to its depths, valued, enjoyed, stowed in memories. Not taken for granted.

Joshua grabbed Michael with one arm and Samuel with the other. He marched them, hooting and hollering, into the living room for a wrestling match for the record books.

Tomorrow he'd have another visit with Bryan. And another until he found his way back.

Chapter 33

At least colder weather made the phone shack less stuffy. That didn't keep Maisy from sweating. Carrying around a baby was like having a built-in woodburning stove always stoked to full blaze. She plopped on the hardback cane chair and tried Nate's number a third time. It rang and rang. Why didn't he answer? He'd said to call him on Sunday evening. She'd waited patiently until after the supper dishes were washed and the babies asleep. The dusk gathered. Tree branches dipped and swayed in a brisk northern wind. They scratched on the shack's roof.

"Come on, Nate, please answer."

"Hello. Maisy?"

Finally. Relief so acute she felt light-headed rushed through Maisy. "Where were you? I've been calling."

"We went out for pizza and I lost track of time. Sorry."

Pizza? Sorry? "Did you talk to your mother?"

"I did." His voice softened. He cleared his throat. "She had some good points. Some things I hadn't thought about."

What good points? The time Maisy had spent with Nate seemed years ago. "So say what you have to say."

"You don't belong living with my parents."

Danki, Gott. "No, I don't."

"You're Plain. You should be with your people."

Right again. *Please, please get to the point.* "Agreed."

"I'm just not sure that extends to our baby."

Our baby? He'd been at school, taking classes, drinking beer, eating pizza, and playing pool on the weekends while she worked in a hardware store to earn money, puked regularly, and lived with her cousin's family because she didn't want to shame her parents any more than she already had.

"What do you mean that it doesn't *extend* to *our baby*?" Maisy dove in headfirst. "You said you wanted to finish college and you weren't ready for fatherhood."

"But I will be. Eventually. My mom and my sister Hadley can take care of the baby until I'm ready. My mom raised decent kids. She can do it again. Hadley has two kids. She's planning on having a whole passel of them. What's one more?"

"I don't know your mother or your sister. I don't know your family. Only you. You and I broke up before we knew about the baby. We weren't even together anymore. We're not family. And you prove every day that having a family isn't a priority for you." Maisy managed not to sputter. With their love of baseball, her brothers would've called this another curveball in a series of pitches from Nate and his family. She kept swinging wildly and missing. "I want my bopli to grow up in an Amish family."

"Hadley and her husband breed, train, and board horses on their four-hundred-acre ranch west of Jamesport. The baby could split his time between there and my mom's." Nate seemed to take no notice of her words. "She'd get a great education. Plus it could be an open adoption. We'd send you pictures and send you emails—I mean, letters—telling you how she's doing. The important thing is she could be whoever or whatever she wants to be."

Amish children grew up around horses, pigs, cattle, goats, chickens, and all sorts of livestock. They grew up on farms, gardening, fishing, hunting, and swimming. "She could be everything except Amish."

"I know you folks don't believe in education, but our baby is half English." It sounded as if Nate had memorized his mother's spiel. He'd bought into it hook, line, and sinker. "Give that half a chance to be somebody."

Like the baby could be divided into equal halves. Her heritage would always be mixed. Maisy couldn't change that. Nate and his mother had good intentions. They wanted what they considered to be the best for this child. Not once had either of them mentioned religion. The most fundamental job a parent had was instilling a love of Jesus in their children.

"You say you're a backsliding Baptist, Nate. What about the rest of your family? Will they pray before meals? Will our baby pray before bed? Will you lead by example? Will our baby know Jesus and live by biblical laws?"

"My folks are good people. They go to church every Sunday. So does my sister and her husband. The baby will have good role models."

Everyone except Nate, who liked his beer and Saturday night at a sports bar. "That's not the same thing. It's not enough. Not nearly enough."

"I don't remember you being so stubborn." Nate's tone held irritation. "I'm trying to do the right thing here."

"I remember you saying it made sense for us to go our own ways." Maybe it was the hormones or maybe it was lack of sleep, but anger sank its fangs into Maisy more quickly these days. "I remember you wanting to *terminate* this baby. That was the word you used. *Terminate.*"

"I was in shock." Nate's voice rose. "I didn't mean it. You caught me by surprise. I helped you get to Kansas City, didn't I? I gave you money, didn't I?"

"Because you felt guilty."

"No, because you were my first crush. My mom called it puppy love. And because men are supposed to step up and do the right thing."

What he'd felt for her had been a teenage boy's crush. What he felt now was a sense of responsibility foisted on him by his mother. Not the foundation for a lifelong love.

"I'm thinking about what's best for our baby." Her baby needed Isaac and Vicky for parents. They would be good parents who would love, care for, and teach their child in the Plain ways. "That's an Amish couple."

"I guess we'll see about that." The anger was gone, replaced by a steely determination. "You do what you have to do and I'll do what I have to do."

"I made a commitment to a couple who don't have their own children. They're desperate for a baby." Maisy gathered all her strength, her longing, her certainty of the righteousness of such an adoption and poured it over her words. "Think how you'd feel if you were in their shoes and I came to you and said, 'Sorry, I changed my mind.' These folks can give my baby more than you can. All you can give him or her is your love. That's not enough."

"A baby should be with family whenever possible."

"So you plan to contest Vicky and Isaac's adoption? Even though you yourself won't be raising the baby?"

"I know you think I'm a spoiled, immature kid and mostly I am. But I'm not stupid. Also, I'm not heartless. Also, I care about you, in my own way."

"What are you trying to say?"

"I can't say, one way or another. I need time to think about this."

"I have to know what to tell Vicky and Isaac. I can't keep them hanging. They deserve to know so they can figure out other options too."

"Just don't do anything until you hear from me."

"I have to wait twelve hours after the baby's born. Then I sign the consent form."

"You'd do that to me?"

"I'm not doing anything to you. I'm doing it for our baby and for the Kings."

A pause followed that lasted so long it seemed as if Nate might have hung up. "Nate?"

"If you need anything, call me. My mom can wire you money."

An attempt to buy her or simply a kindness? Did he really think the baby could be bought? "Thank you but I'm fine for money. I have a good job at the hardware store. I'll deliver here with a midwife. The cost is small."

"My parents would pay for the hospital expenses if you let them raise the baby."

"No need for a healthy baby to be born in a hospital." Maisy hung on to her patience for dear life. "Most Amish babies are born at home."

"Okay. I gotta go. Take care of yourself, Daisy Maisy," he whispered, his voice deep and hoarse. "Call me if you need anything, anything at all."

Maisy closed her eyes and willed away sudden tears. "Thank you. I won't, but thank you."

A click and a dial tone. Maisy laid the phone in its cradle. She didn't move for a long time. Nothing had been decided.

Chapter 34

Joshua shot up from his bed. Noise. Thunder boomed overhead. Heart galloping in his chest, he threw his legs over the side of the bed. *Breathe. Breathe.* Lightning flashed through the second-floor bedroom's double windows. Rain pounded against the tin roof. Hail pinged. Panting as if he'd run an uphill race, Joshua stood and padded barefoot to the window he'd left open. A fierce north wind rattled the rafters. Rain sprayed his face. He wrangled the window down. Lightning crackled, bolt after bolt, creating wild designs across low-hanging clouds.

He closed his eyes. The images ran rampant. Rain, hail, lightning. Fire. Lightning had struck their house in Jamesport. What were the chances it would happen again ten years later? Astronomically slim. His father insisted it would never happen again. Not in a million years.

Somehow Joshua remained unconvinced. He rubbed his eyes and opened them. There would be no more sleep until the storm subsided.

He tromped from the room, headed for the stairs. A stop by his brothers' room revealed all three slept soundly, Michael in his single bed, Samuel and Christopher in their bunks. The girls were equally snug in their bedroom. It was good they didn't suffer from the same malady as he did. He closed the door and made his way down the stairs.

Maybe a glass of milk would help. Not that it had in the past.

A clanging brought him up short. He peeked into the kitchen. His dad, of course. Joshua ambled into the room and paused by the table. "You couldn't sleep either?"

"I was expecting you." Dad stood at the stove, stirring something in an old beat-up saucepan. He laid the wooden spoon aside and turned up the flame on the kerosene lamp. He moved it from the counter to the table. In the flickering light he looked wan and older than his years. "Cocoa?"

"Definitely. With extra marshmallows." Joshua went to the cupboards to dig out a bag of miniature marshmallows. Thunder boomed. He jumped in spite of himself. The bag fell on the floor. "This is a noisy one. I didn't know it was supposed to rain."

"When I was in the feedstore today the *weddermann* on the radio said there was a chance of a severe *schtarem* tonight. Even a tornado watch." Dad poured the cocoa into two oversized mugs. He met Joshua at the table. "We can always use the rain, but I could do without the high winds."

And the lightning.

Joshua dumped a handful of marshmallows in each mug and took his to the window over the sink. Lightning etched a jagged line across the sky, lighting glowering clouds. The sycamore tree's branches whipped in the wind. The trunk swayed. Any leaves left earlier in the day were now gone. "When the rain comes down this hard, it runs off before it has a chance to soak in."

"True."

Joshua sipped his cocoa. The hot liquid burned his tongue. He embraced the sudden pain. It grounded him in the here and now. This wasn't a rerun. He hadn't lived this night before.

"Have a seat, Suh."

"I don't see a bank of clouds on the horizon. I don't reckon a tornado is lurking out there."

"That's gut."

Tornados were commonplace in Kansas, part of the swath called Tornado Alley that blew through Oklahoma as well. Most kids grew up with some experience being awakened by their parents in the middle of the night to trudge down basement stairs and spend a few hours playing card games and listening to the wind howl. Most saw it as a fun game. Unless they'd actually been hit by a tornado and lost everything. "Were you expecting a bad storm that night?"

"Nee. The weddermann said we'd have a schtarem, but no one expected it would be that bad." His father didn't pretend not to know what Joshua was talking about. "I didn't even wake up until Peter ran into the room yelling about smoke and fire."

Neither had Joshua. He and Jacob shared a bedroom with Peter in those days. His older brother rousted them from bed only minutes after the fire started, but it had already engulfed the kitchen. Joshua turned around and leaned against the counter. "It seems like a bad dream."

"If only it were just a dream."

"I don't mean to bring up bad memories."

"Your mudder told me about the talk you had." The lamp's light deepened the harsh sun lines around Dad's mouth and eyes. "Not everyone grieves in the same way, Suh."

"I know. I spoke out of frustration. I have no one to blame for the way I am but me."

"Have a seat." Dad motioned toward the chair across from him. "What way is that?"

"Bryan calls it stuck." Joshua trudged to the table and sat. "I think it's more like walled off."

"So walled off you can't see your way to be baptized?"

"I'm not doing it to cause you pain or to shame you and Mudder."

"There's no shame in making sure you're doing what's right for you." Dad rubbed already red eyes. "But a time comes when a man has to fish or cut bait."

"And you think that time has come for me?"

"It's not for me to say."

A person had to commit to the faith of his own free will. "I'm trying."

"I know. Your mudder told me about the horse training. That's a gut start, right there."

"Nothing has happened yet, but at least the door is open. It's up to me to go through it."

"I'm glad you see that."

Jacob would've wanted that. He would've wanted Joshua to have a life full enough for both of them. To not have a wife and children because Jacob hadn't been given that opportunity made no sense in the eternal scheme of things. Jacob would've told his twin brother to get over and get on with it.

Hail battered the house. Rain poured in sheets down the kitchen windows. The wind rattled the shutters so hard Joshua had to raise his voice to be heard. His hands tightened around the mug. He forced them to relax. "Did Mudder tell you about the other thing too?"

"About the girl?"

Girl. Woman. Maisy. She'd been absent from the hardware store for almost a week. Harvey said she'd been under the weather with a cold. Nothing to worry about. Worrying was a sin. That didn't mean he didn't. She was avoiding him. He'd scared her away with his declaration. He who never talked too much had babbled his way out of her life.

"Jah."

"One step at a time." His father's expression was hidden in the shadows, but his tone was soft. "Otherwise it might be one step forward and two steps back."

"But you don't see her situation as a reason to step back?"

"I can't see the splinter in her eye, what with the plank in mine."

The time Father spent reading his Bible always held him in good stead. He set a good example. One Joshua kept meaning to follow. "Others might not agree."

"Others should keep their noses in their own houses until they can find tweezers big enough to pluck that plank out of their eyes." His father had a way with words. He would've made a good bishop, had the lot fallen to him. "All have sinned and fallen short."

Agreed. "Do you ever wonder how things would've been different if Jacob had lived?"

"There's no sense in wasting time on such thoughts."

Common sense, but that didn't keep the thoughts from wandering through Joshua's brain until they knocked on the door and woke him at four in the morning. "I can't help it. I wish I could."

"You're not the only one. I just hide it better." Father went to the cabinet and came back with a plate filled with three different kinds of cookies. This would be that kind of conversation. "I reckon we'd still live in Jamesport. You'd be married by now. So would Jacob. You'd be a different person. Maybe not as thoughtful, not as quiet. Maybe you'd be the one quick to put a string of words together."

"Maybe."

"Maybe that didn't happen because Gott's plan was for you to be here now in this place." His father set the plate between them. He grabbed one of each kind and settled back into his chair. "You, me, your mudder, Peter, all the kinner. Gott's never wrong. His plan never fails. If we muck it up, He finds another way."

Maybe Joshua was here in this place now because Maisy needed him.

Father's soft chuckle floated in the air. "Even in the dark I can see the wheels turning. Go easy. One step at a time."

One step at a time. Starting with baptism classes. Joshua ate his share of the cookies without further comment. He finished his cocoa.

"More?"

"Nee. I'm going back to bed."

"Gut for you."

Joshua washed his mug and set it in the drain. The drenching rain hadn't slowed. Lightning revealed a stream of water rushing through the backyard where none had been before. "Unless you'd rather have company."

"Nee. I'm gut. I never feel alone."

"You feel him too?"

"I do. Sometimes I hear him laugh that crazy laugh like he's figured out that the joke's on him and he doesn't mind." Father sighed. "Sometimes I hear him whisper that dog's name, like he's still searching for her."

Buttercup. She'd lived to the ripe, old age of seventeen. Her puppies lived on with other families. Life went on.

"Gut nacht."

"See you in the morning."

God willing.

Chapter 35

THE LATE-NOVEMBER SUN SHONE SO BRIGHTLY Maisy had to raise her hand to her forehead to shade her eyes. The previous night's storm had inflicted most of its damage on the Kings' barn. Shingles, tree branches, and leaves decorated Isaac and Vicky's front porch. The potted pink and purple bougainvillea lay on its side, dirt scattered around it. Maisy shoved the dirt back into the pot and set it upright. She brushed her hands together and straightened. Storms like this so late in the season were unusual. Before long snow would replace the rain. Winter would come and then spring.

With spring, the baby would arrive. So far and yet so near. And Maisy would have to deal with Joshua's declaration. His offering was like a gift she was afraid to open. Afraid she wouldn't be worthy of it. Afraid it would disappear like an early morning fog banished by the sun.

"You're here."

Maisy jumped despite herself. Vicky stood at the screen door. Maisy put her hand to her chest and heaved a breath. "I am."

"I was going to wipe down the chairs and clean up the porch. The storm made a mess out here." A towel in one hand, Vicky pushed through the screen door. "I wasn't expecting you until next week for the painting frolic."

They'd decided to repaint the bedrooms and replace the curtains in the house Isaac had inherited from his grandparents the year before he and Vicky had married. The house only had three bedrooms—small for a Plain family. So far the Kings hadn't needed more than one. They wanted to get it done now that Thanksgiving was over and before the Christmas holiday rolled around.

"We need to talk."

Vicky flinched. She sighed. "I pray every day for the strength to face whatever comes next. Nothing has been easy so far. I don't expect that to change now, I suppose."

"You are one of the strongest people I've ever met." *Gott, hold her up through this and every blow to come.* "I'm so sorry it hasn't been easy, that it isn't getting easier."

"Let's go inside. I'll make some tea."

Maisy followed her into the kitchen. The aromas of sausage and fried eggs still lingered in the air. Maisy's old friend nausea reared his ugly head. She took a seat while Vicky flitted about making tea and cutting pieces of pumpkin pie she brought to the table without a word.

When she finally sat across from Maisy, her face had blanched white with rosy spots on her cheeks. "Sei so gut, say what you have to say. You've changed your mind."

"Nee. Not me." Maisy swallowed the bitter pill of being forced into a corner by someone else's expectations and perceptions. It was unfair to her and to the Kings. Not that any of them expected life to be fair. *"In this life there will be trouble. . . ."* "I thought this decision would be mine and mine alone. I'd been led to believe that by my bopli's father."

Vicky's hand went to her mouth. She made a choked sound.

Maisy plowed forward with a description of Sue Ellen's visit followed by Maisy's phone conversations with Nate. "Nate has no legal right to this bopli unless he files paternity paperwork. So far he hasn't done that. He has until I sign the adoption consent form twelve hours after the bopli is born."

Tears welled in Vicky's eyes. She brushed them away with her fingertips. "Did he say which way he was leaning?"

"Nee. He knows I strongly object to my—to this—bopli being raised Englisch. But like so many people, he thinks money and material things will give her a better life than what she would have in a family of strong faith and community. It's a hard thing to fight."

"How can he expect you and us to live like this, not knowing until the last minute?" Vicky laid pieces of pie on saucers. She handed one to Maisy, along with a fork. From her expression she had no idea that she'd done it. "I know I have to be strong. I know it's in Gott's hands, but I sometimes wonder how much more I can take."

"I know. I'm sorry. It's my fault. I should've talked to him first before I approached you."

"Nee. He told you he wanted nothing more to do with the bopli. You couldn't know he would change his mind."

Maisy stirred honey into her tea. If only there were a way to sweeten this news. "I don't want to give you false hope, but at the same time, I feel in my heart he won't come through. Nate is a spoiled boy who still has so much growing up to do. He's not like a Plain man. He hasn't been brought up to be a worker and provider."

"That could be exactly why he decides he wants the bopli." Vicky dropped her napkin over her untouched pie. "He'll be selfish. He'll want the bopli because it's his."

"Maybe."

"I find myself examining my life from every which way, squinting, trying to figure out how I'm supposed to stand up to these blows that keep coming. It's so wrong, but I can't help it when I say why me. Who am I to question?"

"It's human nature. You're not responsible for the tribulations you face. Mine are self-inflicted. I don't dare whine about it."

Yet she did. All too often. Now her troubles had spilled onto this innocent couple. "I'm so sorry for making your situation harder."

"You were trying to help. I thank you for that. We won't give up. We'll pray for Gott's will in our lives and in yours."

"What's going on?" Isaac strode into the kitchen. His shirt was sweat stained and his hands dirty. "I saw the buggy in the yard."

"Want some lemonade?" Vicky popped up and scurried to the counter. "Wash your hands and I'll get you a piece of pie."

"What's going on?" Isaac's gaze stayed on Maisy as he crossed to the sink. "Is everything all right with the bopli?"

It would be cowardly to let Vicky carry the burden of explaining Maisy's visit. "I needed to tell you both about a visit I received from the bopli's groosmammi and the phone calls with his biological daed."

Isaac's eyes went flat. He turned his back, washed his hands, and then moved to the table. "So tell me."

Maisy repeated her conversation with Vicky. Isaac's index finger tapped on the pine table. One leg jiggled. His boot thumped the floor.

"I'm sorry to introduce more uncertainty in your lives, but I wanted you to be prepared for the possibility that Nate could interfere in our arrangement."

Isaac waited until Vicky set the lemonade in front of him. He took a long draught. "We'll pray for Gott's will." He clamped his mouth shut in a grimace, stood, and walked out the back door.

"I'm truly sorry," Maisy whispered, but he was already gone. "So sorry."

"He always goes to the barn when his emotions become too much." Vicky picked up his glass. She paused in the middle of the kitchen, cradling it. "He'll come back later and we'll talk. We'll be fine."

"If I hear anything from Nate, I'll let you know." Maisy went to the sink and set her glass on the counter. She gently removed Isaac's glass from Vicky's hands. "Let me."

Vicky drew back. Maisy followed her gaze through the window over the sink. Dresses in teals, lilacs, and purples flapped on the clothesline. Sun-dappled leaves dropped from the tree branches. Such an idyllic scene with no thought for the turmoil within the house. "Do you think he has enough wherewithal to realize the agony he's putting you and others through?"

"Nee. I don't."

"It must be nice to go through life as the center of your world."

"I ask myself what I was thinking. How could my heart have led me so far astray with a man so lacking in Plain values?" Shame stung Maisy like so many wasp stings. "How could that only have been six months ago? How could we conceive a child under these circumstances when you and Isaac can't?"

"A boatload of questions." Vicky laughed softly but without sarcasm. "I'm afraid it wasn't your heart that led you astray."

The truth still cut deeply, however gently delivered. Maisy brushed her hands across her burgeoning belly. "I just want to make sure this bopli isn't punished for my sin. I can take my punishment. He deserves none."

Vicky picked up the washrag and wiped down the counter, even though it was spotless. "Be sure if Isaac and I are blessed to take in this bopli, you will never have to worry about him. He will have two parents who love him enough to punish him only when he deserves it and with punishment suited to the crime."

A spotlight fell on the years to come. A little boy standing before Vicky, head bent, hands behind his back, lower lip protruding. Yes, he swiped the cookies from the cooling racks. Yes, he knew better than to eat cookies right before supper. Vicky, hiding a smile, would admonish him soundly and let him know he wouldn't have dessert after supper.

"I know you will," Maisy said.

"I can see it."

"So can I."

Gott, let Nate see it too.

Chapter 36

THE DAYS PASSED QUICKLY AS THE Christmas holiday approached. Despite being busy with customers, Maisy still made time for lunch every day. She needed to rest her feet and her aching back while feeding a suddenly voracious appetite. Joshua still managed to pop in and join her, even though business at the furniture store was steadily increasing. Neither of them brought up Joshua's declaration. In the weeks since that fateful conversation, they'd reverted to carefully skirting potentially explosive topics. The weather, the Plank children's antics, stories about crazy customers, simple prattle filled their lunch hours.

Maisy kept her questions to herself. Did she stay here and go to baptism classes with him? Did she go home, back to the life she'd once had? Once that hope had been the bright light she followed to keep from falling into a dark pit. Now the bright light shone in Haven.

The Christmas season brought an even bigger glut of customers to downtown Yoder. The bigger Maisy's belly grew, the slower she moved, making it hard to keep up with the folks shopping for inflatable Santas, artificial Christmas trees, strings of twinkling lights, and nativity scenes. Her back ached, her feet hurt, and sleep was interrupted by frequent trips to the bathroom. Fewer of those trips involved leaning over the toilet to vomit, so that was a blessing.

Working in the store was also a blessing. Everyone had the Christmas spirit. Being busy proved to be a blessing. No thinking about Nate's decision. No imagining what life would be like after the baby's birth.

For all her intentions to avoid entanglements with men such as the one that led to her downfall, here she stood, her feelings wrapped up tight with a man named Joshua. Except Joshua was no English man. He was no teenager. He wanted a life she recognized. Wife, children, a home made together, a life faced together.

That his dream included her seemed like a child's fairy tale. *Tell me, Gott, can something so good come of something so terribly wrong?*

No answer. Instead she concentrated on her work. Christmas Eve fell on a Friday so Harvey had decided to close early and remain closed until Monday. Since Maisy was off on Mondays she had a lovely gift of three and a half days off. Her back, ankles, and feet thanked Harvey.

Humming "Hark! The Herald Angels Sing," Maisy removed Christmas decorations from the shelves in preparation for setting up a snow-removal display. The tiny bell over the front door dinged, which was a surprise. They'd had a dearth of customers on this Christmas Eve morning. They were either home with family or doing last-minute gift shopping in Hutchinson.

"It's me." Joshua stamped snow from his boots while unwinding a black knitted scarf around his neck. His cheeks were ruddy with cold. He held a box wrapped in plain brown paper tucked under his arm. "I think the temperature has dropped ten degrees in the last two hours."

"It's nice that we're having a white Christmas, though." With a deep breath in and out, Maisy traipsed to the front of the store. "Has it been quiet at your place? We've had crickets here."

"Nee, we've had a steady stream of customers who waited until the last minute to buy gifts—lots of quilts especially. Funny how manns don't mind the price tag when they're down to the wire and desperate."

"Is Caleb closing early?"

"Jah, in fact he's shutting down now." Joshua's gaze bounced to the floor. He shifted the package from one arm to the other. "I'm heading home. We have family coming from La Plata. That's why I wanted to stop by now." He paused. His shoulders hunched. "I have a present for you."

A present. Maisy's hand went to her throat. Sudden emotion surged—it felt like happiness or a flicker of joy, the joy that had been missing for the last several months. *Perfect. Danki, Gott.* Now she could give him the gift she'd picked out for him without that persistent voice in her right ear telling her it was a mistake. A person should reciprocate when receiving a Christmas gift.

"You didn't need to do that. It's sweet of you." And it made her decision to get him a gift acceptable. A lovely giddiness enveloped her. *It's just the season. That's all.* "I do love presents, though."

He held out the box. "You've had a lot on your plate these many months. I saw it and thought of you."

Maisy accepted Joshua's gift. It was heavy. Weighty physically. But light compared to the emotion that fell over her shoulders. Was there meaning behind a gift from a Plain man to a Plain woman carrying an English man's baby? What was the etiquette for such a situation?

"Don't overthink it." Joshua smiled. He had a beautiful smile, more precious because he only bestowed it on those he cared for. "Just say danki and open it."

"Open it now?"

"Naturally."

"Wait. I mean, come over to the counter." She trudged to the gate and let herself in. Joshua's gift lay safely stowed on one of the shelves below. She deposited the one he'd given her on the counter and set his next to it.

He shrugged off his coat and handed it and the scarf to her so she could hang it on the coatrack. "What's this?"

"A little something for you from me."

His aw-shucks grin surely matched Maisy's. "You should know I love presents too."

"I do know."

"How?"

"Hannah brought Rachel and Michael into the store last week." Maisy couldn't contain a burble of laughter. "I might have been eavesdropping on their conversation."

"So what did they get me?"

"Ha, like I'd tell you that."

"Fine, so open my gift."

"Me first?"

"Jah."

All thumbs, she ripped off the paper. When the nature of the gift became apparent, Maisy laughed. "A dictionary!" Not just any dictionary, a hardback *Merriam-Webster Unabridged Dictionary*. No wonder the package was so heavy. "Oh, Joshua, danki."

"I see how happy words make you." Joshua shrugged, his tone diffident. His wonder at her fascination with words showed in his wrinkled brow. "You could use some happiness."

"It's very thoughtful." It boggled her mind that he had given so much thought to her happiness. "I know you don't understand."

"I don't have to understand. It's not about me; it's about you."

"How did you get so wise?"

"Practice." He grinned. He was a handsome man who tucked away his tenderness, so it only peeked out now and then.

Maisy smoothed her hands over the shiny cover. The pages called to her. She opened to the Bs. *Bodacious: audacious in a way considered admirable, or impressive. Excellent, admirable or attractive.* Joshua could be considered bodacious. A wave of heat started at her toes and rushed through her body, ending its trek by toasting her cheeks. She swallowed back a nervous giggle.

"Now you."

"You didn't need to get me anything. That smile is all the gift I needed."

"You're sweet. Open it."

He took as little time with the brown wrapping as she had. The shiny new toolbox gleamed in his hands. "How did you know?"

"Rachel and Michael were debating over this or one or two other things. When they settled on the third item, I decided on the toolbox."

"I can't wait to see what those two landed on. Put them together and they're a little narrisch." His grin broadened even though it was obvious he was trying to hide his pleasure. "I should get going. My mudder is baking four kinds of cookies, a raisin cream pie, and a chocolate cake. I'm expected to sample them all."

Maisy followed him to the door. He paused, hand on the door. "Merry Christmas, Maisy."

"Merry Christmas." More words wanted to come out. The one time when she really needed some of those highfalutin words, they failed her. "Are you working after Christmas?"

In other words would she see him before the New Year?

"Caleb is closing the store until after New Year's Day."

So no. "Then I guess I should say *Froh Neiyaahr* too."

"Froh Neiyaahr." His gaze enveloped her. He nodded. "I'm hoping it'll be a gut year for you and for me."

He'd given her another present. The gift of hope. That life might go on. "Me too."

"See you next year."

"See you next year."

That's a promise.

Chaptewr 37

"MA'AM, YOU'RE DRIPPING."

It took a few seconds for Maisy to get past the young customer's use of the word *"ma'am"* when referring to her moments after explaining his dad had sent him to buy something called polyurethane varnish, but he didn't know if it should be matte, glossy, or satin. Belatedly she followed his gaze directed toward the floor around her feet.

A small pool of water ponded around her sneakers. Her baby wasn't due for two weeks. Two long weeks. The new year had started off frigid. February served up more of the same with none of the signs of spring that came with March. The bigger she grew, the more slowly the weeks had passed. Caught in limbo waiting to hear from Nate hadn't helped. Vicky and Isaac had withdrawn from her—rightly so. Only Joshua's determined visits helped pass the time. It seemed this baby would never come. Until this moment when she might decide to come early.

I'm not ready, Gott.

How quickly the tide turned. Maybe it was simply her leaky bladder. The more the baby grew, the more that happened. Kate had deemed painful cramps the previous week as something called Braxton Hicks contractions, also known as false labor.

"Ma'am?" The boy's face flushed with embarrassment. "Aren't you gonna do something?"

Like get a mop? "Ach. Umm. I . . . I . . . let me get Harvey to help you."

Maisy gingerly skirted the puddle of clear liquid. A few drops darkened the hem of her dress. No smell of pee hung in the air—thank goodness. The moment held enough embarrassment for both of them. The customer looked like a college kid out of his league in a hardware store with a woman who knew more about finishes than he did.

Harvey, who labored over invoices in his office, grunted when she knocked on the door. "Come."

"I have a situation."

He scooted away from his computer and faced her. "What's up? An unruly customer who thinks we charge too much for pipe insulation? It's a little late for insulating pipes."

"No." Maisy shifted her feet and put both hands on her belly. The baby had definitely reached pumpkin stage. Watermelon would be more accurate. "I've had a little accident." Heat curled around her face and neck. "I think maybe my water broke."

Harvey stood so fast his chair flew back and hit the bookshelves behind him. His grand-champion catfish-tournament trophy toppled over. "Why didn't you say so, missy? Are you having contractions?"

"Just little ones."

"How far apart?"

"I don't know." After thirty-eight weeks, a person would think she'd be more prepared. After all this time, it still didn't feel real. A twinge hard enough to take her breath away rocked Maisy's stomach. Okay, a little real. "Not regularly."

"It's snowing or haven't you noticed? We're supposed to get seven to ten inches today." Harvey grabbed the phone. "I'll call Caleb and have him send Joshua over here. He can take you to the clinic."

Sudden anxiety riddled Maisy's body with tinny-tasting adrenaline. "No, thanks. I'm going home. Kate is delivering the baby at Amos and Ruth's house."

"Do you have corncobs in your ears, girl?" Harvey tapped in a number on his landline. "It's snowing and the wind is blowing. It'll take two hours to get to the farm. You'll freeze your heinie and maybe the baby's too."

While Harvey talked to Caleb in a staccato that bordered on shouting orders, Maisy trudged to the office's only window. She couldn't see the loading dock or the cars in the parking lot for the blowing snow. This baby insisted on forging its own path, from beginning to end.

Harvey hung up the phone. "Joshua is calling Doreen to take you to the clinic. You should call them to tell them you're coming." He retrieved the receiver and handed it over. "Who knows how many ladies they have in the house this morning. Babies always come at the most inconvenient times."

The hardware store owner had four of his own. He knew what he was talking about.

At the clinic Candy answered with the usual perky lilt in her voice. "Maisy, yay! It's good to hear your sweet voice. Will you be visiting us soon?"

Maisy explained her situation.

"Come on down. We have a full house today, but the entire staff is on hand." Candy's cheerful voice boomed over the line. "The two babies born overnight will go home soon, and the one in delivery now is expected any moment. So don't fret! We'll get you checked out."

When Candy finally stopped for air, Maisy expressed her thanks and hung up. What about Isaac and Vicky? Should she call them? What about Nathan? He hadn't called to ease her mind about his decision. What if this was another false alarm? Betsy could call Isaac from the clinic. Nathan would have to wait until Maisy knew for sure.

"Maisy? Maisy!" Joshua's voice boomed from the front of the store. Everyone was in a tizzy.

"Coming."

Harvey trod so close behind Maisy he stepped on the back of her sneaker. "Sorry, sorry!"

Maisy picked up her pace.

Harvey charged past her and swung the gate open. "Call me or have Candy call me when you know something."

"Someone will. Don't forget about the customer."

"Yeah, yeah, the customer. Don't you fret."

"And I'm sorry, but there's a little cleanup on aisle 2."

"No worries." Harvey grabbed her coat from the rack and thrust it at Joshua. "Is Doreen out front?"

"On her way."

His expression tender, Joshua helped Maisy into her coat and wrapped her scarf around her neck with a gentle touch. His expression said too much. It spoke of a caring she didn't deserve—not from him. If she'd followed God's Word the father of her child would be tugging the scarf up around her chin with shaking hands and a face full of shared excitement, wonder, and anxiety. All the same Joshua's touch brought a wave of comfort, just as his steady presence had throughout the new year. He never said much. He simply made himself present. For lunches. For visits to the clinic. He'd bring her snacks because he was certain she wasn't eating enough. With every move, he showed Maisy she could count on him.

Even when she didn't deserve such care. "Danki." She managed to thank him as if his ministrations were the most normal thing about this day. What else could she say? "You don't have to go with me. I can make it on my own."

"You're not going alone." The tenderness faded into uncertainty. Joshua put his hand on the door lever. "Unless you don't want me to go—"

"Nee, I don't want you to feel obligated—"

"Enough pussyfooting around." Harvey flapped his arms. "Go. Go. You can play games later."

With Joshua in the lead, Maisy stepped into a sparkly winter world. Wind sent icy snowflakes spiraling into her wool bonnet, cheeks, and eyelashes. Frigid air chilled her face and hands. The van wasn't much warmer.

"Sorry, guys, my heater chose today to go on the fritz." Doreen rubbed fat woolen mittens together. "I have a thermos of cocoa if anyone's interested."

Maisy was too busy breathing through a contraction to respond. Doreen didn't seem to mind. Ten minutes later they were at the clinic. A nurse Maisy hadn't met before held the door open for them. "Let's get you into an exam room."

"I'll wait here." Joshua hung back. "Let me know if I should tell Doreen to go home or stay."

"Oh, the daddy comes in too." The nurse waved him back. "Don't be shy. You don't want to miss the big day."

"I'm not the father."

"He's not the father."

They spoke in unison.

Instead she would travel these last few yards of the journey on her own. No Kate. No Ruth. No Vicky. Heaving a breath, she climbed up on the exam table and lay back. She'd come this far with their help. With Joshua's help. With Harvey's help. With Ruth and Kate. They might not be in the room now, but they'd each done their parts. Even Amos had helped—however crotchety he might be.

Maisy stared at the ceiling and counted blessings to the tune of the *whoosh, whoosh* of the baby's heartbeat telling her he was ready for this world, come what may.

"Yes, my dear, you are four centimeters effaced. You're on your way." The nurse patted her knee with one gloved hand. "Did Kate explain to you what that means?"

"Yes."

"You're having a baby today—or maybe tonight—depending on how long he decides to take to grace us with his presence." She peeled off her gloves and stood. "Go ahead and hop down. You can change into something more comfy if you want. There are paper undies in the drawer if you want to change into something dry."

Maisy had nothing comfy in which to change. Her loose dress would have to do. She followed the nurse into the rose birthing room. Even with the wintery weather outside, the room felt like spring with the flowered quilt and bright-white walls.

"Betsy is finishing up catching a baby. She should be with you in a bit. I'll let your friend know you'll be staying."

Maisy gripped the back of an overstuffed chair. "Could you . . . Would it be all right if he comes back?"

"Absolutely. I'll rope him and wrangle him if I have to."

That image stayed with Maisy until Joshua stepped into the room. The petrified look of a coyote with his tail caught in a trap warned her. "It's okay. There's nothing going on you shouldn't see."

"Gut. Warn me when I need to duck and run."

His rueful grin eased Maisy's grip on the chair. She settled into it.

Joshua edged closer. His boots actually crossed the door's threshold. "The nurse said the bopli will be born today."

"It feels like it to me too."

"Are you scared?"

"Jah." Being able to speak the truth to Joshua at a time like this was another gift. Maisy swallowed hard. She could do this. She would do this for her baby and for the Kings. "But that's okay. The bopli will be here before I know it. This'll be a special day for Vicky and Isaac."

"Did you call the bopli's father?"

"Not yet." She studied her hands. They were swollen from the baby and chapped raw from the cold and washing dishes. A contraction ripped through her belly. She leaned forward, hands on her belly, fighting to breathe through it. "Ach."

Joshua took a step back. "Should I get the nurse?"

"Nee. There's a long way to go. That's why I haven't called Nate." *Breathe in. Breathe out.* Part of the reason. Less time for him to contemplate his decision. Less time to act on it. That wasn't fair to him or to the baby. "I should, though."

"What about Isaac and Vicky?"

"It's too soon. I need to know Nate's decision before I bring them down here. It would be a horrible thing to do to them if he decides to stand in our way."

Joshua sank into the other easy chair. "It's better to know than not know, I reckon. Although that's easy for me to say." His expression pained, he stumbled over the words. "I'm not the one trying to figure this all out in the middle of such a mess."

"It's kind of you not to add *of your own making.*"

He shook his head. "No need to rub your nose in it."

"Danki. I should call Nate."

"I'll leave then."

"Sei so gut, don't."

"Are you sure?"

She nodded as she picked up the receiver on the phone sitting on the side table next to the bed. Nate picked up on the first ring.

Or someone did. Titters rang over the line. A girl said something. Another voice responded with a booming laugh.

"Nate?"

"Yeah, yeah. Sorry, these yokels grabbed my phone. I had to fight them for it." More noise and laughter. Nate told them to cut it out, but it didn't sound like he really meant it. "What's up?"

What's up? Maisy breathed through another contraction. Timing was everything.

"Speak up, Maisy. I can't hear you."

"The baby is coming."

"Today?" Nate's voice squeaked. "You're not due for another two weeks."

"It happens."

"I know. I know. I thought I had more time to call you."

"Have you made a decision?"

"Here's the thing." A pause. A door slammed. The noise died away. Had he resorted to the closet again? "The thing is, I met someone."

Met someone? How did that translate? Maisy met people every day. Mostly at the hardware store. "And?"

"We're in love. You'd like Sissy. She's sweet and kind and she's studying veterinary medicine—which would be good for the dairy farm and the horse farm—"

"Nate."

"Yeah, sorry, I'm just nervous. We've been dating for two months, and it was love at first sight."

"What does that have to do with the baby?"

Our baby. The baby his family wanted to adopt.

"Sissy doesn't know about you and me and the baby. I couldn't start out with a big reveal like that. I just couldn't see springing that on her later either. Like, by the way, I have this baby my mom is raising for me or my sister adopted. That could definitely put a chill on things."

The faster he talked, the deeper he dug the hole.

"You're saying you're not going to be the baby's father?"

"That's what I'm saying. I'm sorry, but I can't."

They'd come full circle. To that first day in the pasture, the truck headlights illuminating the ground between the rock and the hard place where they found themselves.

Another contraction hit, this one stronger. She put her hand to her mouth to stifle the groan.

His face worried, Joshua loomed over her. "Should I get the nurse?"

She shook her head.

"What is he saying?"

She shrugged and put her hand over the receiver. "Could you get Betsy? I need to call Isaac."

The worried look fell away. "That's gut, isn't it?"

"Very gut."

Joshua spun around and left the room.

"Maisy, are you all right?" Nate's voice rose. "I'm so, so sorry. I know we made a big deal—"

"Are your mother and Hadley okay with this?"

"Not really. But I told them to respect my wishes. I put my foot down and my dad backed me up. The last thing he wants is a rug rat in the house when they're approaching retirement. Not that he'll—"

"It's fine, Nate. It's a relief. You don't have to worry about it."

"You'll give the baby to that Amish couple then?"

"Yes. It's a gift. It's the right thing to do."

Even if her heart tied itself in painful knots every time she imagined leaving this room without the baby she'd carried in her womb for thirty-eight weeks. "Have a good life. Good-bye."

"Wait, wait." Nate turned up the volume on his voice.

Maisy jerked the receiver from her ear. "At least send me a text—I know, I know, send me a letter, tell me if it's a boy or a girl. And its name."

He was trying so hard to erase this chapter from his life. Wouldn't a picture and a name make it harder? "I can ask the nurse to text you."

"Thanks. I hope the delivery goes smooth."

"Good-bye, Nate."

"Bye, Maisy."

That part of her life was over forever. Now she simply had to figure out what came next.

Chapter 38

THE RIPTIDE OF EMOTIONS SWEPT MAISY back and forth, up and down, wave upon wave. She settled the phone receiver onto the base, but she couldn't seem to take her hand away from it. Nate could close the door and move on, but Maisy wasn't an English teenage boy. Life would go on, but the lessons learned, the scars borne, the losses would remain.

This time the contraction came on slowly, built, built, and built until she gasped. Her lungs didn't want to cooperate. *Breathe. Breathe. Breathe.*

"How are we doing?"

Betsy's chipper voice forced Maisy to tear her gaze from her own belly. "That was a big one."

"How often are they coming?"

"I don't know. I was talking to the baby's father."

"Joshua told me. He's out?"

"He has a girlfriend."

"Isaac and Vicky will be wonderful parents. Your baby will be in good hands. Do you want to call them, or do you want me to do it?"

"I'll do it." They would be so excited. People happy about this birth would make it easier. Vicky could sit with Maisy. They could talk. "It may be a while before they check the answering machine, though."

"That and the roads are bad. I don't think the county can even get out there and clear the roads or salt them."

The machine picked up. They didn't expect a call for another two weeks—if at all. Maisy summoned all her strength to keep her voice from quivering. "It's time. The bopli—your bopli—is coming. I'll tell you all about it when you get here. Please come to the birthing center when you get this message. Or as soon as you can."

She swallowed a half sob and hung up.

"You're doing great, Maisy."

"It doesn't feel like it."

"I've been delivering babies for a while. It's a hard, hard thing you're doing. You have a right to your feelings. You'll feel better if you talk about them. If not to me, then to Kate or Ruth."

"I'm fine. I'll be fine. I just want this bopli to be healthy and happy."

"Absolutely. Let's have a peek then."

The exam was mercifully quick. "Still four centimeters. No rush for the expecting parents to arrive." Betsy stood, yawned, and stretched, her long arms high over her head. Dark circles ringed her eyes. "You can take a nap—which is what I'd like to be doing about now—or visit the kitchen for a snack. Walk the halls. Take a bath. The more you move around, though, the better."

Definitely not a bath. And sleep was out of the question.

"Or I could send Joshua back. He seems very concerned about you."

Maisy contemplated the birthing room made up to mimic a comfy bedroom. This really wasn't the appropriate place for Joshua and her to meet. "The kitchen would be better."

"You got it. Help yourself to the snacks. Drink whatever sounds good. I have to go check on the newest resident of Haven, Kansas, one Todd Eugene Carmichael. I'll swing back by later. But don't hesitate to let one of the nurses know if you need something."

Pain radiated up and down Maisy's spine. Her lower back ached. She rose, hand on her hip, and hobbled into the hallway. Despite the intense pressure on her bladder, walking did feel better. She hiked up and down the hallway a few times. Joshua watched her progress from the kitchen doorway.

"You're working up a sweat? Or working off anger?"

"Nee, not anger. I'm relieved." For the baby's sake. To begrudge Nate his new start was selfish. Especially when it meant he wouldn't stand in the way of the adoption. She did an about-face and started back toward Joshua. "Adoption is what's best for the bopli."

No matter how hard it was for her.

"You'll get through it."

Joshua sounded so certain of that. The desire to pour out her regret and confusion flooded Maisy. She swallowed it back. "Do you want some tea?"

"Let me make it." Joshua moved ahead into the kitchen. "Chamomile or apple-cinnamon spice?"

"Apple-cinnamon spice." She perched on the edge of a kitchen table chair, hands on her knees. *Breathe. Breathe. Breathe.* The contraction passed. "I can get it."

"So can I."

"You don't have to stay. You shouldn't have to do this."

"Do you want me to go?"

"Nee."

"Then hush up and drink your tea."

So she did. Being with someone who saw no need to fill the silence with small talk was a boon. After months of waiting, the time had come. Maisy's hands encompassed her swollen belly. She would hold this baby in her arms for a fleeting moment.

Forgive me, Bopli. Sei so gut, forgive me.

"What are you thinking about?" Joshua's voice was painfully gentle. "Where are you?"

"I'm trying to imagine what I'll do next. The last eight-and-a-half months have been about this bopli. He has filled up every inch of the space inside me and out. Then it'll be over. I'll leave here . . . empty-handed. Alone."

"Maybe you'll leave this building empty-handed." Joshua's voice trailed away. His gaze on his mug, he stirred the tea needlessly. "But you're not alone."

The naked entreaty in his voice coupled with the undisguised longing on his face spoke the words he couldn't. Joshua had tried once before to draw Maisy into something more than a friendship. "Ach, Joshua. How can you want more for me when I sit here in front of you with my fehla so obvious?"

"All have sinned—"

"I know. Everyone keeps saying that. But you're asking me to be more than a friend. You want a fraa. A woman who will be the mudder of your kinner." Maisy breathed through pain that had nothing to do with her labor. "You've never asked me about how I arrived at this predicament."

"I don't need a play by play."

"I took my rumspringa too far. I knew I wanted to be baptized, but I wanted a taste of freedom first." Maisy smoothed her wrinkled apron to no avail. Nothing could take away its wrinkles or her sinful stains. "I took more than a taste. I drank freely from the well. Nate didn't have to convince me. He can't be blamed."

"I don't need to know." Joshua's Adam's apple bobbed. The muscle in his jaw twitched. "You've sought forgiveness and received it."

"I gave myself to another man." Maisy forced the words out in a hoarse whisper she barely recognized as her own. "My deepest regret is that I didn't wait. People who love each other deserve the first kiss, the first embrace, the first gift of love. I can't give you that."

Joshua stared at the table as if mesmerized. "Did you love him?"

"I thought I did. I told myself I did. He said he loved me, but in the end, I knew it wasn't love. So did he."

"I don't care." He raised his head. His gaze met hers. "That's not right. I do care. But I would be the first to truly love you. I can show you the difference."

"I'm here having another man's bopli." Maisy drew a long, shuddering breath. "I'm giving my bopli away. I think I can only handle so much today."

Joshua pulled his chair closer. He ducked his head for a second, then looked her in the eye. "Is it okay if I hold your hand?"

Maisy nodded. She didn't deserve his care, which made it so much more precious.

He took her hand in his. "We will talk about us again. Right now, I'm here as your friend to help you, any way I can. A good friend."

More than a friend. He'd made that clear, not just with his words, but with his deeds. He'd been there at every turn, when others spurned her, when she'd felt alone. He wanted more from her. She wanted to give him more. What would happen when this was over? When she no longer carried this child? Would he see her for herself, for who she was?

"I guess you still talking to me after I threw up on your boots that first day makes you a pretty good friend."

He grinned. "Guess so."

A contraction sucked the air from her lungs. Maisy leaned into it. The pain grew until it absorbed all thought. Finally it subsided.

"Ouch." Joshua took back his hand. He shook it. His fingers were red. "I may need ice for my hand."

"I'm sorry."

"Don't be. It's nothing compared to what you're going through."

He rose and went to the shelves on one wall. "How do you feel about Uno?"

"Perfect."

They passed the time playing Uno, go fish, spades, and blackjack. Joshua made popcorn, then cocoa, then peanut-butter-and-jelly on toasted English muffins. Of all the ways Maisy had imagined passing this time, none had been like this.

The contractions grew worse and came closer together. The snow continued to fall. It cocooned the building in a white gauze that kept them in and everyone else out. No sign of Isaac and Vicky. Or Kate and Ruth.

When the next contraction nearly brought her to her knees, Maisy couldn't sit any longer. Biting her lip to keep from screaming, she heaved herself from the chair. "I need to go back to the room." Her voice was hoarse, barely recognizable as her own. "I think it's almost time."

"I'll be right here if you need me." Joshua stood. He brushed a wisp of hair from her face. His expression held a tenderness that couldn't be mistaken. "I'll be here waiting for you when you're done."

His encouraging smile followed her down the hall and into the birthing room. Maisy held his words of promise close to her heart. She would have to do this part on her own, but she wasn't alone.

She found Betsy drawing a bath in the pink birthing room. "I thought you might consider sitting in some warm water for a bit."

To be unclothed in front of anyone, even this midwife who'd

seen the most hidden parts of Maisy's body, sent a chill through her. "I don't know."

"Just imagine how good warm water will feel on your back. The door will be closed. I can lock it, if you like. It'll just be me and you."

Betsy was right. The warm water did feel good. The ache in Maisy's back eased. She leaned against the tub and concentrated on breathing through contractions that seemed to come one after another now. No time to gather her strength before the next one.

A tentative knock brought her straight up.

"It's okay. It's locked." Betsy hopped up and went to the door. "Who is it?"

"Vicky. It's Vicky and Isaac."

Vicky. *Danki, Gott, danki.* Maisy closed her eyes and breathed a sigh of relief. Her baby would not come into the world in limbo between two mothers. His new mother would be here for the beginning. For that first moment of joy and wonder.

Betsy pumped her fist. "Yay, you made it. Tell Isaac to go have a seat in the kitchen. Then give us a minute."

Betsy helped Maisy into a voluminous cotton nightgown and led her into the adjoining birthing room. Then she opened the door. Her cheeks red and her hair damp with melted snow, Vicky slipped into the room.

"We came as soon as we got the message, but the roads were awful. I thought we would never get here." Her voice was high, the words running together in her excitement. "We almost froze. The wind is blowing so hard. Is the bopli . . . Is he here?"

"You're just in time, I think." Maisy groaned. She eased onto a stool and held out her hand. "Do you want to help me?"

"Jah, jah, I do." Her eyes huge, Vicky drew closer. "Just tell me what to do."

"Just hold my hand. Sei so gut." *So I won't feel alone. So I know someone who loves this baby as much as I do will witness his birth. So I will have the strength to do what I need to do.* Maisy concentrated on the feel of Vicky's hand on hers and her other hand on Maisy's shoulder, rubbing.

Betsy knelt in front of her. "Okay, little one, we're ready for you now."

The room blurred. It didn't matter who else was with her. The pain took all of Maisy's concentration. Time stood still. *Push. Rest. Push, Rest. Push.* When it seemed certain her body would split in two, a tiny baby girl announced her appearance with a fierce cry far too loud for such a mite. She had tufts of wheat-colored hair.

Betsy deposited her in Maisy's lap. "Oh my, she's beautiful and petite."

The tears came then. They weren't a sign of weakness nor regret. Simply the result of understanding what an incredible wonder giving birth to a new life was—under any circumstance.

"Jah, she's beautiful." Maisy touched the baby's red cheeks and kissed her forehead. She favored Nate in the shape of her face and her hair—lots of hair—but she had Maisy's nose and chin.

Let her go. Maisy collected the memory of her baby's slight weight, her bundle of bones and flesh, the sound of her cry, the way she batted her tiny hands in the air, and stowed it in her heart of hearts. She swallowed hard.

Let her go.

She handed the little girl to Vicky. "Meet your daughter, Vicky."

Vicky wept. The more she cried, the more the baby fussed. Candy went to fetch Isaac while Betsy took care of the after-birthing business with Maisy. "She has a good set of lungs. As soon as I'm done here, I'll put the drops in her eyes, weigh her, and such."

"Oh my goodness, she's so sweet." Vicky hiccupped a sob. "You have twelve hours, Maisy—"

"And when the time comes I'll sign the paper." Maisy held out her hand to Betsy. "Help me up. I'll get out of the way so Isaac can come in."

Betsy obliged. "I'll come to check on you in a bit, after I finish with the baby."

Maisy slipped into the other birthing room, closed the door, and leaned against it. She sucked in air and let it out, over and over again. The empty feeling didn't dissipate. She sat on the edge of the bed. She'd just given birth to a baby, yet she didn't feel tired, and she didn't want to lie down. She wanted to be anywhere but here.

"Maisy?" Betsy's voice floated through the cracks of the closed door. "Are you okay?"

"Yes."

"Sweetie, can you open the door, please?"

Maisy wiped her face on the nightgown. She cleared her throat and did as the midwife asked.

Betsy studied her face. "Are you really okay?"

"I am."

"If you need to talk, I'm here."

Maisy nodded. "Right now I just want to go home."

"I can understand that, but you need to stay for a few more hours so we can make sure all is well. You've done some strenuous work this evening. It might be good to get some sleep. That way you'll be here to sign the consent form when the time comes."

"I'm not tired, really. I just want to go home."

"It's okay to take a minute to sort your feelings out about what you've done here today."

Maisy nodded again. *Please, please, stop talking and let me go.* "Could you bring me my clothes from the other room? I don't want to interrupt . . ."

"I'll get them if you promise me you'll lie down for a while. Just an hour or two."

"Fine. But first I want to get some tea." The desire to see Joshua welled up in her. He understood loss. Her baby hadn't died, but she was lost to Maisy. Forever. "My throat is dry."

Her throat ached, but it wasn't from thirst.

Betsy brought her clothes. Her hands shaking, Maisy fumbled with her dress. Her fingers didn't want to work. A small child could make quicker work of it. Her eyes were gritty, her lips chapped and dry. Not tea. Coffee. A single ray of sun made the silver lining shine for a brief second. She could have a lovely cup of coffee, caffeine and all. No more nausea. No more eating dry toast, crackers, and tiny meals. Not one more slurp of ginger tea again. Ever.

Maisy trudged to the kitchen. Her balance was off. A huge weight had been removed from in front of her. Instead it had been deposited on her shoulders. How could something gone feel so heavy?

The kitchen smelled of vanilla cake. Birthday cake.

Maisy halted in the doorway. Candy stood at the counter, a knife in her hand. She loosened a small cake so it slid from the pan onto a saucer. She looked up. "Maisy. Oh, honey, come in. I'll be out of here in a jiffy."

The scent would forever remind Maisy of the soft, silky feel of her baby's skin. The tiny fingers and toes. The outraged cry of a newborn surprised and unhappy at the brilliant light and cold air of her new world.

"No rush."

She edged past the nurse and went to the window where Joshua stood, staring out at a world turned white. The snow had stopped. He turned. Surprise, then understanding flickered in his face. "You're all done, then?"

Maisy glanced back. Candy swiped a dollop of white frosting across the cake with an efficient movement that covered the top and then the sides. She laid the plastic spatula in the sink, grabbed the cake, and bustled toward the door. "I'm out of here."

The lingering aroma floated around Maisy, teasing her. Determined to find in it the celebration of a new life, Maisy faced the window. "Betsy wants me to stay for a few hours so she can check up on me. She thinks I'm suffering from regrets or second thoughts."

"Are you?"

"Nee. I did the right thing." Maisy leaned her forehead against the windowpane. The cold glass cooled her warm skin. She closed her eyes. The image of her baby girl with those endearing tuffs of hair sticking up on her red scalp filled her mind. Her eyes popped open. "You of all people might understand how it feels."

Joshua studied her face with an expression so kind she had to grit her teeth against the anguish that threatened to spill out all over her and him. "How is that possible?"

"I feel as if a part of me is missing. One minute she was in my body. The next minute she was gone."

"I can see what you mean." He blew on the glass and drew two stick figures in the fog, then wiped one away with the side of his fisted hand. "And then there was one. Just me."

"Something like that." Maisy drew two hearts, then wiped one away. "And then there was one. Only my one belongs to someone else now."

"Can I fix you some tea?"

"What I really want is kaffi with milk and sugar, but I'll make it."

"You should sit."

"I'm not sick. I'm not expecting. I'm not anything."

"Not true. You're still Maisy. You still have a life to live." A sudden urgency resonated in his words. His dark gaze pierced the shroud that surrounded her. "You'll be who Gott intended you to be now."

"I don't know what to do next."

"You'll go home to Amos's."

"And then what? Watch Ruth grow big with child and then have a bopli?" The words came out clothed in bitterness. "I didn't mean it that way. I'm happy for them."

"I know you are." His hand came up, wavered within reach of hers, then dropped. "I'll make the kaffi."

He left her standing at the window, staring at the white world just as he had. The everyday, routine sounds of water being poured and coffee percolating added a surreal layer to a day full of strangeness. She inhaled the aromatic scent. The knot between her shoulders eased. Was this how life went on? One small task at a time? One cup of coffee? One pan of bacon frying? The *chug-a-chug* of the wringer washing machine? The breezy sunshine smell of sheets hanging on the line? Small moments that added up to life lived even when it seemed as though it should've stopped.

Joshua returned to her side. "It'll be ready in a few minutes. Do you want to talk some more?"

"Nee. Not really."

"Do you want to play Uno?"

The flicker of humor in his voice touched her. He was trying to feel his way in a situation that must have felt as alien to him as it did to her.

"Maybe later. Maybe we can just stand here and study the

world and wonder how it can change so much from one minute to the next."

"We can do that."

Sweet silence never sounded so good.

Chapter 39

"Where are you?"

Caleb's mild tone, loud and clear over the telephone, didn't fool Joshua. His boss knew where Joshua was. Most likely Harvey had told him. The business owners on Switzer Street talked frequently. They were members of the Yoder Chamber of Commerce. Plus they would've been shoveling their sidewalks and getting their parking lots cleared of three feet of snow.

"I'm at the birthing center."

"Still?"

A million questions teemed behind that single syllable. Caleb was Joshua's employer, but he'd also become a friend. "Still. Someone had to help Maisy get to the clinic in that snowstorm."

"That was late yesterday afternoon."

"Jah, but the bopli took her time getting here, and then Maisy had to wait to sign some paperwork."

"I see."

Caleb saw too much. He likely knew about the adoption plan. Everyone in Haven probably knew about it. "Doreen is on the way. I can be at the store as soon as we drop Maisy off at Amos's."

"Nee. Go home. I reckon you've been up all night. You haven't changed your clothes. Show up tomorrow bright-eyed and bushy-tailed."

"It was a snowstorm. No one could get here." Why did he feel the need to explain to Caleb, the one man who would understand Maisy's situation like others could not? "I couldn't leave her alone at a time like that."

"You don't have to explain yourself to me, my friend. You did an honorable thing. Don't let others try to convince you otherwise."

"I won't."

"I know you won't. Leave it to Gott to sort it out."

"I plan to."

"Gut. Praise Gott for delivering a bopli for Isaac and Vicky, while you're at it."

"Jah." Joshua laid the receiver in its cradle on the table between two chairs in the waiting room. Maisy had gone to freshen up after hours of playing checkers, Uno, and go fish. The sudden dose of caffeine had kept her talking and walking for the duration of the hours she had to wait before she could make that final step toward giving Isaac and Vicky a most precious gift.

"It's time for her to sign the consent form." Betsy stood in the doorway to the hall. "I know you're not technically a part of this, but I thought maybe you would consider providing some moral support."

He'd come this far. Without Kate or Ruth at her side, Maisy had no one. "If she wants me to be there, I'm willing to do whatever she needs."

"I thought so." Betsy cocked her head toward the hallway. "She might not say it, but she does want you there."

How had they arrived at this strange juxtaposition? In this moment it didn't matter. All that mattered was getting Maisy through this painful transition from expecting mother to a Plain woman who had to figure out how to move on.

Joshua followed Betsy into the kitchen. Maisy sat across from Vicky and Isaac, who held the baby wrapped in a crib quilt. Only her scowling face and full head of honey-blonde hair showed, but she made her presence known with steady fussing.

Maisy glanced up from the paperwork on the table. Her eyes were bloodshot. Her lips were chapped, her prayer covering wrinkled, and her hands shook. Too much caffeine. She still managed a slight nod and a ghost of a smile.

"I'm just finishing up." Her voice was steady. "Is Doreen on her way?"

"She is." Joshua took up a spot on the other side of the table, near the cabinet. That way Maisy could see him. "She's taking the Hostetlers home after a doctor's appointment. She should be here in about fifteen minutes."

"Gut."

Maisy picked up a pen. Without reading the document, she signed it slowly, with no rush. She straightened and held it out to Vicky. "I think there's a spot where you and Isaac sign as well."

Isaac let out a whoosh of air loud enough for everyone to hear, even over the baby's fussing. The couple made quick work of the signatures. "I'll hand it over to the lawyer." His eyes were luminous. "Everything else should be in order. Danki, Maisy, for this gift. We are blessed by it. If you ever want to take a peek at her—"

"Wait a bit on that, sei so gut." Vicky was a woman. She knew better what this gift must cost Maisy. "Let us get situated with Elinor Grace. That's what we've named her, for my groosmammi. We'll call her Ellie Grace."

"Elinor Grace." Maisy whispered the name so softly Joshua had to strain to hear her. "Ellie Grace. What a beautiful name. You're right. It serves no purpose for me to visit while you're getting to know each other."

Or ever. That would be like dumping dozens of truckloads of salt into a wound the size of a canyon.

"We'll go then." Isaac rose. He handled the baby like a fragile piece of glass. The fussing eased after he stood. Ellie appeared to have gone to sleep. "Vicky's schweschder and her mudder are at the house, waiting for us."

"It's gut you'll have help."

Isaac nodded. Vicky gathered up their coats. With a final round of murmured appreciation, they followed Betsy from the room.

As soon as they were out of sight, Maisy slumped in her chair. Her hands went to her face.

She needed a moment. Or two or ten or forty. Joshua straightened and moved toward the table. The sooner they left the clinic, the better.

"I'm so glad that's over." Her hands muffled the words. "I was dreading it. But they're so happy. It's gut. So gut to see them happy."

Only someone who knew Maisy well would hear the gravel in her voice. Strange to think Joshua stood squarely in that category after almost six months of deepening friendship. Did she see it that way? Would those times come to an end now? Would she quit her job and return to Jamesport? All questions that couldn't be asked at this moment. She needed time to figure out who she was now. She'd said so herself.

It would be wrong for Joshua to muddy the waters now. Maisy was in the middle of an emotional tempest. Loss and grief and remorse and uncertainty and yes, a smidgen of relief, if she was being honest with herself. A powder keg that might explode before she could right herself.

He could be there to pick up the pieces. Would she want that?

Did he dare risk caring for someone so fragile? In some ways Maisy was more fragile than her newborn baby. If she rejected him, could Joshua take it?

He wasn't a coward. The gain was worth the risk.

Joshua tugged her coat from where it hung on her chair. "You better bundle up. The thermometer on the clinic's porch reads seventeen degrees."

"Danki for being here." She still didn't let her hands drop. Joshua stifled the urge to peel them away. To kiss her fingers and kiss away her hurt. As if it were that simple. Her shoulders hunched. "You went far beyond what any friend should have to do."

Her meaning clamored through the words. That any Plain man should do. Bryan and Joshua's father, maybe others as well, might not understand how Joshua could do this. But Caleb understood it and supported it because he had an inkling of what it might be like to walk in Maisy's shoes.

"It's my honor."

"Why is it an honor?" Maisy finally let her hands drop. She stared up at him and shook her head. "I shouldn't have put you in this position. Bryan won't like it. Your family won't like it. Amos certainly won't like it."

"They shouldn't judge something they can't understand."

"You can understand it?"

Joshua eased into a chair. They had five minutes left before Doreen arrived. "I've been talking to Caleb. Because of the situation with Mason and his mudder, Caleb understands. He was never given the opportunity to know his suh. You gave Ellie's daed his chance and he threw it away. You gave your dochder a chance at a gut life with two people who will love her beyond all measure. You have done everything you can to earn redemption. That's what people will see."

"You're too kind, Joshua Lapp."

He held out her coat. "Let's go. The rest of your life is waiting for you."

The worried look reappeared on her face. It made her seem so much older than she was. Joshua stood and helped her into the coat. He let his hand rest on her shoulder for a scant second.

The rest of our lives.

Chapter 40

IF THE BABY HAD WAITED UNTIL her due date of March first, she would've arrived on a springlike day with temperatures in the upper sixties. The sun warm on her face, Maisy hung the wash on the clothesline in Amos's backyard. The baby. Not her baby. Not Ellie Grace. It took the strength of an ox to think of that tiny being as *the* baby.

Ellie Grace. Such a pretty name. Maybe it wouldn't hurt to pop over to Isaac and Vicky's for a quick visit. Just to make sure the baby was doing well. She might have colic. Maybe Vicky needed someone—like Maisy—to rock the baby while she took a quick nap.

Nee. You can't. They have help. They have family. Ellie Grace is their baby now. Not yours.

The thoughts bulldozed through the ramparts she'd so carefully built to keep them out. Her traitorous body didn't help. Kate called the raging desire to cry "hormones." The physical ache from not nursing had finally subsided, but the emotions still swirled inside her.

Maisy grabbed another shirt from the basket. Little Nicholas's. A baby shirt. He'd grown so much in the months since Maisy took up residence at his house. He sat up, crawled, and squawked *dat* or *mamm* when he wanted attention.

But still a baby.

Maisy wiped her face on her sleeve, then hung the shirt on the line with wooden clothespins next to one of Bonnie's dresses. Another one growing faster than Ruth could sew bigger dresses. Fortunately she had friends and cousins who could offer hand-me-downs. Some of Maisy's maternity dresses fit Ruth, but the material already stretched tight across her belly and she wasn't due until late April. She spent plenty of time with her head bent over the Singer treadle machine, the *thump, thump* of the treadle making music while Bonnie sang to her dolls lined up on the rag-tie rug.

Another reason Maisy should go home. Watching Ruth's belly grow bigger with her baby was like pouring rubbing alcohol on an open wound. Soon there would be a newborn in the house to feed, diaper, rock, and simply hold close. How much more would that baby's cry, his scent, his weight in her arms sting when he was right there in front of Maisy day in and day out?

She'd called and left a message for her parents about the baby's birth. Mother's message in return had asked when she would be home. Maisy hadn't responded. She couldn't. Leaving meant going far away from the baby.

And Joshua. What about Joshua? He hadn't come back to work for Amos yet. Nor had he come into the hardware store after Maisy returned to work last week.

No glimpse of him across the street. Was he deliberately avoiding her? The conversation at the birthing center said differently. He wanted more than friendship. He'd made that clear. So where was he?

Many questions. No answers.

Ruth wanted Maisy to stay to help her with the children and

the baby when he came. It would be hard, but Maisy owed it to her cousin for all she'd done for her. Amos was less inclined to have her stay. Ruth seemed inclined to think he could be won over.

"He's right." She spoke aloud to Sunny, who seemed determined to wrap herself around Maisy's feet. She gave the cat a nudge with her sneaker. "Scooch over before you trip me."

Sunny yawned widely and rolled over on her back. "Be that way." Maisy picked up the last piece of laundry—a quilt crib on which Bonnie had peed. Ruth was determined that at least one of her brood would be potty-trained by the time her new baby arrived.

Bonnie had other ideas.

The *clip-clop* of hooves and creak of buggy wheels gave Maisy a welcome reprieve from her thoughts. She picked up the basket and went to see who was coming. Sunny meowed and followed.

Smiling and waving, Kate pulled into the backyard. "Whoa." She chortled as she came to a halt near the hitching post. "Just the person I want to see. Well, you and Ruth, who's due for a checkup." She hopped from her buggy and trotted around to the back without slowing down. "I brought you all something. Come see."

Maisy did as she was told. Plants of all kinds filled the buggy. Kate curtsied and threw out her arm in a dramatic flourish. "I come bearing gifts. I saw Ruth at church, and she said no one has started the spring gardens—vegetables or flowers. You're way behind the curve, my friend."

Kate might have visited with Vicky and Isaac. She might've seen Ellie Grace. She didn't deliver the baby, so probably not. But maybe. *Stop it.* "Working at the store five days a week and coming home to help Ruth doesn't leave much time—"

"No excuses. You love flowers. You love to garden. You told me so yourself. So we're going to have ourselves a mini frolic." Kate touched the blossoms on a small pot of Shasta daisies, then pointed to another of black-eyed Susans. "We've got perennials that will bloom now and others for this summer. We've got annuals. See the pansies and the snapdragons?"

Without pausing to let Maisy get a word in edgewise, Kate leaned farther into the buggy. "Here are the vegetables. I bought spring transplants, broccoli, cauliflower, and cabbage, plus the potatoes, peas, onions, and lettuce. We'll get out the shears and prune Ruth's apricot and cherry trees so we can get them ready."

"You shouldn't have. How much did you spend?" A flutter of anticipation like wings brushed against Maisy's skin. Flowers were so joyful. Some of God's best work. "I do love daisies. And black-eyed Susans. I'll repay you."

"Nonsense. Run get the wheelbarrow and start moving these to the garden plots. We have to prepare the soil." Kate pushed up her sleeves. "In the meantime I'll have a quick visit with Ruth. Then she can come out with the kinner to help. It'll be a treat and a half."

Indeed it would. For the first time in days—two weeks to be exact—Maisy's mood lifted. She went to work moving the plants to their garden plots. Then she gathered the tools they would need from the potting shed. Kate had included a bag of peat moss and another of mulch in her purchases. The earthy smell was better than any expensive perfume.

Kate would be good company. She made the rounds to expecting moms in the district. She would have tidbits of news, babies born, who was expecting, and all the other news that came by way of her visits to households up and down the back roads of Haven.

She might even have news of Joshua.

Better not to ask. Just wait. Maybe she would volunteer something.

By the time Kate returned, Ruth and the children in tow, Maisy had the rototiller in the garden, creating the neat rows they would need. The vegetable plants were lined up in the order they would be planted. The flowers had their own spot nearby.

With every row tilled, every plant moved, the questions grew and took up more space.

"Gut job. It smells so gut out here." Kate scooped up Bonnie and two-stepped around the wheelbarrow. "Let's get our hands dirty."

"I'm way ahead of you." Maisy held the rototiller steady with one hand and hoisted the other in the air. Dirt smeared her palm and clung under her nails. "This is my favorite time of year—this and when we get to harvest and eat the vegetables."

Focus on the work. Gott help me.

Ruth spread an old quilt on the grass and laid Nicholas, who slept, on it. Sunny immediately curled up in a ball next to him. Ruth scooted back from them both. "I'll cut up the seed potatoes while you start on the transplants."

For a few moments they worked without talking. Who could get a word in edgewise with Bonnie's nonstop prattle—nonsensical songs, gibberish, counting to ten, telling stories only she understood. She took after Ruth, not Amos, no doubt about that.

"Maisy, Maisy!" She sang tunelessly while her fat fingers dug into the damp dirt. A night crawler dangled in the air. "Wormy, wormy."

"Ach, ewww," Kate shrieked. She stumbled back a step, lost her footing, and plopped on her behind on top of a broccoli plant. "Ewww, creepy-crawly thing."

"It's just a worm." Maisy laughed. The surprising sound spun clouds from the sky. The certainty that she would never laugh again slunk away. "Haven't you ever gone fishing?"

"Nee. I do not fish. I don't like bait. I don't like smelly things."

Kate climbed to her feet with great dignity. She brushed dirt from her dress and hands. "I wait for the men to bring me their catch. Then I make a delicious meal for them. They have their job. I have mine."

Maisy grinned at Ruth. Ruth grinned back. She grabbed another seed potato from the sack and slapped it on the cutting board. "It's so gut to see you smile, Maisy, and hear you laugh."

The joy floated, airy and light, just beyond Maisy's fingertips. *The baby would make me laugh.* She pushed the rototiller into the grass, parked it, and picked up a hoe. "I'm trying."

"I know you are. After a while you won't have to try so hard."

"I hope you're right." *Deep breaths. Gott, forgive me for my weakness.* She slid a broccoli plant into its spot and used the hoe to cover the roots, gently packing dirt around it. "How are your visits going, Kate? Any gut news you can share?"

"No bad news, which is gut in its own right, jah?" Kate knelt between rows and started on the cauliflower transplants. "Everyone is happy winter is over. Folks are smiling because spring has sprung. The sun is shining. They're getting outside to plant their gardens."

"That's gut. That's gut." *Just do it. Just ask.* "What about Vicky and Isaac? Are they doing well?"

"They are wunderbarr, according to Vicky's mudder." Kate leaned back on her haunches. She raised her hand to her forehead and peered up at Maisy. "Ask me what you really want to know."

"I wondered how the bopli was doing."

"I haven't seen her, but when I talked to Sadie, she said Ellie Grace is a gut bopli, a good eater. She has her days and nights mixed up, but they're managing. They're blessed."

"Jah, they are."

"Gott blessed them."

"I know."

"I reckon Gott used you to bless them." Ruth's attempt to make

Maisy feel better was sweet, but none of them—least of all Maisy—could claim to understand God's plan. He could use her sin for something good. No one denied that. Whether He intended this outcome all along was beyond comprehension. "And now you take the baptism classes and get baptized."

Was she talking about here in Haven or in Jamesport? Her open face with cheeks pink from the sun held no ulterior motives. Suddenly weak-kneed, Maisy leaned on the hoe. "Mudder wants me to come home."

"I can understand that. She's your mudder. She misses you. I'm hoping she'll understand if you stay a little longer."

"Ruth isn't the only one who wants you to stay." The change in Kate's tone signaled Maisy to take a peek at her. The older woman had a sly expression on her round face. "I went by Bryan's house yesterday to pick up some clothes from Esther that she's donating to the thrift store. Guess who was coming out to his buggy when I pulled up?"

"I have no idea."

"Joshua."

That Joshua had been visiting with Bryan was no secret—not to Maisy. "He's working through some things from his past."

"And his present."

"Amos talked to him just the other day." Ruth had that same sly look. "He's not needed at the furniture store anymore so he's starting back here for a few weeks, until we can find someone else. He says he has a job opportunity at a horse farm. He's going to learn to train horses."

"That's wunderbarr. It's a gut sign too. It's something he and his bruder Jacob talked of doing as kinner." Maisy's airy tone was perfect. Chin up, she smiled at Ruth. "In the meantime we'd better stock up on maple syrup. You know how he loves pancakes."

Maisy would see him again. Finally.

She knelt in the dirt next to Bonnie. She had to work on Tuesday. Why had Joshua waited until then to come back to the farm? It didn't matter. Their paths would cross at breakfast and supper. They were bound to run into each other in the yard or on the porch, in the living room. The pressure from his hand on her shoulder in the moments before they left the birthing center reappeared for a second. The light in his eyes when he yelled "Uno," the careful way he set the coffee mug in front of her. His steadying presence while she signed away her rights to her baby. If Maisy's life was a puzzle, right now Joshua served as a big, important piece of that puzzle—whether he knew it or not.

"You needn't pretend." Kate shook her dirt-encrusted finger at Maisy. "You're among friends."

"I don't know what you mean."

"But you do. Vicky's mudder had heard all about how Joshua stayed by your side during the delivery. She said he even waited nearby while you signed the consent form. What kind of man does that?"

"A very gut man."

"We all know Joshua is a gut man." Ruth paused long enough to pick up Nicholas, who'd chosen that moment to open his eyes and squawk. "That's why he's spent the last year working with Amos out here. It's not the money. There's not much to be made in farming these little plots of land. Joshua's gaze followed you at the supper table. He had the look—"

"There was no look. Don't give Joshua a burden he shouldn't have to bear, sei so gut."

"You're not a burden, Maisy." Kate popped up from the ground. Her scowl matched her tart tone. "You've been given another chance to live your life according to Gott's rules. Take it."

"Whatever Gott has planned for me, I'll be obedient."

"Even if that means leaving yourself open to the possibility that He means for you and Joshua to be together?"

Maisy raised her face to the heavens. God knew the number of hairs on her head. He knew her name before she was born. He knew she would fall. How it must've hurt His heart to see His child stumble. Opening herself up to another man required faith in God's plan. Joshua wasn't Nate. He'd proven he could be trusted, over and over again.

"Gott's will be done," she said.

"Amen." Kate snatched Bonnie up into her arms. She danced a funny jig. Bonnie shrieked with laughter. "Gott's will be done. Gott's will be done." Kate sang her words of praise to a tune only she knew. "Gott is gut. He is great. He is our Lord and Savior. The great I Am."

"Aren't you getting ahead of yourself?"

Giggling, Kate put her free hand to her heaving chest. "I can't breathe. I'm too old to be so silly, aren't I, Bonnie, sweet Bonnie?" She didn't give the little girl time to answer. "Ask me what Joshua was doing at Bryan's. Go on, ask me what he said he was doing there."

"If he was talking to Bryan, it's likely none of our business." Maisy had her own repertoire of tart tones. "Maybe he doesn't want you spreading his business around the countryside."

"Nee, nee. Joshua knew telling me was like telling you and Ruth, my dear friend." Kate deposited Bonnie on the quilt next to her brother and then sat down herself. She tugged off dirty sneakers and socks with a blissful sigh. "I have dirt in my shoes. I hate it when that happens."

"Kate!" Maisy and Ruth spoke in unison. "What?"

"Joshua has been counseling with Bryan. That's what he called it. *Counseling.*" Kate tickled Nicholas, whose giggles sent Bonnie into Kate's lap seeking her own. "That's what he said. Then he said—and this is even more important—he's started baptism classes. He's finally ready to join the faith. Isn't that wunderbarr?"

"It is. So wunderbarr." Maisy stabbed the ground with the hoe. Joshua had done it. He'd disentangled himself from his unhappy past. He'd be able to treasure memories of his brother while making new ones. "I'm so happy for him. He's moving on with his life."

"Why do you think he's doing that?"

"Because he's at peace with his past and ready to embrace his Plain faith."

"Jah, for sure. But there's more."

There couldn't be more. Once Joshua was baptized he could no longer have anything to do with Maisy. Not until she'd been absolved of her sin and was able to be baptized as well. She shook her head and kept hoeing.

"Have you considered being baptized here?" Kate laid her hand on the hoe to still it. "If you wanted to stay in Haven."

"We'd love to have you stay." Ruth abandoned the seed potatoes. She slipped over to stand next to Kate. "You've been through so much. You've stood the test. You're ready."

"Going home would mean carrying on while knowing everyone knows." Just as everyone in Ruth and Kate's district knew. "I'm not a coward. I can face them. On the other hand, leaving here could be cowardly in a way."

"Because Vicky and Isaac live nearby." Ruth patted Maisy's shoulder. "You would see them around town. There's no denying it."

"And at church." Kate wrinkled her nose. She had smudges of dirt on her cheek and over one eyebrow. "There's gut in that. You'll see how their bopli grows and changes—at a distance."

"We can't pretend the bopli wasn't mine." Maisy tightened her grip on the hoe. Her knuckles hurt. "We can't ignore the circumstances of Ellie Grace's birth. Vicky and Isaac plan to tell her she's adopted when she's old enough to understand. It hurts my heart to imagine what she'll think of a mudder who gave her away."

"You can't pretend, it's true, but you can stand on the promise that Gott will see you through." Ruth grimaced. She rubbed her belly and sighed. "He will handle every situation in His wisdom and His grace and His mercy. All we have to do is be obedient."

"Obviously I got an F in obedience."

"Nee, you brought that grade up to an A." Kate's smile warmed Maisy even more than the sun. "You did a hard thing and did it with grace."

"Now all you have to do is keep an open mind about Joshua," Ruth added. Her smile matched Kate's. "You don't have to decide right away about going home or baptism. Just keep an open mind."

Did Joshua have an open mind? What was he thinking? Kate and Ruth could draw all the conclusions they wanted, but theirs was wishful thinking, nothing more.

Gott, sei so gut, don't let me regret having an open mind, sei so gut.

Chapter 41

THE GARDENS WERE PLANTED. KATE WENT home after promising to return in a week to check on Ruth and help with weeding. Maisy kept busy. That was the key to not thinking. Serving supper. Washing dishes. Putting Nicholas and then Bonnie to bed.

Ruth and Amos sat in the living room, working on a puzzle of a farm scene together. They deserved some alone time without Maisy intruding. She should be exhausted. Her body drooped, but her mind still yammered. She swept the kitchen floor a third time. She scrubbed already clean counters, wiped down the playpen, and rearranged the pantry.

Sleep remained out of the question. If she closed her eyes, the dreams would come. Vivid dreams in which she held Ellie Grace in her arms, rocked her, and sang sweet lullabies. The baby's plump fists waved. She grabbed one of Maisy's fingers and hung on. Finally, she sighed and drifted off to sleep, leaving Maisy to marvel at her perfectness.

Think about something else. Anything else.

Perspiration dampened her cheeks. It was stuffy in the kitchen. A walk. A walk would be good. Maybe then she'd be tired enough to sleep. If she didn't she'd be a mess at the hardware store in the morning.

Maisy pushed through the back door and slipped down the porch steps. Automatically her body angled toward the barn. No, a walk, not a buggy ride. Sunny trotted across the yard and joined her. "There you are. I wondered what happened to you." The cat hadn't turned up for lunch or supper. "Have you been out there mousing?"

Sunny didn't deign to answer. Maisy picked her up and stroked her long, sleek back. The cat's purr revved. Mutual comfort. But not enough. Not nearly enough. Maisy's steps carried her to the barn as much as she told herself she couldn't, she wouldn't.

In minutes she had the horse hitched to the buggy. Half an hour later she pulled into Isaac's yard. Her head demanded she turn around and head home before making this mistake. Her heart refused to listen. *Just a peek. Just a touch.* Isaac and Vicky would understand.

The front door opened. Isaac's dark frame filled the space, silhouetted by the living room lamp's light behind him. "Maisy, what are you doing here?"

Swallowing hard against the ache in her throat, Maisy hopped from the buggy. She trudged to the bottom step but didn't take it. "I just thought—"

"You shouldn't be here." Isaac moved onto the porch, but he still blocked the open door. The solar porch lights revealed his grim expression. "We agreed."

"I know. We did." Maisy gripped the wooden railing. "I can't stop thinking about her. I thought maybe if I could see her and know how she's doing, I could get past it."

"I don't think so." Isaac spoke softly, his voice full of compassion, but firmly. "I reckon it'll make it worse. She's fine. She's gut.

She's a gut eater. It would be nice if she slept more, but it's okay. Vicky doesn't mind."

She wouldn't. Ellie Grace was Vicky's dream come true. "I could rock her sometimes while Vicky gets a nap."

"Nee. Vicky's mudder is here. Her schweschder comes by two or three times a week. Her friends help out." Isaac rubbed his eyes with rounded fists like a small child. "I even take my turns during the night. That's one of the few advantages of bottle feeding."

Maisy's chest still ached at the mere mention of feeding Ellie Grace. "I'm sorry. I shouldn't have intruded."

"Go home. Sei so gut. That's the only way this will work."

Did he mean home to Amos or home to Jamesport? "I promise I won't come back."

"Who is it?" Vicky came to her door. She held Ellie Grace wrapped in a thick crib quilt. Only the back of her head showed. Maisy stumbled back a few steps when her body screamed to race up the steps to see her baby—not her baby.

"I'd better go. I'm so sorry."

She whirled and raced to the buggy. *Don't stop. Don't slow down. Do the right thing. Let go. Gott, help me let go.*

"Maisy? It's okay. She's okay. She's asleep."

Vicky's high voice floated on the night air. It mingled with Isaac's lower tones, murmuring something too soft for Maisy to hear in her headlong scramble to get in the buggy and be gone.

She allowed herself one final glance back after she had safely turned the buggy around. Isaac had his arm around Vicky. He was leading her back into the house, the baby between them. They were a family, complete and in no need of anyone else.

Maisy swallowed tears and urged the horse to pick up his pace. She didn't belong here. She'd given her daughter the gift of a happy life with a couple who already loved her with the love of parents who wanted nothing more than to be mother and father to her.

Let it go. Let her go.

God's voice couldn't be clearer. "How?" Her face raised to the heavens, Maisy spoke aloud to the cloudy night sky. "How do I do that?"

Chapter 42

A SUPPER OF MEAT LOAF, FRIED potatoes, okra, and corn bread sat like a stone in Joshua's gut. Lights in the living room windows at Amos's place signaled somebody was still awake. If it was Amos, so be it. Joshua had his duffel bag under the seat. He would tell his boss he decided to arrive early so he'd be ready to go to work in the morning. A true statement. But not the whole truth.

Maybe Maisy had gone to bed already. Then their talk would have to wait. Maisy had to work tomorrow. Joshua didn't want to wait. Waiting would be easier. No, it wouldn't.

Don't be a coward.

If Joshua didn't reach out soon, he'd miss the chance. Maisy hadn't returned to Jamesport yet, which was surprising. Harvey said she asked to come back to work only a week after the baby was born. She didn't say for how long, and Harvey didn't ask.

Joshua halted on the gravel road near the barn, a good four hundred yards from the house. His horse tossed his head and whinnied. "Yeah, yeah, be patient, Job. I'm thinking."

Coming over this evening to talk to Maisy had seemed like a good idea in the after-supper glow of good food. That way his presence the following morning wouldn't be so awkward. Awkward for whom?

Talking to Bryan about what the bishop liked to call Joshua's spate with God had been bad enough. The discussion regarding Maisy was worse. Bryan urged Joshua to take the baptism classes and be baptized while working for John Shirak. When these aspects of his life were in order, then he could consider his options among the single women in the Gmay. Then and only then, *if* he still had an interest in Maisy after all that time, *then* he could act on it. The bishop claimed Joshua had been drawn into Maisy's terrible emotional situation and that accounted for his feelings for her. They would die away with the emotional overload, Bryan was sure. In the meantime slow was better.

A slow, measured approach to the rest of Joshua's life didn't work. He'd postponed the rest of his life too long. The time he'd spent with Maisy had opened his eyes. She'd had the wisdom and the strength to do what was best for her baby. She chose her faith despite the pressure from Nate and his mother. Maisy never lost her faith—even in the darkest hours. Her strong faith beckoned to Joshua, that light in the dark that Bryan had assured him was Jesus.

He planned to be baptized and he couldn't wait to tell Maisy. To share the peace and joy that came from knowing he didn't have to keep struggling anymore. She of all people would understand. He wanted to share that and so much more with her. Starting as soon as possible.

The thud of horse's hooves sounded on the sun-dried dirt. Joshua peered over his shoulder. Buggy headlights bounced in the darkness with every rut. Dark shadows behind the lights hid the driver. Who would be coming to Amos's house this late in the evening?

The answer came a few minutes later. The buggy pulled into

the drive several yards from Joshua's. He peered past the lights. "Maisy? Is that you?"

"Joshua?"

Her voice held brokenness. But also hope. As if she might be glad if it were him. Dueling emotions trampled Joshua. *Fix the brokenness. Earn the hope. Be worthy of the hope.* "Jah. It's me."

"What are you doing here?"

"I came to see you. Where did you go this time of night?"

No answer. Joshua moved his buggy so he could come alongside hers. The lights no longer shone in his face. Her head bent, Maisy studied the reins in her hands. The darkness hid her expression. "Maisy?"

"I had to get out of the house. I needed some air."

"So you decided to hitch up the buggy and take a ride all on your own?"

"It's safe out here. I'm not afraid to be alone."

For all the defiance in her tone, she still hadn't looked at him. Joshua leaned closer. "What's going on? Did something happen?"

"Nee. Why are you here tonight?"

Joshua wrapped the reins around his hands, then unwrapped them. He could ignore her odd behavior and bare his soul or he could try to find out why she seemed so sad—and so guilty. "Let's put your buggy away and I'll take you for that drive. How about that?"

"Ach, Joshua." Finally her head came up. She chewed her bottom lip. "You're so kind."

Did she simply think of him as a kind man, a friend, someone she could count on in a hard season in her life? If that was the case, he would have to accept such a limited, if honorable, role in her life. *Sei so gut, Gott, let it be more than that.* "Is that a jah?"

She nodded. Joshua jumped down from his buggy and led hers

back into the barn. A few minutes later she was situated on the seat next to him. He struck out for the long, winding dirt road that would take them past the neighboring farm. After several minutes of silence, he tried again. "So why don't you tell me what you were really doing. Did you go somewhere?"

"I couldn't sleep. I needed fresh air."

"You said that."

"I keep dreaming about the bopli."

Joshua gritted his teeth against a flood of painful empathy. He, too, had dreams that caused him to avoid bedtime. Not even sleep allowed her to escape the reality of her decisions—from the one that led to her carrying an English man's baby to the one that gave a kind and good Plain couple the gift of their deepest desire. "That must be hard."

"I thought if I could just see her, just one more time, maybe then I could stop thinking about her and wondering and imagining."

"You went to Isaac's?"

A truly terrible idea.

"I knew it was wrong. I knew I couldn't really knock on their door and ask to see her." Maisy's voice quivered. The words came slowly. They were thick with pain and self-recrimination. "I knew it, but I couldn't stop myself."

"You're only human."

"I've proved that over and over again. I haven't learned my lesson. I still do things because they make me feel gut instead of being obedient to Gott's will."

Going to Isaac's didn't make her feel better. The truth was written on her wind-reddened face. Worse, in fact. "Did you see her?"

"Nee. Not really. Isaac stopped me at the porch steps."

"He did the right thing."

"Vicky came to the door with . . . the bopli in her arms." Maisy stopped. Her fingers clawed her dress's cotton material in thick bunches. "I could only see the top of her head. I knew then I had to leave. I had to flee or I would never be able to leave her. I ran back to the buggy and flew down the road."

"In the end you had the strength to do the right thing."

"Only Gott gives a person that kind of strength." Her sigh held regret tossed in a river of wonder. God could still love a sinner like her. And him. "I can't believe He hasn't given up on me yet."

"Bryan says Gott is patient and merciful because He wants all His children to repent and come to their Savior. He leaves the flock of sheep to rescue the single lamb."

"That's me, the lost sheep."

"Not so lost now."

"I don't know about that."

"I do. You're kind and gentle and smart and a gut person."

Quiet reigned. Maybe he'd said too much. That would be a new one for Joshua. Running at the mouth wasn't his style.

"Kate said you're coming back to work for Amos for a few weeks." She tugged at her sweater sleeves until they covered her hands, then tucked them under her arms. "You don't start until tomorrow. Why did you come here so late in the evening?"

Now or never. Still Joshua hesitated. His gut twisted. Despite the cool spring breeze, sweat dampened his face. "I came early because I wanted to talk to you."

He felt rather than saw her stiffen in the seat next to him. "About what?"

"About us."

There it was. Out in the open. Two explosive words. What if she said there was no us? What if she'd leaned on him while expecting but no longer needed him? Maybe he would remind her of what she'd been through. He would have to see her every day and act like it was fine, just fine, no harm done. Or what if she'd decided to go home to Jamesport, and he never saw her again?

"After everything that's happened, are you sure you still want there to be an us?"

Very sure. Maisy gave him joy in a hundred ways. Her love of big words and romance novels. She was funny, smart, and determined. Look at how she'd taken to the job at the hardware store. She was kind, loving, and generous. Everything about her served to make her desirable.

Joshua guided the buggy to the side of the road and stopped. He couldn't have this conversation and drive at the same time. Too much was riding on it. "I do. I believe there's an us whether you like it or I like it. I think we need to find out for sure."

"You're not really sure then?"

"I'm sure, but you went through something traumatic. You're still going through it. Bryan thinks all those emotions color how we feel about each other. I don't think so. I think we saw who we really are together. I just don't want to assume how you feel."

So many words. His mouth was dry. His tongue thick. This talking about emotions morning, noon, and night might be the death of him. *Gott, give me the words. Let her hear my feelings when words fail me.*

He was new at talking to God. It still felt strange, like a foreign language he'd learned as a child but no longer spoke fluently.

Maisy turned in the seat. In the moon's light her skin was pale, her blue eyes dark. "I have to ask you something."

"Ask me anything."

"How can you really know who I am when there's no bopli in the picture? You've only known me as a woman expecting an Englisch man's bopli. You don't know me in any other place or time."

Where to start? It wasn't about her outside, although she was pretty. Maisy was everything he'd thought before, plus she was plainspoken. She was herself. She admitted her shortcomings and worked to do better. He could talk to her. Furthermore he wanted to talk to her. He could count on one hand the number of people who fell in that category.

"People show their true colors when they go through hard seasons. I've seen you at your lowest. You've seen me. We don't have anything to hide." Joshua inched closer. He laid his hand on top of hers. She sat so very still. "I can be myself. I like you. More than I've ever liked a woman."

Maisy didn't respond, but her sharp intake of breath was answer enough. Joshua turned her hand over so their hands met palm to palm. He slid his fingers between hers and let them become entwined.

"I hoped. I dreamed that you might have feelings for me like I have for you." Her lips twisted. Sadness etched a story around her mouth and eyes. "How can you even think of . . . touching me . . . knowing what I've done. You deserve more. You deserve a woman—"

"Don't tell me what I deserve. I know what I want." The words burst from Joshua. He could no more control them than he could control the way she heard them. "It's taken me a long time to get here. You're the only woman I've ever thought of this way."

She closed her eyes and shook her head.

Joshua touched her face with his free hand. "Open your eyes. Look at me."

She did both. In that moment she was the most beautiful woman in the world. He kissed her softly, slowly. She let go of his hand and raised hers to his face. They were warm and soft on his cheeks.

The kiss went on and on. He couldn't breathe. He didn't want to breathe. Or he wanted to breathe her in. Finally she pulled away. She didn't simply lean away, she scooted to the end of the buggy's seat. She clasped her hands tight in her lap. The sadness had fled from her face, replaced with uncertainty, hope, surprise, and most troubling, regret.

"Don't back away, sei so gut."

She touched her fingers to her lips for a brief second. "This is what got me into trouble before."

"Nee, this is different."

"How? How is it different?"

"Because it comes with the feelings I have for you." Making her see the difference might be the most important argument Joshua would ever have. He searched for words that could describe the beauty of a love that was so much more than the physical. Something so much more than Maisy had known with Nate. "It comes with the hope that we'll always be together. That someday we'll be mann and fraa. That we'll have kinner. That we'll grow old together."

She sighed deeply. "That's such a lovely picture. All that from one kiss?"

Uncertainty clutched at his heart. "Didn't you see it?"

"I did, but I didn't dare hope you would too."

Joshua breathed again. "So you're willing to try."

"I'm willing. But it will take time. I'm still recovering from childbirth. The physical part is so real and I have no bopli to make up for it. I'm reminded by my own body what I've done and what I've given up. And there's all these weird feelings like I want to cry all the time. Kate says it's hormones and it will stop eventually. Even then I don't know how to start over. I don't want to make the same mistakes again."

"I don't mind taking time if we take it together. I'm counseling with Bryan. I've started baptism classes." He tugged her close. "In a few weeks I'll start work at a horse farm. All this will take time. There will be time for us to get to know each other as special friends. Time for us to talk."

"Talking?" She leaned her head against his shoulder. Her fresh scent of soap and womanliness calmed his heart. She laughed softly. "I know how much you like that."

"For you I can do it." He chuckled. He never chuckled. Men like him didn't. "What about you? What about your baptism?"

"I want to be baptized too."

"Here?"

Her hand sought his again. She had a strong grip. "Jah. If Bryan and the others will consider it. But I need to talk to my eldre first."

"It won't bother you to be so close to Vicky and Isaac?"

This time she didn't answer right away. Joshua let the silence ride. Maisy rubbed her fingers along his, her touch light but firm. She traced the scar on his index finger and sighed. "It will be hard. It is hard. My feelings can't change from one minute to the next."

"It'll take time." Joshua relaxed against the buggy seat. At last, after ten years, time didn't seem out of whack. "Take all you need."

"Do you mean that?" She shifted and raised her head. "I don't understand how you can be so accepting of what I did and the consequences. How can you wait for me to get over what I did?"

"What you did was human. I'll tell you what I told Bryan—which he didn't like much, by the way. I reminded him of the Scripture you've heard a thousand times—we've all sinned and fallen short of the glory of Gott."

"He didn't like having Scripture quoted to him?"

"Nee. I reminded him that it's not my job to judge you or

forgive you." The memory of Bryan's rueful expression made Joshua smile. "The only job I want is to love you."

"Ach." Maisy leaned her head on his shoulder. "We need time to know each other in a different season."

"That's what I was thinking, and to give Bryan his due, that's what he was trying to tell me."

"So how much time do you think it'll take?"

Joshua put his arm around her and hugged her close. "However long it takes."

"Gut."

It was very gut.

Chapter 43

A ROOSTER'S UNMISTAKABLE SQUAWK FILLED THE telephone line. Maisy pulled the receiver from her ear until the noise died away. She always knew she'd reached her parents' phone shack. That nosy rooster loved to stick its beak into the family's business. Why it chose to hang out at the shack no one knew, but its presence today was a comforting sign that not everything had changed in Jamesport while Maisy was in Haven. She settled back on the cane-bottomed chair with its slightly crooked legs that made it into a rocker.

"Mudder?"

"Ach. This rooster is so annoying."

"It's okay. He just wants to keep you company."

"I'm keeping Mudder company." The high, sweet voice had to belong to Sarah. "I was with her in the garden when Daed came running to say you were on the line."

"He didn't come back to the shack too?"

"Nee. Your onkel is here." Mother picked up the conversation, but Maisy could still hear Sarah's excited breathing. Her imagination sketched an image of her sister squeezed on to Mother's lap, the two of them sharing the receiver between them. Both had dirt on their aprons and hands. Their cheeks were pink from a sunny spring day. Sarah would talk for days of getting to be on a "grown-up" phone call, and Mother would let her. "They're planting oats today. He had to get back to the field."

Her father hadn't asked any questions when Maisy told him why she was calling. He hadn't said much at all. More of a grunt or two. He was gone before she could ask him what she really wanted to know. Did he forgive her? Did he want her to come home? Would he be okay with her staying in Haven? "I wanted to tell him . . . about what I've decided to do."

"Aren't you coming home?" Sarah spoke first. "The kinner are asking for you."

Ten-year-old Sarah—no, she'd turned eleven in January—was a little mother figure now. Maisy forced herself to sound cheerful. "I'm hoping to come home for a visit, but there's so much going on here with Ruth in a family way and starting baptism classes."

"You're taking baptism classes in Haven." Mother jumped on that subject immediately. "Why not come home and be baptized in your district? Isn't it hard to watch another mother care for your bopli?"

Her tone cried out "I don't understand." Maisy groped for words. She was never at a loss for words. Except now when she needed them so badly. "I've put down roots here. I have a gut job. I have a friend."

"A friend?"

"A man."

"Ah."

Maisy's mother could pack so much meaning into two letters, one syllable.

"He's been a good friend to me since my first day in Haven.

His driver brought me home from the bus station." Maisy rushed to explain what couldn't be explained—not in a phone call. "He's taking baptism classes too."

"I'm glad you've decided to be baptized." A big *but* loomed in Mother's words. "I thought you would come home. You could take the classes here."

Live at home again. Pick up where she'd left off. Only now Jamesport would be like starting over instead of Haven. Here everyone knew her story. They'd watched her redeem herself. In their eyes she'd done the right thing. Her decision had helped a couple they all knew and loved.

Was it cowardly to stay here? In Jamesport no one knew of Isaac and Vicky's plight. They would know Maisy's mistake drove her from her parents' home and that she'd returned without a baby.

Fear wouldn't keep her from returning home. She would face family and friends. But then she would come back and live the life she'd come to love in Haven. With Joshua. "I'll come home to visit when I can, but right now Ruth needs my help." The answer, so obvious in its simplicity, made Maisy sit up. The chair rocked. She grabbed the spindly table that held the phone with her free hand. "Why don't you all come here? Come to Haven for my baptism. I miss seeing your faces. Say you'll come."

"Jah, jah, say we can go, Mudder." Sarah's squeals forced Maisy to pull the receiver from her ear again. "I want to see Kossin Ruth and meet her boplin."

"It'll be your daed's decision." Mother made the statement in all seriousness, but Maisy knew, and Sarah probably did, too, that their mother would have plenty to say before Father made the decision. "He has a lot of work to do here."

"I understand." Maisy squashed her want into a box too small for it. If they came to Haven they could meet Joshua. They would see why she had to stay. "You'll like him . . . the man. He's a gut person."

"He must be."

Mother didn't have to elaborate. Her tone did it for her. Any man who would take Maisy as she was—a woman with deep stains on her character—was special. Maisy eased her grip on the receiver. "If I finish the classes and all goes well, I'll be baptized in May. There's plenty of time to plan a trip."

A year ago in May she'd been flitting about St. Joseph with Nate, line-dancing, bowling, going to movies, and making out on his truck's tailgate. That life could change so much in a year boggled the mind.

"I'll write." Mother's words held a note of finality. There was no need to prolong a telephone conversation. That's what Father would say. "You do the same. Let us know when Ruth's bopli is born."

"I will. I'll write." Questions crowded her, like kids who wanted to be at the front of the line for recess. How were her brothers and sisters, her nieces and nephews, how was life in Jamesport? How was Skeeter? "I really liked getting letters from you, Sarah. Write me with all the news, okay? Everything. If Danny gets a hangnail, I want to know."

"Danny tried to hitch up the cart last week." Sarah giggled. "He let Blaze out of the corral. Daed had to run after him."

"It wasn't funny." Given Mother's chuckle it must've been a little funny. "Anyway, we'd better get back to the garden. It's almost time to start lunch."

Maisy didn't want to hang up. Every choice she made had an effect on the journey ahead of her. The curves, the bends, the forks in that road made it impossible to see her destination. Only the assurance that God had a plan for her, that He knew her destination, made it possible for her to say good-bye on that silly note. "Talk to you soon."

"Jah. Soon. Gott willing."

Chapter 44

"*BABY STEPS*." THE IRONY IN THAT phrase didn't escape Maisy. Bryan had used it with all the kindness of a man who'd never walked in the shoes of a woman who'd given up the right to watch her baby take her first steps. Maisy's steps toward claiming her Plain faith and her life with Joshua could be described as mincing steps, maybe. Steps in slow motion, perhaps. Anything but the halting, falling, get-back-up steps of a baby.

She held Nicholas's fat fingers as he waddled in that bowlegged, arms-in-the-air way that a baby taking the leap of faith from crawling to first steps had. Slobber trickled down his chin, thanks to the teeth trying their best to burst through his sore gums. He crowed, tugged free, and sat on his diapered bottom.

"Gut job. Gut job, Bopli."

Maisy swooped down and picked him up. She spun around the room. His giggles built to a crescendo of shrieks. The sweet sounds of a happy toddler. All her childbirth aches and pains were long gone in the six weeks since Ellie Grace's delivery. Even the hormones had been sent packing. April's beautiful spring days lit up the scenery even as showers grew green grass and flowers burst into blooms. The windows were open, allowing a breeze to blow through the kitchen, mingling with the aromas of stuffed pasta shells and baking cookies.

She had two baptism classes behind her and two more to go. Every day she came a few steps closer to letting go of her longing for Ellie Grace. Maybe today would be the tipping point— holding Ruth's baby and feeling nothing but joy for her new second cousin.

Maisy settled Nicholas on the floor. He hiccupped a giggle and threw his arms in the air. "More. More."

"How about a drink of wasser instead?"

"Wasser, wasser."

"I believe that's a jah." She poured water from the pitcher into a sippy cup for him and a glass for her. For a few seconds she paused, tensed to hear any sounds from the bedroom. Kate would call her if Ruth needed anything. She'd woken up this morning in labor. A third child usually came quickly, but this little one didn't seem to be in any hurry. Amos had Bonnie out at the corral taking her first horse-riding lesson—passing the time until Kate told him to come in for the birth. It was almost lunchtime.

The screen door squeaked. Probably Amos and Bonnie. Maisy glanced up from checking on the cookies. Joshua wiped his boots on the rug. He slid his straw hat back and smiled. "Guder mariye."

"What are you doing here?" Not having Joshua close by had been an adjustment, but a necessary one. His apprenticeship was going well. He loved working with horses. Their evening buggy rides were filled with stories about the horses he was training and the life he hoped to make for her and their children one day. "I wasn't expecting you until this evening."

"Kate called John's. She thought it might be gut for me to come around early."

In the midst of doing her job as Ruth's midwife, Kate still had time to think of Maisy and the pain this day might cause her. "She's such a gut friend, but she needn't have bothered you. I'll be fine."

"I know you will, but I'm here now." Joshua raised his head and sniffed like a hound dog. "Smells good in here. I'm hungrier than a bear after a winter of hibernation."

"That's gut because I made a huge batch of stuffed shells, but no one has shown up to eat them." Maisy returned his smile. She closed the oven and hustled to the counter where the glass pan of pasta sat on a trivet. "Nicholas and I were about to snarf them up all by ourselves."

"I went down to the barn first and talked to Amos. He is on his way in, but not to eat. He's trying to be stoic faced, but he's walking on cactus needles waiting for this bopli to arrive." He cocked his head toward the hallway. "No word?"

"Kate came out for some cold lemonade about an hour ago. She said it was slow going."

"Things are moving along at a good clip now." As if she'd heard her name bandied about, Kate bustled into the kitchen. "Tell Amos to come back. Ruth is asking for him."

Within minutes, Joshua had delivered the message, and Amos was headed for the bedroom he shared with Ruth. Bonnie stood on a step stool washing her hands and jabbering about the horse she rode "all by herself."

"You might as well sit down." Maisy carried a plate and silverware to the table for Joshua. "I think it'll just be the kinner and us."

Joshua helped Bonnie finish cleaning up and took care of his own hands. They settled around the table with Bonnie in her booster seat and Nicholas in his high chair. Even the little boy knew to bow his head and clasp his hands during prayer.

"Aamen." Nicholas echoed Bonnie's boisterous response to Joshua's amen. "Bopli aamen."

"That's right, Nicholas." Joshua tousled the boy's hair and then gave Bonnie equal time with a pat on the shoulder. "Now eat your shells. Maisy did a lot of work stuffing every one of them."

This was what it would be like. If they were husband and wife sitting down to a meal with their children, every day could be like this. Joshua would be a good father. He still had that touch of childish curiosity and wonder—even the tragic event in his life couldn't rub it out. Or maybe it was because of that tragedy that he cherished moments of innocent fun.

More tomato sauce ended up on Nicholas's face, hands, and shirt than in his mouth, but he managed to gum some of the pasta. Bonnie did a better job of hitting her mouth. However she drew the line at green beans, instead filling up on hunks of homemade bread.

A cry stopped Maisy in the act of setting a plate of still-warm butterscotch-pecan cookies on the table. That cry. So familiar. A red-faced, squalling, beautiful baby girl squinted against the world's bright light. She squirmed against Maisy's chest for a scant few moments. Then she was gone.

Maisy drew a long breath. She swallowed. "Eppies for everyone. It sounds like Bonnie and Nicholas have a new bruder or schweschder to celebrate."

"Bopli, bopli." Bonnie banged her spoon on the table. *"Mei* bopli."

"Mei bopli." Nicholas said whatever big sister said. Lacking a spoon, he banged his sippy cup on the high chair instead. "Bopli, bopli."

Joshua clapped in time while Maisy handed out the cookies—which put an end to the impromptu music. Cookies trumped banging, as much fun as it was.

Another baby in the house. Maisy bit into the cookie, letting its sweetness drown any remaining bitterness. Ruth needed her help. Maisy was glad to be able to repay her kindness and hospitality. She heaved a breath and concentrated on the cookie.

Joshua laid his cookie on his napkin and picked up his coffee cup. "Everything okay?"

"I'm so happy for Ruth and Amos."

"Me too."

More coffee. More cookies.

"Will you be all right with it?"

Maisy busied herself cleaning up Nicholas over his dismayed squeals. "I'm fine. I promise."

"You don't have to hide your feelings from me."

"I'm not hiding them." She stopped wiping Nicholas's hands long enough to focus on Joshua. "I'm imagining what it would be like if this were our house, our table, and our kinner. If we were sitting here eating eppies and drinking kaffi like an old married couple, how wunderbarr that would be."

"Me too." Joshua swept cookie crumbs onto his hand and deposited them on his plate. "It's a nice picture."

"Very nice."

"Look who finally decided to show up." Amos limped into the kitchen. He held the baby wrapped in an old, soft blanket. "Meet Finn."

Finn was wide awake. His owlish eyes peered up at Maisy with what surely was curiosity at this big new world. He had a wide face with a long nose—like his daddy. A spritz of damp hair—hard to say if it was brown or blond—shot up from his head like a cowlick. Too soon to say what color his eyes would be. Maisy took it all in. A boy. A boy was easier. Silly, though that was.

"He's definitely your son." Joshua had risen and gone to Amos.

He did what Maisy wanted to do it. He touched the blanket, then the baby's cheek. "What a big bu."

"He is. Kate says he's nine pounds, two ounces, and twenty-two inches long." Amos couldn't contain his pride. "I reckon he'll be a good farmhand one day."

He laughed and Joshua joined in. Leave it to men to think ahead to the practical matters in the future of a baby boy only in this world thirty or forty minutes. Maisy backed away so Amos could introduce Bonnie and Nicholas to their new family member. He sat down and let them crawl into his lap for a closer peek. Finn seemed as interested in them as they were in him.

"Such a calm bopli." Maisy focused on clearing the table. She had plenty of dishes to wash. Best to keep busy. "You'd think he'd be tuckered out after all the work of being born."

"Nee, it's Ruth who's tuckered out." Amos gently removed Nicholas's fingers from his little brother's nose. "She's resting while Kate cleans up the room."

"Shall I fix them plates?"

"That would be gut." He guided his new son's fingers so they wrapped around Bonnie's small index finger in a tight grip. "He's holding your hand, Dochder."

"He is, he is." Bonnie squealed. "Look, Maisy, bopli holds my hand."

"You'll have to be a gut big schweschder and take care of your little bruder." Maisy helped Bonnie and Nicholas down. "It's time for your daed to eat. You two can play with Finn later, after you've had your naps. Your mudder will need your help so you need to rest up too."

Amos stared at his plate with an aimless grin that erased six years, taking Maisy back to the day he married her cousin. They'd been so young and so excited. So ready to embrace their future. They'd had some hard times since then, but blessings too.

She made quick work of fixing their plates. "Would you like me to take them back?"

"I'll do it. If you don't mind holding him." Amos's tone was soft. His gaze was warm, direct. He knew this was hard. He wanted her to have this time to take this next step. This baby step. "The kinner can play until I get back. Then you can put them down for their naps."

She nodded. He stood and handed over the precious bundle. He tucked silverware wrapped in napkins under one arm, picked up the plates, and slipped from the kitchen. By now Finn's eyes were drooping. He whimpered and snuggled against her chest. Maisy dropped into the closest chair. He smelled like baby. She adjusted the blanket so she could see his face better.

"Okay?" Joshua eased onto the closest chair. "Anything you want or need to say?"

"I know Bryan is right. I still have a chance for this. Gott is merciful and gracious." Maisy stared at the baby's red, swollen face and his bruised, smushed nose. He was so beautiful. "I'm on the right path now. I don't ever expect it to be easy, but going through the trials with a man like you will make it easier, make it special."

Joshua cleared his throat. "I feel the same way." His voice was hoarse. "I'm glad you can say what I can't."

His relief shone on his face. Maisy giggled. She couldn't help it. "Don't worry. I'll always have twenty-five words for your every one."

"I'll be glad to hear every single one of them." He smoothed his hand across her cheek. "World's wordiest special friend."

"Am I your special friend?"

"I surely hope so." He slid an arm around her and leaned close. His scent of sweat, sun, and soap enveloped her. "I still have a long way to go before I'm in a position to support a family. I've made a start, but I'll need to save money for a house—"

"I'm saving most of the money I make at the hardware store. You're not in this alone."

"I just want to make sure you're still willing to wait."

They had time to do this right. They would take the time to find their way together. Everything in the right order. Maisy kissed baby Finn's cheek. One day she would hold her own baby—hers and Joshua's. *Thy will be done, Gott.* "I'll wait as long as it takes."

Chapter 45

JUST LIKE THAT, THE BAPTISM SERVICE ended. Maisy pinched her arm to make sure she wasn't dreaming. After months of anticipation, nerves, and study, the trickle of holy water from her hair down her cheeks had happened so suddenly on a mid-May Sunday morning. She patted her still-damp cheeks. *Danki, Gott. I didn't fall on my face or faint or giggle hysterically.* If God found that prayer odd, so be it.

The air, filled with fine dust and hay bits that hung in the shafts of light peeking through the barn's wooden slats, hung dank and heavy. Perspiration dotted her forehead. Maisy scanned the crowd in Bryan's barn while singing the last hymn. Everyone she loved packed the benches. Father sat with Amos, Joshua's father, and her brothers. Mother, Nora, Sarah, and the little ones crowded the bench next to Ruth and her babies.

Maisy's gaze didn't seek them out. It wanted one person in particular. Joshua, also newly baptized, sat with his brothers not far from Maisy's menfolk. Only what Bryan would call intestinal fortitude kept Maisy from staring at him during the final hymn. A baptized member of the church concentrated during worship, even when she brimmed with joy. Or especially because of that joy.

The muggy warmth, the smell of sweat, even the lingering scent of horses and manure only made her feel more at home.

She closed her eyes for the final prayer and added her own postscript. *All is right in the world. Danki for that, Gott. Danki for my family's safe trip here. Danki that they could be here. And danki for this community of believers. Danki for Your grace and mercy, and forgiveness I don't deserve.*

The prayer ended. Everyone surged toward the doors. After a three-hour service no one was bashful about the need for food and drink. That didn't stop them from hugging Maisy and welcoming her to the fold. Whatever her past transgressions, she was a member of their church family now. Smiling so wide her face hurt, she forged through the crowd, leading the way for her mother and the children. Ruth and her brood brought up the rear.

Vicky stepped into the aisle. She held Ellie Grace, now three months old. "Bewillkumm. I'm so happy for you." She lifted her voice to be heard over dozens of buzzing conversations and laughter. "Gott bless you and keep you."

No words could express how much her welcome meant. "Danki."

"*Hallo.* I'm Sarah, Maisy's little sister." Sarah squeezed between two older women who'd stopped to chat in the middle of the aisle. She stood on her tiptoes and peered at Ellie Grace. "Your bopli is so sweet. What's her name?"

"Ellie Grace. She *is* sweet." Vicky bent down so Sarah could see. Ellie Grace's blue eyes were bright and her cheeks pink. She babbled. Her arms batted air. "She's a gut bopli. She didn't give me a bit of trouble during the service."

She had Nate's face and coloring, but Maisy's eyes. Sarah and Mother had never met Nate. They wouldn't see the similarities. It didn't matter. Ellie Grace would have all of Vicky's personality, her way of talking with her hands, and her airy laugh. It was so good to see her laugh. Maisy planted a quick kiss on the baby's forehead. "Good job, Ellie Grace."

Vicky met Maisy's gaze over Sarah's head. "My mann and I are blessed."

Maisy waited for the sorrow, the grief of loss and regret, the anguish, to pierce her to the bone. None came. God had answered her prayers. "She's getting so big."

"She eats all the time."

"Me too. Mudder says I have a hollow leg." Sarah threw her arms in the air. "See how tall I'm getting? I'm almost as tall as Mudder."

Not quite. "Then we'd better get you to the picnic tables. You don't want to miss out on all that food. If the buwe get there first, there won't be anything left. I need to get inside and help serve."

"Not today." Vicky shook her finger at Maisy. Her gaze encompassed Mother and Maisy's sisters. "You're excused on the day of your baptism. Enjoy time with your family before they return home."

Good advice and a nice reprieve. Vicky stepped aside and allowed them to go first.

Finally they made it outside where brilliant sunshine and a swift breeze awaited them. Mother's arms came around Maisy in a quick hug. "That was her, wasn't it?"

Maisy leaned into the hug. "Jah."

"How do you feel?"

"Gut. Like Gott made gut happen from my mess."

"I'm happy for you then."

Her words were like balm on a wound that healed more each day.

"There's someone I want you to meet." Maisy drew back, but she held her mother's arm. She let her gaze rove across the yard, out to the corral, and back to the picnic tables set up in long rows outside Bryan's sprawling wood-frame house. Leave it to Joshua to disengage from the crowd so quickly. He seemed to be having a conversation with his horse tethered near the buggies. "There he is. Of course he'd be with the horses. He prefers them to people."

"I can't say that I blame him." Her mother chuckled. "Sometimes I feel the same way."

Leaving Ruth to herd the children toward the open tables, Maisy tucked her arm through Mother's and headed toward Joshua. He looked up as they approached. He shoved his black church hat back and nodded. Always the one for conversation. Her twenty-five words for his one. Maisy grinned. "Joshua, this is my mudder, visiting from Jamesport."

With a welcoming smile, Joshua ran his hand down the horse's long neck. If he found this meeting awkward, it didn't show. "I saw you sitting together and figured as much. You're two peas in a pod."

"I wanted to thank you for all you've done . . . for my dochder." Mother's cheeks reddened. Her gaze flitted to the road and back to Joshua. "Your great kindness will never be forgotten. She tells me you're the reason she's staying here in Haven."

"I know it's hard for a mudder not to have her kinner close." Joshua's voice softened. "But Jamesport isn't so very far. In the meantime just know your dochder is loved."

Mother nodded. "I expect we'll be back one day for a wedding." The words held a query. She didn't come right out and ask, but she came close.

Joshua nodded. "Gott willing."

"His will be done."

"In the meantime Harvey needs me at the store." Maisy rushed to fill a pause fraught with conflicting emotions—missing loved ones while embarking on a future sure to be full of everything she longed for. "And Ruth has needed me as well."

Caring for Finn had been a surprising, sweet antidote for the loss of her own baby. Maisy rocked him, sang lullabies, and changed his dirty diapers whenever Ruth needed a break. Any time she wasn't working at the store, she spent doing chores like washing the endless mounds of dirty diapers generated by Nicholas and Finn. Bless her heart, Bonnie was finally potty-trained.

Even Amos had come down on Maisy's side. He saw how much Ruth relied on her. If he saw the looks that passed between Maisy and Joshua at the supper table or the way she disappeared after the children were in bed, he said nothing about it. His words of support had tipped the scale, at least from Father's perspective.

One hand to her forehead to block the sun, Mother peered over her shoulder toward the house. "I'd better get back up there. The buwe will eat your bishop's fraa out of house and home if I don't stand between them and the food."

"I'll be right there," Maisy called after Mother. "Save me a piece of apple pie."

Her mother waved in response and kept walking.

"Now I know where your sweet disposition comes from." Joshua slipped his hand over Maisy's. "She's a kindhearted woman who wants what's best for her dochder."

"How did it go with my daed?"

"Gut. He and my daed hit it off right away. I didn't have to say much."

"You wouldn't have anyway."

Teasing Joshua felt good. It felt perfect. The weight of Maisy's worries dropped away. They'd both jumped a major hurdle this day. Committing to their faith brought joy and relief. No more floundering. Maisy would never forget the lessons learned, nor would she repeat her mistakes. A clean slate awaited her. Maisy sneaked a peek at Bryan's yard. The multitude of visitors filled the space.

They talked, laughed, and ate, unaware of the changed lives a few hundred yards away.

Maisy ran her hands across Job's withers. His warmth and aliveness matched her own. His presence helped her keep an even keel, kept her from floating away in a cloud of bright hope for a future filled with the family life she'd always wanted.

Joshua slid his hands across the horse's back. His fingers touched hers. She met his gaze. His eyes said everything he couldn't. He would never bowl her over with his words. He didn't have to. She didn't need declarations of love from him. Everything he did, every move he made, reflected his love for her.

He glanced toward the crowd and then at her. "We're on our way."

"There's no one I'd rather walk this road with."

"Come here, sei so gut."

Maisy slipped around Job, who tossed his head and neighed as if to give his stamp of approval to the conversation and his role as their buffer from the rest of the world. Joshua took her hand and pulled her close. After he popped up to glance over the horse's back, he ducked down, cupped her face, and kissed her in a long, slow kiss that celebrated not only this day but every day to come.

Breathless, Maisy pulled away first. "I'm so happy I'm almost afraid."

"Afraid?" Joshua put his hands on her shoulders. "You have nothing to fear. Just remember what you've been through and survived."

"Because of what I've been through, I know life won't always be like it is today."

"That's true. The difference is we'll go through whatever comes together."

Maisy wrote the rest of the conversation on her heart. She

needed no big words or definitions. No words at all, really. Joshua's touch, his eyes, his lips, the heart he wore on his sleeve told her everything she needed to know.

She'd found her way through the angry thicket of shame and remorse to redemption and hope. She was home.

Acknowledgments

My writing career wouldn't be possible without my readers, so thank you for giving me this great gift. Being able to sit at my desk each day and write these stories is a dream come true.

As always, my heartfelt thanks goes out to editors Becky Monds and Julee Schwarzburg for your understanding and patience as I endeavor to produce stories in the midst of medical treatments that muddle the brain, dampen the spirit, and mess with the precious pipeline between creative thought and fingers on the keyboard. Thank you for seeing the forest and the trees when I can't.

To my husband, Tim, thanks for putting up with me.

Above all else, thank You, Jesus, for the gift of creativity, the ability to tell stories, and the time to write them.

Discussion Questions

1. Maisy decides to leave Jamesport and go to Kansas without discussing it with her parents first. She says it's to spare them the shame. Do you think she did the right thing? Should she have stayed in Jamesport? Why or why not?

2. After he's had time to get over the shock of Maisy's announcement, Nate tells Maisy they could get married. She says no because she would have to give up her Amish faith. If you were in Maisy's shoes, what would you do? Is it more important for her baby to have both his/her mother and father? Or is Maisy's faith more important?

3. Joshua questions whether a good God would've allowed his twin brother to die in a fire, while the dogs he intended to save made it out safely. What would you say to Joshua to help him understand that God is always good, no matter the circumstances?

4. Does Joshua's suffering serve a purpose? If so what do you believe that purpose is?

5. What about Vicky and Isaac's suffering? Do you see a greater purpose in it?

6. Maisy wonders how it's possible that she so easily became pregnant with a baby at a time when she didn't want one, while Vicky and Isaac had been unable to have one no matter how hard they tried. We see this over and over in our broken world. How do you explain it?

7. Scripture says that God can make good come from all circumstances. What good do you think He made come from the death of Joshua's brother Jacob? What good came from Maisy's becoming pregnant with an English man's baby out of wedlock?

8. It's become more and more common in today's world for unmarried couples to have babies. The Amish rely on Scripture to support their view that father and mother should be married. What are some situations in which you think a woman might choose not to marry the father of her child? Is there Scripture that can support both sides of the question?

From the Publisher

GREAT BOOKS

ARE EVEN BETTER WHEN THEY'RE SHARED!

Help other readers find this one:

- Post a review at your favorite online bookseller

- Post a picture on a social media account and share why you enjoyed it

- Send a note to a friend who would also love it—or better yet, give them a copy

Thanks for reading!

About the Author

Photo by Tim Irvin

KELLY IRVIN is a bestselling, award-winning author of thirty novels and stories. A retired public relations professional, Kelly lives with her husband, Tim, in San Antonio. They have two children, three grandchildren, and two ornery cats.

Visit her online at kellyirvin.com
Instagram: @kelly_irvin
Facebook: @Kelly.Irvin.Author
Twitter: @Kelly_S_Irvin